JUDY MERCER

SPLIT IMAGE

POCKET BOOKS
New York   London   Toronto   Sydney   Tokyo   Singapore

This book is a work of fiction. Names, characters, places and incidents are products of the author's imagination or are used fictitiously. Any resemblance to actual events or locales or persons living or dead is entirely coincidental.

POCKET BOOKS, a division of Simon & Schuster Inc.
1230 Avenue of the Americas, New York, NY 10020

ISBN: 0-671-55603-7

First Pocket Books paperback printing August 1999

10 9 8 7 6 5 4 3 2 1

POCKET and colophon are registered trademarks of Simon & Schuster Inc.

Cover design by Tony Greco

Printed in the U.S.A.

CRITICS CAN'T GET ENOUGH OF ARIEL GOLD—IN THESE SUSPENSE BLOCKBUSTERS BY NATIONAL BESTSELLING AUTHOR

JUDY MERCER

A People magazine *"Page-Turner of the Week"*

SPLIT IMAGE

"A tantalizing thriller. . . . [a] cunning game of truth or consequences."

—*People*

"Mercer hits her stride. . . . A tantalizing end. . . . Mercer manages wit and dialogue as well as ever. It's great fun to watch an intelligent author—and her intelligent heroine—advance."

—*Kirkus Reviews*

"Perfect for those who like their mysteries on the light side . . . [with] a bit of romance in the bargain."

—*Booklist*

DOUBLE TAKE

"Stylish . . . inventive. . . . It's one of Mercer's triumphs that she ties the [plot lines] together without straining credibility. . . . She makes Ariel's predicament plausible."

—*San Francisco Chronicle*

"*Double Take* has it all—an amnesiac heroine . . . a guilt-driven, aristocratic Charleston family . . . a chance encounter with a stranger on a beach, [and] a mysterious disappearance."

—*Richmond Times-Dispatch*

"Mercer's second Ariel Gold thriller has a fetching cast and an ingenious plot device. . . . Mercer is a bright author with a fine sense of humanity."

—*Kirkus Reviews*

FAST FORWARD

"A riveting delight, a veritable banana split of a mystery."
— *Washington Times*

"Wow! . . . *Fast Forward* is smooth and smart, with enough thrills to satisfy even the most jaded mystery reader. Judy Mercer's characters are so real that . . . you may have to restrain yourself from phoning them just to chat."
— Susan Isaacs, author of *Compromising Positions*

"An action-packed thrill ride that's full of unexpected twists and turns. . . . Reminiscent of Jonathan Kellerman at his best."
— *Booklist*

"A winner. . . . Packed with puzzles within puzzles, *Fast Forward* delivers layered suspense and a heroine readers will root for."
— Nora Roberts, author of *Temptation*

"*Fast Forward* is that rare thriller that delivers much more than it promises. . . . Mercer doesn't miss a beat."
— *The Orlando Sentinel*

"An irresistible first-person voice—clever, caustic, and brash."
— *Minneapolis Star Tribune*

"*Fast Forward* leaves no time for pause. . . . Full of classic suspense. . . . Written by a talented, skillful storyteller, this finely crafted thriller has come out a winner, if not an international sensation. . . . This read will be a ride to remember."
— *The Macon Telegraph* (GA)

"Suspenseful and compelling. . . . Judy Mercer fast forwards to the head of the pack of new mystery and suspense writers."
— Nancy Pickard, author of *The Whole Truth*

"Thrills from beginning to end . . . *Fast Forward* is an [appro]-priate title. . . . It was so good it seemed to take no time at all to get from beginning to end."

—*Herald-American* (Syracuse, NY)

"Credit Mercer with a rare imagination . . . skill and wit . . . and a Machiavellian penchant for plot. . . . *Fast Forward* is a good yarn, well told."

—*Los Angeles Times Book Review*

"*Fast Forward* couldn't be a faster read if it tried. . . . [It] grabs the reader on the first page . . . and doesn't let go until the last, when all the loose ends are finally tied. . . . Perfect escapism, fantasy, and intrigue for anyone wanting to forget the world for a while."

—*South Bend Tribune* (IN)

"An irresistible new voice. . . . What raises this tale heads above the average . . . story is our heroine's pluck and indefatigable sense of humor. The result is a suspense novel with heaps of wit and not a little charm."

—*Alfred Hitchcock Mystery Magazine*

"A good shivery tale . . . Judy Mercer has developed an appealing heroine for her first novel. . . . A pleasant page-turner."

—*The Pilot* (Southern Pines, NC)

"The reader experiences all the suspense, uncertainty, fear, and confusion that Ariel feels. . . . [You'll] find a gem in this well-written mystery with a twist."

—*The Gothic Journal*

"Engaging, fast-paced . . . with just the right combination of terror and compassion. . . . The ending, like the rest of the book, is a pleasing combination of the slick and the jagged."

—*San Francisco Chronicle*

Books by Judy Mercer

Fast Forward
Double Take

Published by POCKET BOOKS

For Ronnie and Rick Mercer,
brothers and friends

Thanks to Dean A. Alper, attorney at law; Bruce W. White and David Pearlburg, Fraser Yachts Worldwide; and Sgt. Rick Keaton, Marin County Sheriff's Department, for their answers; to Bill Petrocelli for his generosity of heart; special thanks to my literary agent Joy Harris and able cohorts Leslie Daniels and Kassandra Duane, to my editor Linda Marrow and colleague Kate Collins, and to Patricia Porter, each for her friendship and insights; and to Larry for laughing, listening, and questioning in all the right places.

Who never doubted never halfbelieved.
Where doubt there truth is—'tis her shadow.
                    —P. J. Bailey
                    Festus: A Country Town

SPLIT
IMAGE

1

CAN YOU DIE OF FEAR?

People do. Ariel Gold has read the freaky stories; everybody has. She hadn't really believed it, hadn't understood how it was possible. She knows now. Terror swallows you whole. It crushes your lungs so that no matter how desperately you struggle for air, you're suffocated by panic. Your heart, its pumping amplified to deafening drumbeats, its fragile valves engorged by fright, simply swells and bursts.

Ariel tried to swallow. She'd never been so thirsty. Water, cool, clear, and wet, was a mirage shimmering in the sea of lights that blinded her.

The worst thing was that this was her fault. She should never have listened to the manipulative arguments that brought her to this moment. She had no one to blame but herself, her stupid, insidious ego, soaking up the flattery, whispering temptation. If only she could go back to yesterday. She'd say no. She'd scream no. She'd laugh in their faces. But it was too late.

The man in her field of vision was smiling, a fake

smile, and his lips were moving, mouthing incomprehensible words. She couldn't concentrate on what he was saying because her guts had knotted with an ominous, roiling cramp that caused her to break into a sweat. She could smell her fear. She had to hide it. No matter what, she couldn't let them see it.

She blinked as the sweat trickled from her scalp, down through the crud caked on her eyelid, stinging like fire as it hit her eye and became, she imagined, a black rivulet. Quickly, furtively, she dabbed at it. Her hands had taken on a life of their own, trembling as if they were palsied. The shakes were starting again. They came in waves, starting at her knees, vibrating up her body through her elbows into her hands, rattling bones that felt brittle as old china.

Just then, a red light flicked on: a single, demonic eye. It was all she could see. It grew, paralyzing her, filling the room, taking the oxygen from the air. All her fear, all her panic, was focused on that glittering red point. It signaled that there was no going back; she'd run out of time.

Ariel opened her mouth. Knew in that second that the power of speech had vanished. Knew absolutely that she could no more speak than fly, but no one else could help her now. She had no choice. A cheek muscle jittered as her face formed itself into grim seriousness.

"The story you're about to hear," she said, gazing directly into the camera lens, "will shock you."

2

"WOULD I LIE TO YOU?" HENRY HELLER SHOUTED through the rest room door, spreading open hands to demonstrate his sincerity. "I admitted you sounded a little shaky the first sentence or two, didn't I? But you snapped out of it. I'm telling you, you really weren't bad after that."

The door opened and Ariel tottered out, blowing her nose.

"And you *looked* terrific," Henry said. "The camera loves you."

Ariel gave him a nasty look. Her eye makeup, what seemed like layers of it, troweled on, was streaming down her chalky face. She snatched up another tissue and blotted. It came away black. She thought she was about to throw up again, but the urge passed.

"We should've opened with your segment," Henry advised himself. "You had too much time to think. If you'd just told me you were going to be nervous—"

"*Nervous*? I was *nervous* when we rehearsed. I was *nervous* when I was getting made up. I was nervous when we were scrambling to get in the late-breaking stuff fifteen minutes before airtime. What nervous is to what I felt when the countdown started is what a sneeze is to a grand mal seizure!"

"But why didn't you say something before? We'd have worked out some way to tape you this first time—"

" 'First time'? Like there's going to be a second time?" Ariel's stomach lurched, and she tasted bile. "You think I knew how I was going to feel? I couldn't have been more terrified facing a firing squad! Have you ever hyperventilated? Have you ever felt like you were going to toss your cookies, live, in front of thousands of people? 'First time,' my . . . !"

Henry knew that if he smiled just then he was toast, and physical contact didn't seem wise. He sensed more compliments wouldn't go over too well, either, but the fact was she'd owned that story, almost from the first second.

Yesterday, the brand new Lexus of Chloe Ford, one of the newsmagazine's three correspondents, had been rear-ended. Screaming whiplash, she'd been raced to the nearest emergency room. With little option, Henry made the decision to vamp what was already in the can. Then a story Ariel had been developing broke wide open, and he had his brainstorm.

She's watched every *Open File* that ever aired, he argued first with the higher-ups and then with her; she helped put dozens of the shows together herself. She knows every technique of every network newsperson who's ever beamed sincerity into American living rooms. She's well-spoken. She's good-looking.

She had vindicated his judgment.

Her story was dynamite, an exposé targeting a little-known man named Leeman Parker. Parker himself couldn't be located (Ariel couldn't even put hands on a picture of the man), but according to her sources, he was the leader of a cult called Canaan. The cult was big but destined, allegedly, to be smaller. To be, imminently and in a blaze of mass suicidal glory, extinct. The Canaanites, as they referred to themselves, believed that the command came from the Almighty via his messenger, Leeman Parker, and that it applied to the children of the flock as well as the adults.

Ariel had personally scrounged for every chilling fact.

Her initial edginess on camera had promised something worth waiting for. The vibrato in her voice had come across as intensity. What the director had excitedly described as "fire in her eyes" had probably been a spasm in her colon.

"The whole idea of my taking over for Chloe," Ariel was saying, "was a fiasco. I'm a producer, Henry. I can finally say that without apology. After a year—more than three years if you count the ones I don't remember—I've earned the right. I'm not 'talent'!" She thrust a thumb and forefinger, half an inch apart, into Henry's face. "I came *that* close to making the whole show an industry joke. We weren't thinking, Henry, not you, not me, and not any of the other geniuses who hatched this rotten egg."

Distractedly, she plowed fingers through blond-streaked hair, stiff with spray and sticking out now like a frazzled haystack. The tantrum had turned her face tomato red, and from the ruin of smeared mascara, her green eyes, raccoonlike, glittered.

"Did I mention," Henry said, "how great you look on camera?"

"You've got a week," Ariel said, "to figure out how to

do this show with two correspondents or to find a third because, bossman, it ain't me."

She gathered up coat and purse, and bent to retrieve her briefcase from beneath a desk. Her limbs felt weak, limp as overcooked spaghetti. She'd go home. Pet her nonjudgmental dog. Drown herself in the shower, or a bottle. And watch the tape of tonight's show. Just to see if it was as bad as she thought.

"I'll see you in the morning," she told Henry as she left.

He watched the door sigh pneumatically closed behind her and to its blank metal surface said, "I guess that means you want to be alone tonight."

3

"SHOULD'VE HELD EYE CONTACT RIGHT THERE," ARIEL told Jessie. She fished the last marshmallow out of her cup and, dribbling cocoa on the remote, hit rewind. "See? Intimidation. I admit it. I got anxious. Rushed it. Bad timing. Sucky timing!"

The big German shepherd opened one eye, briefly, and then sighed heavily back into sleep. The tape had been replayed relentlessly. Jessie hadn't been especially interested even on the first go-round.

Ariel clicked off the VCR. "I looked fat," she said, and got up to stir the fire beside which Jessie slumbered.

She'd arrived home feeling bleak and resigned to very shortly feeling bleaker; there was no question of sleep or anything else until she'd seen the tape. Her first reaction had been relief: it could've been worse. The second viewing changed her mind. That's when, whirling dervishly, she'd built the fire, showered, put on her oldest, warmest robe, dumped out a drink, and made cocoa. Three mugs and too many marsh-mallows later, the woman on the screen was just some ditz without one recognizable feature or mannerism.

She sat down to share Jessie's rug, and the shepherd obligingly shifted, resting her head on her mistress's nearest knee. The phone, which had rung several times, rang then. As before, Ariel ignored it. She didn't want to hear false compliments, and anybody who really did believe she'd done okay couldn't have much taste.

Other than *Open File* staff, a blur of faces she'd rushed past in her race to the loo, the only person she'd talked to was Henry. Tact and flattery weren't his long suits. Had he looked her in the eye when he'd claimed (Henry's idea of effusiveness) that she "wasn't bad"?

Ariel had a sudden hunch about why he'd engineered tonight's experiment. Back in the fall a New York show had come after her with bigger bucks, nice perks, and a coordinating producer title. She'd turned them down. From one or two comments Henry had made, she suspected he worried: that she might come to regret the decision, that she'd grow restless and want more, that next time she'd say yes.

She would not. She wasn't up to starting over again quite yet.

Ariel was a thirty-three-year-old woman with one year of history. That was it. Everything prior to twelve months before was gone from her memory as cleanly as if it had been excised with a scalpel. The surname she'd learned from a driver's license was inherited from a dead and unremembered husband. The house in which she'd found herself was inherited from adoptive parents she knew only from yellowing photos. As she'd quickly discovered in her present, pastless existence, there'd been no close friends around to remember.

If Ariel was no longer the hard-core loner she was told

she'd once been, she remained, essentially, a private person. Only those she'd grown close to knew of her handicap, which was diagnosed as traumatic amnesia. Only in her weakest moments did Ariel question whether it was something else entirely.

Going in to work the next day was an act of courage.

Ariel found a dozen red roses on her desk and a thick stack of message slips. There were even telegrams. Dazed, ducking her head, she murmured graceless thanks to yet another staffer and opened one of the wires.

BOFFO ETC. HONEYLAMB YOU SMOKED! NEXT STOP NY? WIN.

Win Peacock, a former *Open File* correspondent, was now with *Life/Time*, the competitive newsmagazine about which Henry worried. From time to time it was the prodigiously handsome Win himself who worried Henry; their competition was of a personal nature.

She was opening another wire when her phone buzzed, and Tara Castanera, Henry's assistant, said, "You don't have a brother with a Midwestern accent, do you?"

"A what?"

"He's on line one. Brother somebody, he said."

"I don't have a brother."

"A nutter! Ah, the price of fame. I'll tell him to get lost. Meantime, more floral tributes on the way in, and your bona fide relative's on three."

Ariel looked up to see an intern approaching her workstation with a basket of flowers the size of a small tree, said thanks to both Tara and the intern, and punched three.

"Some reason you didn't let me know you were takin' to the airwaves?" asked her grandfather.

B. F. Coulter, septuagenarian Southern gentleman and self-made multimillionaire, was Ariel's only living kin. Stumbled on by accident, he was by far the happiest discovery of the last cataclysmic year. He was also a master of righteous indignation. "Answer me!" he demanded, having given her no time to do so.

"You saw it then," Ariel said, and grimaced, muttering, "Did everybody in America see the thing?"

"I can't speak for my fellow countrymen but I, personally, didn't see squat, not havin' been let in on your plans."

"Look, I'm sorry. I'll send you a tape. But watch fast; it'll be the last time you get a chance to see me make an ass of myself, on the air anyway."

"Don't bother. Woman I know was tuned in. Heard your name in the intro and put the show on tape for me. I'll watch it on the plane—I'm flyin' to L.A. this afternoon—and call back when I have."

The sharp click of disconnection was his exclamation point.

Ariel was reaching for the little envelope tucked in with the flowers when the phone buzzed again.

"Call on two," Tara said. "A Jack Spurling. Claims no kin but says you know him."

"I don't." Ariel plucked the envelope from behind a yellow daylily. "He didn't say what it was about?"

"You want me to ask him?"

"Never mind," Ariel said, and picked up, trapping the receiver between ear and shoulder as she slit open the envelope. Her "Hello" was preoccupied.

"Good morning," a male voice replied. "It's been a long time."

"Oh?" Ariel mumbled absently, fumbling with the card enclosure.

"I don't need to ask how you're doing. I caught you on the tube last night. Good work, Ariel! I'm proud of you!"

Ariel's hands stilled, the card forgotten. She didn't get personal calls from her past. It didn't happen. The voice was warm, familiar. Familiar in its attitude, that is; to Ariel, it was utterly unfamiliar. "That's . . ." *That's what?* she thought. "That's nice to hear," she said, and swallowed. After a short and awkward silence, she prompted, "How long has it been?"

"How long . . . ? Oh. Two years, almost to the week. I'd say that seeing you after all this time, virtually on the anniversary, was a sign, but . . ." Ariel heard a quiet chuckle. "After hearing about that madman on your show, I hesitate to blame anything on spiritual intervention. We make a big enough mess of our lives all by ourselves, don't we? God knows I have."

What in the world? Ariel thought. This had to be another crank call. What had Tara said his name was? Sterling? Not Sterling; Spurling.

"Did I catch you at a bad time?" he asked.

"No, I just . . ." *I just don't have a clue whether you're an old friend or a nut case.* "Look . . ." she said, and couldn't for the life of her think where to go from there.

"I know you must be busy. I only wanted to tell you how much I enjoyed your—what would you call it? Debut?"

"Thank you."

"And, Ariel, you *looked* so good! I almost didn't recognize . . . I mean, you look different from how I remember . . ." He groaned. "I'm digging myself a deep hole here. Please, take that as a compliment, will you? However inept."

"No problem."

"I've offended you."

"No, really. Mr. Spurling, I'm sorry, but I'm afraid—"

" '*Mr. Spurling*'?" A moment passed before he made a sound in his throat, something between a laugh and a snort of surprise. "Well, *Ms. Gold*," he said, and his voice had cooled by noticeable degrees, "sounds like you *are* different from how I remember you. I won't take any more of your time. Good luck with your new career."

"Mr. Spurling?" Ariel said into a dead phone.

"Ariel?"

She looked up to see Henry. Even in her distracted state, she couldn't miss his sly, sweeping glance at the messages and telegrams and flowers littering her desk. "You want to come into my office a minute?" he suggested.

She'd no more closed the glass door to his cubicle before she said, "Does the name Spurling mean anything to you?"

Henry took longer to change gears than usual. Depositing his long, lean bones into his circa 1950 swivel desk chair, which elicited a squawking plea for oil, he rested his bearded chin in splayed fingers and his deepset dark eyes on Ariel and said, "What?"

"Spurling. Somebody I knew two years back, he says. Since he's slipped my mind—along with everything else from before a year ago—I was asking if you knew who he was."

"I do not believe this! I spent a good chunk of the night worrying about you. Why weren't you answering your phone? I had visions of you working yourself into nervous prostration. Making yourself really sick."

"You worry too much."

"Is that right? Listen, when you're dealing with a

woman who could be the poster person for posttraumatic stress disorder, no worry is too idle."

"Oh, for heaven sakes, Henry! You make me sound like a hysterical—"

"Some people consider amnesia the product of hysteria, and you were hysterical and you are, it is a fact, amnesic."

"Stop yelling! They'll hear you out there!"

"I am not yelling," Henry yelled, "and amnesia is not a social disease!"

"Whatever it is," Ariel said quietly, "it's my business."

"Ariel . . ." Henry came around the desk and took her by the shoulders. Rarely did he touch her at work in even the most casual way, and it was an indication of his concern that he did so now. He pushed her gently but firmly into a chair, and said, "You're acting like last night never happened. You want to tell me what's going on?"

Ariel dropped her eyes. She noticed she was still holding the card she'd plucked from the huge floral arrangement. "Encore!" it said. It was from one of the sponsors.

"Ariel? I got the distinct impression—after you pitched a fit and broke out in hives and so on—that you were disenchanted with going on camera." Henry perched on his desk and waited. "Well?"

"Well what?"

"Well, have you changed your mind? We need to know. Chloe's in traction. She's out of commission for the foreseeable future. We've already gotten a couple of calls from agents looking to see how the land lies. What should we tell them?"

"Whose agents?"

"Nobody we love so far, but the day's young."

Ariel chewed on a cuticle.

"You're going to have to stop that if you're going to be talent," Henry observed. "I noticed last night that you could use a manicure."

"What are they saying upstairs?"

"If they weren't saying good things, we wouldn't be having this conversation. In fact, I was told to escort you up when you came in."

"What do you think?"

"I told you already. Apparently, you don't trust my judgment."

"You're biased."

"Not where this show's concerned."

"I watched the tape," Ariel said. "Once or twice. I'd think: not too bad, not for a first-timer. Then I'd know the greenest weekend anchor from some tank town in a wheat field could've done better."

"Listen to me, okay?" Henry thought for a few seconds before he said, "If you don't want to go on camera, fine. But if you say no, say it because that's not the direction you want to go, say it because you're content with what you're doing now. Base your decision on facts, not this fun house-mirror distortion of yourself you carry around.

"You were good last night. You've got a solid news background, electronic and print before that, and even if you can't consciously remember all that experience, it didn't go poof. It's percolating around in your head somewhere. You know this show. You know our audience. You've logged untold hours putting the shows together and that includes watching tapings, studying interviews, *doing* preliminary interviews."

"They weren't in front of an audience."

"They showed us what we needed to know. You think we would've taken a chance otherwise? Yesterday, putting you on was a stopgap measure. You and the camera clicked. You need rehearsal, you need polishing, you're going to have to lose a couple of gestures." He demonstrated one of them, a sincere, open-handed appeal that reminded Ariel of Ross Perot and made her flinch.

"I did that, didn't I? Did I do that more than once? How many times did I do that?"

"Easily fixed. That's the easy part."

"Easy! Henry, I dropped *g*-endings. My *r*'s came out uhs. 'Mistuh Parkuh,' I called that creep last night! Did you *hear* that?"

"So work on it, but don't lose it altogether. That Southern softness you've picked up from Grandpa is good camouflage." Henry grinned. " 'Mistuh Parkuh' is probably one angry 'suckuh' about now. You better hope they put him away or he might just come after you one of these days. Him or one of his disciples."

"That's supposed to be a positive argument?" Ariel crossed her arms. "I don't know, Henry. This whole thing is just so . . . unorthodox."

"What, that you haven't gone the regular route? Courting the camera, working your way up from the smaller markets? Hey, Lesley Stahl was a producer before she went on the air, too. She didn't even get into the news business until she was nearly thirty."

"I looked fat."

"You sound ridiculous. You used to be heavyish. You used to be frumpish. But you used to be in touch with reality. Amnesia's worked wonders for you, and I'm the last one to complain about the changes, but the truth is, you used to be easier to deal with, too. Tell me something: how much would you guess Jane weighed?"

"How much . . . ? I don't know. One-twenty maybe? Why?"

"Your sister, God rest her soul—your gorgeous, tall, hollow-cheeked *twin*—graced the cover of every fashion magazine in the so-called civilized world. You weigh, what? Ten pounds more than she did? So how come you're too fat to grace the TV screen?"

"Five pounds more, not ten. Funny you should mention Jane. Last night, in that first second right when I started to speak, she came into my mind. I know I can't make you understand this, but . . . we did that show. She and I together, like one person."

"Ariel . . . yes or no?"

Ariel picked at her thumbnail, caught herself, sighed, and stopped. " 'Failure,' " she said, " 'has gone to my head.' "

"Is that a yes?"

"I'm still working my own stories," she stipulated. "That doesn't change."

"I'll call upstairs," Henry said.

4

"HOW MANY VALIUM DO YOU THINK I COULD TAKE next week and still pronounce 'allegedly'?" Ariel asked, only half joking.

Her grandfather patted her head as if she were a bird dog that showed promise but hadn't quite gotten the commands down, making soothing sounds and exchanging a look with Henry.

"You won't need valium," B.F. said. "You're a Coulter."

"I'm a klutz. The more coaching I got, the more wooden I got. By six o'clock I was Pinocchio. I was talking like Eliza Doolittle with marbles in her mouth. I'm tired of myself."

"Changed your mind, have you?"

" 'The only man who can change his mind is a man that's got one.' I've obviously lost mine."

"Stop carryin' on. I told you I was proud of you. Henry told you you were fine. Your executive producer told you he loved you. Western Union and FTD and Pacific Bell brought you raves from sponsors and competitors and friends and enemies from coast to shining coast the whole day long."

" 'Fifty million Frenchmen can't be wrong.' "

"Stop her before she quotes again," Henry said.

" 'Stronger than an army is a quotation whose time has come.' I'm too tired to think of anything original to say."

Sam, Henry's fourteen-year-old son, had wandered in and was foraging through what little was left of dinner, Chinese take-out.

" 'What costs nothing,' " he said, " 'is worth nothing.' "

"Pardon?" Ariel said, as Henry simultaneously said, "Good God! Now she's got him doing it!"

Sam waved a tiny white strip of paper and, through a mouthful of fortune cookie, said to Ariel, "You ought to write these things. I can't remember junk I spend hours memorizing, and I'm not an amnesiac or amnesic or whatever you call it."

"Call it past-impaired," Ariel said, and Henry watched her fight a yawn. She and Sam had become friends over the last few months, especially during those times when he was on the outs with his mother, which was more often than not lately. Sam felt important, being among the select few who knew about Ariel's secret malady. It was exotic to the boy, the stuff of action adventure, and Ariel a heroine: an identical twin whose sister had been murdered, whose memory as of that moment ended as abruptly as her sister's life.

She managed to crack jokes about amnesia, much as surgeons learn to banter over the operating table or policemen over a corpse, but misplacing over thirty years of one's life is not a minor inconvenience and Ariel was not a woman of small curiosity. Those years, Henry knew, itched like a missing limb.

"I've got more free megabytes than you, see?" Ariel

was teasing Sam. "A head full of unoccupied brain cells. Blank as white rice. So I store useless information. Of course, *I*—unlike you—can't play Bruce Hornsby's entire body of work by heart. Or Ray Charles's or Paderewski's—"

"You couldn't play with the sheet music in front of you either," Sam said. "You couldn't play if—"

"All right, all right, Mr. Piano Man! Hey, you never said if you watched the show last night. Did you?"

"Yeah. Why isn't that Parker jerk in jail? He's got to be schizo."

"On what charge? And he's MIA anyway. Wandering the desert was what I was told, seeking 'final purification.' But what I was asking was, what did you think?"

"I just said. I think he's mental."

"About me, Sam! How did you think *I* was?"

"Oh. Great. Did anybody want that last egg roll?"

As he went past on the way to the living room, Sam let one eyelid drop in a wink only his father could see.

"If we can dispense with the accolades," B.F. said, "I'd like to invite you two to dinner this weekend." The restaurant he named was the newest gourmet mecca, and reservations were at a premium.

"What's the occasion?" Ariel asked.

The old man's eyes flickered just noticeably afield when he said, "A celebration of your new career," and reached for his coat. His kiss was almost perfunctory, and Ariel watched him go with a tingle of unease.

"B.F. and trendy restaurants?" Henry asked. "Since when?"

"Since when he's entertaining somebody important to him."

"You qualify. We're off, too. Get some rest, love." Henry's kiss was not perfunctory.

Ariel rested against him and breathed in the warm, distinctly Henry smell of soap and bay rum tinged with a distant echo of cherry pipe tobacco. If Henry had ever smoked, it was nothing she remembered. But, then, Henry's wardrobe tended to be considerably older than their acquaintance or her memory problems.

She felt his sigh, long, deep, and regretful. While Henry was careful to observe the proprieties in their workplace, he was even more circumspect around his son.

Ariel had no quarrel with the former; she was no less professional than he. Furthermore, she found the secrecy seductive. She'd catch herself watching a worldwise, assured, and impersonal Henry interacting with some network bigwig or defusing a crisis—knowing he was totally unaware of her, knowing everyone else was totally unaware of *them*—and the rush would almost make her lightheaded.

In their off-hours, like right now, self-restraint was less appealing. Which wasn't to say she didn't understand.

Henry's most recent ex-wife, Sam's mother, was kicking over the traces. Since the boy had moved in with his father a few months before, she'd decided it was her turn to live, and she didn't believe in hypocrisy. Henry didn't begrudge her right to the pursuit of happiness, but hypocrisy, in his opinion, was underrated. Sam wasn't comfortable coming face-to-face with strange men when he dropped by his mother's house.

Henry couldn't have found himself falling profoundly in love at a more inopportune time. He felt angry at his ex-wife's goings-on and guilty because of the double standard that implied. He was protective of the still-fragile bonds he and Sam were forming after too many years of absenteeism on his part. He understood Sam's confusion because he remembered his own pubescent sexual ferment. He ought to understand; he was thirty years past pubescence and he was frothing.

"I'm living every modern woman's dream," Ariel whispered. "Being courted by an old-fashioned gentleman with noble intentions."

"If you knew what I was thinking, you wouldn't think I was so noble."

"I'm close enough not to miss what you're thinking." She grinned into his shirt buttons. "You're a man of firm resolution."

Henry nuzzled. "Couldn't we send Sam away to camp?"

"In January?"

"It's summer in Australia."

"Oh!" Ariel jerked away. "A letter came in today from Milly Chillcut. She's agreed to the interview."

"You're kidding! Why didn't you tell me?"

Millicent Chillcut was the daughter of an Australian pop star of international celebrity; she had also been an adolescent kidnap victim, and she'd lived to tell about it. The thing was, she never had, not in the nine years since. The kidnappers had never been caught, and, fueled by her silence and the speculations of creative media, public curiosity had never died.

"I didn't think you'd get anywhere near her," Henry said. "Why now? I wonder. Why after all this time would she talk to the press?"

Muttering to himself about logistics and scheduling changes, he told Ariel to start setting it up first thing the next morning and then called to Sam, "Let's go!"

They heard Sam, in turn, calling for Stonewall. Shortly, the boy came in, eagerly trailed by the nondescript little dog. He'd briefly been Ariel's; she'd given him to Sam. More accurately, Stonewall had given himself. He had a spotted history. Before being Ariel's, he'd been her sister Jane's, a shelter rescue. Ariel had never been able to decide whether he was opportunistic or an angel in scruffy, golden-colored fur, aiming his loyalties where they were needed.

Just now he gave Ariel not a glance. Sam did, though. Ariel caught him giving both her and his father a good long look, and the expression on his face was impossible to read.

5

THE NEXT DAY WAS A KILLER. BY THE TIME ARIEL STAG-
gered home, she knew everything there currently was to
know about the Chillcut kidnapping. That would have
been enough were she still only producing the story; now
it was merely the preamble. Her flight to Australia was set
for the following day, the interview for Friday, and the
butterflies in her stomach were as big as buzzards. They
had plenty of room to flail around. It was after nine, and
she hadn't eaten since breakfast. The available menu was
limited. After a very brief debate between canned sauer-
kraut and a leftover pork chop of uncertain vintage, Ariel
changed into sweatclothes and, with Jessie for company,
headed to the nearest market.

Too many impulse buys later, she was trying to steer
a lop-wheeled cart across the market's parking lot. Her
thoughts were as erratic as the cart—things she still
needed to do, like postpone dinner with her grandfather—and it took her a second to spot her minivan. At
first she didn't see the man beside it.

He wasn't merely passing by.

He stood a yard or so from the vehicle and, from what she could see in the shadow-pocked light, he appeared to be looking through the passenger window. He was wise to go no closer, she thought, and took her keys from her handbag. The point of the key could do a certain amount of damage but not as much as the large German shepherd poised still and watchful in the shotgun seat.

The man made no move as she approached. She stopped with the cart and a sensible distance between them and loudly cleared her throat. He jumped. She pressed a button on her keychain, releasing the rear lift hatch door. Jessie could now make a fast and impactful exit and, on command, she would.

"Something I can help you with?" Ariel asked.

"No, no, I was just . . ." He plunged his hands into his pockets and took a step backward. By accident or design, he'd backed farther under the sheltering darkness of an avocado tree that overhung that area of the parking lot. Wind stirred the leaves, and shadow patterns flitted across his face.

He nodded toward the van. "The dog. He's yours?"

Ariel considered the wisdom of having this tête-à-tête. She listened, vainly, for the sound of fellow shoppers in the vicinity. "*She* is, yes," Ariel said with unmistakable finality.

"Beautiful. I used to have one a lot like her. Well, I didn't mean to . . ." He broke off. There was surprise in his voice when he said, "Ariel Gold?"

Ariel had already realized that he sounded familiar. She peered at his face, uncertain, and thought: Who? Is it finally happening? Am I going to remember someone from before?

"Yes?" she said and before it was out of her mouth, another thought came: he knows me from TV. It was the first time she'd been recognized on the street, and it threw her for a loop.

"This is wild!" he exclaimed, and started toward her. Ariel tensed. Out of the corner of her eye, she caught movement: the rear door of the van opening. "Jessie, stay," she ordered.

"I can't believe this!" the man was saying as WEIRDO FAN RUNNING AMOK? flashed hysterically through Ariel's mind and, at the very same time: *Why didn't I at least put on lipstick!* Her dismay obviously showed on her face.

"Hey!" he said, embarrassed, laughing a little. "Don't you recognize me?"

Ariel stared. He was a stranger. Forty, she guessed, or close to it. Clean-shaven. Dark hair. Better dressed than the average late-evening grocery shopper (including herself). He wore dress trousers and a button-down shirt open at the neck, a tweedy-looking sportcoat. He was a substantially built man, with two inches, maybe three, on her five-nine, and he'd straightened to every millimeter of it under her scrutiny. "Ariel?" he asked. "Ms. Gold?" His eyes narrowed. Had Ariel been capable of remembering anything about the man, it would have been those eyes. The irises were so light they looked colorless, like water. The lashes and eyebrows were heavy and dark, and one brow had a peculiar, thread-thin white streak running through it.

"I see," he said, his mouth going flat. "Of course you recognize me, and that's the problem, isn't it?" Abruptly, he turned to leave.

"Wait a minute!" Ariel was hooked.

He stopped.

"Actually, I don't recognize you," she said.

"How could you not . . . ?"

"I'm sorry if I should, but I don't."

"Jack Spurling?" He asked it rather than stating it, defiantly, as if he suspected Ariel of pulling his leg.

"Spurling . . ." The name clicked. "You called me at the studio."

"And here I am, in person."

"Who exactly are you, Mr. Spurling?"

"My God, have I changed that much?"

"Apparently."

"I don't suppose a murder trial rings any bells?"

"Whose murder?"

"My wife's."

Ariel frowned. "And the person on trial . . ."

"That would be me."

Ariel's hands tightened on the grocery cart. If she aimed it at him, the cockeyed thing would probably veer off and turn over. It was more protection as a barrier, a ramming weapon if need be; Jessie was better protection still. Ariel heard a low, restless rumble from the van.

How, she had time to wonder, could there be a murder trial going on of which she was totally unaware? And if he was telling the truth, if he wasn't just yanking her chain, what was he doing running around free? "You're . . . out on bail?" she asked.

"What?"

"You're on trial for murder, you said. You're not in jail. Bail's not usually granted for murder suspects unless . . ."

"Ariel," he began, and took a step toward her.

"Stop right there." Ariel braced herself for whatever might happen next.

What happened was that Jack Spurling made no move

except for the smallest shake of the head. Even in her skittish state, Ariel could read nothing threatening in it.

"My trial, for God's sake," he said, "was nearly two years ago. I don't know which has been the worse hell, when it was going on or all the time since. Every time somebody looks at me the way you're looking at me now, I wish they'd found me guilty and gotten it over with."

There was an audible movement in Ariel's van, a shifting of uneasy dog flesh, and Spurling said, "Go on. Calm that poor animal down before she hurts herself."

Ariel watched him walk away, striding across the lot and into the market, his back held even straighter than before. "It's okay, Jess," she said, and raised the lift hatch to soothe the agitated dog. "It's okay. He's nobody to worry about."

She buried her face in warm fur as a shiver rippled across her shoulder blades. The wind had begun to whip up, she noticed, and there was a chill in it.

"I'm glad you called," Henry said. "I've been thinking about opening the Chillcut piece with that still shot of the police—"

"Henry, have you ever heard of a Jack Spurling?"

There was a pause before Henry said, "Excuse me for interrupting, Henry. No problem, Ariel; obviously, what you've got to say is more important."

Ariel had headed for the phone as soon as she arrived home, and she was peeling off her coat as she talked. "Okay, I'm sorry, but have you?"

"Have I what?"

"Heard of him?"

"Are you talking about John Spurling? Guy tried for murder a couple of years ago here in L.A.?"

"He calls himself Jack, but that's the one."

"Sure, I've heard of him. What about him? Is that who you were asking me about the other day? John Spurling?"

"Yes, and you never answered me then, either."

"Ariel, what's the question?"

Ariel unwrapped the roasted chicken she'd bought and began slicing into the breast. "Well, tell me about him."

"Flattering as it is to be your personal databank, I might suggest you look through a file you yourself put together. You've probably got it there someplace."

"What file?"

"The one you compiled back before the trial, when you were so hot to do a piece on him."

"I was?" Ariel stopped mid-movement, knife in hand. "Did we do the piece?"

"No. Why this sudden burning need to know about Spurling?"

"I already told you he called and, as it happens, I ran into him tonight. Since *he* knew *me*, I was at something of a disadvantage." She pulled open the vegetable crisper, looking for a tomato she seemed to recall. It had expired in a puddle of gray-flecked slime. "Oh, for . . . !" she muttered. "So are you going to tell me?"

"You know, Ariel, you may no longer report to me, but I don't believe it's the other way around yet."

Ariel blinked. Where had that come from? Carefully, she said, "Sorry if I sounded high-handed. It's just that it was . . . awkward. You know? He knows me, and I'm standing there looking stupid. Like I'd been lobotomized."

"You could have simply explained why you didn't remember him."

"That's not funny."

"You're right, it's not. Sorry. Look, I've got to go. I've got to pick up Sam from his basketball game."

Thinking he could've already told her the man's life story by now, Ariel said, "Oh, well . . . it's waited two years, it can wait till I get back. It's not like the man wasn't acquitted, after all."

"What are you talking about? He *wasn't* acquitted."

"Well, he's walking around free."

"Check your file, babe. It was a local case. California: the home of hung juries. His hung high. Have a good trip."

Thoughtfully, Ariel hung up. Overriding curiosity about a two-year-old murder was a suddenly more pressing concern. *The Open File* wasn't a rigidly hierarchical organization, and she'd given little thought to the fact that Henry was no longer her superior. That should be a good thing; life should've become simpler. She had a feeling it hadn't.

6

ARIEL TRAVELED OFTEN. SHE WENT WHEREVER research or preliminary interviews or a need for face-to-face persuasion took her. Most were day trips: the unglamorous, behind-the-scenes scutwork of producing. By comparison, Australia was an odyssey. The upside-down weather and accents and characters were exotic. The pace (and deference) was exhilarating. The Chillcut kidnap story was a coup.

It had been an international sensation. The mother a fabulously famous pop star, the victim a beautiful child, and the ending happy but unresolved. Before the ransom could be paid, Milly had turned up unharmed. She couldn't or wouldn't talk then, and because of her silence in all the years since, the incident had become legend. The public, accustomed to the tidy wrap-ups of TV drama, craved resolution. The interview was any news correspondent's dream; because it was taped rather than live, it was Ariel's.

When she arrived back in Los Angeles, rough cut in hand, Henry hugged her openly, if briskly. He was grabbing for the tape at the time, and heading for the nearest edit bay. Several other staff members crowded into the small room, too, making Ariel almost as nervous as she'd been during the taping.

With one eye on Henry and one on the monitor, she listened again as the shy young woman finally told her story. Simply, softly, Milly told of terror: of men with covered faces, rough hands, and hard voices. Of desperation: long hours left alone in an old freight car, abandoned near a remote stretch of train tracks. And, finally, of deliverance: the night a different man had come.

He was tough-looking, she said, but he'd treated her gently. He unlocked her prison. He gave her water. He walked her a great distance along the tracks until they reached a house, and there he'd left her. To this day, she didn't know who he was.

Ariel watched herself frown. Why, she'd wanted to know, had Milly kept such a thing to herself.

"He asked me to. I promised," the girl explained. "He could've collected a reward. Been hailed as a hero. He must have had . . . a reason to hide."

Asked why she'd decided to break her silence, Milly handed Ariel a piece of paper. "This came in the mail last week."

When the show aired the following night, the viewing audience saw a closeup of the words printed on the cheap, lined paper. "Helping you was the one thing I did in my life I was proud of. God bless you."

The public ate it up. *Open File*'s parent company was suitably pleased with the ratings. Media worldwide followed up the tale of a mystery man who'd requested only one thing: anonymity.

"You see this?" Henry asked the next day, dropping that morning's L.A. *Times* beside Ariel's computer.

She glanced at the headline: "Bodies Believed to Be Chillcut Kidnappers Found Buried." "I did. I convinced Milly to tell the police what she'd told me. They were digging up the area around those train tracks before I left."

"How'd she know the men were dead?"

"She didn't know it for a fact." Ariel paused as a man she recognized as a newly hired electrician passed her workstation. He was an odd-looking duck, she thought idly. Grim.

"Yeah?" Henry called her back to the conversation.

"She'd always believed her rescuer killed them. It's another reason she never gave him away."

Henry nodded, started to leave, and then changed his mind. He perched on a corner of her desk and, watching Ariel thoughtfully, said, "You're not going to have a story like that drop into your lap every week, you know."

"It didn't drop; I prodded."

"Uh-huh. It might not be possible to tape every week, either. Time may come when you'll need to go on live again. How will you handle that?"

Ariel scowled, hit Alt-Block on her keyboard, and zapped a paragraph. "Fear can be positive. 'If it doesn't paralyze you, you can use it.' Jim Brown said that."

"Yeah? What did Jim say about becoming a household face? A commodity? Public property? You've got fans already, you know, and critics. Can crackpots be far behind?"

"No kidding. One of the more amusing letters I've gotten was from one of 'Mistuh Parkuh's' cultists. It wasn't noticeably religious in tone."

"Be glad it's just a letter."

"There've been phone calls, too. If you're trying to

bring me down to earth, you're doing a good job. I thought you wanted me to do this."

"What I want is for you to be careful. Parker's still running around out there somewhere, you know." Henry stood. "Are we still rescheduled for dinner with your granddad tonight?"

"Eight o'clock. I'll pick you up."

"Whatever." He hesitated. "In case I forgot to say so, you done good with the Aussie."

"Thanks."

"But that's last week's news," he added as, smiling sweetly, he left.

"What that is, buster," Ariel muttered, "is two for two."

She was in various stages of development with three different producers on three different pieces. She'd slept a total of four hours the night before. It was midafternoon and she'd forgotten to eat lunch, again. She was having the time of her life.

Ariel's "other car" raised questions, eyebrows, and comments wherever she drove it. One of some four hundred built in 1954, the sole year of production, the Darrin was the last hurrah of Kaiser-Fraser before the company folded its tent. The sleek little sports car looked as contemporary today as it had when it rolled off the assembly line, and it looked like no other car on the road, then or now. Ariel didn't drive it often, but tonight seemed appropriate. The Darrin had been a gift from her grandfather.

"You know anything more about this command performance dinner?" Henry asked from the other bucket seat.

"No more than you do." Ariel turned right onto

Beverly Drive, catching a glimpse of moon between the
towering royal palms that lined both sides of the street.
"B.F.'s being mysterious."

"Speaking of mystery men, did you look for your file
on Spurling?"

"I did." Even in the fast-track flurry of the previous
week, the incident with Jack Spurling had been on her
mind. "There is no such file. I'd put everything I found
from pre-amnesia on computer. There was nothing
about Spurling."

"Probably tossed. It was a while ago, and the story
was ditched before development."

"There was something about Spurling. He looks
so . . ." Ariel recalled the man's clear-eyed gaze. "He
looks so not guilty."

"So you thought two years ago and so, obviously and
fortunately for him, did at least one person on his jury.
In fact, as I recall, it was more like about half
of 'em."

"I would've thought a deadlocked jury would have
set up our kind of story to perfection. So why didn't we
do it?"

"Scooped. One of our trash compactor competitors
did him first."

"Oh. Sleazily, no doubt."

"Sleazily and unauthorized—without his cooperation—but first. And, as to deadlocked juries, in this neck
of the woods they're a dime a dozen."

"Yuk, yuk. Why didn't they retry?"

"Spurling lucked out, timing-wise."

Shifting down, Ariel passed a creeping rental car whose
driver was either lost or rubbernecking, on the lookout
for movie star homes. "I don't follow," she said.

"Think about what had been eating up the headlines

everywhere in the country at the time: the high-profile cases from Rodney King to Reginald Denny to the Menendez boys to Lorena Bobbit. Oh, and the Kennedy kid—I mean, the Smith kid—and O.J. in the offing. You couldn't get a good, positive conviction if you had the crime immortalized on film and replayed it every fifteen minutes. Especially in California! Hell, the riot was still a vivid memory then. Nobody wanted to be responsible for another one!"

"Spurling being found guilty or being retried wouldn't have started a riot."

"I'm talking climate of the times. Hey! Watch out for that guy backing out of the driveway!"

Ariel swerved. "I saw him. How come you get so careful when somebody else is driving?"

"Jury members were scared," Henry went on. "Remember the King civil suit? Some irate citizen confronted a couple of jurors and 'accused' them of being 'Rodney King jurors.' Laid into them about wasting taxpayers' money. King's attorney asked for a mistrial on account of that. If you were unlucky enough to serve on a jury, you ended up demoralized." He shrugged. "Or you landed a book deal."

"Still, Henry, I don't—"

"You know what the deadlock rate in the country was? For felony trials? About five percent. You know what it was in L.A.? Thirteen percent."

"I've seen that *Open File* piece, along with every other one you did back then."

"Spurling's jury split within weeks of the Menendez mistrial."

"But why would that have precluded—"

"It didn't preclude, it impacted. You had this highly publicized, very expensive double-jury trial, patently guilty defendants looking like they might get off because of legal shenanigans, as the public saw it . . . and then you had Spurling, a media minnow by comparison. The D.A. had bigger fish to fry, bad guys he *had* to go after the second time. 'Be damned with how much it's going to cost,' as he put it."

"So he let Spurling slide."

"Probably seemed like the better part of valor, not to mention smart politics, and I'm guessing he didn't have any new rabbits to pull out of the hat in a second go-round anyway."

"That still seems—"

"Besides, with Spurling, public sympathy was with the defendant. People believed him. They liked him, and they didn't much like what they'd heard about his wife. The victim."

Ariel realized that she'd lost track of the fact that there'd been a victim, a wife. A woman who'd died. "What happened to—"

"Slow down. There's the restaurant."

Ariel steered to the curb and surrendered the Darrin to the grinning valet. He didn't, quite, gun it as he left.

"What's wrong?" Henry asked, watching her watch the car's departure.

"Just tired, I guess. Thinking about Spurling." She paused. "Having a premonition."

He picked a dog hair off her black coat. "About Spurling?"

"About B.F."

Henry reached to open the restaurant door, but a doorman beat him to it. "What about him?"

The maître d' approached, menus the size of Moses' tablets cradled to his chest, and Henry and Ariel were being led to a table before she could respond.

"*That* about him," she said, and squared her jaw.

The red-haired woman seated on B.F.'s left wore a welcoming smile and deep purple sueded silk that shouldn't have worked with her hair but did. Her right hand rested on his arm, and a marquise diamond the size of a plum glittered on her ring finger. She was attractive and exceedingly well maintained for fifty-plus, which Ariel guessed she was. She looked thirty-five years younger than B.F. rather than the mere twenty-five years younger she probably was.

B.F. had come to his feet. His expression was one Ariel hadn't seen before, a combination of boyish shyness and pride. He looked, she thought, like he was about to bust his buttons.

Whatever he was saying ended with "Darlin'," and for a second Ariel thought he was addressing her. He wasn't. Pure green jealousy, hot as lava and just as mindless, seared her veins. It required a muscular effort to smile as B.F. made the introductions. Her name was Sarah. "Sissy," she inexplicably said, chuckling in a lady-like way. The diamond flashed as she laid her hand on B.F.'s. "That's what my friends call me. I do hope you will, too."

Ariel watched the woman pat her grandfather's hand possessively. *Sissy?* She couldn't foresee a time when she would utter the word.

Henry was a tall man; B.F. was both tall and built on a grand scale. "Sissy" was small and fine-boned. Beside them, she looked like a doll. She made Ariel feel like Big Foot.

Knees buckling, Ariel plunked into the chair that Henry shoved under her. Apparently, he'd been trying to seat her for some time.

"We don't meet many television celebrities in Tulsa,"

the redhead said, "so this is a thrill for me. That first show? I got so excited when they introduced you I could hardly get the tape into the VCR."

So that's "a woman I know," Ariel thought: the one B.F. said taped the first show for him. She mumbled "Yes?" and, after a thuddingly empty silence, "Thank you."

"You're from Tulsa?" Henry hastened into the conversational gap.

"Met her at the country club there," B.F. said, "last time I was out on business. Sissy's got a ten handicap."

Handicap? Ariel's eyes narrowed. Then she realized he was talking about golf. "*You* were playing golf?" she asked her grandfather. "You hate golf. I heard you say fossils could turn into thirty-weight in the time it took to play one game."

B.F. gave her a look that plainly said "That's enough" before he said, "I'm flexible. I'm thinkin' of takin' it up."

"He really should," Sissy said. "He doesn't get nearly enough exercise. For a man so"—she smiled at B.F.— "lively."

Ariel picked up her dinner knife, looked at it as if she didn't know how it came to be in her hand, and put it down again. The waiter appeared, and the other three became engrossed in his recitation of the evening's specials. Ariel buried her face in the menu.

The meal was excellent and eminently civilized. Champagne bubbles whispered in crystal, cutlery clinked busily on china, and Sissy deftly wove conversation. Responding to her interest, Henry explained his criteria for what made a good *Open File* subject, told newsroom war stories, and bragged, modestly, about Sam. B.F. was urged to tell about having once met George S. Patton, an event of which

Ariel had been totally unaware. When several gambits directed Ariel's way were only moderately successful, Sissy contented herself with including Ariel obliquely, as in, "We women know better than that" or "Unlike Ariel, I can't eat dessert; it goes right to my middle."

Ariel, who ordinarily watched her caloric intake with grim discipline, shoveled in another forkful of chocolate soufflé and smiled sweetly before she turned to B.F. and asked, "Where's Sarge these days?"

"Montana," he said, "fishin'."

Ariel thought it was a mighty poor time for her grandfather's cook, bodyguard, and cynical old friend to be AWOL. To Sissy, she said, "Have you met Sarge McManus?"

Sissy hadn't but she was looking forward to it. So am I, Ariel thought.

"How can you say you weren't rude? Of course you were rude!"

"Henry, I was merely quiet. I was listening."

"Quiet? You were a lump. You acted like headhunters had shrunk your brain and sewed your lips together."

Ariel slowed for a stop sign. Changing gears, she asked, "Did you see that ring?"

"What ring?"

"How could you miss it? When the light hit it, people two tables away were blinded by the glare. You don't reckon he gave that thing to her, do you?"

"I'm surprised you didn't ask. I've never seen you like this. What's wrong with you?"

"What do you mean, what's wrong? How can you be so thick?"

"You're jealous."

"I am not. I'm concerned about my grandfather, about his being taken in by that . . . woman."

"You think she's after his money?"

Ariel rolled her eyes.

"Why," Henry asked, "do you assume that's the case?"

"*Why?* He might as well have a target painted on him. He is wealthy. He is more than twenty years older than the woman."

"I'm eleven years older than you. You're an heiress."

"No, I'm not. Not if I choose not to be. It's not the same thing. Are you being deliberately obtuse? He's nearly eighty."

"So he's no longer a man? He is, and still an imposing-looking one, too. He's sharp, he's witty, he's a world-traveled captain of industry. He's still active, and he's as far from being a fool as any man I know."

"Active! You mean *'lively'!*" Ariel mimicked. "Anybody can be foolish if the con person's cunning enough."

"You see Sissy as cunning? I think she's a charming woman."

" 'Sissy' is smooth as snake oil. She had you two chattering about yourselves like *Tonight Show* guests with a new movie to promote. You were practically babbling."

"One who gracefully draws other people out is considered a good conversationalist in some circles."

"Is that right? Did you happen to notice that she never said one thing about herself?"

"As I said, one who—"

"Not one thing, Henry. Nothing. That's unnatural. That's deliberate. What's she hiding? Who is she? Where'd she come from?"

"Tulsa."

"Well, little Miss Tulsa better watch out when Sarge McManus gets a hold of her. After thirty years as a cop, he's got contacts all over this country. If she's ever so much as spit on the street, he'll find out."

Henry laughed. "I can't quite picture Sissy spitting on the street, can you?"

"I can picture a grown woman who calls herself Sissy doing just about anything."

7

ARIEL'S THIRD *OPEN FILE* PIECE STARTED TAPING THE next morning, days ahead of schedule. The focus was frivolous lawsuits, a subject the public loved to hate. After the intensity of her first two shows, one tangling with a genocidal religious fanatic and another spent coaxing painful memories from an emotionally scarred kidnap victim, Ariel welcomed a chance to lighten up. She was having so much fun she forgot to be scared. That changed in one heart-stopping second.

They were on the studio set, and Ariel was in the middle of taping the intro when she heard a scream. Before she could react, there was a grating noise directly above her head. She jumped to her feet just as a bank of lights swung free, grazing her shoulder as they slammed across her chair, overturning it, and both chair and lights crashed to the floor. She had time to see feet and then legs and torso as a figure dropped from the ceiling grid above, time to glimpse the steel wrench clutched in a fist before she was grabbed from behind and snatched away.

Ariel didn't see what took place immediately after

that. She was being hustled in one direction while two security guards came flying from another, and everyone on the premises seemed to be yelling or running or both. It wasn't until an hour or so later that she began to grasp what had happened. She'd almost stopped shaking by then.

The man was the new electrician she'd thought peculiar from the start. He claimed membership in Canaan, the cult whose leader she'd "blasphemed." He claimed, in fact, to be Parker's lieutenant, assigned the sacred mission of "transporting" Ariel.

"Azrael, he's calling himself," Henry told her.

"Oh, great!" Ariel shuddered. "The Angel of Death!"

"We don't know yet," Henry said, "if the guy even knows Parker, let alone if he was told to attack you."

Ariel took another turn around her office, chafing her arms, trying to appear calm. There seemed to be something wrong with the heating system. "What I want to know is how he got hired on here."

"Stolen union card." Henry shrugged. "But a real electrician apparently."

"What I'm even more interested in knowing is whether he's the only one with the 'sacred mission.' "

"Yeah." Studying his fingernails with great concentration, Henry asked, "Are you also interested in knowing that the camera never stopped rolling?"

It took Ariel a minute to get his meaning. "You're unbelievable," she whispered. "Aren't you missing something here, Henry? That man meant to . . ." She stopped, considered the situation, and, finally, scowling, said, "And just what do you see as the new angle for this action-packed little segment? The Perils of Ariel?"

"We'll think of something. And, Ariel, you can't deny it: this one literally *did* drop in your lap!"

"Lucky me. I hate to think how excited you'd be if those lights had come down one second sooner."

Henry did something then that was unprecedented. In plain view of anyone who cared to see, he hugged her long and hard. Her face buried in his shoulder, Ariel shuddered and, at length, relaxed. That'll be three for three, she found herself thinking, and she'd already begun researching the next one. She wouldn't be dealing with a would-be killer; she'd be interviewing a man who might have already killed and, so far, gotten away with it.

The confrontation Ariel had planned for her grandfather might prove almost as perilous. She decided to get it over with that same night.

"How about coming for a late supper?" she invited when she called. "I've got a new recipe for grits. A casserole with jalapeño peppers and cheddar and—"

"Spare me the nouvelle grits, Ariel Gold. Grits are like lilies; they don't need gildin'. What time you want me?"

B.F. arrived looking as robust and satisfied with life as Ariel had ever seen him. He was wearing a new jacket, expensive and—she had to admit it—becoming. His eyes twinkled whenever he mentioned Sissy's name. The mentions were entirely too frequent in Ariel's opinion. She hadn't figured out yet how to voice her opinion.

While she made coffee, she worked up her nerve, and when she brought in the carafe, she was primed. She found B.F. bemusedly petting Jessie. He looked up and said, "She's good company, isn't she? Listens to every word you direct at her like it's the wisdom of Solomon."

"She's listening for a word she recognizes. Any connected with food or an outdoor experience will do. Listen, B.F., I need to—"

"Still," he said as if she hadn't spoken, "a person can get lonesome, can't they? I'm glad about Henry."

"Henry?" Ariel put down the coffeepot with a clunk. "That was an interesting non sequitur."

"Not really. We were talkin' about companionship. Henry's a good, straight shooter, and any fool can see he's crazy about you. You feel the same?"

Meaningfully, Ariel said, "I don't believe in forming . . . attachments just because you're lonely."

"Uh-huh." B.F. smiled. "You'd also need to feel—"

"Affection, of course. And trust."

"You would, yes, and—"

"Common interests. That's important. So is time, to get to know the person, so there're no . . . surprises when it's too late, when you could be hurt."

"Very true. A real *mature* attitude. Of course, if we all took it, the race might've died out a while back. What else?"

"Speaking for myself," Ariel said, remembering who'd made and who'd grasped the humorous comments during last night's dinner (and who hadn't), "and I think I speak for you, too, a good sense of humor is vital."

"And attraction?"

"Well, sure . . ."

"Grand passion? A stirring in the blood?"

"That—"

" 'The triumphant twang of a bedspring'?"

Ariel opened her mouth and then, wisely, closed it.

"Good!" B.F. nodded. "That's all right, then. Sounds like you two'll do fine."

"So what's the problem?" Ariel asked Henry first thing the next morning. "You don't look enthusiastic."

"I don't? I am. It could be good. Following up on an

unsolved murder and the man who was accused and not exonerated, only let go. I like it. What did Chris think about it?"

"I haven't discussed it with our esteemed executive producer yet. I've been busy researching. I can see why they didn't retry."

"The evidence against Spurling was purely circumstantial, wasn't it?"

"Not purely but nearly. A yachting party. A bunch of pleasure seekers. A middle-of-the-night argument, overheard by somebody's tipsy date. Mrs. Spurling disappears. Nobody sees her go overboard. There's no body, no witness to anything, no obvious motive."

"Which is why the charge was manslaughter and not murder." Henry consulted his beard, thoughtfully. "The wife was supposed to be a wild one. Parties. Drugs. An arrest record."

"Arrest record? I didn't see anything about that. For what?"

"I don't remember. Nothing major. Public disturbance or something like that."

"I don't know much about her yet. Spurling's attorney tried to try the victim, but he couldn't get past the judge with it."

"Well, she was gorgeous, that much I do remember."

"I know. I saw her picture."

Eve Spurling had been a blond. She'd looked young, maybe ten years younger than her husband, and her smile seemed wistful. Was it? Or was it knowing what had happened to her—knowing, at least, that she was dead—that lent the grainy newspaper photograph poignancy?

Ariel had, of course, seen pictures of Jack Spurling, too. In one snapped after his arraignment, his mouth had been hard, his pale eyes grim. With anxiety or anger? Was that the face of a killer, shuttered to hide guilt, or wouldn't anyone—grief-stricken, frightened, and wrongly accused—look just like that? Ariel had studied each of several photos carefully; the scar that now split his eyebrow hadn't been there two years ago, and the man had aged more than two years could account for.

"Talk was," Henry was saying, "Mrs. Spurling was fond of night life, and if Mr. Spurling didn't happen to feel like barhopping, she wasn't averse to finding somebody else to tag along with her."

"What was the 'talk' about him?"

Henry shrugged. "That was one of the prosecution's problems; there wasn't any. Nobody had a bad thing to say about him. Seems everybody who met him liked him, man, woman, and child."

"I liked him," Ariel said, realizing that she had.

"You did two years ago, too."

"Yeah? I did?"

"Yeah, you did." Henry was struck by the curiousness of the situation: Ariel, in effect, sharing her own opinion. He wondered, not for the first time, what it would be like to remember nothing about yourself before a certain hour of a certain day. To remember nothing you'd ever seen, or done, or felt, not as a child and not as an adult. He found he couldn't imagine it. Being unable to see into your past seemed as logic-defying a prospect as being able to see into the future. "Yeah, you did," he repeated, and frowned, at what he couldn't have said. "Now I think about it, you were practically starry-eyed about him."

"You're kidding! Stuffy, uptight old me? Why?" Ariel sounded like a kid, captivated by a bedtime story.

"How do I know? We didn't have a heart-to-heart chat about it. About that or anything else. I hardly knew you then. All I can tell you is you were convinced he was innocent. Adamant about it."

"Based on . . . ?"

"Beats me. Wishful thinking? Keep something in mind, Ariel, will you? When you interviewed Spurling two years ago, he was behind bars. Harmless as an animal in the zoo. He isn't behind bars anymore and, whatever you thought then and whatever you think now, we still don't know if he did what he was accused of. Don't let yourself forget what that was."

"I'll carry brass knuckles when I meet with him."

"You think Spurling will work with you on this thing?"

"He's been in a kind of limbo all this time. I'd have to believe he'll be thrilled."

8

"UNDER NO CIRCUMSTANCES WHATSOEVER," JACK Spurling said.

The refusal caught Ariel entirely by surprise. She inhaled to launch into a protest, and the nacho she was swallowing caught in her throat. Choking, coughing helplessly, she thwacked her breastbone, sucked air, and coughed some more.

"Hey, easy!" Concern flashed across Spurling's face, and after only the smallest hesitation, he was up off his bar stool and behind hers. "You okay?" His arms looped around her ribs, and his clenched fist was ready against her abdomen. "Ms. Gold?"

"I'm okay," Ariel managed to squeak. "It's okay. It went down." She felt Spurling release her. "I think, in view of . . ." Her voice failed, and she went into another coughing fit.

"Easy. Take your time."

After a few swallows of water, Ariel said, "In view of the circumstances, I think you can go back to calling me Ariel."

"The circumstances?"

"You saved me from an ignominious end." Feeling foolish, Ariel joked. "Hey! You save somebody's life, you're responsible for them forever. Didn't you know that?"

"If there's nothing between you and death but me, then you're in deep trouble, lady. Ariel." The concerned half smile on Spurling's face had faded. "Besides, I didn't do anything."

Ariel couldn't believe how clumsily she was handling this meeting, which, in effect, had been handed to her on a platter.

Spurling's number, she'd found, was unlisted. There was no personal or business listing in his name. From old news stories, she knew he'd worked with his father-in-law, a man named Winters, that they'd owned a chain of upscale home furnishings stores. When he was arrested, Spurling disassociated himself from the business (against his father-in-law's wishes, interestingly), and it had been sold within the year. Winters retired. Ariel located him in Colorado. He refused to talk to her. She was deciding where to go from there when coincidence intervened.

It was that same evening, just before six, and Ariel was picking up her dry cleaning. The small interior design shop next door—Winterset, according to the sign—had caught her eye before, and she stopped to admire the window display: antiques, mostly, comfortably juxtaposed with fabric and wallpaper scrolls and flowers. On a discreet card propped in the window were the hours and below that, the name of the proprietor: J. Spurling.

Ariel blinked. Could it be? But the shop was just across San Vicente from the grocery where she'd run into Spurling the week before, and the name wasn't a common one.

She went in. Jack Spurling had seemed pleased to see her, and readily agreed to meet her at a nearby café as soon as he closed shop. He didn't look pleased just now.

"Joke," Ariel said. "Lame attempt."

"Overreaction." Spurling shrugged. "Knee-jerk."

"Your reflexes looked pretty good to me."

"Right. I'd probably have cracked your ribs." He blew out a sigh and said, "I am really out of practice."

"At the Heimlich maneuver?"

"At socializing."

"With the kind of business you're in? That's hard to believe."

"Different thing. The way I work is, you talk, I listen. I watch you awhile, see how you dress, how you relax and eat and drink, what you read . . . then I'll make you such a 'space,' as my colleagues say. You're old wood."

"Pardon?"

"Cherry. Burled walnut. Tiger maple. Lived with, worn to a warm patina. Rich accent colors. Lots of books. Good reading light. Down cushions. Traditional but . . ." Unexpectedly, he grinned. It took up only half his face, and Ariel could almost hear the rusty jaw muscles creak with the effort. "A little quirky thrown in."

"Can I move in tomorrow?"

"That's where you live already unless I miss my guess."

"You're good at what you do."

"I like it."

"Takes more than liking it to be good at it."

"Okay, I'm good at it. I love beautiful things. *Good* things. What happens when . . ."

"When what?"

"When an artisan listens to what's inside him and creates something fine. Furniture, fabric, whatever. It's . . ." He exhaled. The air went out in a rush, and he grimaced in embarrassment. "But enough about me. Let's talk about you. What do you think of me?"

Ariel chuckled. "You're not the typical interior designer, are you?" She caught herself. "What I mean is . . . you're more down to earth than, um, what my idea of interior designers is."

Spurling watched her writhe, and then laughed full out. His eyes crinkled. They were technically gray, Ariel supposed, but they were so light and clear that looking into them was like looking through rock crystal. "That is not what you meant, and you know it." Still smiling, he said, "This is the damnedest thing."

"What?"

"You act as if we've never talked before. How can it be that you don't remember me? Although I have to admit, you're not the way I remember you either."

"Really?" Uneasy with the drift the conversation was taking but tempted, as always, to know more about herself, Ariel asked, "How's that?"

"Apart from the physical differences, the weight loss"—he waved a vague hand—"the clothes, the hair . . . Do you mind my saying these things? I could hardly not notice. You're a lot more outgoing than you were two years ago. Easier, funnier. Must be love."

"We seem to have gotten way off the subject we came here to discuss."

"The subject *you* came here to discuss. You didn't mention anything about doing a show on me when you invited me to meet you."

"Would you have come if I had?"

"Probably. You're a smart, good-looking woman, a TV star. I lead a boring life these days. Thank God."

"Why won't you cooperate with me in doing the show?"

"Because I'm not certifiable yet."

"And that means . . . ?"

"Did you see me cooperating last time? Did you see me cooperating when that tasteless, brainless competitor of yours did their show on me? Did you see me writing my memoirs? Did you see me doing the talk show circuit? I left my business, a lucrative business. I got my phone number unlisted. When I started my shop—starting over was the pits, by the way, and it's still uphill—I didn't use my name on the shingle. I keep quiet and I keep my privacy and my sanity, what's left of it."

"You can't mean to live the rest of your life like an ostrich."

"Oh, yeah?"

"Did you kill your wife?"

"That is a really ugly question."

"Forgive me. Will you answer it?"

"I already have, countless times."

"Okay, you didn't. Wouldn't you like to prove it?"

"The way our system works is, I don't have to prove I didn't; the other guys have to prove I did. They tried. They couldn't."

"If you didn't kill her, what have you got to be afraid of?"

"I assume you're just pretending to be that naive."

"We can help you lay this thing to rest once and for all."

Spurling abruptly dropped his head, shaking it impatiently, as if he were dealing with a mental defective. He stared at some object on the floor, or at nothing, for some time before he asked, "Have you ever gone through the dregs of hell? Had people look at you as if

you were some other, lower life-form? Had your freedom taken away from you? Been so frightened, so pow-
erless, that you couldn't think? That you weren't even
sure anymore if you *had* done the unspeakable thing
people were saying you'd done?"

He pointed to the eyebrow about which Ariel had
been curious. "You see this?" The dark hairs were cleanly bisected by a thin, diagonal slash of pure white hairs,
and the line continued as a fine but noticeable scar for
about an eighth of an inch above the brow. It lent
Spurling a diabolical look, rather buccaneerish, but it
wasn't unattractive. "An angry citizen recognized me on
the street a year or so ago. Just walked up and popped
me, out of the blue. Seems his son was found guilty of
some felony—unjustly, of course—and he was express-
ing his opinion of a legal system that punishes the down-
trodden and lets the 'rich' get away with murder. It
wasn't an unprecedented type of incident. Now tell me,
do you honestly believe I'd take part in resurrecting all
that?"

"I'm not talking about putting you back on trial."

"Of course you are!"

"Jack, what do you think happened to your wife?"

Spurling's face slammed shut. "It doesn't make any
difference what I think. The only thing that matters is
what I know: I didn't kill her."

"Wouldn't you like everyone else to know, too?
You've got to hate the doubt in people's eyes, the speculation. You've got to want people to know, once and
for all, that you're innocent."

With a disgusted sigh, Spurling said, "One thing certainly hasn't changed from two years ago, and I do
remember this, vividly. You're still relentless."

"Tell me about that, when we met before."

"What?"

"I don't know why I said that. Never mind."

"Do you realize that I *can* be retried? I wasn't exonerated. Double jeopardy doesn't apply."

"Living with that has got to be horrible! The sword of Damocles. Will you consider working with us on this? Think about what it would be like to get on with your life! Jack? Will you at least consider it?"

Spurling's fingertips tapped the table. Ariel held her breath. He leaned toward her. Quietly and with finality, he said, "Under no circumstances whatsoever."

9

"WELL," HENRY SAID, "SO HOW DO YOU PLAN TO approach doing this without Spurling's cooperation?"

"I don't know."

"It *can* be done without him."

"I know."

Henry was shuffling through papers on his desk, but he was eyeing Ariel over his half-glasses. "There's plenty of footage from before the trial and during."

"I know that."

"We can talk to the other members of the yachting party. Talk to the attorneys and the cops, to Eve Spurling's friends, her family."

"She didn't have any brothers or sisters, and her mother's dead. Her father won't talk to me. I tried."

Henry yanked his glasses off his nose impatiently. "What is with you? You sound like some wan damsel about to succumb to a fainting spell. I thought you wanted to do this story?"

"I want Jack Spurling, Henry. That's what's with me. I need *him* to do the story I want to do the way I want to do it. My idea was to follow up on his life since the trial. What it's like to be on the fringe of society, neither guilty nor innocent, to live day after day with . . . well, dammit, with the sword of Damocles hanging over your head. Purgatory from a personal point of view. From *his* point of view."

"Mercy, nurse, and pass the hankie! You'll forgive me, dear, but unless we can come up with some new evidence or a new way of looking at old evidence, what you're talking about here is a big yawn. Don't sulk. I'm right."

"I'm not sulking, and I know you're right. I also know that if we can't get Jack to go on camera, it's going to be next to impossible to communicate his innocence."

" 'Jack'? 'Communicate his innocence'? Since when are we editorializing, Andy Rooney? What happened to professional detachment? What happened to two sides of the question? What happened between you and 'Jack' last night?"

"You wouldn't ask that kind of thing if I were one of the male correspondents, if I were Alec or Bill."

"Actually, if you were Alec, I probably would. However, let us not go off on a tangent. Tell me this, if it doesn't offend your sensibilities: Why, if your new friend Jack is so blameless, is he unwilling to be our partner in this worthy endeavor?"

"You know what? I wonder if I would in his place. As things stand, he can live a fairly normal life. Quiet. Dignified. No press chasing him around with cameras and raking up nightmares. He's trying to build a business. His clients don't know who he is. They don't associate their decorator with—"

"Decorator? *That's* what Spurling's doing now?"

"As I was saying, they don't associate him with a two-year-old scandal. He's been forgotten, and he's glad of it. What's the likelihood after all this time that we'd come up with any evidence that pointed away from him? Would the gain of raising questions be worth the pain? At least, as things stand now, he's free."

" 'Freedom's just another word for nothing left to lose.' "

"Very good! I wish I'd thought of that one last night. On the other hand, there's 'Let sleeping dogs lie' and 'If it ain't broke, don't fix it' and 'We forgive the guilty, especially if they confess, but not the innocent, especially if they don't confess' and—" Henry's look stopped her. "I also wish," she said, "that I'd pushed him on something I let slide."

"What?"

"I asked what he thought happened to his wife. He closed up so fast I could hear the bolt sliding into place."

"What did he say?"

"That it didn't matter what he *thought*."

"Sounds like he's got a theory. If he had more than theory, his attorney would have used it. You read the transcript. There wasn't anything like that, was there? The defense never suggested an alternative scenario to Spurling's doing her in?"

"Well, sure, in a generalized way. He said any number of things could've happened. Like Eve Spurling could've met with an accident, that she could've fallen overboard. It was the wee hours, and the boat was moving. There was still some partying going on, a good bit of noise."

"Who was driving?"

"A hired crew. They didn't hear anything—a scream or a call for help or anything—but it was a big boat, the

Princessa Ora, by name. A hundred and thirty-six luxuriously appointed feet. Several decks."

"Remind me: Where was Spurling supposed to have been, and how did they determine when she went into the drink?"

"They couldn't pinpoint the timing, but she was last seen at about one o'clock, give or take a little either way, when she left a card game in the main saloon. The impression among the other players was that she intended to come back, that she was just going to her cabin for something. Aspirin, one woman said."

"Aspirin, huh? It might have been a pill, but I'll lay odds it wasn't Bayer. And I'll also bet the lapse of memory was agreed on and that there was some fast and furious jettisoning of other interesting 'medication' by the rest of that jolly band before the Coast Guard came on board."

"Whatever, she wasn't seen again. Jack raised the alarm that she was missing about forty-five minutes later."

"He didn't leave the saloon with her?"

"He wasn't there. He'd gone to bed around midnight, he said."

"What about the argument you said somebody heard?"

"Okay, that was the girlfriend of one of the guests. A woman named Leesa—that's Leesa with two *e*'s, if you please—Canady. Little Leesa had overpartied early on—a combination of sunburn and alcohol—and gotten sick and gone beddy-bye. She said she was awakened by voices on the deck, a man and a woman, both upset, the woman crying. It was the Spurlings, she said. She heard 'Jack,' and she heard him call the woman 'Eve.' She swore she recognized the voices, and she wouldn't budge from that."

"What were they arguing about?"

"They were only near her window for a minute, and she could only make out a word here and there, but—"

"A plastered dame? Who couldn't hear what they were saying but recognized their voices?"

"She claimed she was cold sober by then. She did say she definitely heard the word 'stupid' from him, and she heard a slap."

"A slap?"

" 'The sound of a palm against flesh,' was how she described it."

"Or the sound of water slapping against the hull of a boat."

"Followed by a gasp and more crying and high heels moving away from her window, fast."

Henry made a face. "I don't know . . ."

"Nobody else in the party admitted to having an argument that night, then or at any other time, on the deck or anywhere else, and nobody else was missing at quarter of two."

"I don't suppose Spurling admitted to having an argument either, did he?"

"He says he was asleep at the time. Trouble is, he wasn't."

"Who says?"

"The boyfriend of the little lady with the big ears. Mr. Boyfriend—I can't think of his name—came to his and Leesa's cabin not long after this overheard scene, and Leesa was all worried and insisted that he go to the Spurlings' cabin and see if Eve Spurling was all right. I gather this pair was still in the early stages of romance because he actually gave in and did it."

"And?"

"And there was nobody there, he said; neither man

nor wife. The door was ajar, he looked in, the bed was empty and unslept in."

"How did Spurling account for that?"

"He said the gentleman must have gone to the wrong cabin. He said he left the saloon at midnight, that he went straight to his cabin and was asleep within fifteen minutes. The next thing he knew was when he woke up at one forty-five and found himself in bed alone. He went looking for his wife. She was not on the boat."

"Let's say that *was* Eve Spurling the young lady heard on the deck. What're the chances it wasn't her husband with whom she was having a dispute?"

"There were several men aboard. A half dozen? Ten? I don't know. I assume the police checked everybody's whereabouts."

"And they all had corroborated alibis? Where, for example, was Leesa-double-*e*'s boyfriend before he came to bed? It's worth considering that, at least from what you've said, those two are the only ones disputing Spurling's story. What was it again he said to you last night?"

"That what he thought didn't matter. That only what he knew mattered. Or words to that effect."

Henry shook his head, sucking his upper lip thoughtfully. "I can't believe you didn't go after him on that."

"I was too caught up in eloquent persuasion. Which fell flat."

"So that's it? You're going to drop the whole thing?"

"Don't be ridiculous and don't patronize me. I'm dropping it, Henry, darling, 'under no circumstances whatsoever.' "

10

SARGE MCMANUS, B. F. COULTER'S UNORTHODOX MAN
Friday, was back in town.

Fresh from the wilds of Montana and two weeks of
floating the Smith River, fishing the Big Hole, cooking
over a campfire, and raising a beard, he answered the
phone when Ariel called her grandfather's L.A. condo.

"Just got in this morning," Sarge told her. "Your
granddad's not here right now. He's at a golf lesson."

"At a golf lesson," Ariel repeated, and hit the *S* on her
keyboard so hard two lines of sibilation hissed across the
monitor before she could control her finger. "He is
not!"

"He is," Sarge disagreed cheerfully, "and about time,
too. I've been after him to take up some kind of exercise
for years. You know, he's already looking healthier?
Which doesn't make any sense since until today, he
hasn't actually exerted himself past pulling out his
charge card. Have you seen all the stuff he's bought? 'I
got me a bag full of Callaways,' he tells me and starts
pulling 'em out to show me, like I know a putter from a

crowbar. 'Metal woods and irons,' he says, 'and look! A Big Bertha titanium driver.' He's bought a shelf full of how-to videos, and—"

"Knickers and argyle socks," Ariel growled.

"God knows. He seems to think that if he's paid for it, he'll know how to do it. Today starts the hands-on phase, though. *I'd* pay to see that! I can't figure what's got into him."

"I'll tell you what's got into him. Claws."

"Huh?"

"Of the female variety. He hasn't told you all about *Sissy?*"

"What're you talking about?"

"It's not a what, it's a who. Calls herself Sissy."

"Ariel—"

"Her real name is Sarah . . . something. I didn't catch her last name, but it doesn't matter what it is since she has in mind to get herself a new one. She's after B.F."

Silence deep as a Siberian snowdrift and twice as dangerous met this news. As it stretched, so did the satisfied smile on Ariel's face.

Sarge McManus was a consummate skeptic. Native mistrustfulness had been honed to a sharp-edged tool during the thirty years he'd spent as a Los Angeles cop and, more than once during those years, it had kept him alive. "Benefit of the doubt" was not a concept with which he was comfortable; where B.F. Coulter's welfare was concerned, it was not a concept with which he was familiar.

"Are you making some kind of joke?"

"Sarge, he's suddenly taking up *golf.*"

"What's golf got to do with this woman?"

"She plays. That's where he met her, at a country club in Tulsa, he said. He's flown her out here. Well, I don't know that he flew her out; she was out. She may still be, for all I know, set up in a love nest somewhere. He invited Henry and me to dinner to meet her. She's a good twenty-five years younger than he is. She's a very attractive redhead. She's sporting a big diamond ring already. She smiles under her lashes at him and caresses his hand on the table and talks about how 'lively' he is."

"That doesn't sound like B.F."

"Really? He's getting livelier by the day."

"I mean being taken in by some woman, or by anybody else for that matter. You're about the only person I ever saw him accept at face value, no questions asked. He's not gullible."

"No, but I think he's lonely. And, my friend, if I recall correctly, his lack of gullibility didn't prevent your checking *me* out pretty thoroughly."

"Yeah? Some dame turns up from noplace, claiming to be B. F. Coulter's heir, an heir he didn't know existed? His granddaughter's just been murdered by a person or persons unknown, and you show up claiming to be her *twin sister*, for crying out loud? What? I'm supposed to shake your hand and say 'Welcome to the family'?"

"I didn't claim anything. I didn't even know who I was, let alone who he was, and I wasn't after his money, and I'm still not, and you know it. And it's no mean feat to look like and behave like a woman you never met unless you are, in fact, her twin."

"When enough money's at stake, no feat's too mean."

"My point, exactly. Now, when are you going to start finding out about the Tulsa belle?"

It was Ariel's day for conversations with policemen, retired and otherwise. In her line of work they were indispensable resources. The one she called after hanging up with Sarge was a detective lieutenant. He was also a good friend, one of the first she'd made as an amnesiac and one of the few who knew she was. She invited him to lunch. "I'll pay," she said.

"I can't afford it when you pay," Max Neely said. "What do you want now?"

Ariel had gotten the names of several of the yachting party from accounts published at the time of Jack Spurling's trial. The rest she got over barbecued beef at a café in Santa Monica.

"This is a poor excuse for a barbecue sandwich," she grumbled.

The giant-economy-size redhead across the booth had ordered two, wolfed down the first as if it were an appetizer, and was voicing no complaints about the second.

"They don't even have real barbecue on the menu," Ariel said.

"Tastes real to me." Max licked his fingers clean of sauce before wiping them with a napkin. "You think it was fake cow?"

"That's just it; it was beef. Barbecue's pork."

"Barbecue is whatever you slap on a grill and set fire to and put sauce on."

"Not in the South."

"We're in L.A., Gold, and that don't mean lower Alabama." He reached for the menu and checked out the desserts. "They got pecan pie, though. I'll have a piece to honor your cherished newfound heritage." He signaled a waitress, ordered the pie, and waved to somebody he recognized at the counter, almost simultaneously.

Unlike the average big man, Max functioned in high gear. He almost crackled with energy, right to the crinkly tips of his baby-fine sandy red hair. He moved fast, talked fast, and laughed every chance he got. When his humor was too black for comfort, it paid to remember that his work was often a cesspool and his personal life had been no day at the beach; he was a widower, and his wife, Ariel had heard, had taken a long time to die.

Max's pie came, and he sampled it before he said, "I meant to tell you, I've been watching your bits on the show. Pretty good."

"Try not to turn my head."

"These names you wanted; they have to do with your show?"

"Is that a problem?"

Max twitched a shoulder. "It wasn't our case, and there's not anything confidential about who was on that boat. I am curious why you're poking these particular coals after all this time. If you knew something we didn't, you'd say so, wouldn't you?"

"Sure, I would."

"Sure, you would."

"No, really. I ran into Spurling and got interested is all. Reinterested, I should say; from what I'm told, we met two years ago."

"Oh, yeah? Before, huh?" Max said, twirling his forefinger in the direction of his forehead.

"Cute, Max. Yeah, before."

"How're you doing with that situation? Any breakthroughs?"

Ariel shook her head.

Max chewed pie glumly. "Wonder how many good memories I'd be willing to give up if I could wipe out the bad ones, too."

"You don't get to barter."

"What would you remember? If you could choose one thing?"

Ariel didn't have to think about it. "What happened the night Jane died."

"Your sister was killed by mistake, by a zoned-out creep with an IQ that would have to heat up to reach room temperature. He mistook her for you. You got hurt in the head when the bomb went off. End of story."

"Barely the prologue, Max. Did I see her? Did I recognize her? Did I speak to her? Did she and I just happen to be at the same place that night, and at the same time, or was it something . . ."

Max gave her a one-eyed squint. "Was it 'something' what? Fate?"

"Forget it."

"Forget it is right! Next thing, you'll be getting holy messages like Leeman Parker and his bunch of space cadets."

Ariel shuddered. "If the messages those people get are as creepy as the ones they send, I'm glad I'm not in the divine loop."

Ordinarily, Max would've jumped on the implication of that statement with both feet, but right now he had other things on his mind. "You don't go around dropping kooky little tidbits like that, do you? Or talking about your amnesia?"

"Oh, yeah, right! Like I think it's an asset? Are you crazy? You think the people at Woolf Television would've kept me two minutes if they'd known I was a head case? If it hadn't been for Henry's help . . ." Ariel shook her head. "There is no upside to amnesia, Max, and no possible good reaction. One, you'd get the people who don't believe in it. Period. Amnesia's a gimmick for a TV movie; it doesn't happen in real life. Then you'd get your morbidly curious. To them, I'd be an oddity. A freak." Ariel tapped her head with her fore-finger and rolled her eyes. "Wiggo! And then . . . let's not overlook the kinder folks who'd just pity me. No thank you."

Scratching his nose, Max grimaced. "Yeah, well, all that aside, there's another thing you ought to think about, now that you're a TV star."

"I'm not a TV *star*."

"You're on TV. And the better known you get, the riper you are for extortion. Even regular personalities are targets, but people find out you got no memory? You can't deny anything about your past because you don't know anything? Hoo! It's open season. They'll come out of the cracks to fill it in for you—and offer to sell their lies to the highest bidder. Or you just get some crankcase who claims he knew you once upon a time, who claims to be your oldest, dearest friend or your long-lost lover. Add to the equation that you've got a zillionaire for a grandfather . . ."

"The people who need to know know," Ariel said firmly, "and they know to keep it to themselves." I hope, she thought. Hearing Max voice her own anxieties made the "barbecue" she'd eaten come back to life. "Getting back to Jack Spurling . . ."

"Spurling, yeah. You just happened to run into him, you said?"

"Last week. He has a business near my market, on San Vicente."

"What kind of business?"

"Environmental consultation," Ariel surprised herself by saying. She wasn't in the mood to see Max wiggle his pinky or smirk.

Max frowned. "Like with the government? The EPA or something?"

"No. Indoor. Antiques, art, like that. You have the list from the cruise?"

There were seventeen names: twelve guests, six men and six women, and five crew, all men.

"Must be a big boat," Max commented.

"A hundred thirty-six feet. Six guest cabins. The *Princessa Ora*. Could you do one more thing for me? See if any of these people ever ran afoul of the law? Oh, and Eve Spurling . . . I heard she was arrested once. I'd like to know what for."

"Okay."

"*Okay?*"

"I'll see what I can find out. No problem."

"In exchange for . . . ?"

"You learn anything new, anything at all, you tell me."

It was no more than Ariel had expected; she agreed easily, picked up the check, and began to fish for money.

"I'm not kidding, Gold. No judgment calls, no delays."

"All right, all right. I said yes."

"And there's one other thing."

"What?"

"Tell me, what exactly is an 'environmental consultant'?"

Ariel was less than six minutes late getting back to her van. Half a block away she could see the pink paper under her windshield wiper and, beyond the van, the meter maid's little jitney chugging righteously away. She snatched the ticket off the windshield and aimed the van east, back to the studio.

The traffic was normal for L.A. That is to say, a breeding ground for acts of homicidal rage by otherwise docile citizens. Blue-haired librarians tailgated and sat on their horns. Sunday-school teachers blasphemed out open car windows. Mild-mannered bookkeepers cut off their fellow motorists and fought pedestrians for the crosswalks. Ariel rolled up her window and turned on the classical music station, smiling peaceably at anyone who looked her way and exhausting her knowledge of alternate routes.

At the studio a message from Jack Spurling waited on her voice mail. She called him.

"You sidestepped an implied question last night" was the first thing he said after hello. Ariel had no idea what he was talking about and said so.

"We were talking about love," Jack said.

"We were? When?"

"When I mentioned the changes in your appearance and behavior since last we met and surmised that love was at the root of it."

"That was a question?"

"You're sidestepping again. God, I told you my social skills were shot. I'm trying to ask you out. I didn't want to be turned down, so I was . . . Are you involved with somebody? Or . . . you're not *married* again, are you?"

Ariel's hand tightened on the receiver. "You knew I was married?" How well acquainted had she been with this man? "That I was once, I mean?"

"Of course I knew. Will you go out with me?"

Ariel hesitated. The story aside, this man just might be able to tell her something new about herself. There were so few people who'd really known whoever she used to be. Few? Make that no one. Had he?

There was, however, Henry to consider.

She and Henry had no "arrangement." They'd never discussed exclusivity, but she hadn't needed to. She couldn't imagine being involved with one man and wishing to go out with another. But this was different. And there *was* the story to consider, she reminded herself. While Jack had made it clear he wouldn't discuss it further, Ariel was confident she could work the subject in. Henry would approve.

Who was she kidding? Like she'd approve of Henry romancing his sources? So, she wouldn't tell Henry. So then she'd feel triply duplicitous: to Henry for sneaking behind his back, and to Jack, both for letting him believe she was uncommitted and for socializing under false colors.

"Yes," she said. "How's tomorrow night?"

"But we had plans tonight," Ariel said to Henry, quietly, and waited until the intern who was dropping off afternoon mail moved on before she said, "I already bought dinner. Salmon, your favorite, and fresh dill."

With a hitch of his head toward his office, Henry led the way. Closing the door behind them, he said, "Ham Snyder's only going to be in town tonight. I haven't seen him since we were at the *Plain Dealer*, a few centuries ago when I was young and full of oats."

"Were those the oats that broke up marriage number one? Or was it two? I lose track. Why is it again that I'm not invited to this nostalgic reunion?"

"Don't be nasty. You're welcome to come, but I warn you, we'll be telling old war stories. Lying about our fearless exploits during crises you're too young to remember even if you could."

"Gosh! The Teapot Dome Scandal. Black Friday. That sounds like fun. I'd love that."

"Okay, the real reason I don't want you along is because you wouldn't like Ham."

"Why not?"

"Let's just say he's not enlightened in every respect."

Ariel translated mentally. "You mean he's a sexist."

"I mean he hasn't achieved a higher plane in regard to gender neutrality. Come on, Ariel, does it really make a difference whether you and I have dinner together tonight or tomorrow night?"

It did, because she'd be with Jack the following night. A corkscrew of guilt twisted through her midsection. "You're right," she said. "I'm being selfish. Of course you should go out with Ham. I can't remember the last time you just let go, you know? And had fun? But Henry, if it's all the same to you, let's do our thing Sunday night instead of tomorrow night." She counted on Henry's relief at her backing down to squeeze by without an explanation, and she almost made it.

"Okay," Henry said. "Why?"

"Why? Oh, you mean why Sunday instead of tomorrow?" Ariel would not lie. She'd devote one night of her life to subterfuge, but she wouldn't outright lie about it, not to Henry. "Just better for me. Things to do. Hey, let's do something totally different, why don't we? Do you dance? Isn't that funny? I don't even know. Of course, I don't know if *I* dance."

"Why are you babbling?"

"Why, indeed? Have a good time tonight. And do say 'Oink' to your chauvinist friend for me."

11

IT WAS SHORTLY BEFORE DUSK, AND ARIEL WAS STRAPPING on Jessie's leash for a walk when her doorbell rang. She found Sam Heller on her front porch with Stonewall beside him. Stonewall wasn't one to stand on ceremony. The little yellow dog barked hello and climbed Ariel's legs in a brief, hyperactive fit of affection before scooting through them, dragging his leash behind him as he headed straight for the treat jar in the kitchen.

"Won't you come in?" Ariel said dryly. "You, too, Sam." Sam had never paid her a visit alone and uninvited. "What's up?"

"Is it okay to drop by like this? I know Dad's out with somebody else tonight—a guy, I mean, not a woman—so I figured you wouldn't be busy. I kind of wanted to talk to you about something."

The statement gave Ariel pause. It confirmed that Sam was aware she and Henry enjoyed more than a professional relationship, and that he assumed it wasn't a casual one. It suggested, at least to Ariel, that he might

be here to ask questions about it and, more dismaying-
ly, that he might be here to voice his opinion of it.

"My life's not quite so circumscribed as you imply
but, as it happens, you're right; I'm not busy."

"What does circumscribed mean?"

"Limited. How'd you get over here?"

"On my bike."

"With Stonewall?"

"He likes to ride in the basket. I fixed him a
harness."

"Your dad know you're here?"

"No. I wanted to talk to you, you know, without
him."

Uh-oh, thought Ariel. "We were just going for a
walk," she said. "Get Stonewall. Come with us."

They walked to the north end of the neighborhood, a
compact, cloistered tract of perhaps eighty houses, the
oldest built in the thirties. A few, unfortunately, had
been mansionized during the last decade, but most
retained a quaint *Father Knows Best* character Ariel
loved. She knew every house and was on vaguely familiar terms with much of the flora, and the fauna as well.
She could call nearly all the neighborhood dogs, if not
their owners, by name.

Whatever Sam wanted to talk about still hadn't been
broached when they turned south again.

"Notice the scent?" Ariel asked him. "Really subtle
and clean? It's that acacia tree." She pointed to a brilliant yellow mass of fuzzy bloom.

"Yeah?" Sam gave it a polite glance.

"Getting nippy," Ariel said, and zipped her jacket.
"Why do you suppose forty-something seems so much
colder in Southern California than anywhere else?"

Sam smiled vaguely.

"You know this whole neighborhood used to be bean fields? The freeway hadn't been built then, of course. Sepulveda Boulevard was the only big north-south route in this area."

"Umm," said Sam, whose interest in history and geography was on a par with his interest in horticulture and the weather.

"Stonewall doesn't heel too well, does he?" Ariel noticed.

"Sometimes."

"You should make him stop at curbs, though. He used to be pretty good about that."

"Jessie's, like, perfect," Sam contributed.

"I can't take credit. She was professionally trained when I got her." They were on a short street that dead-ended at the neighborhood's westernmost border. "Tell you what. There's no traffic here. Let's give Stonewall a little refresher course, want to?"

Sam showed more enthusiasm than he had thus far, relieved, Ariel thought, to be diverted from trying to formulate an opening to his subject.

She put Jessie on a down-stay on the sidewalk. "How much," she asked, "do you know about training for basic commands?"

"Some. A little. Not much."

"Okay, tell him to sit." Sam did. Stonewall, after a reluctant, undecided wiggle of his posterior, complied.

"Praise him. Good. Take off his leash. Now, hold your hand up—like a traffic cop. Back away while you tell him to stay. Just once. Don't tell him but once. Back away. Keep backing. Wait a few seconds. When you practice this, increase the time gradually, all right? Now, say c-o-m-e," she spelled out. Sam said "Come." Stonewall did. Praise and petting followed. The simple exercise was repeated. The third time there was outside interference.

A tabby cat darted from ivy cover in front of the nearest house. Stonewall lost interest in Sit and Stay and took off in hot pursuit. At that moment a man came out the front door of the house. It was one of the original houses of the neighborhood, unaltered from its modest prewar construction, as unchanged as if it were trapped in amber. The man was around sixty, surrendering into dilapidated, flabby late middle age.

"That dog's supposed to be on a leash," he yelled from his porch.

Ariel looked toward Sam, giving him the chance to call his dog. He did. Stonewall had disappeared. In the murky, still flatness of twilight, it was hard to tell where he'd gone.

"That's the law," the man was yelling. "They're supposed to be on a leash."

"I'm so sorry," Ariel said, and smiled. "We'll get him. Just give us a minute." Sam called again, louder. "I live down the street," Ariel said. "We were doing a little training."

"Do it at your own house. I've got cats. That damn dog will scare my cats."

Totally unconsciously, Ariel let a little sweet Southern slide into her voice, as if she were reverting to her native tongue. "He's not a bit aggressive, sir. Just playful. Sam? Run get him."

"You stay off my property, boy!"

Ariel felt her smile solidify. Jessie stirred behind her. "I'm afraid we can't get the dog without coming into your yard. May I? It'll just take a minute." She murmured "Stay" to Jessie and, with a look that told Sam to do the same, she took a few determined steps up the man's walkway. A gray-haired woman appeared behind him, holding the screen door open, looking worried.

"Warren?" she said.

"Get back in the house, Lila."

"Let them get the dog."

"I said, go back in!"

Lila gave Ariel one quick, apologetic look. She might have been the voice of moderation in the family, but she knew when to hold them and when to fold them. She retreated, and the screen door slapped shut.

Ivy rustled, and the cat came flying, a silent missile, one second earthbound and the next scaling a tulip tree. Stonewall cornered the house, his tongue a flag. He and the cat, in his opinion, were having an excellent chase. As he passed the homeowner, the man kicked. Stonewall yelped and scurried out of range.

"Don't do that!" Ariel was within a few feet of the dog and ready to scoop him up.

"Get away from here!" the man said.

"I'm trying to do that, believe me! Don't kick him!"

The man trotted toward Stonewall, temporarily hemmed in by porch furniture, and kicked at him again.

"I said stop that! This minute! This has gotten out of hand. You scare the animal, I can't get him, okay? Just stay still."

Stonewall picked the worst possible moment to growl. Warren lost whatever control a frustrated middle age and bilious nature might have left him. He pushed past Ariel and raised his foot. Behind him, she raised her own. She aimed it precisely at his coccyx and put her full weight behind the kick. Warren hit the deck, knees first. He groaned. Stonewall headed for higher ground.

Ariel felt as though she'd been injected with rocket fuel. She resisted the impulse to boot him again and keep on stomping. Her vision cleared. Breathing hard, she said, "Let me help you up," and bent to do so. She could see the freckles on his scalp beneath thinning hair. He slapped her hand away.

"I'll sue you," he said. With more agility than Ariel would have credited him, he got to his feet and began backing toward his door, pointing his finger and wagging it furiously. "I'll sue your pants off! I'll sue you for everything you're worth!"

"Are you all right?" Ariel asked. "Did you hurt yourself?"

"You stay away from me!" He'd opened the screen door and put it between himself and Ariel. She could see his wife behind him, wringing her hands. "Don't you touch me!" he warned. "I'm suing!"

"Fine, sir. You do that." Ariel smiled. She could feel the muscle at the corner of her mouth jumping like a live wire. "Good night."

She turned and marched down his walkway. Sam had Stonewall in his arms. Jessie was where she'd been told to stay, but she didn't look happy about it. Ariel snatched up her leash. "Is Stonewall okay?" she asked. "Good! Then, let's get out of here." They were in the next block before Ariel began to giggle. "I hope the old vinegar puss can't sit down for a week," she said, and laughed out loud.

"Do you think he'll really sue you?" Sam asked, round-eyed.

"Probably."

"Doesn't that bother you?"

"It will tomorrow. Tomorrow he can hire a lawyer and spend every cent he's got and sue me silly, but right now I feel too good to give a rip. If I'd known how good losing your temper felt, I'd make a point of doing it at least once a day. I'm hungry. Do you like salmon?"

"You're kind of crazy, aren't you?"

"I hope so, my young friend. Just enough to stay sane."

Ariel was snipping dill onto two perfectly grilled salmon tails when she asked, "Didn't you say you wanted to talk to me about something?"

"Yeah." Sam tossed salad and sucked on his cheek and blurted, "What do girls like, anyway?"

"What do which girls like?"

"Any girls. Since you're one—I mean, since you used to be one—you ought to know, I thought."

"Sit down. Let's eat. And start at the beginning."

An angel, it seemed, had descended to earth, embodied in the form of one Laurie McCutcheon, the thirteen-year-old sister of a friend of Sam's. This apotheosis of femininity had fair hair ("kind of the color of a collie, the tan part, not the white part") which she wore in a long braid, and golden-brown eyes ("you know how a football looks brand new?"), and she was smart ("not like a brain but, like, she doesn't squeal or giggle or talk about dumb, girlie stuff"). She knew more about baseball than any girl Sam knew ("I mean, way more! She and Phil—that's her brother—they play this game like *Jeopardy!* except that baseball's the only category, and they play for money!"), but the best thing about her was that she was a "serious" musician, a violinist.

"She's got a nice body, too." Sam's face flamed, but he didn't drop his eyes when he said it.

Ariel scratched her cheek. It didn't itch, but it gave her a second or two to stall. She had the weirdest sensation that she was talking to an unformed, adolescent Henry, thirty years younger. The boy looked so much like his father. Long bones. Fine long fingers that, in Sam's case, could span an octave without straining. A slightly yellow cast to the skin, the kind of skin that would tan in a day. Dark hair and deep-set eyes. But the eye color wasn't Henry's. Henry's eyes were dark. Sam's were light. They were his mother's eyes. "Laurie sounds perfect," Ariel said.

"Even Phil likes her."

It was on the tip of Ariel's tongue to ask if Sam wasn't a little young yet for girls, but she felt reasonably sure that would be a mistake. "What you asked a while ago," she said instead, "about what girls like? Explain."

"I want her to like me and to know, you know, that I like her, but I don't want to sound like some nerdy retard, and I don't want to get shot down. So, how do you impress girls? And not sacrifice your self-respect?"

"That's tough. I'd have to take a little time to think about that. I'm flattered you're asking me but why, exactly, are you? I mean, why me?"

"Out of everybody I know, you were the one I decided would most likely steer me right. You're a girl, you're smart, you got my dad interested in you so I figure you understand guys, you're not a parent so you don't have these prejudices people get when they have kids, and you're straight with me like I'm a human being instead of some kind of junior person. You don't change your voice when you talk to me, you know what I mean? Plus, you're kind of sharp looking; you're not a dog or anything."

"Thank you." Ariel was fascinated. "What else?"

"I know I can trust you not to go blabbing what I say. You never told Dad that time about how I covered up for Eric when he stole those CDs or what I said about his dad beating up on him."

"No, but I was sure glad when *you* told him."

"So, did you think yet?"

"Oh, boy," Ariel said and hoped common sense was

as good as experience. "Well, the first thing is, girls aren't interchangeable. They're individuals. But you and Laurie have a lot in common, it sounds like, so put yourself in her place, and behave the way you'd want her to behave toward you."

"Yeah?"

"You respect her, right? Then treat her that way. Listen to her when she talks. If she looks especially nice or does something well, tell her so. You don't have to gush. Everybody likes to be made to feel good. Treat her like a lady. Unless she's a rabid feminist, open doors for her, offer your arm sometimes."

"You're kidding! The guys see me doing that, I'm dead meat!"

"You'll be the one with the girl, won't you?"

Sam looked dubious. "Anything else?"

"Just the basic stuff, like no girl I know is impressed by crudeness. You'd know better than to belch or whatever around her, wouldn't you?"

Sam squirmed just enough to suggest that he hadn't necessarily known better one hundred percent of the time. "You said tell her if I like something about her. What if I *don't* like something? How far can you go with telling girls the real truth?"

" 'It has always been desirable to tell the truth, but seldom if ever necessary.' "

"What?"

"Nothing. I was trying to be funny. Generally speaking, I recommend being honest." She thought that over. "But some things are better left unsaid. The trick, Sammy, is knowing which ones they are."

12

ARIEL WAS DOING SOMETHING SHE HAD VIRTUALLY NO experience of. She was dressing for a date.

Granted, it wasn't a real date. It was a fact-finding mission, and a professional engagement. Granted, too, she'd gone out with Henry many times, but that was long after he'd become her dearest friend, so it hadn't been as if she'd had to sell him a bill of goods. And granted, presumably, the man to whom she'd briefly been married had paid court, but since she didn't remember, it didn't count. For all practical purposes, she was a thirty-three-year-old novice at this dating business, and she couldn't make up her mind what to wear.

Long gone were the monochromatic, form-concealing clothes she'd favored before amnesia liberated what she'd decided was her alter ego. At the moment, everything she'd bought to replace those sad garments looked no more appealing. Jack Spurling had made reservations, so he'd told her, at a "good" restaurant. Black and relatively slinky was probably appropriate attire. The dress she considered first was black, and too slinky. The next three candidates were, to differing degrees, too big for her now. Hangers were slid aside, one after the other, and Ariel grew more indecisive with each.

She dropped to her dressing table bench and looked at her carefully made-up face in the mirror. "What are you doing?" she asked herself. "Tonight's business. Strictly business."

The doorbell rang. For a panicked second, she thought it was Jack. He was nervous, she sensed, about this evening, but surely not so nervous that he'd show up half an hour early? She threw on a robe and went to the door.

One of her favorite people on earth had come to call. Uninvited, unexpected, and, at this particular moment, inconvenient, Marguerite Harris planted a kiss near Ariel's cheek, handed her an envelope, and, in a conversational style unique to herself, said, "*Bonsoir*, cupcake. I was intending to leave this in your mailbox, but I saw your lights blazing and, as it's been an age since we've seen you except on television, I decided, don't you know, to deliver the invitation *personne à personne* so that you could RSVP right now. Hello, my sweet Jessie, you beautiful girl." Marguerite bent to rain air kisses in the vicinity of the shepherd's head without interrupting herself. "Not that you're allowed to say anything but yes, so say it, and I'll be on my way and you can finish getting dressed. To go . . . ?"

"Out to dinner. Come in. Invitation to what?"

"The opening of *The Spa*, naturally, and supper afterward, with Carl and me, of course, and a few close friends. It's Friday night, and you will be there, right? Of course, you will. Well, I won't keep you. You're going out with darling Henry, I suppose?"

Ariel laughed and clasped the tiny, much older woman who lived two houses away in a quick hug.

Marguerite never seemed to age. ("How could I get any more wrinkles?" she would ask; "I've only got so much face.") Under penciled brows her blue eyes were as avid as ever ("Call it like it is, dear: nosy"), and her frizzled hair, as if it had been exposed too long to the elements, was the color of rust. Her lips and nails were cardinal red tonight, but her mode of dress was rather more conventional than usual. She was dwarfed by an enormous greatcoat, formerly owned, perhaps, by a cossack, and it hung open to reveal peacock blue satin pajamas and a glittering aquamarine brooch the size of a bar of soap. On her child-sized feet were marabou-trimmed mules. She looked like a wizened lady of the night; she was, in fact, an acclaimed playwright and had been since the Truman administration. *The Spa* was her newest play, the first she'd written in years.

"I'm not going out with Henry," Ariel said. "It's a business thing. Come pick out something for me to wear, will you? I've gone through everything six times, and I can't make up my mind."

It wasn't as foolhardy a notion as Marguerite's own garb might suggest. She dressed to make a statement: a Bronx cheer. That wasn't to say that she didn't have a critical eye for costumery both on and off the stage.

With one sharp look that plainly said For a business thing you're so worried about what to wear?, she led the way to Ariel's closet and began running over the options and asking questions. "A 'nice' restaurant, did you say? As in good food or as in see and be seen?" She reached for a hanger. "Umm, doesn't matter. This one." She thrust a trouser suit the color of burnished bronze into Ariel's hands. "Sets off your hair color marvelously, but don't wear that pin you wore with it last time. Too timid. Where are your baubles, dear?" Accessories were chosen just as decisively, and Ariel set and wound the dress watch Marguerite picked out. "The gentleman is due in ten minutes."

"Is the gentleman someone I'd know?"

"Maybe." Ariel buttoned the pants and slipped on the jacket. "John Spurling is his name."

"John Spurling? I know that name from somewhere. From the news? Yes, definitely. Is he in politics? No. It's something unpleasant, but it's not politics. Spurling, Spurling . . . Oh, my dear!" Marguerite's forehead wrinkled as her eyebrows soared. "What an extraordinary business you're in! It does occur to me to wonder whether it's wise to engage in business with a 'gentleman' accused of murdering his wife. Is it?"

"Accused, not convicted."

"Yes, rather left up in the air wasn't it? Interesting, don't you know, that these days people want justice only in the abstract? When they're reading their newspaper over the breakfast table, they're death on crime—rabid as a lynch mob and staunch as the pilgrim fathers—but put them in a jury box? Stand a living, breathing defendant in front of them and throw in a glib lawyer shoveling smoke and, all too often, they can't get off the pot.

"You look lovely. Call me when you get in tonight, will you? Just to put my mind at ease? I assume it won't be late since this is a *business* affair?"

Marguerite was hardly out the door when Jack Spurling arrived. He was, definitely, nervous.

"I stopped at a florist on the way over," he said, and handed Ariel a sheaf of elegant white calla lilies. "I almost decided on an orchid corsage so big it would've covered your whole chest and made you look like a prom queen, but I thought, overkill maybe?"

Ariel laughed, and then wasn't sure he was joking. For all her confident assurance to Marguerite, she was more than a little nervous herself. She admired the lilies and introduced Jessie.

Jack held out his hand to be smelled. "My shepherd was named Alcindor, Al for short."

"Alcindor?" Ariel watched Jessie sniff and then sit back to see if the stranger would offer anything more interesting than an empty hand. "When did you have him?"

"Oh, I was a teenager. Fifteen. I got him for my fifteenth birthday, I think." Jack was eyeing his surroundings and, Ariel thought, starting to relax a little. "I wasn't far off, was I? In fact, I was right on. Rich colors. Warm. Lots of books, comfortable seats to read them in . . . nice! That armoire is very fine."

"Thanks. Any top-of-the-head suggestions?"

"If I were a baker, would you be hitting me up for free croissants the minute I walk in the door?"

"Good point," Ariel said, and excused herself to put the flowers in water. When she returned, she said, "I'm guessing you're from Milwaukee?"

"Excuse me?"

"Are you from Milwaukee?"

Jack blinked, to rather dazzling effect with his thick dark lashes and pale eyes. "How'd you know that?" he asked.

"Ah-ha!"

"You can't know that from my accent. I don't have one." Looking at Ariel as if she were a witch, he said, "How'd you know?"

"Elementary. Quick, rough mathematics tells me you got Alcindor in the early seventies?"

"Yes?"

"Nineteen seventy-one, maybe?"

He stopped to calculate. "Yes?"

"You're a basketball fan."

"Yes? I mean yes, I am, but I don't see—"

"Everybody in Milwaukee was a basketball fan in nineteen seventy-one. The Bucks won the championship. They took it in four straight, a sweep. Thanks largely—not to detract from Oscar Robertson—but thanks largely to Lew Alcindor, who was NBA top scorer that year *and* MVP, regular season and play-off."

A slow smile of incredulity had crept over Jack's face. "And from that you got—"

"Oh, it wasn't such a long shot." Ariel laughed, realized she was chattering, but couldn't seem to stop. How *do* you socialize with an accused murderer? "Teenage boys," she said, "often name their pets after their idols. Nineteen seventy-one? Let's see . . . if you'd been into baseball, especially if you lived in Atlanta, you might've named your dog Hank. If you'd gotten Alcindor for your *sixteenth* birthday, he'd probably have been named Kareem."

"I could've been from L.A.," Jack pointed out. "He was still Alcindor when he played for UCLA."

"But that was in the sixties. He graduated in the late sixties and didn't come back to town till, what? Nineteen seventy-five? Seventy-six?"

"You're amazing."

Ariel held up a restraining forefinger. "Wait," she said. "One last factor in my reasoning is that, statistically speaking, it was more likely that you were from somewhere else. Not many of us over-thirty types are actually from L.A. originally. Most are like you: imports."

"How did you know all that stuff about Alcindor? About the Bucks and everything?"

"I like basketball, too, but it's mostly because I helped

research a piece on him a few months ago, and . . ." She slipped on her coat. "I have some odd quirks, Jack. One of the few useful ones is a photographic memory." Almost under her breath, she said, "Ironically enough."

Jack shook his head, slowly. "You're a dangerous woman. Talking to you, a person would have to be careful to keep his story straight."

"If he could be convinced to tell it."

Ignoring that, Jack asked, "Why ironical? And if you're memory's so superior, why'd you blank out on me?"

"Another quirk, I guess," Ariel said, and changed the subject. He wouldn't get an answer to that question that night, that week, or at any other time.

The restaurant was on Rodeo Drive and was "nice" as anticipated. The food was a treat for the eyes, what there was of it was tasty enough, and the prices were suitably absurd. The diners were either instantly recognizable or looked as if they thought they should be. Quite a few of the faces of both groups, male and female, were as slick and tight as the skin on a drum.

"Good ol' Southern California," Ariel remarked when she called it to Jack's attention. "Have you ever noticed," she asked, "how the veterans of too many lifts resemble chimpanzees?"

Jack glanced around. "I don't think I'm with you on that one."

"Around the mouth." Ariel drew her forefingers down the faint curved lines that parenthesized her own mouth from nose to outer lip. "See these? Everybody with any mileage on them has these things." She stretched the skin back toward her ears, and the lines vanished. "Muzzle mouth, see? Now, the woman at the next table . . . the one you spoke to when we came in?"

Ariel raised her water glass and, over the rim, surreptitiously, aimed her eyes at a sixtyish woman dressed in black spangles from high neckline to hem.

"Patsy Dalton?" Jack glanced the woman's way. "She doesn't have any," he murmured. A mischievous grin caught the corner of his mouth and, very subtly, he made a scratching motion near his armpit. "Uhhh," he grunted, Cheetah-like.

Ariel snorted, inhaling water through her nose. "Who is she?" she sputtered, patting herself down with a napkin. "Anybody semi-famous?"

"First wife of a producer famous enough to be stinking rich and now smooching with wife two at that table over in the corner."

"How do you know them?"

"Patsy Dalton, bless her, is my client. Wife two wants to be, but if I took her on, Mrs. Dalton would take her trade elsewhere. She redecorates every time she feels bored and unfulfilled; she feels bored and unfulfilled a lot."

Their waiter approached just then, and once they'd ordered, Ariel asked, "How'd you get into interior design?"

"You mean what's a nice heterosexual boy like me—"

"You're touchy about that, aren't you?"

"I just get tired of it. You wouldn't believe how often the husbands of my clients ask that question. They think they're being cute. One of these days I'm going to plant a big wet one right on some jerk's kisser. See how funny he thinks that is."

"Better take up judo first. And that's not what I was asking anyway. You owned furniture stores before. I'd have guessed that was more in the line of buying, finance, human resources, like that. Business. What you do now is art."

"Just because I know Belle Époque from Bauhaus doesn't mean I can't be a good businessman."

"But what you did before was—"

" 'Before,' " Jack said, "was another life. I was another person."

"I can relate to that."

"Really? Why?"

"I have bottomless fonts of empathy. You still haven't said how you came to be in your line of work."

"The trial . . ." Jack shifted slightly in his chair. "All that happened taught me life's too short and way too uncertain to waste it doing something I don't enjoy. Or to give a damn if other people have a problem with what I do enjoy. The design aspect of our business—my father-in-law's and mine—was what I did best. He introduced me to my first client."

"Your father-in-law thinks well of you, obviously."

"And surprisingly?"

"Well . . ."

"He knows I didn't kill his daughter. Bread?" Jack offered the basket. "Did I tell you how lovely you look this evening?"

"Not that I recall."

"You remind me of somebody. I noticed it when I first saw you on the tube."

"Who?"

Jack shook his head. "It won't come to me."

"Jack, about your wife . . . The last time we met, I asked what you thought happened to her. You said it didn't matter what you thought. But what *do* you think?"

A very long ten seconds passed during which Ariel watched the light eyes across from her chill to ice water. "I'd hoped," Jack said, "that we could at least make it through the salad course."

It would have taken a more hardened woman than Ariel to hold his gaze.

"Oh, well," Jack said. He took a roll from the basket, looked at it, and then tossed it back in. "You jump in a swamp with alligators, you don't expect to come out with all your toes."

"I am in the news business, Jack. You can't really expect me to—"

"Credit me, Ariel, with enough intelligence to take into account what you do for a living, to know that you weren't going out with me just because I'm such a good-time guy. And one thing I do remember about you is that you're one single-minded lady." His mouth might have softened by a fraction. "Persistent as a case of the shingles. But still . . . call me a cockeyed optimist, but I really thought we might have one pleasant evening before you started in with the questions."

"Alligator?" Ariel said with a small shake of her head. "Shingles? My! Kind of makes me wonder why you asked me out."

"I hope it won't hurt your feelings if I say that, right now, I'm wondering the same thing."

"I'll make you a promise."

"Oh, yeah?"

"I won't bring up the subject again."

Jack gave her a sidelong look.

Ariel smiled, tentatively. "Until the dessert course."

"Skip dessert, okay?" Without any change of inflection or expression, he asked, "Why did you pretend not to know me?"

Ariel took a roll and a moment to butter it, and her voice was casual when she said, "Why would I pretend? You called yourself Jack; it threw me off. You were always John two years ago. And it has been two years.

I've worked a lot of news in two years, and, let's face it, you've changed a lot since then. You said so yourself. We both have."

"Two whole years, huh? A woman who remembers who the NBA champs were in nineteen seventy-one can't recall a man she had a number of in-depth conversations with two years ago? A man in a jail cell, accused of murder?"

"Memory's a funny thing."

"Hilarious, judging from the expression on your face."

"It plays tricks on you sometimes," Ariel said. "Like these conversations we had . . ." She took a small bite of the roll, and immediately wished she hadn't. Her mouth was too dry to swallow.

Uninformingly, Jack said, "What about them?"

"I don't remember them being all that 'in-depth.' Just what did I say that stuck so deathlessly in your mind?"

" 'Deathlessly' might be stretching it a bit."

"Oh. Well, maybe you're making too much of it, period?"

Jack stared. "I don't . . . Are you embarrassed about the things you confided? Is that what this is all about? It is, isn't it! You're a TV personality now, and you think I'm going to"—he waved a hand as if tossing crumbs to pigeons—"tell all? *Me?*"

"What would I have to be embarrassed about?"

"Nothing. But maybe you don't see it that way. It was obvious to me at the time that you didn't go around broadcasting your private business. I doubt that's changed."

" 'Private business'?" Her laugh was meant to be light; it sounded, even to her, like glass splintering.

With his forefinger, Jack smoothed the scar that sliced his eyebrow. He did it, Ariel had noticed, whenever he was perplexed or stressed. "Tell you what," he said. "Let's have it your way. We chatted about our birth signs, okay? And inflation. And—"

"No, I'm serious. If you remember—"

"I remember how happy you were that one day. So full of your news you couldn't hide it. I'd thought you were such a sobersides, but you were smiling fit to kill." He smiled to himself then and, frustratingly, said, "I promise, I'll never tell a soul you weren't the unremitting professional, okay? That you actually stopped asking questions for a few minutes and broke down and acted human."

"But—"

"Want to try it again?"

It wasn't that hard once Ariel got into the swing of it. She didn't bring up his past again, or hers. She didn't ask about his wife's death and, incredibly, it seemed to her when she thought about it later, she forgot he might have been responsible for it. The evening slipped by quickly, flowing on shared interests, snagging on divergent opinions. They were arguing when they got to her house, about immigration. She was talking about natural human instincts; Jack was talking about money, the bottom line.

His headlights swept the house as he pulled into her driveway, finishing his argument with, "And that's one point you can't refute." Ariel didn't. Her mind was no longer on the conversation but on how to handle the next few minutes. He cut the engine and then the lights. It was suddenly loudly quiet. The car's roomy interior seemed to have shrunk to the size of a cupboard, and the two of them filled it.

"Wait a minute," she said. "Turn your lights back on."

When he did, her gaze quickly raked the patch of house they illuminated. The pale blankness of the garage door. The bricked walkway and the grassy yard on either side of it. "Something's wrong," she said, and leaned toward the windshield. "Something's not . . ."

"What is it? What's the matter?"

It took several seconds more to figure out what she'd seen but registered only subliminally. "It was pitch dark," she whispered.

"What?"

"Before you turned your lights back on."

Jack doused the headlights again, and everything went black.

"I left my outside lights on," Ariel said.

"Power failure?"

"Just my house?" She was out of the car, streaking to the porch. The porch light was shattered. She assumed the light over the garage was, too. The door had something splashed across it and so did the front windows, something that looked like blood, but the door was still locked. She could hear Jessie snuffling and scratching on the other side. Jack had to take the keys when her fumbling fingers refused to work.

The dog tore between them into the yard. Feverishly, she sniffed at the ground, growling in her throat and following her nose from trampled flower beds to sidewalk. The fur on her back was erect as a Mohawk when she stopped, looking around with the air of a warrior too late to battle. Ariel deactivated the alarm and called her inside.

Jack was looking at the muck on the door. He touched it, and his fingers came away sticky. He sniffed them. "Paint," he said.

The living room was exactly as they'd left it. Ariel rushed from room to room, flipping on lights. Nothing inside the house had been disturbed. She collapsed onto the sofa, trembling, and was horrified to realize that she was on the verge of tears. Jack had been beside her as she made her frantic rounds, and he watched her now with an expression of concern.

"Hey, now. Everything's okay," he said. "It's not a tragedy. Just some screwball passing by, probably. Bored kids."

"You don't understand," Ariel said, and tilted her head back, blinking to stem the flow. Jessie nuzzled at her knees, nervously. "Just give me a second; I'll be fine."

"Where would I find brandy?" he asked. Ariel pointed to the sideboard in the dining room and made herself breathe deeply, practicing the pranayama she'd learned from yoga. When he came back, he found her exactly as he'd left her, as if she were frozen into position.

"Here," he said. He handed her a glass and sat down. "Now what is it I don't understand?"

"Nothing I want to talk about, Jack. Sorry."

He fiddled with his tie, loosening it, and said nothing.

"It's just that . . . the house has been broken into before. Twice, actually, but who's counting?" Ariel tried a smile and failed miserably. "Both times were . . . devastating. It all came back for a few seconds there. It just . . . hit me."

"You don't look to me like a woman who cries easily or throws around words like *devastating*. What happened?"

Ariel was framing a polite way to avoid the question when she realized she couldn't think of one good reason not to answer it. "It was because of a story I'd been . . . researching for a long time. A man came after me with a knife. Jessie attacked him. He stabbed her. I shot him."

"You . . . killed him?"

Ariel nodded. She gave Jack an edited and rather disjointed account of the events that had taken place the year before: the botched break-in and the car bomb that had almost proved fatal. It had proved fatal for her twin, who'd been mistaken for her. To her immense surprise, she found herself telling him that, too, and about her adoption and learning about it too late to know her sister or their parents.

He heard her through. His eyes were so nearly translucent Ariel felt she could see his mind tracking, trying to assimilate the information, and, she knew, catching her hesitation, as if she were on the verge of saying more.

"And?" he said.

"And . . ." In the space of an instant, for far less time than it had taken to say them, Ariel heard Max Neely's words from just the day before. *People find out you got no memory? You can't deny anything about your past because you don't know anything? They'll come out of the cracks to fill it in for you!* And her confident response. *The people who need to know know, and they know to keep it to themselves.*

"And nothing," she said to Jack. "That's not a bizarre enough story for you?" She took a shaky breath, and managed a smile. "You can see why I don't tell it often," she said. "You look dazed."

"It is quite a story. Your twin, she was identical?"

"Jane. Yes." Ariel shook her head. "We came within feet of each other, within seconds, the night she was killed. If she'd stayed at the restaurant a little longer, if I'd gotten there a little earlier . . ."

Suddenly, Jack's expression changed to outright incredulity. "Restaurant? You're talking about Jane Macaulay? Jane Macaulay, the model? You're kidding me."

"You're not being especially tactful."

"No! I just didn't realize that's who your . . ." He looked more dazed than ever. "My God, of course! *That's* who you reminded me of. But you said identical. Jane had—"

"A cleft chin, I know. A scar, actually, from a childhood accident, my grandfather told me."

"And your nose . . ."

"Mine was fixed," Ariel said impatiently. "Jack, how could you possibly remember Jane's face that well?"

"I knew her."

"What?"

"Briefly. Not well. She was a client of mine not long before . . . before she died."

It was Ariel's turn to be dazed. "You're not lying about this?" she said sharply. "I mean, I'm sorry, but that would be the cruelest thing you could possibly do to me."

"No, Ariel, I'm not lying."

"Tell me," Ariel said urgently. "Tell me everything you remember about her. Every detail. I don't care how small."

"Well . . ." After several minutes' thought he said, "I liked Jane, a lot. I thought she seemed real, you know? Through and through. No ego trips, no pretensions." He paused. "She wasn't gorgeous, not like you'd expect a big-time model to be, and she sure wasn't anything as banal as pretty. I guess it was that her face and the camera clicked. It picked up the life, the humor. Her face was . . . it was interesting." He gave Ariel a little grin. "Like yours." Abruptly, he asked, "Did you ever meet her husband?"

"Once. After she died. I didn't much like him."

"Neither did I. I wonder if she did. She didn't seem . . ."

98

en

JUDY MERCERJUDY MERCER

"Didn't seem what?"

Jack was shaking his head. "I just figured something out. You weren't ever in her house, were you?"

"Once. *The Open File* did a story about her murder."

"I'll bet you felt right at home, didn't you?"

"Instantly. I didn't know then, about us. About who Jane was. Her house was more elegant than mine, but still . . . I could've picked out every fabric, every piece of furniture."

"That's why I was so right on about what your place would be like. I was associating the two of you without even knowing it. You know what? You act more like her now than, well, the way I remember you."

"What do you mean by that?"

"It's late. I'm getting punchy. Look, are you okay? To be by yourself?"

"The alarm warning sign—or Jessie barking—stopped them earlier. They won't come back, not tonight anyway."

"I'll go then," he said, but he didn't immediately make a move to do so. "Hey," he said softly, "thanks for talking to me. For letting down your defenses."

"You're easy to talk to," Ariel replied. *Way* too easy, she thought. The man did have a way about him. As she'd apparently done at least once before, she'd confided in him—things deeply private to her—and she'd done it with hardly a qualm.

13

"I ASKED YOU TO CALL ME WHEN YOU GOT IN LAST night."

Ariel shifted the receiver and blinked at the clock before she said, "I know you did. I'm sorry, Marguerite, I didn't think about it until very late, too late to call."

It was eight o'clock Sunday morning, and the telephone had awakened Ariel out of a deep sleep. It had been after two when she'd gone to bed. Even then, sleep had been some time coming.

"You're forgiven," Marguerite said. "I saw your lights when you got home."

"What else did you see?"

"If you're asking whether I stood vigil to see what time your business associate left your house, I did not. One can only insinuate oneself so far into the private life of one's friends and expect to remain friends. There is a certain line, don't you know, that one simply doesn't cross."

Ariel chuckled. "You'd have to have hindsight to see it, Marguerite, but what I was asking was, did you see anyone at my house last night while I was out?"

"What's happened?"

"A little mischief out front. Petty vandalism. You didn't have any problem, did you?"

"Oh, Lord, what now! No. I mean, I don't know. I haven't been outside yet. I'm on the portable, so just bear with me a minute, and we'll soon see."

Ariel could hear the light tapping of high heels on hardwood, and Marguerite's husband, Carl, asking where she was going, and Marguerite saying (to him, presumably) "Oh, don't be such a nosy old duffer" before she said, "Okay, I'm outside. You've put me in such a dither I forgot we would've seen if anything had been amiss when we came in last night, but that's neither here nor there, is it?" Ariel heard static, and Marguerite saying, ". . . important thing is whether you're all right. Are you?"

"I'm fine. Just angry."

"Of course you are!" More static. ". . . front door! And your windows! What is that? It's not . . . ?"

"It's paint."

Whatever Marguerite said next was lost, broken into crackle and disjointed words. "Marguerite?" Ariel yawned hugely and covered her eyes with her hand. "Where'd you go?" Then, quite clearly, she heard what sounded like a door slam shut, and for a bleary-minded second she thought Marguerite and her portable phone had somehow gotten into her own house. She glanced at Jessie, curled on her rug and unaroused, and said, "Marguerite, where are you?"

"In the entry hall, why?"

"Whose entry hall?"

"My own, of course."

"Oh. I thought . . . I think I must still be half asleep." Marguerite growled. "Oh, if only we'd been at home last night! I'd have enjoyed routing some hooligan. More, certainly, than I enjoyed the terminally boring party we had the poor judgment to attend. The only person there still evincing signs of life was the bartender, who was actually quite interesting. He has the ability to communicate with animals. If you ever need anyone in that line, let me know; I'll give you his name. Don't bother calling the Spencers."

Ariel made a supreme mental effort. Spencers. Neighbors. The couple who'd moved into the house between the Harrises and herself. "The Spencers communicate with animals?" she asked.

"Not that I'm aware of. Their house is unharmed, too, and they're out of town this weekend, so they couldn't have seen anything. As to Calvin and Marie across the street, when they have their TV on, they don't see or hear anything else.

"For whatever it's worth"—Marguerite had settled down to business—"whoever did that was there after nine-fifteen, when Carl and I returned home. I confess; I did ask Carl to slow the car as we passed your house. I would not have missed that paint."

Ariel's phone beeped, and she excused herself to Marguerite. The other call was Max Neely. He had some information for her, he said; he'd be by with that and doughnuts when he went off duty in half an hour.

The detective was frowning when she opened the door to him. "Who did this trash?" he asked. "They didn't get inside?"

"I don't know who; I wasn't here. It's just what you see, and lights broken." Paint, Ariel noticed then, had been splashed over her flower bed, too. It looked like an abattoir. Helplessly, she said, "I half expected to see some sort of message, but . . . Oh, I don't know! Come on in."

"Message?" The bag he shoved into her hands was still warm, and the fragrance when she opened it was essence of ambrosia, manna, and nectar of the gods. "Oh, Max, they're the old-fashioned buttermilk kind, and just out of the oven! Where did you get them?"

"Place I know. What message?"

Over coffee and caloric suicide, Ariel told Max about the attack by Leeman Parker's follower, the electrician-cum-avenger, "Azrael," and about the letters and calls she'd gotten over the last week and a half. But by the middle of last night, she told him, she'd convinced her-self (wanted to believe) that this incident was unrelated, that it was (as Jack had assumed) the work of nasty kids. "Don't you think so?" she asked. "If this was a message, wouldn't it have been spelled out?"

"Like 'Repent' written on the door? Paint's kind of a wimpy substitute for the real thing, but it is red. Could be some kind of cleansing thing. Symbolic blood of the lamb or whatever." Max chewed and thought. "It wasn't kids," he declared.

"Why not?"

He shook his head. "There's something spiteful about it. Vindictive. Feels like a woman."

"Max!" Ariel exclaimed, distracted despite herself. "I've never known you to be misogynistic before!"

His forehead creased.

"Chauvinistic, maybe," Ariel said, "but not misogy-nistic."

"You finished? Good. What does that word mean?"

"Misogynistic? Disliking women."

"I thought so." His almost lashless eyes bright with indignation, his mouth drooping, Max looked like a wounded cartoon bear. "Why," he asked, "would you think I don't like women? I like you. I always have, even back when you were kind of a mutt."

"Thank you."

"I loved Marcie."

"I know you loved your wife, Max."

"I'm getting pretty fond of a widow lady that owns a bakery near the stationhouse. I like her daughter, too. Nice kid. Wants to be a writer."

This was the first Ariel had heard of a budding romance and, despite the fact that Max had been alone for several years, she was surprised. "These are her doughnuts, then. Can I meet her? How old is the daughter? You know, Henry has a son—"

"No, you cannot meet her, not now. Maybe never. The observation I made, Gold, was not indicative of any personal bias; it was based on evidential experience and many years of professional observation. There was a certain restraint with what happened here. Boundaries uncrossed. If you will notice, the paint was utilized in such a way as to do the most superficial damage, and to make it difficult to clean up, that consideration being familiar to a woman, who more often than not is relegated to do the cleaning up."

Rather dazed by this pontifical Max, Ariel said, "I see."

"This does not suggest a delinquent youngster on a tear and in a hurry. Boys would tend to be more heavyhanded. They would be more likely to stomp your flowers. Paper your trees and shrubs with tissue. Dump garbage. A further observation is that the perpetrator of this misdemeanor did not employ a spray can, the artistic weapon of choice for a teenager."

Ariel burst out laughing. "Indeed," she agreed. "Pray continue."

"The color, as you may have noticed, is not your standard primary red; it is more of a, ah, geranium shade, perhaps. A color more likely to be in the possession of a female, wouldn't you say?"

"I have a question."

"And it is?"

"Where in that knotty head of yours did you come up with 'geranium'?"

Max slouched in the chair and reverted to his normal voice. "It's written on the paint can, which is still out there, dumped by your porch. Nobody else in the neighborhood got hit but you? Okay, you were singled out." He finished off his third doughnut and dusted his hands. "Any chance Heller's got a girlfriend you don't know about? Or one of his ex-wives got taken by a jealous fit? Wants him back?" When Ariel merely rolled her eyes, he persisted. "Are *you* fooling around with somebody else that might have a hot-tempered lady friend?"

"Of course not."

"Has *anybody* been bothering you besides these cuckoos of Parker's?"

"No."

"Then why are we even speculating? The obvious answer's the right answer. Any of those letters or phone calls been from women?"

"Calls. I didn't talk to her myself, but a woman—Tara Castanera says she thinks the same woman—called several times."

"Aha! Has Parker got a wife? Or an adoring acolyte? We'll check it out. Has 'Azrael'? What's his real name anyway?" Sighing, he said, "You've got that bark in the flower beds, so there aren't any shoe prints—I looked—but I'll get the paint can gone over. Thing is, though, this *is* just a misdemeanor." He raised his hands in a what-can-I-say gesture. "Your burglar alarm working okay?" When Ariel nodded, he said, "You're public property now, Gold; change your number; get it unlisted."

"Fine, but the phone book's still got my address in it, so I don't think I'd be accomplishing much."

"Well, whatever the message was, it's been delivered. Now I had a long night, and I want to get to bed, so let's get to why I'm here." Max took a notepad from his pocket. "The crew and passengers of Eve Spurling's last, fatal maritime adventure. Seventeen citizens," he said, "although not necessarily of our own fair land, with more sheets than you'd usually have in a group that size unless you were doing a survey at San Quentin."

Ariel's ears perked up, and she grabbed the notepad.

"Don't get excited. Just one crime of violence, and no convenient murderers to take the onus off Spurling."

"But still, Max, a boatload of people with records—"

"It's not the *Minnow*, and one of the deckhands sure ain't Gilligan, but I wouldn't say it's a boatload of—"

"I can't read your writing," Ariel complained. She handed the pad back and, saying "Translate, will you?" found a pad and pen.

"William Mott," Max read. He squinted, took drugstore bifocals from his jacket and, slipping them on, continued. "Deckhand, male, South African Caucasian, twenty-two, charge: possession of heroin, convicted, deported. Peter Doyle, cook, male, American Caucasian, forty-three, charge: harassment, charges dropped . . ."

"Harassing a woman?"

"Girlfriend. To continue. Charge: assault and battery, convicted, probation—"

"Slow down; I can't write that fast. Same woman?"

"A new romance. Next, Linda, aka Candy Charvat, passenger, female, American Caucasian, thirty, charge: prostitution—"

"Charged before or after the Eve Spurling murder?"

"Both. Ms. Charvat's been picked up more than once."

When Max finished reading, Ariel checked over her notes, counting. She had two people with drug charges; one with harassment and assault and battery; one with prostitution; one with a list of various white-collar crime charges a yard long; and one with grand theft and attempting to bribe a police officer. "Six out of seventeen people with records!" She was stunned. She simply couldn't put the man she'd been with the evening before in this picture. "The Spurlings certainly had a lovely circle of friends!"

"Keep in mind the crew were strangers until this charter, and the guests were mostly near-strangers to Spurling. They were his wife's pals. And it's seven out of seventeen; you forgot about the wife herself."

"You're right, I did."

"Drunk and disorderly; did community service." Max stifled a yawn. "Have fun with the Ship of Felons there. I'm going home."

The phone rang while Ariel was seeing him to the door. "I remember where it is," Max said and shuffled to it. Ariel heard it close behind him as she picked up the receiver.

"Good morning," a male voice said, and for a second Ariel thought it was Henry. She felt a pang of discomposure before Jack said, "It's me. Ariel, have you given any thought to who made that mess at your house?"

"You're joking, right? How about half the night? But I

know who it was. I just had a lengthy and enlightening conversation about it with a detective friend."

"Detective?" Jack sounded taken aback.

"Max agrees. It was a 'Canaanite.' The story I did on Parker? There've been problems with his people."

"Oh."

"Why do you say it like that? Did you have some other theory?"

"No, no. I just couldn't sleep either and, well, you know how weird you get around four in the morning. I got this idea that maybe . . ." He laughed a little. "Listening to myself in the cold light of day, it sounds like I think the world revolves around me. Nobody even knew we were out together, for crying out loud."

"You thought my visitor had some connection to you?"

"Just imagination working overtime. Forget it."

"Why would that even occur to you?" One of Max's questions popped into Ariel's mind. "Are you involved with someone, Jack? A love affair, I mean, somebody who's a little—"

"A love affair!" Jack's laugh was thin and, if such a thing could be read into a laugh, evasive.

"You don't have to be uncomfortable," Ariel said. "We've gone out once."

"And the once we went out, this!"

"Coincidence. Unless there's something you're not telling me."

"What's to tell? It's just paranoia. Being on the receiving end of hate mail will do that to you."

"After all this time you still get—"

"Ariel, you're right. It's coincidence. Forget it, okay?"

But Ariel couldn't. The vandalism was the work of Canaan; probably, as Max theorized, a lone woman

Canaanite. Still, Jack had been evasive. He'd had some reason, right or wrong, to associate what had happened with their being together. Some similar incident? Something that had happened to Jack?

For the first time Ariel fully comprehended that his wife's untimely end was not a dead issue, a forgotten incident resigned to yellowed newspaper pages. It was at least conceivable that there might be a very live person out there who, after all this time and for reasons at which she couldn't begin to guess, kept up with Jack; a person who knew when he went out and with whom he went; a person with an ax to grind.

14

HENRY SOUNDED UNLIKE HIMSELF WHEN HE CALLED late that morning. Tense, or nervous. Definitely short on chat. Ariel couldn't get a reading on his mood. By seven o'clock that evening, when she'd complied with his cryptic request that she "put on something nice" and come to get him rather than the other way around, she felt feverish with free-floating, guilt-induced anxiety. There'd even been one infinitesimal speck in time when she'd wondered if it had been Henry who, somehow learning of her duplicity, had been the wielder of the paint. After that wholly, dementedly disloyal flash, she'd felt even guiltier.

When she arrived at his house, she could hear music coming from inside, a vocal, turned up high enough that she could feel vibrations through the boards of the deck. There was no reply to her knock, but the door wasn't locked. She went in. The music was Johnny Mercer, the singer female and husky voiced. "My fickle friend," she sang, and Ariel's foreboding became a solid rock in her hollow stomach. She called Henry's name.

"I lost you to the summer wind," the vocalist wistfully regretted.

There was no sign of Henry, but lights were on, dimly, and a fire blazed in the fireplace. Ariel glanced around uncertainly.

The first time she'd been here, several months before, she'd been taken by surprise. She'd expected divorcé grunge, something appropriate to the helter-skelter sty that was his automobile; the souvenir-crammed, paper-strewn warren that was his office; and the lackadaisical attitude he exhibited toward his wardrobe. She'd found instead a neat bungalow, livable in ways important to Henry.

The music system was state of the art. The sofa and chairs were showroom-impersonal but undeniably comfortable (one was a leather recliner the color of predigested baby food). There were telephones everywhere including the bathroom, and a fax machine–copier in the office now converted to Sam's room. The bathtub was a large Jacuzzi, a necessity rather than a luxury for a tall man who did cruel things to his backbone all day long, and the king-size bed was piled with pillows, some of unusual configuration (the experimental purchases of a man who reads in bed and is convinced there's a way to do it comfortably).

The only signs she'd seen of a past littered with wives were two or three items of uncoveted furniture. A scarred pie safe. (Henry didn't bake.) A plastic parson's table in Sam's room (ugly but sensible for a boy who couldn't be expected to think about water rings). A massive rolltop desk kept closed, Ariel assumed, to hide the clutter nowhere else in evidence.

She draped her coat over a chair, shivering ever so slightly. She was wearing the black dress, the slinky one,

and there wasn't a lot of fabric to it. She started for the
fireplace, about to call out again, when she caught a
whiff of something. She sniffed the air. The unmistakable fragrance of garlic and onions filled it. The fragrance of anything cooking at Henry's house was, in her
experience, an unprecedented phenomenon. She followed the scent to the dining room. The table was set
for two. There were flowers and candles and a bucket of
ice—a water bucket, actually—with champagne tucked
inside.

From behind her, Henry said, "I thought I heard you
come in."

He was holding a large spoon, one hand cupped protectively underneath to catch drips, and he was wearing
a bibbed apron. Beneath it was what appeared to be a
tuxedo. "Want a taste?" he said, and held out the spoon.
"It's good."

"Henry?" Ariel looked from the spoon to his eyes, as
dark as chocolate, and, rather breathlessly, asked, "What
is it?"

"Chili. That's all I know how to make."

She let him guide the spoon to her mouth. He
opened and closed his own along with her, reflexively, in
the way one does when feeding a baby. "So?" he asked.

"It's . . . wonderful."

The music, Ariel realized, had stopped. In its absence,
the hush seemed absolute. "Is Sam here?" she asked.

"No."

"Oh."

The music resumed, this time an instrumental: a low,
mean sax, sinuous as curling smoke.

"Everything looks so nice," Ariel said.

Henry twitched a shoulder. "Cleaning lady was here
yesterday."

"I didn't know you owned a tuxedo."

"My award dinner uniform."

"You look very handsome in it."

"Jack Palance probably looks passable in a tuxedo."

"Just say 'thank you.' "

"Thank you. You look beautiful."

"Thank you."

"That must be what they mean by a *little* black dress.'"

Ariel's mouth twitched. "Henry, what brought all this on?"

"Well, you see, dancing's something I don't do too well."

"Pardon?"

"You mentioned that you'd like to go dancing. That's fine by me, but I don't dance well enough to do it out in public."

"I see," Ariel said and, slowly, thoughtfully, she nodded. "I believe I follow your thinking." She smiled. She went to Henry and, very gently, slid the spoon from his fingers. She licked the last vestige of chili from it, thoroughly, making sure she got it all, and laid the spoon on the table. Then she reached behind him and untied the apron. She slipped it over his head, mussing his hair a bit, and when she'd smoothed it down, she laid the apron, too, on the table. Finally, she put her arms around his neck. "Tell me," she murmured into his ear, "how well do you dance in private?"

"That, Henry, was the best," Ariel said. "A ten." She sighed with languid, sated satisfaction. "I am a happy woman."

"My pleasure," Henry said, and poured champagne for them both. "We aim to please."

She took a sip. "You're a man of many talents, Henry Heller."

"Well, my repertoire may be limited, but 'what there is,' as Tracy said about Hepburn, 'is cherce.' "

Ariel lifted his hand from where it rested near hers and kissed the knuckles lightly. He felt a shiver run through her.

"Was that from contentment?" Henry asked.

"That was from the fact that I'm underdressed. Do you have a sweater I could put on?"

"I'll get you something, and build up the fire, too." When he'd accomplished these things and helped her into a soft old flannel shirt that smelled pleasantly of laundry softener, he said, "Don't laugh, but, actually, I was a little nervous."

Ariel laughed.

"I said don't laugh."

"Why would you be nervous, you idiot?"

"Oh, you know how it is when you're out of practice. I kept thinking I was forgetting something."

"Well, you didn't forget anything important. If you left anything out, it wasn't missed. It was perfect. Everything was. The music, the candlelight . . ." She lifted her glass. "Everything."

Henry dabbed at a speck of something on the corner of Ariel's mouth, muttering, "Better in you than on you."

She guffawed. "Interesting philosophy."

"The result of an all too brief era of feeding an infant. Sam was a messy eater. Be brutally honest. Was it really okay?"

"Henry!" Ariel got up from the table, wrapping the flannel shirt around herself and her slinky black dress. "Stop fishing." She lowered herself onto his lap. "The chili rated a cook-off blue ribbon, okay? A delight for the palate. I will no doubt continue to savor its pungency throughout the night." She cupped his face with her hands, pulling it close. "And the salad"—she nuzzled his nose with hers—"with all those pretty little nasturtiums in it? Worthy of a *Gourmet* cover. But the appetizer, Henry . . . my, my." Her lips touched his, teasing, and then lingering as she whispered, *"Pièce de résistance."*

"Ummm," Henry said.

"Um-hm, and most effective."

"Effective?"

"I did have quite an appetite."

"I noticed." Henry nibbled at the hollow of her throat. "I can't take credit for the salad, you know. Store bought."

"But you can definitely take credit for the appetizer." The conversation, then, became nonverbal. A CD ended. The fire crackled in the silence. With a sweep of violins, another CD began.

"Henry?"

"Hmmm?"

"Aren't you ready for dessert?"

15

Monday morning found Ariel with a relatively open calendar. That night's show, Henry's big-idea episode inspired by "Azrael" 's attack, was in the can. It had turned out to be good, a gripping montage of journalists—not just Ariel—in the line of fire. Ariel headed for her workstation, ready to tackle the Spurling story in earnest.

Her chair was occupied by the producer hired to replace her. His belongings, including a lunchbox and a prickly and rather evil-looking potted cactus, had taken over her desk.

"Did somebody forget to tell me something?" Ariel asked, not altogether joking.

"Oh, hi," said the producer, whose name was Gabe. Cheerfully, he said, "You didn't know? You're outta here."

"Excuse me?"

Gabe pointed, not toward the exit but to Chloe's old office. It was swathed in dropcloths, and an overalled man was rolling fresh paint onto the walls. The large lump in the middle of the room looked to be a desk and, according to the new plaque on the door, it was Ariel's.

"Guess they wanted to surprise you," Gabe said.

"Guess it worked," Ariel said. Inconvenienced but pleased, she retrieved what she needed, found a vacant desk, and went to work with the passenger list from the *Princessa Ora*.

Although neither Leesa Canady nor her companion, one Wally Hatcher, had had any known brush with the law, Ariel decided to launch her investigation of Eve Spurling's death with them. They were, as Henry had pointed out, the only ones on board the yacht who gave damaging testimony against Jack.

Hatcher had lived in a west L.A. suburb called Pacific Palisades two years before. Since then, he'd sold a successful PR business and retired to Palm Springs, where Ariel eventually tracked him down. He'd just come in from playing eighteen holes, and he sounded as though he'd lingered at the nineteenth.

"A TV show?" he said muzzily, after Ariel had explained her reason for calling. "Tell me again what it is you're after?"

She went through it again. "So," she said then, "could I set up a time with you to talk about the night Mrs. Spurling died?"

"No way."

"It wouldn't take long, Mr. Hatcher."

"Read the trial transcript. Whatever I know's in there."

"Now, sir, you can see that my talking about the testimony on the air isn't the same as talking to a witness face-to-face."

"A taped interview?" Hatcher's voice cracked. "That's what you're saying? Bring cameras and all that here? Not a chance, little lady."

"Probably just a tape recorder to start with, to do a preliminary interview. It might not get any further than that."

"It's not going to get that far."

Oh yes it is, Ariel thought, fingering the busy little apparatus connected to her telephone. "May I ask why you're reluctant to talk with me?"

"Not reluctant. Adamant. That blasted little boat trip almost ruined me. It almost cost me my marriage, and my wife is one hard-nosed woman. No way am I stirring up that hornet's nest again."

Ariel was momentarily stumped; she hadn't known Hatcher was married. "I can appreciate your position," she said. "Tell you what: talk to me for a few minutes right now, will you? I'd be grateful if you'd just tell me in your own words about that night."

"Why should I?"

"Because I asked nicely?"

Ariel heard a snort and then a noise easily identifiable as ice cubes dropping into a glass. "I'll tell you this," he said. "I liked Spurling right off the bat, and whatever he did to his wife, he didn't do anything to me. I've always felt crummy about having to testify against him." From the sound of it, Hatcher paused to take a drink. "I wish to high heaven I'd kept my nose out of it."

For the next several minutes Ariel heard, punctuated by the rattle of ice cubes, what was pretty much a recount of what she'd already read.

Hatcher had left the ship's saloon when a card game there had broken up for the night. It was between 1:00 and 1:30; he could be no more precise. He'd gone straight to his cabin, where he'd found Leesa in a tizzy about the scene she'd overheard out on the deck. ("Girl stays in a tizzy," Hatcher said. "She's an actress. If there's no drama going on, she invents some.") Leesa pleaded with him to go to the Spurlings' cabin and check on Eve, to make sure she was okay. ("Pretty please, babe? Just go knock on their door?") He knew he'd get no rest (or anything else) if he didn't, so he gave in. He found the door ajar. He knocked and stuck his head in. The cabin was empty, the bed made up. He didn't see either Spurling there or anywhere and, except for three or four diehard stragglers, he saw no one else during his foray. End of story.

"The lights in the cabin were on?" Ariel asked.

"If they weren't, the light from the hall was enough to see what I just said. Look, I was in, out, boom—you know? What I'd have said if anybody had been in there, I don't know. I felt like a chump. I'd considered just hanging around in the hallway five minutes and telling Leesa I did what she wanted. I wish I had."

"The 'stragglers' you saw. Who were they, do you remember? And where'd you see them?"

"Who? Gosh, that was so long ago. . . . On the way down I saw the Jameson couple." He chuckled. "They were kissing. Hugh and . . . Myrna? Myra? Myra, I think."

"Maura."

"Yeah, that's right! Tall brunette woman. Dynamite figure."

"I don't know what she looks like, but the records list a Maura L. Jameson. Did you see anybody else?"

"Yeah, coming back I did. Karen somebody. She was with one of the guys."

"Karen Lucas," Ariel supplied. "She was the companion of a man named Barry Verlyn." She was also one of the two people aboard who'd been busted for possession of a controlled substance.

"Yeah, she was with Verlyn. That's right. He died, you know? I saw it in the paper not too long ago."

Ariel hadn't known. She crossed his name off her list. Less Eve Spurling and Jack, that left thirteen viable names: nine guests and four crew; the deported deckhand was a lost cause.

Ice tinkled in a glass in Palm Springs, and Ariel asked, "Had you been drinking that night?"

"Sure, I'd had a few. I never claimed otherwise. It was a pleasure cruise. I wasn't driving the boat."

"How did you know which cabin the Spurlings were in?"

Hatcher groaned. "You sound like his lawyer!" he said. "We went there the afternoon we set sail. Had a kind of mobile bon voyage party that ended up in our place—we had the master stateroom—but we traipsed through everybody's cabin."

"Was the Spurlings' cabin in close proximity to any of the others? Like, say, one and then another leading off the corridor?"

"Well, sure."

"Was it numbered?"

"Yeah, it was numbered. Look, I know where you're going with this—"

"You remembered the number of the Spurling cabin? From the bon voyage party?"

"No, I didn't remember the number. It wasn't an ocean liner, little lady; there were only six cabins. I just remembered which one it was, all right? This was covered at the trial, and I'm sure as hell not going to be interrogated again."

"Did I sound as if I were interrogating you? I'm sorry. I'd better read the transcript, hadn't I, and stop wasting your time rehashing. You know what would be helpful? Your feelings. The sort of opinions you wouldn't be allowed to express on the stand. You liked Jack Spurling, you said. Did you like his wife, too?"

"Eve? She could be a lot of fun." He laughed. "She's the only person—outside the movies, I mean—I ever saw actually jump into a fountain. It was at this bash a few months before she died. She pulled a hired waiter in, too, trying to get him to tango with her. His tray went flying. Canapés landing on everybody!"

"What did Mr. Spurling think of that?"

"I don't remember if he was there."

"Did you know Mrs. Spurling well?"

"I didn't know either one of them all that well. Him I'd only met a couple of times."

"How did the twelve of you happen to hire a yacht together?"

"Spur-of-the-moment thing. It was a good-time group. Showed up at the same parties, the same restaurants; you know how it is. Always ready to try something different. Or some*body*." He laughed again, a suggestive chuckle this time. "Some of that bunch, maybe, were a little closer than others."

"Closer?"

"Oh, yeah, it was . . ." Hatcher stopped abruptly. His voice, all loose-tongued, in-vino-veritas amiability, became businesslike. "That's all I'm prepared to say about that."

"Are you still in touch with Leesa?"

"I don't give out that kind of information over the phone, and we already take the newspaper. Goodbye."

I do believe, Ariel thought as she pressed Stop on the tape recorder, that the wife just walked in.

She thought about what she could deduce from what Hatcher said.

Jack had been on less familiar terms than Eve with the other party members, and some were "maybe" on familiar terms with persons not their partners. Was Eve one of them?

Hatcher hadn't known the number of the Spurlings' cabin, which wasn't easily distinguished from others except by the number. He'd relied on his memory of where he'd been partying two days before, and he wasn't sober when he sought out the cabin. At least four other people were out and about at the time. Could the empty cabin have been the Jamesons'? Or that of Karen Lucas and Barry Verlyn?

And, most interesting, Leesa Canady was of a creative bent: titillated by drama, and creating it where it didn't exist. Had she imagined any of the conversation she claimed to have overheard, or had she perhaps embellished it?

Ariel hadn't been aware that Leesa was an actress, which told her all she needed to know about how successful an actress Leesa was. Her number was listed in the San Fernando Valley directory. It came as no surprise that she'd be "so happy" to answer any questions at all. "On camera?" she asked hopefully. An appointment was made for nine the next morning.

The Jamesons, Hugh and Maura, had divorced since the Spurling trial and just before Hugh Jameson's own trial, which Ariel researched before she contacted the man. He owned a large construction firm. A number of pieces of heavy equipment had come to be in his possession through a complicated and illegal scheme involving smoke and mirrors, and leaving a paper trail followed by an enterprising detective. Jameson had made an injudicious proposition to him. The lawman hadn't found the proposition appealing, and Jameson had served time for both grand theft and attempted bribery.

Jameson's criminal activities, presumably, had no

bearing on Ariel's investigation. But, also presumably, it was the adverse publicity resulting from those activities that made him leery of any journalist calling for any reason. Ariel couldn't get past his secretary. The woman was a velvet-voiced guard dog possessed of faultless courtesy and steely protectiveness. She frankly intimidated Ariel, who left a message and then turned her efforts toward locating the ex–Mrs. Jameson.

She found her listed in west L.A. The Bel Air address was no more than five miles from Ariel's own house, and for every mile you could add another quarter million in market value. The address suggested fences and gates and electronic scrutiny that would bar access even more effectively than did the velvet-voiced guard dog. Maura Jameson, however, was accommodating. She would see Ariel at twelve-thirty the following day.

The search for Karen Lucas, the other passenger Wally Hatcher saw during his Good Samaritan trip to the Spurlings' cabin, was unsuccessful. She was listed in none of the current local directories, and she was, Ariel soon found out, a fugitive. She had been convicted of possession, cocaine, a few months before Eve Spurling's fatal cruise and, according to the terms of her probation, was ordered to participate in a rehabilitation program. She'd shown several times and then disappeared. There was no hunt afoot for her. Given the number of fugitives on the books for far more serious crimes and the drastic shortage of manpower, the search for Karen Lucas wasn't just low priority; it was no priority.

Ariel did find a listing for a couple named Palmer, Carolyn and Ronnie, but she didn't find them in. She left a message.

She was interrupted at that point to be told that the painter was done, and the rest of the day was taken up with getting her new office in order and work on other stories. She did phone Winterset, Jack's shop; it was, the recorded message informed her, closed on Mondays.

Being awakened by the ringing of a telephone is never a good thing. Ariel jerked awake, knocking some of the newspapers beside her to the floor.

She'd dozed off in her study. The article she'd been reading was about a girl who'd confessed to killing a foster mother she claimed was abusive. The woman was garroted, and her body was found in the trunk of her car. The girl was thirteen. Grisly details of the story had worked themselves into her interrupted dream, and Ariel felt a sense of foreboding even before she lifted the receiver.

"Hello?" she said, her voice rough crackle. She cleared her throat and said it again.

"Ariel Gold?" The words were an urgent murmur, the voice a woman's. Ariel said yes, but the only response was quick, shallow breathing. She was about to slam the receiver, hard, into the cradle, when she heard, "I left a message for you. Did you get it?" Without waiting for an answer, disjointedly, her nearly whispered words colliding with one another, the woman said, "Doesn't matter. Better to tell you straight out. What I want to say . . . I'm sorry about what happened. I am! But—"

"Who is this?" Ariel demanded. Squinting against the bright desk light, she looked automatically at the clock. It wasn't the middle of the night; it was only ten-fifteen.

"I can't come out and say my name, you know that! But, Ms. Gold, no *real* damage was done! That's what I want you to think about!" The voice dropped even lower. "I know I can't expect people to understand about him. He's . . . sick, but he's mine. All I have. So, please, just let it go. Will you do that? Forget him!" Ariel heard the voice catch and choke, and then she heard a click.

"Hello?" she said pointlessly.

She paced, rubbing her stiff neck. She checked her machine for a message; there wasn't one. She checked her alarm. Why, she fumed, couldn't these Canaan people talk straight? The call had to be repercussion from tonight's *Open File*. So was her caller Azrael's woman? Or Parker's? Was "what happened" the attack in the studio or did the woman even know about that? Had she even seen the show? Maybe she was harking back to the incident with the paint.

Ariel drank a glass of water and then another, and spent some time checking all the locks in the house. She got a lot of work done that night because she wasn't the least bit sleepy anymore.

16

LEESA CANADY LOOKED LIKE SHIRLY TEMPLE. TO BE accruate, she looked like Shirley would look if someone had stretched the perky tyke to nearly six feet, pumped voluptuous curves into the right places, and dressed her in skin-tight leather. The actress's spectacular height was topped by unruly golden curls, her eyes were as big and blue as hydrangea petals, and her voice burbled. She had to be at least thirty, but her baby-fine skin didn't seem to have made the trip through three decades with her. Nor had her brain.

"I watched your show last night," she told Ariel when they were settled in her living room. "After you called, you know, I was curious? You really looked the part!"

"Looked the part?" Ariel asked.

"*You* know what I mean! The newscaster type." Leesa dimpled and then snatched a pair of Cary Grant hornrims off the coffee table, slid them onto her pert nose, and arranged her face into sternness. "Intellectual," she pronounced, her voice descending into the alto range. "Serious. Tailored clothes." She whipped the glasses off. "Do you have to memorize your lines? I read that you people use cue cards. I've seen *Broadcast News* three times. I love the William Hurt character! He was so cool. And what's that other one? *Network*. I thought it was depressing, though, didn't you?"

Evidently, it was a rhetorical question. Leesa paused only for breath before she began to tell about how she'd once auditioned for the role of a weather girl. "Should I say 'weather person'?" she interrupted herself to ask. "Anyway, I got called back twice, but I didn't get it. The girl that did was petite and, see, the male lead wasn't exactly tall?" She named a well-known actor of modest height. "You see the problem?"

"I do see, yes." Ariel smiled and pushed the record button on her tape recorder. "What I'd like to ask you about," she said, "is your . . . role in the Eve Spurling tragedy."

Leesa's endless legs had been folded lotus style on the sofa, but now she put both her feet on the floor, sat up to her full, startling height, and crossed one ankle over the other demurely.

"It was a small role," she said, "but, as badly as I felt for Jack, I had to play it out. A woman was dead. I had to come forward with what I had heard." Well rehearsed by countless tellings, Leesa said, "A man and a woman were out on the deck. They were arguing. She was crying. I recognized the voices of Eve and Jack Spurling." She paused for effect. "They were near my window for only a minute. They spoke in agitated whispers, but one or the other of their voices would suddenly peak on a word. I heard her call him Jack, and I heard him call her Eve. I distinctly heard the word 'stupid.' And then I heard a slap: the sound of a palm against flesh."

The descriptive phrase, Ariel recalled, was the one Leesa had used on the stand, verbatim.

"Eve gasped, as if in shock or pain or anger, and she said something I couldn't distinguish. She was crying too hard. And then I heard the sound of high-heeled shoes moving quickly away."

"And what time was that?"

"I don't know. It seemed like the middle of the night to me, just being waked up like that, you know? Scary."

"Yes," Ariel agreed. "What did you do then?"

"I looked out the window, but they had gone. I worried for a little while, trying to decide what to do. Eve wasn't an intimate friend, but she was a friend. I was concerned for her, of course. I couldn't just sit and do nothing, so I began to get dressed. I intended to find her, to make certain she was all right."

"What you heard . . ." Ariel smiled to soften any offense her observation might give. "What you heard doesn't sound like a life-or-death matter. No threats, out-of-control rage, that sort of thing. It sounds like a simple domestic argument, the kind every couple gets into from time to time."

"Are you saying I overreacted?" Leesa leaned forward earnestly. "You didn't hear them," she said. "You could feel the anger! And that slap. Oh, Ariel, I am really, really death on spousal abuse. That is really, really one of my pet peeves. You don't know me, but I am not the kind of person who just stands by."

"Good for you! And, of course, as it turned out, you were right to be concerned. What happened then?"

"Well, I finished dressing, and then I did my face . . ."

Unsure that she'd heard correctly, Ariel asked, "Your face?"

"Uh-huh . . ." As the woman screwed her face into concentration, Ariel realized that what she'd seen as flawless skin and dramatically perfect features was, in fact, the result of a makeup job so professional it was almost imperceptible. "About that time," Leesa said, "here came Wally. He'd been playing cards or something, and I thought, wouldn't it be better if a man handled the situation? Just in case of trouble? So Wally went. You know about what he found? I mean that they weren't in their cabin and so on?"

"Yes, I talked to him."

"You saw Wally?" Leesa's guileless eyes widened in anticipation. "When? How is he?"

"I called him yesterday. He sounded fine."

"He told me he was separated from his wife, you know, when we were together? I don't want you to think I fool around with married men. I mean, he *was* married, but . . ."

Ariel made understanding noises and guided Leesa back to the subject. "You were shocked when you found out about Eve's disappearance?" she asked.

"Oh, Ariel, I was just sick! If Wally and I had kept looking for them, if we hadn't let it go like we did, she'd still be alive, wouldn't she? It really brings me down when I dwell on it."

"You can't blame yourself," Ariel said. "Twenty-twenty and all that." When Leesa frown-smiled uncertainly, Ariel explained: "Hindsight. It's always twenty-twenty."

"Oh. That's good. That is so true."

"What I was really asking, is: based on your observation of the Spurlings together, how shocked were you? Had you seen any suggestion of trouble brewing? Any fights?"

"They asked me that at the trial, but Eve and Jack didn't really hang together a lot. I saw them on the sundeck sometimes, but he'd be reading and she'd just be working on her tan. Eve tended to be a lot more into the party thing. You know, cards and dancing and just kind of drinking and horsing around. Jack swam. Fished." Leesa shrugged. "I saw him in the cockpit or bridge or whatever you call it with the guy running the boat, the skipper, one time. I guess he was interested in the equipment or something."

"So until that night you'd seen no incidents of volatility? Of, uh, hot temper?"

"Oh, yeah! You better believe it!"

"You had?" Ariel was surprised. "You'd seen Mr. Spurling lose his temper before?"

"Not Jack. *Eve.* I saw her lose her cool a few times, especially if she was tipsy. I'll tell you, and I don't mean to speak ill of the dead or anything, but I'd have been less shocked if it had been her that killed him instead of the other way around."

Ariel had made a call early that morning to the Ft. Lauderdale offices of Delafield Worldwide Charters, the company that owned the *Princessa Ora.* The yacht was currently chartered, captained by the same man who'd been aboard for the Spurlings' cruise, but it was in Pacific waters, en route from Cabo San Lucas, and would dock at Long Beach in a week. Delafield had a branch office in Century City. It was only fifteen minutes from Maura Jameson's home, and the manager was available to talk with Ariel at three.

She wanted to shoot the intro to the piece aboard the yacht. It might be a hard sell. The publicity would be priceless, and free. Whether the owners of a pleasure vessel would consider the "death ship" aspect a trifle negative, however, remained to be seen. Ariel was plotting the camera shots in her mind as she made the turn from Bellagio Road into the Jameson drive.

The high fence and electronically protected gate were just as she had imagined. The grounds, she saw when she was admitted, were something else. There was no lawn, just slate terracing, bark beds, and gravel walkways, and not a single flower bloomed. Whoever had done the landscaping favored a color range from dull gray-green to brown. Every plant and tree was spiky. Century plants. Needle and fan palms. Clumps of fescue and pampas grass. Huge igneous rocks were strewn about, the effect random, as if they'd rolled down from a volcanic eruption. It was all meant to be minimal and chic, Ariel supposed, but if it was a reflection of the owner, then Mrs. Jameson was in a state of severe depression, or she was one angry woman.

The house was just as forbidding. A monolithic structure of poured concrete, steel, and glass, it was all straight lines and acute angles. To Ariel, it looked like a futuristic prison.

A maid answered the door and let her into a room so open and colossal that it seemed at first to constitute the entire house. Three stories high at its vaulted apex, it was canopied on one side by a vast expanse of steeply pitched glass. At its center a concrete pillar stretched thirty feet upward to dark, exposed girders, and the only curved line in sight was a steel and mahogany staircase that swept to the partial second floor. On the one solid wall hung a frenziedly vivid contemporary oil painting. Ariel was backing up, trying to take it in, when she heard a soft sound behind her.

The staircase was made for dramatic entrances, but

Maura Jameson couldn't take advantage of its potential. She limped down step by step, holding carefully to the railing. In addition to the elastic bandage on her ankle, she wore scuffs and plain gray sweat clothes. A towel was wrapped turban style around her head, and her rather pale face looked freshly washed.

"Hello," she said, glancing at Ariel but concentrating on her footing. "I'm afraid I've forgotten what you said your name was. Let's go into the living room. Ruth will bring drinks. I've asked for tea, but you can have whatever you like, of course."

She didn't offer to shake hands.

Leading the way into the area beneath the glass ceiling, she let herself down onto one of two available seats, a sofa consisting of white duckcloth-covered cushions piled on a tubular steel frame. Wincing, she lifted her injured ankle onto the cushions. Having no option other than to stand, Ariel took the matching chair.

Mrs. Jameson was in her early forties, Ariel guessed, taller than average, with brown eyes under well-shaped brows. She was, as Wally Hatcher had said, a brunette; a dark widow's peak was visible at the towel's edge. The sweatclothes she wore were too bulky to judge whether she had "a dynamite figure," as he'd also said, but the lady did have a lovely face. Lovely and lived in. There didn't seem to be anybody at home just now, however.

"Ariel Gold," Ariel said.

"What?" Her hostess looked mildy startled, as if she'd forgotten Ariel's presence. She'd been gazing at the view beyond the floor-to-ceiling windows. It was spectacular, certainly, but even that expensive vista could hardly account for so short an attention span.

"You said you didn't remember my name," Ariel said amiably. "It's Ariel Gold."

"Oh, of course. Sorry. I'm no good with names."

"Quite a place you have here."

"Thanks. It suits me. You don't happen to smoke, do you?"

"No."

"Neither do I, really," Maura Jameson said, and smiled vaguely.

The maid came in bearing a tray. Tea, as promised, but a tantalizing variety of tiny sandwiches, too, which presented Ariel with a minor dilemma. She was, she realized, starving. But it would be hard to interview this brittle lady with her mouth full. She swallowed saliva, murmured no to cream and sugar, yes to lemon, and looked around the stark room. A forged iron sculpture the size of a washing machine dominated it. Rather desperately, Ariel asked about it, and her hostess brightened. She even began to show signs of focusing. She was talking about David Smith's influence on Alain Kirili and Kirili's influence on the sculptor who'd done her piece when, abruptly, she said, "Forgive me if I'm a bit foggy, but I had to take a little painkiller. I seem to be rather accident prone lately." She pulled the towel from her head and finger-combed short, dark, damp curls. "Today I tripped on the tennis court. A day or two ago I cut myself carving chicken. Last week . . ." She laughed a little. "You didn't come to discuss my clumsiness, did you? Poor Eve. To think, I once had the arrogance to pity her."

Ariel hurriedly wiped her fingers on a linen napkin and produced her tape recorder. "May I?" she asked.

"I can't think what you expect to hear that merits recording." For several seconds Maura stared at the machine. Whether she was gathering her thoughts or was simply absorbed by the slow turning of the cassette,

Ariel couldn't tell. At length, musing, she said, "Time was, I suppose, when Eve would've been called 'madcap.' An old-fashioned word, I know—shades of Zelda Fitzgerald!—but it fits. Madcap, gay, devil-may-care. Bent on squeezing every minute of the day and night for the last drop of pleasure. She *was* fun to be with, and generous. If you admired something in a shop, she'd want to buy it for you. Eve loved to buy things."

"Yes?" Ariel prodded when the other woman stopped as if she'd made her point or lost track of it.

"Once we were at her house . . . I went into a closet for some reason, looking for an umbrella or something. I saw stacks of boxes—shoe boxes and dress boxes from half a dozen shops—that had never been opened. Clothes with the price tags still on them. I began to notice that things she'd bought when I was with her, pictures or, I don't know, vases or whatever . . . they were nowhere to be seen. I expect they were still boxed up somewhere." She shifted her weight, obviously uncomfortable, and glanced longingly toward the staircase, that distant, steep route to her bathroom and the medicine cabinet there. Her tone was detached, almost offhand, when she said, "I came to see all that impetuousness, that frivolity—that grab-life-by-the-scruff-and-shake-it-for-all-it's-worth attitude of hers—for what it was."

"And that was?"

"Eve had no center at all. She was a desperately sad woman trying to fill an emptiness with possessions, with constant activity, with people. Throngs of people. She would have denied it; she was so lacking in introspection that she didn't know it was true. If the emptiness threatened to surface, to thrust itself into her awareness, she'd pour another martini and drown the specter."

"You've given her psyche a lot of thought," Ariel observed, and it occurred to her to wonder how introspective Maura Jameson was. "Knowledge is power," she thought—if you know it about the right person. "Why," she asked, "would your feeling pity for her be arrogant?"

"We're not talking about me; we're talking about Eve."

"Sorry. I'll stick to the Spurlings."

"Stick to Eve. I haven't given Jack Spurling's psyche any thought at all."

"Did he kill his wife?"

"I don't know."

"You have no opinion?"

"No opinion I'm going to share with your television audience." Maura adjusted her ankle again and grimaced, muttering, "This thing's starting to throb like the devil."

"Do you think it's possible that she killed herself?"

"Of course it's possible. If anybody's capable of killing other people given the right circumstances, anybody's capable of killing herself given the same."

"Let me rephrase the question. Do you think she did kill herself?"

"No."

"You said she was a 'desperately sad woman.' Why are you so certain that, on that particular night, she might not have been able to 'drown her specter'?"

"I flatter myself that I'm a fairly observant person, Ms. Gold, and Eve seemed to me no more unsettled than usual that night. She may have imbibed more than usual of one thing or another, but who hadn't? When she left the card table, she did not leave in agitation. She did not cast lingering, meaningful looks of farewell over the assemblage. She popped up, said she'd be right back, and went to fetch an aspirin. There's no reason whatsoever to suppose that, somewhere between the saloon and her cabin, she was overcome by melancholy and pitched herself into the sea."

Ariel suppressed amusement at both the image Maura evoked and her increasing sharpness as the painkiller wore off. "The 'assemblage' consisted of . . . ?"

"My former husband and me. A stupid man named Wally Hatcher. A couple named Palmer. Carolyn and Ronnie Palmer. Those other people—Vail and that Charvat woman—had left by then."

"Karen Lucas wasn't in the game? Or—"

"Now, why do you ask about her in particular?"

"I meant to ask about her and Barry Verlyn both. When Mr. Hatcher was checking out the Spurlings' cabin, he noticed several people still up and about: you and Mr. Jameson and Ms. Lucas and Mr. Verlyn."

"Oh. Well, they weren't there. Barry had been gone quite a while, to bed, I'd assumed. His girlfriend left at the same time."

"You seem disappointed."

"The adjective, I would say, could be aptly applied to me."

"I mean in my reason for asking about Ms. Lucas." When Maura merely shrugged, Ariel asked, "Did you see her later at all?"

"No."

"Mrs. Spurling left the card game at what time?"

"I imagine you've done your homework on all this? Then you know we were none of us watching the clock. It was one-ish."

"And how long after did the rest of you continue to play?"

"Until Hatcher spilled his drink all over the cards."

"That would be about how long?"

"Ten minutes? Fifteen?"

"And you all left the saloon then? So Mrs. Spurling may have returned and found you gone?"

"Or, for all we knew, she'd taken her aspirin and gone to bed with her headache. None of us, including me, were especially concerned about her at the time. Tell me, have you talked with Hugh, my esteemed ex-husband?"

"Not yet."

"Waste of time. As much as I'd like to see him inconvenienced in any way possible, up to and including being suspected of murder—Eve's or anybody's—he and I were together every minute."

"Where did you go after the card game broke up?"

"To the top deck. The front of the boat. Spooning in the moonlight. In those days, you see, we were still spooning."

Impetuously, Ariel asked, "What happened?"

"Turn that thing off," Maura said, pointing to the tape recorder. When Ariel did, she said, "I married late. Mid-thirties. I waited for 'the right man.' I was ridiculously in love. I felt sorry for every woman who didn't have what I had: a decent, honest, faithful husband. The man I thought I knew did not exist outside my imagination. The man I married was a cheap crook and not even a very smart crook, and a casual adulterer with piss-poor taste. I have found that divorcing him and helping to put him behind bars and taking him for every penny I could grab, including the contents of a few accounts he thought cleverly hidden, isn't especially satisfying, but I will eventually move on to a more positive state of mental health. You caught me at a low ebb.

"Now," Maura Jameson continued, "Was there anything else you wanted to ask about that night?"

Sensing that the woman's tolerance level had been reached, Ariel got up to take her leave. At the door, Maura surprised her by asking, "Have you talked to Karen Lucas?"

When Ariel replied that she had been unable to locate her, Maura said, "It shouldn't be hard. She's part owner of a real estate agency, so she said. Somewhere in the Valley. Sherman Oaks? One of those towns?"

Ariel had little hope of the lead, but she made a note of it. "She must be long gone from there," she said, "or the police would've found her when she first violated her parole."

"Parole?"

"Cocaine possession. She was ordered to take part in a rehabilitation program back before your cruise. She was a no-show not too long after."

"Are you saying that she's missing?"

"You could put it that way."

"Very interesting," Maura murmured, and she would say no more.

Ariel was en route to the Delafield Charters office when her car phone rang. Ronnie Palmer had picked up her message from the day before. He was calling from *his* car, on speakerphone. His wife, Carolyn, said "Hello, there" from the other seat.

Unlike the other cruise couples, the Palmers sounded happily married and, evidently, they had no lasting traumatic memories of the trip on which Eve Spurling had died. They were driving, even as they spoke, to Newport Beach to board the *Stay Happy*, a ketch bound for Baja.

"We've got about seven minutes," Ronnie advised

Ariel, "and then we'll be blissfully unavailable for ten days." Ariel heard a giggle and then a *"Whoo!"* of surprised feminine laughter. Carolyn, she thought, had just been goosed; if the Palmers kept that stuff up, they were going to miss the boat. "So, Ms. Gold," said Ronnie on a chuckle, "what can we do for you between here and the marina?"

Quickly, they went over the events of the evening in question; the Palmers' account was nearly identical to Maura Jameson's. By now, Ariel had pulled over to a curb. Reviewing her notes, she said, "So after the game broke up, you two went directly to your cabin together?"

"We did," Carolyn agreed. "Directly!" Ariel heard a metallic jangle (a charm bracelet?) and a soft *whap!* as if Carolyn had given her husband a playful punch on the arm. These two, she thought, were going to plow into a semi if they didn't watch out.

"Maura and Hugh Jameson went up to the flydeck?"

"Yes?" the couple said in concert, rather eagerly, as if they were contestants on a game show awaiting clues.

"And," Ariel said, "Wally Hatcher went to his cabin, where he talked briefly to Leesa Canady, and—"

"Went on his mission of mercy," supplied Ronnie, "and then back up to the arms of his young blond Amazon. They were in the master stateroom on the main deck; the rest of us were in humbler accommodations on the lower deck."

"Which is where Karen Lucas and Barry Verlyn had gone, right?"

"Right," Ronnie said.

"But they were seen later by Mr. Hatcher, out and about."

"If Wally says so," Ronnie said.

"That leaves only Jack Spurling and a . . . Bob Vail and his companion, Linda Charvat."

"That leaves only Jack," Carolyn put in with a catty edge to her voice. "Those other two were at the bar until about a half hour before we all left the saloon. The way they were acting then and later, when their frolicking got out of hand, I'd say they were too preoccupied with each other to have any interest in a third party. Although, God knows, that wasn't always the case."

Ariel smiled at a meter maid who strolled by, an eye on the 15 Minute Parking sign beneath which Ariel sat, and asked, "Were you two aware that Ms. Charvat was a professional prostitute?"

"What?" yelped Carolyn.

"Yeah," said Ronnie. "Some of those folks' lives are a bit more fast-track than ours, a bit more, shall we say, on the fringe? Bob Vail's a client of mine, an important client. The Charvat woman was his current playmate then. She didn't last long, as I recall."

"You were saying that their 'frolicking got out of hand'?"

"It was one-forty in the morning," Carolyn said indignantly, "and those walls weren't thick. They sounded like they were sticking pigs in there! I was still dressed, so I went out into the hall, to ask them to tone it down. Hugh beat me to it. He was already banging on their door, and Jack was in the doorway of his own cabin. Then Barry opened his door, too. When Jack realized we were all safely in our nests, he asked where Eve was."

"And then he went looking for her?"

"Yes," the Palmers chorused.

"Did Mr. Spurling look as if he'd been asleep? As if he'd been awakened by the commotion?"

"He was in pajama bottoms," Carolyn said. "Barry was, too. Jack was barefoot, and his hair was wet and kind of messed up."

Ariel frowned, made a note, and asked, "What about Karen Lucas? Did you see her?"

"Yeah, through the open door, behind Barry. She was in her little twin bed." Ariel heard a snicker, she assumed Carolyn's. "It's funny what you can learn about people's relationships from what they wear to bed, you know? Like Karen's pj's were man-tailored. Maura was in this elegant peignor set. Wally was nude under his robe—I could tell—and little Leesa had on see-through baby dolls. Her face was made up, for the love of Pete!"

"Hey, hey!" Ronnie exclaimed then. "There she is, the *Stay Happy*. Look, Caro! Man, is she gorgeous!"

"Well, bon voyage," Ariel said. "Oh, one more question. How did Mr. Spurling seem when he realized his wife wasn't still with all you guys? Surprised? Upset?"

"At first just kind of annoyed," Carolyn said. "He threw on a robe and went looking. Hugh went, too. Then Jack told the captain, and Hugh came and got the rest of us and, and we all looked. By then Jack was seriously worried. Gosh, who wouldn't be?"

"You think worried?" Ronnie asked his wife. "I thought he looked scared."

The manager of the local Delafield Charters office was a strong-featured, middle-aged man named Charlie Sisson. His office was practically papered with photos of sleek yachts shot from every angle, but he made Ariel think more of stables than marinas. His skin was tanned to the color and texture of an old saddle; his thin, oiled hair was as coarse as a mane above wide-set eyes and a long horsey face. He wasn't noticeably enthusiastic about *The Open File* shooting aboard his firm's yacht. His opinion might be a forerunner of similar opinions but, in and of itself, it was immaterial; Sisson was in no position to grant or deny permission.

"The facts bore out," he assured Ariel, leaning back in his chair and draping one knee over the other, "that we were in no way responsible for that poor woman's death. Every regulation was observed, every safeguard taken as always. But let's be realistic; five crew can't watch twelve guests every minute. It's not possible. Still, blame attaches. I'll pass on your request, but I'd be surprised if anyone at corporate would even consider it."

"We'll make the request directly," Ariel told him mildly. "If they feel as you do, it's not a major problem. We'll go to one of your competitors, one with a yacht of similar configuration, shoot on their boat, and explain to our viewers that Delafield wasn't interested in resolving the tragedy that occurred on the *Princessa Ora.*"

The manager glared and thrust out his considerable jaw. Ariel held his gaze and felt sleazy. Hardball wasn't her game and, she could see, it was getting her nowhere she wanted to go. "Sir," she said, "let's not worry about that now, okay? That's down the road. Maybe my own bosses won't think shooting on the yacht's a good idea. I'm kind of new at this, and I think I may be getting a little Hollywoody." She gave him an abashed grin and stopped herself from saying more.

Sisson folded his arms across his chest. "Was there anything else?" he asked. It wasn't an offer; it was a dismissal.

"Yes, thanks," Ariel replied, keeping her grin and herself firmly in place. "I'd like to talk to the crew members who sailed with the Spurlings."

"They're at sea."

"All five?"

"The captain is, and two crew. One's not with us anymore; he left the country. One's taking some vacation time."

"The crew at sea . . . they come into dock next week, right? In Long Beach? Would you have a problem with my talking to them then?"

Tapping fingers against bicep, Sisson appeared to consider the request but, as Ariel expected, his thoughtfulness prefaced a negative answer and, she had to admit it, a reasonable justification.

"I've watched your show on TV. I've even seen you on it. You people are pretty responsible journalists, I think, compared to most of those magazine-type shows. Still, Delafield would be dumb to set you loose on these fellows, wouldn't we?

"In the first place, the crew was questioned by the police, intensively, two years ago. Even then, when their memory of the night was fresh, no one had any information that could shed light on what happened. Point two, these aren't sophisticated men; I mean, in regard to PR skills. You want to go over my head, fine, but I'm confident I'll be supported on this. One of them could get defensive, or creative, dazzled by the spotlight, so to speak, and, in all innocence, say something that could be misinterpreted.

"Nevertheless . . ." He paused as if he were again considering his words before he came out with the suggestion Ariel had been expecting. "We're responsible citizens. We want to do everything within reason to cooperate. Now, an officer of the company would be a different story. Someone trained in communications . . ."

Ariel watched with secret amusement as Sisson relaxed into cooperativeness, casually unfolding his arms and smiling. "I'm sure," he went on, "that Delafield would be amenable to having a more . . . appropriate representative appear on your show."

"You mean you're willing to be interviewed?" Ariel asked. "Now that's a happy compromise! I'll certainly hope to include you along with some of your people who were actually at the scene."

Sisson's smile broadened, went static, and, as he digested what she'd said, died. "I wasn't offering to appear *along with*," he said. He went squarely on the offensive then. Planting his feet on the floor and his elbows on his desk, he said, "Frankly, Ms. Gold, I don't see what you're going after with this thing. What you think *you're* going to dig up that the authorities didn't."

"Frankly, Mr. Sisson," Ariel said, "I'm beginning to feel the same way."

She realized that she was telling the truth. She'd strayed far afield from her original idea: to profile a man in a highly unusual limbo, a man who'd dropped through the slats of the legal system, neither cleared nor convicted, neither absolved nor condemned. Without new information, the story was a rehash of what anyone could learn from old newspapers; in short, no story. So what *was* she "going after with this thing"? To provide resolution? Right! With a boatload of nonwitnesses? She had one crew member packed off to his homeland and the rest unavailable for comment. Of the passengers, the one most central to the issue, Jack, was silent as the grave; two, Eve Spurling and Barry Verlyn, were in the grave (watery or otherwise); and one, Karen Lucas, was out in the ether somewhere. Leesa Canady, Wally Hatcher, and the Palmers had only reconfirmed what they'd sworn under oath, and Maura Jameson had shed no light on anything except the victim's psychological quirks.

But, Ariel told herself, that left three passengers with whom she had not yet talked. Surely, one of them or one of the crew, even if they were unaware of it, had seen something significant, heard something significant.

Significantly was how Sisson was looking at his watch. Her time was up. She was passing through the reception area when she noticed a rack of advertising brochures, and she stopped to look. "Feel free to take some," called a woman at the service counter.

Ariel looked over the rows of slick four-color folders. One invited her to "Experience the legendary enchantment of Greece," and another promised to be "Your Ticket to the Caribbean sun." A third praised sparkling Pacific waters and Mexican ports of call and featured the *Princessa Ora* on the cover. She was taking it from the rack when the outer door opened and a man wearing work clothes came in. She gave him no more than a quick, reflexive glance, seeing a tanned, muscular man with thick iron gray hair. His equally casual return glance, she could hardly fail to notice, became a once-over, slow and thorough. His lazy smile suggested that he liked what he saw.

"Do it," he said.

"Excuse me?"

"You thinking of chartering? Do. I recommend the amenities."

Ariel smiled. He was on the rough side, but he was attractive. He was—the word leaped to Ariel's mind—*dangerously* attractive. The gray hair was misleading; as he moved closer, she could see that he was in his midforties at most. His eyes were the color of much-washed denim, as if the sun in which he obviously spent time had leached the blue, and fine lines radiated from the outer corners. His full lower lip was caught between teeth so white they looked sun-bleached, too. He was a virile-looking individual, and there was no question in Ariel's mind that he knew it.

"Thank you," she said. "I just might."

"Excellent." He winked, creating some ambiguity as to just what it was he was commenting on.

"You *have* chartered, I take it," Ariel said. "You used Delafield?"

"More like they use me, pretty lady."

Ariel heard a throat being cleared, and she noticed that the saleswoman was eying the man fixedly. She seemed to be telegraphing some sort of silent message. He wasn't receiving. "I'm a chef," he explained, "seagoing. I do a duck à l'orange to die for, and my chocolate mousse? Pure sin. The sweetest, lightest thing that ever melted on your tongue."

Ariel resisted licking her lips, barely. A quick smile flitted through his eyes as if he knew it. "I'm on vacation right now, but I'll soon be back in the galley of that craft or one like it." He tapped the brochure in her hand. "Sure hope I'll see you aboard some day," he said, and ambled away.

Ariel unfolded the brochure; her mind wasn't on the pretty pictures. She was trying to eavesdrop on the conversation between the man and the saleswoman. He leaned against the counter, completely at ease, but she was obviously incensed. Her eyes flicked toward Ariel, and Ariel caught the word "customers" and then "Sisson," the manager's name, at which the man laughed, a low, unintimidated rumble. He turned to give Ariel a grin, inviting her to share his amusement. The woman hissed "Doyle!" and grasped his arm.

Ariel's eyes widened. He caught the reaction, and his own eyes turned curious, holding hers for a long moment before he returned his attention to the other woman. His "B.S." was clearly audible, and the last Ariel heard was something angry about a paycheck. She stuffed the brochure into her handbag and left.

Once in the parking lot, she stopped, considering her next move. Doyle was the name of one of the crew members on the Spurling cruise. The cook. The cook who had a nasty habit of harassing and beating up on women. And she'd thought she was being figurative when she judged him "dangerously" attractive!

She had to get to him, now, before Sisson or some company higher-up warned him off talking to the press. She swallowed revulsion. So he was a bully. A creature on the lowest rung of the evolutionary ladder. But he was on that yacht two years ago, he loved to hear himself talk, and he was not going to be abusive in broad daylight. Ariel found an inconspicuous place to wait.

Time passed. The saleslady emerged, dropped letters into a mailbox, and went back inside. A lovey-dovey couple Ariel imagined were honeymooners or soon-to-be honeymooners drove up. Necking and giggling, they went into the building. Waiting patiently, idly, was not something at which Ariel excelled. She had second thoughts, and third ones. She grew antsy and hungry. She thought of those lovely little sandwiches she'd passed up at Maura Jameson's. She thought of duck à l'orange. She thought of how ridiculous she must look, lurking behind a pittosporum bush like a fourth-rate private eye. After half an hour she began seriously worrying about time.

She, personally, was spending too much of it on this story. She had to get something going or she'd be told to drop it. At best, she'd be directed to stop husbanding it so unprofessionally, to start assigning interviews to producers. She couldn't let that happen. A producer couldn't find out what she needed to know: whatever Jack could tell her about herself. But her reluctance to delegate went beyond that, Ariel realized. The story compelled her now. As a friend? To prove once and for all that a man with whom she was simpatico was innocent? That he was as ignorant of what happened to his wife as Ariel herself was?

What if she actually lucked into some previously overlooked evidence? What if she did find out what happened that night, and what if what happened was that Jack Spurling murdered his wife? There wasn't, Ariel had to admit, a plethora of alternative suspects.

The winter sun had altogether lost its warmth. Ariel was getting cold, but she'd been handed this Doyle character on a platter, and she would take advantage of the break.

Doyle's sullen expression when he finally emerged was not reassuring. Thinking himself unobserved, he bit the end off a cigar and spit viciously. Ariel watched him light up, take a few puffs to get the cigar going, and walk off toward a dusty pickup truck. He was getting in when she approached him from behind.

"Mr. Doyle?"

He jumped, banging his head on the roof, hard, and barked an obscenity before he saw that it was Ariel who'd called his name.

"Sorry I startled you," she said. Rather hoping that he had, she asked, "Did you hurt yourself?"

"You been waiting for me?" His surprise quickly became obvious satisfaction. Rubbing what was probably going to be a goose egg, he said, "Well, by God, pretty lady! Aren't you something!"

"My name is Ariel Gold, Mr. Doyle. If you've got a few minutes, I'd like to talk to you."

"Ariel. Nice. Well, Ariel, I've got from now till Monday morning. How'd you know my name?"

"I heard the woman inside say it."

"Vilma! Prune-faced cow was warning me off 'fraternizing' with 'prospective customers.' " He laughed in delight, and his remarkably white teeth flashed against olive skin. He was galaxies away from being Ariel's type—physically and, certainly, in any other respect—but even she could feel the raw current he generated.

"Looks like," he was saying, "old Vilma the virgin was on the wrong track as usual. Goodness me!" He waggled his cigar Groucho style and said, "Have we got a little *fraternizing* on our mind?"

Ariel made herself smile pleasantly. "I'm afraid," she said, "it's you who's on the wrong track, Mr. Doyle."

"Call me Pete."

"All right. Is there somewhere nearby we could go to talk?"

"How about my place? It's not too tidy, but it's private, and I've got nothing but time till Monday. We can do a lot of talking."

"I had more in mind a cup of coffee, and I've only got an hour before my next appointment. Is there a café in walking distance or should I follow you in my car?"

"You're not kidding, are you?"

"Afraid not."

"Too bad." Doyle's face lost its blithe cockiness. He clamped the cigar between his teeth. "I don't get it," he said. He crossed his arms and probably it was deliberate that the bicep muscles bulged. "You're not a cop, I can tell, and you don't look like some kind of do-good agency snoop. What are you, a lawyer?"

"No. Look . . . Pete. I should've explained in the

beginning, but we kind of got off on the wrong foot.
I'm in television—"

"Television?"

"Yes, the news business. What I wanted to speak to
you about is a cruise you worked—"

"What cruise? What're you talking about?"

"A cruise two years ago. A woman named Eve
Spurling died."

"That's ancient history, and it's got nothing to do
with me." He snatched the cigar from his mouth and
threw it to the ground, grinding it to bits with his heel
before he turned to get into his truck. It was a vehement
reaction, and it took Ariel by surprise.

"Mr. Doyle . . . Pete. Hold on! I'm talking—or trying to talk—to everybody who was on that yacht. Not
just you."

"Yeah, fine." He pulled the truck door closed and,
through the window, said, "Go chat with the dead lady's
rich playmates. I'm hired help. I don't know nothin',
and the nothin' I don't know satisfied the cops."

"I believe that, okay? I'll explain exactly why I'm but-
tonholing you this way, but . . . could we go somewhere
else? Sisson doesn't want me talking to you or any of the
crew from that job. If he sees me here, sees me with you
against his express wishes, well . . ."

Doyle glanced at the Delafield office and back to
Ariel, and she could see that he was torn. Clearly, he was
more than willing to thwart his boss in any way he
could, but he looked to be measuring that indulgence
against something else, and making up his mind. Ariel
had been interested in talking to the cook; at that
moment she became determined to talk to him. If need
be, she'd stand behind the truck and block his exit with
her body. More sensibly, she propped her forearms on

the windowsill and said, "Come on, Pete. What can it hurt? If you know anything I can use, if you saw something or heard something that gives me a new direction to go in, we might be able to do a little business."

He sucked on his lower lip. It wasn't the studied come-on it had been the last time she'd seen him do it. "Just you, right? I mean, no cameras or tapes or anything like that?"

"If you say so."

"All right," he said. "Sure. Why not? Go south to Pico. There's a diner about a block east." He looked again at the Delafield office and said, "Better get your car and follow me."

It took no more than ten minutes, even against late-afternoon traffic, to drive the short distance. It was more than enough time for Doyle to have thought things through. He'd regained his cool.

"So, what's in it for me to talk to you?" he asked point-blank as soon as they were seated in a booth.

"That's hard to say." Ariel studied the plastic-coated menu. She was hungry, but she couldn't see herself maintaining control of this conversation with ketchup on her chin. "If you're just going to repeat what you said two years ago, I'd say very little."

"I thought you were ready to ante up. I don't see anything in the pot yet."

"And I don't see, yet, that you're holding any cards." Ariel laid the menu aside and waited for Doyle's move. It was unexpectedly subtle—or, maybe, he was playing by different rules.

"You really on TV?"

"Yes."

"That's something. Imagine me with a TV personality! A real lady, too. Big-time TV?"

"Medium time. Medium budget."

Doyle laughed. "You're all right. I like you. You want a burger?" he asked. "Or a steak sandwich? They're good here."

Ariel glanced around. They were the only customers in the place. "I don't think so, no."

"What's with the attitude? This joint isn't fancy enough for you? I know food, okay? I make it a point to know where they keep a clean kitchen, serve decent food. If I say the beef's good here, the beef's good here."

Ariel regrouped. Who would've thought a man with such tender sensitivities would also think it was just fine to punch women out? "I'm just not hungry," she said. "Is the coffee good?"

The waitress arrived, a woman whose name, embroidered on her uniform, was Gwen and whose downturned mouth and defeated shoulders suggested she'd been on her feet too long. Doyle flashed her a smile. It was no more than a gesture, an automatic "Hiya, babe" response to female flesh. She straightened as if she'd been injected with a jolt of pure B-12. Her mouth curved, her chest shot out, and her pencil was poised to take down his every syllable. The transformation wasn't lost on Doyle. "You're new, aren't you?" he asked. "Are you guys getting ready to close up? It's not too late to get a sandwich, is it?"

Gwen assured Doyle that she had all the time in the world.

"Tell Manuel," Doyle said, "that it's for Pete."

When she'd promised to pass on his message and had lovingly recorded his order for a draft and a steak sandwich, medium rare, open face on sourdough and smothered in sautéed onions (there was no such thing on the menu, but that was no obstacle), and jotted down Ariel's black coffee, she sashayed away.

Doyle excused himself to go to the men's room. He was gone long enough for Ariel to think about what she'd ask when he got back. To rethink it. To question (as she did more often than anyone knew) what the heck she was doing, running around interrogating people. Posing as a bona fide news correspondent. More times than not, like now, she was flying by the seat of her pants and if she was lucky, "coming in on a wing and a prayer." Gwen brought her coffee. Ariel cradled the mug in cold hands. How she got away with this masquerade was more of a mystery than any *Open File* story.

Doyle came back smelling like soap. He slid into the booth and got down to business. "Okay, say I was able to tell you something about that night I didn't mention to the cops. Are we looking at money or not?"

"Possibly."

"What kind of money?"

"Depends on what you tell me."

"What if I was to tell you Spurling lied?"

Ariel's heart bumped. "Lied about what?"

"About him being in his cabin when he said he was."

"*Did* he lie about it?"

"How much would that particular lie be worth?"

"Backed up with proof that it's he, not you, who's lying?"

Doyle rubbed his nose. Grudgingly, he said, "I can't back it up. What was I supposed to do, take a picture of him? Like I knew it meant anything at the time?"

"You saw him?"

"Yeah, I saw him."

"Where? When?"

"Around one. On the main deck, forward."

"Doing what?"

"Nothing. Walking."

"Going where?"

"Not far, for sure. We're not talking the *Queen Mary* here. Okay, toward the aft deck and then inside. After I passed him, I heard him open the door and go inside."

"Was he moving slow? Fast? Did he seem upset?"

"Fast. How would I know if he was upset? It was dark."

"If it was so dark, how can you be sure it was Spurling?"

Doyle's order arrived. His plate, Ariel noted, was garnished with a proud sprig of parsley. "How can you be sure it was him?" she repeated when the waitress, reluctantly, left. "And why didn't you tell the police?"

"Because it was none of my business." He began cutting into his steak, precise slices, neat and efficient.

"Pete?" Ariel watched him chew. "This takes me nowhere. You say you saw a man in the dark. You say well enough to recognize him, but you couldn't even tell what kind of expression he wore. And you didn't bother to mention it when you were questioned."

"So I'm not a good citizen," Doyle said around a mouthful of beef. He cut another wedge and, with his fork, scraped off onion. "Here, try this."

"No, thank you."

"Why not? I know the cook. I'm going to hire him one of these days when . . ." He shrugged. "Dream on, Pete. Come on, have a bite. No lie, it's good."

"I'm sure it is." Ariel forced saliva back into her throat and took a sip of coffee.

Doyle watched her, and for a few beats it was touch and go whether he'd take offense.

"Actually," Ariel lied, "I'm a vegetarian."

"Oh." Forking the bit of steak into his mouth, he said, "You'd like my eggplant gratin. Killer."

The word recalled Ariel back to the subject. "Pete, a woman died on that cruise. Jack Spurling was charged with her murder. You're admitting you knew he was lying under oath, and you stood by and let him get away with it. Why would you do that?"

"I said already."

"Did you make a deal with him? Like you're trying to do with me?"

Doyle laid down his knife and fork. "No," he said, "I did not make a deal. Maybe if I'd heard he had the kind of bucks that would have made it worth the risk, I would've. But I didn't see any sign of that and, frankly, I didn't feel like giving the guy grief."

"You're telling me you refrained from blackmailing Spurling out of compassion?"

"I'm telling you, lady, that I don't care who killed the bitch. If it was him, more power to him."

Slowly, Ariel lowered her coffee mug to the table. "What did she do to you?" she asked, guessing. When Doyle didn't answer, she said, "You made a play for her, didn't you? She turned you down."

"That's not the way it was."

"Then how was it?"

"She came on to me. Don't you give me that look! I'm telling you, she did! You think because I read you wrong I don't know when a woman's coming on to me?"

"I think it must happen to you practically every hour of the day, so, yes, I'm sure you know it when you see it. So then what happened? She came on to you and . . ."

"She was touching me when she didn't need to. You

know what I mean, lady, so don't say you don't. She put her hand on mine when she complimented me on a meal, and she let it lie there just a little too long, and she let her fingernails drag along my arm when she moved it. She'd give me looks out of the corner of her eye. Pose herself in her little bikini. All that mating dance crap.

"One night she came in the galley. Said she was looking for olives or some damn thing. I knew what she was looking for. I took her up on her invitation. She let me. Started breathing heavy, making little moaning noises. Letting her head drop back—you know what I mean?—offering her neck and pressing against me like she was begging for it. Then when she really had me going . . ."

Ariel knew what must have happened next, but she also knew to wait and let him say it himself. It took him a minute. He sniffed, explored the back of his teeth with his tongue, and then, his eyes averted, said, "She pushed me away. She laughed." He looked full on at Ariel. "There's a word for women like her," he said, "and if ever there was a—"

"I know the word."

"She gave me this look like I was a hair she found in her soup and said, 'I don't think my husband would approve, do you?' I couldn't believe she was serious. She was trying to be cute, I thought, so I went after her again. She tried to slap me. Can you believe that? Like a bit out of some old movie! Even then, I still didn't get that after all the come-on—I'm talking two days of giving me the eye!—she was going to blow me off! I thought, maybe she's the type that's turned on by a little persuasion. So I grabbed her. She started to scream. I put my hand over her mouth. When I moved it, she said, 'I'll see you fired for this.' "

"Then what happened?"

"Nothing. She left."

Ariel doubted that, but she didn't press. "When was this?" she asked.

"I don't know. A few nights into the cruise."

"The night she died?"

"No!"

Doyle had apparently lost his appetite. He slammed the beer bottle to the table, got up, and walked out. Ariel threw down a twenty and hurried after him.

The parking lot was dusky now and empty, as far as she could see, except for her van and his truck. "Pete, wait." She caught up with him, and he stopped, looking impatient.

"When you saw Spurling on the main deck . . . he was alone?"

"Was when I saw him."

"Do you remember a couple named Wally Hatcher and Leesa Canady? Do you know if the cabin they were in overlooked that deck?"

Doyle gave Ariel a sour look. "I don't know who was in which cabin."

"They were in the master stateroom."

"Then it did."

A man came out of the diner. Since he hadn't been a customer, Ariel assumed he was an employee. He gave Doyle a big grin and a wave, calling, "Yo, Pete!"

"Manuel! *¡Hola, varón!*"

The other man gave a different kind of wave then, a stiff-fingered jiggle that, universally, suggests admiration. "Hey, *que linda! ¡Buena suerte!*" he called, and, laughing, he crunched off across the gravel and disappeared around the side of the building.

Doyle was still grinning when he turned back to Ariel,

a completely natural, open-faced grin. It looked alarmingly good on him. "My future sous-chef," he said.

"What was he saying?"

"Nothing bad. Complimenting me on my taste."

"Pete, you said it was 'around one' when you saw Spurling. What were you doing up at that time of the morning, anyway?"

"You've really got a one-track mind, don't you? I'd been having a beer with one of the guys, one of the crew, okay? I went topside, up on the flydeck, to smoke a cigar before I turned in." He resumed walking toward his truck. Ariel followed.

"You didn't see Eve Spurling?" she asked.

Doyle sighed.

"I'll take that as a no. You didn't see anyone else at all?"

They'd reached the truck, and Doyle opened the door and began to climb in. Ariel thought for a second that he was going to drive off without another word, but he paused, one foot on the truck's floor. "I *heard* somebody else," he said. "A woman."

"Heard somebody where?" Ariel asked urgently. "How do you know it was a woman?"

"She was on one of the decks because the interior's all carpeted. What I heard was high-heeled shoes on wood."

Ariel frowned, trying to assess the implications. Eve had left the card game shortly before or after one o'clock. Had she run into Jack then and gotten into the argument Leesa heard? Leesa also heard high-heeled shoes, walking away from the argument. If Doyle saw Jack leave the deck to go back inside, *and afterward heard high-heeled shoes on the deck,* then Eve was still alive at the time. *Alive and alone with Doyle?*

"Hey, Ariel?"

The change in Doyle's voice brought her back with a jolt. Within minutes he'd gone from anger to good humor to . . . what? His smile was sly. "I thought you had an appointment." He looked at his watch. "Fifteen minutes ago? You don't seem in much of a hurry."

"I let the time get away from me. I've got to go." Ariel took a step back, twisting her heel in the loose gravel. He reached to steady her, grasping her forearm. She looked down at his hand. He wasn't hurting her, but he also didn't let go.

"Why the rush? You're late already," he said softly, "if you really do have an appointment at all."

"I do."

"What are you afraid of?"

"I'm not afraid."

"You are. You're stiff as a board. Are you afraid of me?"

"No."

"No? Something's got you nervous. You're shaking. I can feel it." The smile was gone; his expression had turned dead serious. "God, you're pretty!"

Ariel said nothing. She made a halfhearted try at freeing her arm. He held fast.

"Could it be you're scared of what you're feeling right now?"

Ariel's mouth was suddenly as dry as dust. She licked her lips.

"I'm not usually wrong about women," Doyle said. "I can count the times on one hand. I don't think I was wrong about you." The diner's neon sign went dark, and a second later the bright fluorescents inside were turned off as well. "You tell me if I was wrong."

Ariel's eyes flicked toward the building. Doyle grasped her chin, turning her face back toward him. The parking lot seemed suddenly very quiet and very empty. For a long moment neither of them moved. Then, against her resistance but with surprising gentleness, he began to draw her to him. "Forget them. Look at me."

It was a superfluous demand; she couldn't drag her eyes away. Her mind was racing. She was intensely aware of his smell, a combination of sun and soap and sweat. It wasn't disagreeable.

"You're one very classy lady, you know that? Pretty. Smart as a whip. And I think you're up front. You're not a tease, are you?"

"No," Ariel whispered. She heard herself and, more forcefully, said "No, what I mean . . ."

Doyle's lips curved.

Ariel felt her skin contract, from scalp to face to arms. She could hear his breathing, heavy and fast. She felt as if she'd stopped breathing altogether. "Pete," she said, "this isn't—"

He pressed his forefinger against her lips. "The kind of men you're used to . . ." he said. "Do they know how to make you happy?" His finger moved, skimming her lip, her cheek, her neck. "Do they? Clever guys, I'll bet—hotshots—and sophisticated. Dressed in clothes with the right labels. Smelling like some designer's idea of macho man. I'll bet even their bedsheets have designer labels. But, tell me the truth, do your kind of men make you happy?"

He brought her captured arm to his mouth and kissed the tender skin at the inside of the wrist. Ariel's fingers were an inch from his eyes. With one swift rake of her nails, she could have drawn blood. Her hand remained as it was: open, inert.

"Listen to me," he murmured. "There are two places on this earth that I know what I'm doing. The kitchen and the bedroom. I am very, very good in the bedroom. You know why? Because I love it. I can make you feel things, Ariel, that you never felt before." His eyes had grown heavy-lidded. The pupils were black wells.

"Good night!"

Ariel jumped. The call had come from the door of the diner, where Gwen was waiting for a second woman to lock up. Ariel pushed herself away from Doyle. He didn't try to hold her. She put a good three feet between them and said, "Good night." It wasn't addressed to the waitress. "I'm going," she said.

Doyle made no move to stop her. "Is that what you want?"

"If . . . if what you told me pans out, I'll see what I can get for you money-wise."

Doyle's chest visibly lifted and fell with his breathing. His expression was unreadable. After a moment he said, "Whatever. I don't care. If I was smart about money, I'd be working in a four-star restaurant, not a galley."

Ariel nodded and went quickly to her car. Until she made the first turn, she could still see the light from his truck cab in her rearview mirror. He hadn't moved.

17

THE STEAK WAS PRECISELY RIGHT, CHARRED ALMOST TO A cinder on the outside, pink and tender inside and oozing with juice, and the salad was a work of art: a crisp jungle of greens and reds and oranges, sweet and tart on the tongue. The Cabernet had been saved for a special occasion, and its ruby color was brilliant in the firelight.

With her dinner before her, Ariel sat at her gateleg table, a recent acquisition. It was a pretty thing and set up just as she liked it in front of the fireplace. Beside her plate was *Child of the Century*, Ben Hecht's autobiography. It was out of print, and she'd special-ordered it. It had come in yesterday's mail, and she'd looked forward to the simple act of turning to the title page. The book lay unopened.

The steak was congealing, the salad grew limp, and the Cabernet was untasted. The last, Ariel rectified with a long deliberate swig.

"Ever so good," she told Jessie, who dozed nearby. Jessie sighed, at peace with a fine world, having been taken for a vigorous walk and then fed dinner. Jessie had a full stomach and a clear conscience.

"Music!" Ariel said. "I forgot music. What do you think? Mozart? Respighi? Hoyt Axton?" She didn't move from her chair. She pulled the collar of her robe tight to her chin and tried to find comfort in the sheer luxury of cashmere, a gift from her grandfather, never worn until tonight.

The fire crackled loudly in the silence of the room.

Ariel couldn't remember when she'd felt this low. She couldn't remember if she ever had. That's the funny thing about amnesia, she told herself; you can't remember. Funny thing. She wasn't laughing. "Dog," she said quietly, "you've got an idiot for a mistress."

The episode with Pete Doyle had shaken Ariel. Not the fear she'd felt; fear she could live with. What she couldn't reconcile with her self-respect, with her own image of who and what she was, was that—for one small, mindless black hole in time—she'd also felt excitement. *Call it what it was,* she told herself: *desire.* And he'd read her like a headline. What would've happened if they hadn't been interrupted she didn't know. She didn't even like the man! What was to like? He was a bully. A convicted abuser. What else was he?

Tonight Doyle had said outright that Eve Spurling deserved to die, that she had it coming to her. If the encounter between the two of them actually happened (and why would he make up such a humiliating incident?), then he had motive for wanting her punished. He certainly wouldn't have told the police what he told me, Ariel thought; a man on parole for battering a woman? Maybe he tried to pick up where Eve cut him off. Maybe it got out of hand.

It was possible—probable—that she was the only other living person who knew about that sorry scene. It was also possible—probable?—that right about now he was regretting that he'd let himself be needled into spilling it. Right about now, he might be seeing her own behavior in a similar light to Eve's. *A woman who thinks she's too good for "hired help." Toying with him. Teasing. Promising. Not delivering.*

Nuts! Ariel told herself. He probably didn't even hear your last name, and he never did ask where you worked. Which show you're with. Which *network* you're on.

She got up and made sure she'd set the burglar alarm.

The Delafield manager knew her full name and where she worked. Even if Doyle didn't get the information through Sisson, it would be an easy matter to find her. She was listed in the phone book, the address conveniently supplied. Also, Doyle had seen her license plate when she left the parking lot. In fact . . . how difficult would it have been for him to follow? Sure, he hadn't jumped in his truck and torn out after her, but she'd caught every light. She'd been in no hurry driving home. Straight home. And she hadn't been in her right mind at the time. She had never once looked back, looked around, thought about the possibility that he might come after her.

Then where is he? That was an hour and a half ago. If he followed you, where is he? Getting the lay of the land? Planning to come back later? This is a creature of impulse we're talking about here, a man driven by testosterone, not strategy.

She got up again and took her nearly untasted food to the kitchen, where she wrapped it and put it away. She hoped the act of clearing up would clear her mind. Jessie hoped it meant scraps. They were both disappointed.

The sensible thing to do, Ariel knew without having to think about it, was to tell somebody else what she'd learned. She'd been behaving, she realized, like the old

Ariel she'd heard about: a Lone Ranger, an outrider who couldn't function as a team player. Nobody at *The Open File* knew, except in general terms, where she'd been today, from the interviews with Leesa Canady and Maura Jameson to those with Charlie Sisson and Pete Doyle. She ought to call Henry. She couldn't, just then, face calling Henry. Henry trusted her, and Henry knew her too well.

Nice somebody knows me, she thought; *I'm not recognizing myself.* She had the wit to smile at such an observation from a total amnesiac who, one year ago, literally didn't recognize herself. She didn't remember her past; she felt no kinship with the woman people told her she once had been; she could only theorize—as she might with a character in a novel she was reading—about that woman's feelings.

But, contradictory as it might sound, at no time had she truly doubted her sense of self. From the first she'd had an innate understanding of who she was now, of her values and her virtues, such as they were, and her failings as well. On some fundamental level, she knew who lived inside the body she found herself occupying; she recognized herself in her eyes, and she'd always been able to look herself in them.

Enough with the breast beating! You didn't do anything!

Ariel drifted back to the fire, her mind back to Doyle. Stroking her dog and staring into the flames, she faced a fact: she believed he was telling the truth about seeing Jack on the deck that night. She saw no reason to lie. Doyle's interest in money had been skin deep, an opportunistic reflex. She didn't see him as calculating enough to come up with the story in order to make Jack a scapegoat if he, himself, had killed Eve. If that were his plan, he'd have told the police, not her. More to the point, he was never considered a suspect, or if he was, he'd been cleared.

"It's time to apply logic," she informed Jessie, "about what happened to Eve Spurling. So . . ." She gathered her thoughts. "To cover our bases, we start with option A. 'The reports of my death are greatly exaggerated.' She's not dead at all."

It took little pondering to see that it was no option at all. *If she's alive, where'd she go?* They were miles from land. A lifeboat or tender would've been missed. It was conceivable that she hid and slipped away after they docked, but why would she? The notion of an accomplice rendezvousing with the boat and spiriting her away was too stupid to entertain. *Forget A. She's dead.*

B: She accidentally fell overboard.

It wasn't impossible. Eve wasn't sober. The waters had been calm that night, but the yacht was moving; a person could slip. *So why didn't she call for help?* Had she somehow injured herself or passed out? Ariel would keep B in reserve.

C: She killed herself.

She sounded rash enough, and, from what Maura said, she was not a happy woman. But, as Maura also said, her behavior on that particular night wasn't that of a suicidal person. Would Eve have manifested despair if she felt it? Would a woman who refused to face her own despondency show it to others? Ariel didn't know enough about Eve's mental state to make an educated guess. With the information currently at her disposal, she could make no case for suicide. Which left one option: she was killed by someone else, unintentionally or otherwise.

At this point Ariel knew of no one with a motive except Pete Doyle. Getting back at somebody for taunting you and rubbing your nose in it might not sound like a grand and noble vengeance but, God knows, people are killed for less. He not only had motive, he had a bad temper and a history of violence against women. Talking to the two who'd brought charges against him, the one who'd dropped harassment and the one who'd held firm on assault, was a necessity. Ariel would get their names from public records.

Doyle said he'd been having a beer with another crew member before going topside to smoke. It was important to talk to that man. To ask what Doyle's state of mind had been. To ask if he'd seen Doyle return to the galley. And how long he'd been gone and what his demeanor was on returning. Ariel tapped her nails against her cheek. Had the shared drink taken place? Could she find out who, if anybody, the other party was? Slim chance.

Okay, Doyle had motive; he had opportunity as well. Was he capable of murder? He was strong, in good shape physically. Ariel knew that one thing for a fact. But emotionally? She pondered that one long and hard. Every instinct told her no. If Pete Doyle had caused Eve's death, Ariel believed, he hadn't planned it ahead of time and he hadn't meant to do it; it had been a case of heated passion getting the better of him. She put him aside for now.

Next, Jack. An image flared in her mind's eye: his face, contorted with rage, his hands choking or striking. Leesa had heard a slap. *Did he stop with a slap?* Ariel's eyes squeezed shut. Treat this as a puzzle, she told herself. *Just a puzzle. Nothing that has anything to do with real people.*

She didn't want to believe Jack killed his wife. She freely admitted it to herself. She also admitted that he could have. She was convinced he had not told the truth when he said he was in his cabin, asleep from twelve-fifteen on. Doyle said he saw him on the deck "around one." Hatcher said he wasn't in his cabin at some undetermined time between one and one-thirty. No one could place him there until one-forty, when he was seen by several people. One of them, Carolyn Palmer, said his hair was wet. Would his hair still be wet from a shower an hour and a half earlier? No. Would he, if he'd been awakened by the "frolicking" next door, have stuck his head under a faucet before going out to complain? Unlikely.

Ergo, he was not in bed when he said he was; he was up and awake, and he was out on the deck, and he was lying about it. If he didn't kill Eve, why lie? If he did kill her, why, period?

Eve was a troublesome person. A neurotic, demanding person. She drank too much and got unruly when she did. According to Leesa, it wasn't uncommon for her to "lose her cool." According to Maura, she spent a lot of money frivolously. She may or may not have fooled around but, according to Pete, she fooled around with the *notion* of fooling around. There must have been times when she embarrassed Jack, when she drove him wild. Enough to kill?

Jack had never once talked about his wife, about their relationship. The truth was Ariel didn't know *jack* about it.

"Ha-ha," she said aloud, bleakly. "Like it or not, Jess, he had opportunity. If we don't have motive, we have reason to believe there was frequent provocation. Maybe this one night he got pushed beyond endurance? We've certainly got no evidence of premeditation, no more than the prosecuting attorney did two years ago."

The shepherd yawned and adjusted her head on her paws, making herself more comfortable.

"Right. Let's move on. Who else had motive and/or opportunity?"

First, Ariel considered the other four crew members. Presumably, they hadn't known the victim before the cruise, but neither had Doyle. She had no information as to where any of them was during the critical time. She'd talk to the three from the *Princessa Ora* next week, with or without Delafield's permission.

The passengers all appeared to be nonstarters; they were almost, to a man and woman, provided with corroborating, alibi-providing witnesses. But were they? They were also, to a man and woman, sloshed. How long would it take to do away with someone on a yacht on the high seas? Who would've noticed if someone left to relieve himself or make a phone call and didn't come back for five or ten minutes? Ariel winced in frustration. She had no reason to connect any male passenger to Eve, and she didn't have enough information about them to waste time speculating. What about the women? If Max Neely was right about the sex of the person who'd run amok with the paint, the female of the species should be at the top of her list. After last night's anonymous phone call, over the top!

Leesa was one of the few who, to Ariel's knowledge, had been alone during the time in question and, at six feet tall, she was no delicate flower. Still, Ariel couldn't believe the dippy girl-woman was capable of murder. She couldn't even imagine it.

Maura, too, was taller than average, and she was athletic. She was also a disturbed and unhappy woman. Her husband had been unfaithful to her; with her good friend Eve? Ariel got her tape recorder from her purse, found the bits where Maura had talked about Eve, and listened. She decided against it. There'd been no trace of jealousy or rancor in anything said about the dead woman.

Carolyn Palmer had been with her husband; Linda Charvat, noisily, with her employer; and Karen Lucas with her companion, but Barry Verlyn was dead and Karen was . . . missing. Ariel remembered that Maura had focused on that fact, and on Karen herself. Why? Ariel shook her head, sighing. She wasn't likely to get the answer to that question from Karen; even the police couldn't locate her.

The phone rang. Ariel hesitated, then answered it.

"Can't find anything on the woman," Sarge McManus said.

"On . . . ?" For a confused second Ariel wondered how he knew about Karen Lucas. "Oh! You're talking about Sissy."

"Of course I'm talking about 'Sissy.' Sarah Alice Hardaway, widow of Martin Abbot Hardaway. Age fifty-six. Resident of Tulsa, Oklahoma. Registered Democrat. Active in local charities. Model citizen. Has no record of any kind. Not even a traffic ticket."

"Hmmm," Ariel commented. "How old was her husband and how long were they married?"

"I haven't got that yet, but I will."

"Have you met her?"

"I haven't yet," Sarge said, his voice grim, "but I will."

18

EARLY THE NEXT MORNING ARIEL FLEW TO DENVER TO tape an interview for the next *Open File*. The story was a bizarre twist on interfering in-laws that she believed would divide the viewing audience into warring factions. Her subjects were seventy-year-old grandparents charged with kidnapping their only son's newborn baby. The sire was dead and had been for three years, but he'd left sperm on deposit. The baby was borne by a woman who'd answered an ad placed by the grandparent "wannabes," a woman eager to become a mother. She'd been exhaustively interviewed. She'd signed a contract guaranteeing the grandparents an active role in the child's life. She'd decided after the birth that they were fruitcakes, and she was welshing on the deal.

Ariel left the elderly couple with mixed feelings. She was sorry for them, but she wasn't sure the baby's mother was wrong in her assessment. She'd be taping the other side of the story the next day in L.A.

In the meantime, the crew with whom she'd worked was heading east on another story; the producer was staying in Denver overnight to visit family; and, because the taping had gone off without a hitch, Ariel had over four hours to kill before her return flight. She picked up a Colorado map and saw that Boulder was about half an hour away. Jack Spurling's father-in-law lived in Boulder.

As it turned out, Mitchell Winters lived on a remote spread south of Boulder, and Ariel was driving up the snow-encrusted road to his house forty minutes after she made the decision to go there. She hadn't called ahead. Winters had been as frosty as his name the time she had called, back when she was trying to locate Jack, and she didn't figure he'd be any friendlier today.

Frosty described more than the attitude Ariel anticipated. She'd thought ankle boots, gloves, and a wool coat would be adequate for a trip to Colorado in January. They would have been for the day as she'd planned it, hurrying from airport to heated car to heated house and back again.

When she got out of the rental, it was like stepping into a meat locker. She wrapped her coat into a double layer across her body and breathed air so cold it hurt. Exhaling a fog of condensation she expected might turn into ice crystals, she took in the scene beyond the cleared acreage of the ranch: miles of forest gradually climbing to distant white-tipped, humpbacked peaks. They were dwarfed by an infinite slate-colored sky, swallowed in silence and lonely as grief.

The crunch of her boots on snow was loud. The house was as silent as the landscape. A big, rustic ranch, a combination of log and stone, it was closed and still. There was no sign of life, no smoke issuing from the chimney, and no cars, although the attached garage, also closed, might conceal a car. Ariel adjusted her bag on her shoulder. She hadn't decided what tack to take with Winters, assuming he was even at home.

Just then, a sharp cracking noise cut through the silence. It echoed violently against itself in the vast open space and, within seconds, before the echo died, there came another. Ariel dropped into a crouch, certain beyond doubt that what she was hearing was rifle shots. She plastered herself against the car, trying to judge where they were coming from. The next one reverberated endlessly. Sound carried crazily on the empty air, and the echoes played havoc with her sense of distance and direction. She didn't know whether she was blocked from the shooter's view or totally exposed. Was it a hunter? Or was she the game?

Even before another shot rang out, Ariel had her car keys in hand. If this trigger-happy nut was gunning for her, then he had pitiful aim; she'd heard no hit or ricochet, and he didn't seem to be getting any closer. She wasn't planning to hang around while he improved. She reached for the door handle, ready to bolt. In the moment she braced herself to move, it came to her, what blind panic had prevented her from catching before: the measured cadence of the reports. *Thwack!* And in three seconds, *thwack!* And in three seconds . . . If it was a gun, it was target practice.

She angled her head and listened. It wasn't target practice, and it wasn't a gun. It was an ax, close by, splitting wood.

Ariel rested her forehead on the hand that still clutched the door handle, weak-kneed and red-faced. "Okay, okay," she muttered. " 'Just because you're paranoid doesn't mean they aren't out to get you.' " When her heart had stopped jumping around like a boxed-up frog, when it had settled to a rhythm as steady

as the woodchopper's, she straightened up. Brushing
snow off her coat, she noticed that she now had a big
run in her hose.

No one answered the doorbell. The broad, sheltered
porch surrounded the entire house. Ariel walked around
to the side and called out. The regular whack of steel
against wood continued uninterrupted. She followed
the sound to the back of the house, where wooden steps
descended to the yard. Beside a shed, what looked like a
smokehouse, was stacked half a cord of wood, and
beside that was the woodchopper, still hard at it.

He wore earphones, and a tape player was hooked
onto his belt. His lips moved along with whatever song
he was listening to. The ax went up and then down;
wood chips flew. Between descent and ascent, Ariel saw
him make a face and grumble some complaint, directed,
she assumed, at the log presently undergoing dissection.

She hesitated. Obviously, he hadn't heard her, was
unaware that he was not alone. A man wielding an ax,
especially a man who wouldn't be happy to see her,
wasn't that much more appealing than a man wielding
a rifle.

Just then, ax raised, he paused. For a second he was as
rigid as an animal first sensing danger. Then, awkwardly
but with startling speed, he gave the earphones a shove,
knocking them cockeyed as he pivoted toward where
Ariel stood. His feet were braced, his knees bent. He
looked like Pete Sampras waiting for the match-deciding
return at Wimbledon, but what he had firmly gripped in
both fists was considerably more serious than a tennis
racquet.

"Whoa! Hold it! It's okay!" Ariel cried. "Mr.
Winters?" Feeling foolish but a lot more concerned
about the ax than how she might look, Ariel held up

both gloved hands, palms forward. "Sorry to startle you, but I rang the bell. I did call out."

The man's shoulders relaxed, millimeter by gradual millimeter. He didn't relax his grip on the ax. "What do you want?" he asked.

"My name is Ariel Gold. I telephoned last week? From L.A.?"

Winters—if he was Winters rather than a handyman hired to replenish the firewood supply—frowned. He looked fit enough to be a laborer, slim and straight of back in his down vest and jeans and oil-tanned boots, but he was no kid and he didn't look like any laborer she'd ever seen. He was gray-haired; in his late fifties, Ariel judged, maybe a young sixty. He had an expensive haircut and a lean, clean-shaven face. There were good bones under it, and intelligent gray eyes looked out of it. He was, definitely, more L. L. Bean than J. C. Penney.

"You're the woman from the TV show?" he asked. "From *The Open File?*"

Ariel admitted it.

"You're alone?"

Even more reluctantly, Ariel admitted it.

With one mighty swing, Winters buried the ax in a stump. Ariel flinched when it hit. He started toward her. She backed up. Then, calmly and with no animosity she could detect, he looped the earphones around his neck, flipped the off switch, and said, "You'd be wiser not to sneak up on a man out here in the middle of noplace." Peeling off work gloves, he crossed the yard and held out his hand. "Mitchell Winters," he said. "You look frozen. Let's go in the house."

It wasn't all that toasty inside, and Winters went straight to a kitchen hearth that looked big enough to roast an ox, with room left over for one or two shoats if not a full-grown hog. As he twisted paper into spills and made a neat, efficient pyramid of wood, he said, "I'm warm-natured. Fast metabolism, I guess. I know I keep it too cool in here for normal people." He glanced up, smiling. "This won't take a minute."

Ariel was goggle-eyed, not just at Winters's behavior, but at the kitchen in which she found herself. It was huge. The floor was stone pavers, the walls rough plaster and old European tiles, the cabinets antique pine, and the massive carved range hood . . . could it be stone? she wondered. The whole kitchen looked as if it had been transplanted from a farmhouse in Provence, picking up just what was necessary in the way of modern conveniences en route. A third of it, the end where Winters now worked, was what realtors currently liked to call a "keeping room." It was thoroughly masculine, imaginatively put together, and deceptively simple. Ariel had a hunch she was seeing Jack Spurling's handiwork.

The wood burst into flame. Winters gave it a couple of smart pokes and then turned his backside to it, gesturing Ariel toward the oversized leather sofa facing the hearth and himself. She would have preferred that he move over and let her have the hearth, but she sat. The leather was stiff with cold. Winters seemed as relaxed as if Ariel were his favorite neighbor. "Mr. Winters," she began, determined to know why a man who had been anything but cooperative when she'd telephoned was suddenly Mr. Congeniality.

He interrupted. "You want coffee?" he asked, already on his way to the coffeemaker. "I do. I've got some made."

Removing the tape player from around his neck and setting mugs, milk, and sugar on the counter, he asked, "So, Ariel, did you come all this way just to talk to me?"

"I was here on other business," Ariel said shortly. "Mr. Winters—"

"Mitch."

"Mitch, do you mind telling me why we're all of a sudden buddies? Not a week ago you all but hung up on me."

"A week ago I hadn't talked to my son-in-law. I told him you called, that I'd said 'no comment.' He vouched for you. Said I was a grown man and if I felt like talking to you, it was up to me."

Ariel cocked her head. "But Jack wants no part of this."

"He also said, 'It was your daughter who died. You've got a right to know what happened to her. You've got a right to see her killer punished.' "

Ariel accepted a steaming mug. "For him to put your feelings ahead of his—and he does feel strongly about letting this lie—he must think a lot of you."

"I think a lot of John—Jack, as you call him. He's right. It's time poor Eve's death is resolved, and John cleared, beyond a shadow of a doubt.

"Do you know the man still gets hate mail? Even threats? I know because I was with him once when he got a crank call. Every now and then some crackpot who thinks he got away with murder crawls out of the slime. Reads some story and thinks it's up to him to see John punished. I'm afraid that one of these days . . ."

He paced a few feet, stopping to warm himself at the fire. He was, Ariel took note, neither as warm-natured nor relaxed as he'd made out to be. "John's still young," he said, "and even God can't change what's past. He needs to get on with his life unencumbered. Without this suspicion dogging him. He ought to have a wife who's capable of being a wife. He ought to have a family."

Ariel set down her coffee, and reached her hand into her purse. "A wife who's capable of being a wife?"

"You heard me."

Letting her frown ask the question, Ariel said nothing.

"I shouldn't speak ill of the dead?" Winters sat, heavily and suddenly, in an armchair. "I take full responsibility for my daughter. That requires, however, that I acknowledge what Eve was. To be accurate, what kind of person her mother and I made her." He stopped himself. "I won't say this stuff on the air, Ariel, let me warn you."

Ariel nodded, and left the tape recorder in her purse. "That's fine," she said, and pushed Record. "But *I'd* like to understand."

"Nothing complex about it. Eve got what they call mixed signals, on every single level, all through her formative years. Elaine, my late ex-wife . . . I'll say it straight out: Elaine came from 'new money.' Appearance was everything. Eve had to get into the right schools . . . I'm not just talking about college; I'm talking preschool on. She had to have the 'right' friends, had to wear the 'right' clothes. Had to know how to write 'proper' thank-you notes and communicate 'appropriately' with the servants." Winters's mouth twisted in what might pass for a grin. "I thought you just knew those things like you knew how to dress yourself."

"You came from a different background?" Ariel murmured.

"Oh, my family had run through our respectably *old* fortune by my generation, but we limped along on past glories. Silver-spoon-in-the-mouth shabby gentility." He laughed. "Of course, the spoon had been sold off by then, along with all the other silver. The lovely Elaine and her nouveau riches looked good to me.

"What I'm sure you've already figured out is, I was a helluva worse snob than Elaine." His gaze was level when he said, "After too few years—once the physical attraction wore thin—everything about her began to set my teeth on edge. To be painfully blunt, she embarrassed me. Every time she used that ridiculous, carefully cultivated voice—'Oh, darling, *must* you?'—I'd mock her. I'd give Eve a big wink. Trouble is, I didn't give the child anything else. Nothing real to counteract the phoniness. No principles, no values. How could I give her what I didn't have?

"I did teach her one thing, by example. When you don't like something, when life gets unpleasant in one place, why, the thing to do is go somewhere else. Forget your troubles and have a good time, life's too short, et cetera."

"That's what you did? Went somewhere else?"

"Elaine and I had a couple of trial separations, but she talked me into coming back, 'for Eve's sake.' The truth was, Elaine didn't want to be a divorcée. Eve was twelve when I left for good."

The fire didn't need attention, but Winters got up to stoke it. "I notice," he said, "that you're not asking about the result of this admirable upbringing. Has John talked to you about Eve?"

"I've talked to other people who knew your daughter." Ariel had no trouble recognizing in these origins the Eve Spurling she'd heard described: a sad, frivolous woman on a madly spinning wheel, trying to outrun the emptiness of her life, the hollowness at her core. Winters was watching her; she had the uncomfortable feeling that he could see her thoughts. "How did you and Jack get to be so close?" she asked.

Winters's eyebrows formed a vee, but his mouth

curved in a friendly enough grin when he said, "What's all my soul baring got to do with finding out what happened to Eve?"

"Probably nothing. I'm just nosy."

He laughed. "And I guess I must be lonely today, or I'm getting to be an old windbag. I liked him from the day Eve brought him around. Sure, he was glib—he knew the right things to say—but I sensed substance under the smoothness. A man comfortable with himself. I could see she was in love. Him, too.

"This was . . . nine years ago? Closer to ten, probably. Eve would've been in her very early twenties then. I convinced myself that the damage Elaine and I had done wasn't irreversible, that Eve was still malleable. And John was just enough older to be a steadying influence." Winters's eyes lost focus, and he might've been talking to himself when he said, "I think a man with a little more age on him, a little more experience, can be good for a woman, don't you?"

Assuming it was a rhetorical question, Ariel didn't reply. After a moment, Winters snapped out of his reverie. "Where was I?"

"You hoped John might be a steadying influence."

"Hardly fair to expect him to fix what we'd broken, was it? When a shrink hadn't been able to."

"Eve was in therapy?"

"Oh, sure. But you've got to be able to face your problems for that to work. John looked like a much more pleasant solution, a quick fix, and Eve was happy as a kid with a new toy for a year or two. Playing the role of young matron, Junior League, all that. She wanted a baby, too, badly. I'm not sure why it was such a big thing to her, so consuming. Maybe she thought since she had firsthand knowledge of how not to raise a child, she'd be a fine mother. Maybe she just wanted someone whose love she could be absolutely sure of. It was when she found out that wasn't going to happen that she started to fray."

"She wasn't able to conceive? Or was it . . . ." Ariel visualized a woman in love with a husband who couldn't give her the thing she most wanted and needed, the hellish conflict that could cause.

"It wasn't Jack," Winters said. "Eve had had an abortion years before. She'd been damaged somehow, internally. Can you imagine? In that day and age—it was well after *Roe* versus *Wade*—she'd gone to some . . . She'd been under eighteen, you see, and you had to have parental okay then. She hadn't wanted us to know."

Winters's voice caught, and Ariel waited the second or two it took for him to get his face straight. "Well now," he said. "Next I'll be collaring strangers on the street, rambling and raving."

"Maybe it was just time to let go of all this. To start to forgive yourself."

"The only person whose forgiveness matters is dead."

"I expect you know better than that."

"You sound like a friend of mine, a priest, matter of fact. Dick lets me get away with no B.S. He's a crafty listener, like you." With a meaningful look, Winters said, "With my friend the priest, though, I don't have to worry about confidentiality."

Ariel shook her head, feeling only moderately guilty about the recorder; she didn't plan to air anything without his knowledge. "Don't worry about me. You're just helping me to understand."

"Good. If you understand the man John is, you'll see why I say he didn't harm Eve. He couldn't live with himself if he had. He couldn't face me if he had. And if you understand how Eve was, you'll see why I don't believe she was killed by someone else."

"What are you saying?"

"When she was fifteen, she took pills. Enough pills. If Elaine hadn't found her, she would've died. About a year, maybe two, after Eve found out there'd be no baby, she tried again."

"But . . . Mitch! Why didn't Jack tell the police she was suicidal? That could've made all the difference!"

"He didn't know. I didn't know. Elaine didn't tell me until just before her own death a year and a half ago."

"But the second attempt was after they were married. . . ."

"He was off on a buying trip. It was pills then, too. Eve got scared, changed her mind. She called her mother. Good old Elaine, ever the one for appearances, made sure everything was hushed up, again. Money well spent as far as she was concerned."

"Your ex-wife was still alive when Jack was tried. She didn't realize what this information would've meant to his defense?"

"I asked her the same thing, of course. She said that in her judgment Eve's 'little episodes' were immaterial."

"Immaterial?"

"I know. The truth is, Elaine despised John. He was not her idea of a suitable husband for her daughter. No name, no money of any consequence, no one she could brag about. She decided that he was guilty if for no other reason than to prove that she'd been right about him all along."

19

IF THE PLANE HADN'T BEEN DELAYED, ARIEL WOULDN'T have been on it. Fortunately, the catering truck had held up departure. The other passengers were cranky; Ariel was out of breath and grateful to have avoided the highway patrol as she'd sped to the airport.

The meal, unsurprisingly, hadn't been worth waiting for. Ariel nibbled briefly at something beige and gave up the effort. A second glass of wine on an empty stomach wasn't a better idea, but it seemed like one at the time.

Her ideas in regard to Jack Spurling were getting murkier by the minute. When she'd asked Mitch Winters if he'd told Jack about Eve's suicide attempts, he'd said of course. And what had Jack done with the information? What he did, Mitch told her, was nothing. He considered the news carefully, said thank you for telling me, and explained why it would go no further.

It had been six years, Jack had reasoned, since Eve's last try, and that one was halfhearted. There was nothing in her behavior before or during the cruise to suggest that she wanted to end her life, and her friends on board would no doubt testify to that. Finally, Jack said that having survived the trial, he would not rake up trouble and heartache with nothing more than ugly speculation about Eve's frame of mind.

It was too bad, Ariel reflected, that the man's witch of a mother-in-law was dead; she'd like to shoot her. A line from a Flannery O'Connor character popped into her mind: "She would of been a good woman," said the down-home talking character, "if it had been somebody there to shoot her every minute of her life."

Ariel noticed that her glass was empty again. Looking for the stewardess, she craned to see past her seatmate, a pale woman with too much makeup and too much hair, tortured into a frizzy aureole. The woman was less finicky than Ariel; she'd finished her dinner down to the crumbs and was reapplying lipstick of a plum color so deep it looked almost black against her white skin. She looked, Ariel thought, rather like Elsa Lanchester in *The Bride of Frankenstein*, especially when she bared her canines at a little mirror, checking for smudges. Ariel blinked away the image, put her glass down, and rested her muddled head against the window.

The glass was cold, and a black void reigned beyond it. Far, far below was a tiny, geometrically perfect grid of lights. Why, Ariel mused, did city layouts that seemed so haphazard at ground level seemed so precise from the air? Perspective, she decided, worked wonders. Too bad she'd lost track of hers.

Fishing out her address book, she found the number for Jack's shop and placed a call. Despite the fact that it was after seven, that's where she found him.

"Oh, good," he said. "You got my message."

"What message?"

"Apologizing for not calling till today. I'd like to see you."

"That's fine because I'd like to see you, too."

"Good! I was afraid you might be upset with me. I don't suppose . . ."

"I am upset with you. What don't you suppose?"

"I'll be leaving here in half an hour. Can I come pick you up? Take you out someplace casual?"

"No, I don't believe I care to be taken out of where I'll be in half an hour. Not unless you're Captain Marvel and you've got an extra magic cape with you, or a parachute."

"Ariel, does what you just said make sense to you?"

"Certainly. 'A lady's imagination is very rapid' *but* . . . 'We haven't all had the good fortune to be ladies.' Not bad." She laughed. "A brilliant verbal marriage, if I do say so myself, of Jane Austen and Mark Twain."

"You're in quite a mood, aren't you? But if Jane married Mark, she'd be Jane Twain."

"Ah, but 'never the twain shall meet.' " The plane seemed to descend slightly, and Ariel's ears closed. "Did I ever tell you I'm acrophobic? Funny, though; I ain't afeared of flying. That's, say, if . . . Ma Kettle married Erica Jong. She'd be Ma Jong."

"Are you by any chance a little high?"

" 'There is nothing wrong with sobriety in moderation.' " Ariel caught herself before she actually snickered. It gave her pause to realize how easily she'd fallen into silly, comfortable sync with Jack. It gave her pause to realize how unprofessionally she was behaving. "Jack, your late wife tried to kill herself," she said. "Twice." Noticing that she'd caught her seatmate's attention, she turned to the window before she said, "You knew that over a year ago, yet you didn't see fit to mention it to your attorney or anybody else. Are you nuts?"

"How did you find out about—"

"Tell me, was the third time the charm? Oh, please, forget I said that. That was inexcusable. It's just that I don't get it. When you found out the woman had tried suicide, not once but twice, why didn't you—"

"Why are we discussing this on the telephone when we could be talking face-to-face?"

"Because I'm on a plane, en route from Denver to L.A."

"Denver . . . ? Oh. I see. Mitch. Why am I surprised? You're going ahead with this show, aren't you? With me or without me. Whether I like it or not. Whether it destroys me or not. You don't know what you're doing, Ariel."

"You don't know how often I notice that, Jack."

The silence that ensued was relatively expensive. At three dollars a minute, Ariel figured it was about two dollars' worth.

"Are you being picked up at the airport?" Jack finally asked.

"No."

"Did you drive out?"

"I took a cab."

"What time are you landing?"

Ariel told him.

"I'll meet you at the gate," Jack said.

"There's her plane, Dad!" Sam popped up. "I'm going over to the gate."

Henry grabbed Sam's arm and pulled him, protesting, back into the molded plastic seat between himself and a heavyset woman chowing down on a pastry. He relaxed in his own seat, crossing his legs and continuing to watch the dark-haired man with the weird pale eyes that looked like they belonged on a Siberian husky.

The man had been pacing the area nearest Ariel's arrival gate for several minutes, looking from his watch to the increasing activity on the tarmac. When the plane had come into view, he'd moved to the window. He crossed his arms now, fidgeting as the jetway was adjusted to meet the plane.

Henry wasn't sure this character was who he thought he was. He wouldn't have remembered him from two-year-old news photos, but the name had come up quite a few times in the last two weeks.

"Dad?"

"Hush, son. Just sit tight a minute."

Passengers began to trickle and then to flow through the door. The stout woman beside Henry swallowed the last of the pastry quickly and, licking her fingers clean, hurried over to the gate. A teenage boy who looked just like her emerged, and she fell upon him, hugging and crying and blocking Henry's view. When, still locked together, they moved aside, he caught sight of Ariel.

"There she is," Sam said, but, taking his cue from his father, he didn't move.

The waiting man had also spotted her. He gave a little wave. She nodded. He started toward her. A foot or two away he stopped and said something to which she smiled a response. No touching took place. In fact, the tentative greeting was almost more concerning to Henry than an effusive one would have been. That awkward body language made his stomach clench.

"Who's he?" Sam asked, totally mystified.

"A man named Jack Spurling, I do believe. Looks like Ariel's still at work. We'd better let her be."

Spurling took the tote bag Ariel carried and hoisted it to his shoulder. Saying little to one another that Henry could see, the two of them began walking in the direction of the terminal.

Sam stood. "But what's . . ." Looking from their receding backs to Henry, he said, "I thought *we* were going to take her? What did we come all the way out here for?"

"To learn one of life's important lessons, I guess."

"What lesson?"

"That trying to surprise a woman is generally a crummy idea." Henry pushed himself from the chair. "The surpriser's liable to end up the surprisee." He grinned although he didn't much feel like it. "Come on, Sam Bones. Let's go console ourselves with a good hot bowl of greasy chili someplace, and I'll share more of the wisdom I've gleaned from my vast experience of the fairer sex."

He draped his arm over the boy's shoulder, noticing for the first time how nearly on a level it was with his own. "Now, I'm fairly sure it was W.C. Fields," he was saying as they joined the last of the passengers making their way toward the terminal. "Or was it Groucho? Said something on the order of: 'Women are like elephants; they're nice to look at but I wouldn't want to own one.'"

"Who's W.C. Fields?" Sam asked.

20

"HAVE YOU HAD DINNER?" JACK ASKED.

"I just got off a plane," Ariel responded. "Don't ask silly questions."

"I like airline food. I even like hospital food."

"You get weirder with everything I learn about you."

Jack's smile came and went so fast it was no more than a muscle tic. They'd reached his car by then, and Ariel waited while he put her tote bag into the trunk. He seemed preoccupied. In fact, she sensed, he was wound tight as a new steel spring. He beeped the passenger door unlocked, but he didn't open it. "So you went to see Mitch," he said.

"Yes."

"How is he?"

"Good. I like him. He's working on liking himself, too."

Jack nodded.

"He's concerned about you," Ariel went on. "He'd like to see you get this thing resolved so you can get some peace yourself."

"Jumping from the frying pan into the fire ain't the way."

"Proving you're innocent is."

"Aren't there any stories in this world besides mine? Any *real* news you could latch on to? A revolution or sextuplets or—"

"Jack, why didn't you tell your attorney about Eve's suicide attempts? Let him decide whether the information would warrant a new trial? Mitch mentioned that she'd been in therapy. Maybe the psychiatrist could've shed light—"

"Ariel, forget it! Eve didn't kill herself."

"You know that, do you? All right, I'll accept that. But if you know so much, then tell me. What *did* happen to Eve?"

He jerked the door open. Ariel made no move to get in. Then, in a move so sudden it was almost frightening, he slammed the flats of both hands against the car roof and, straight-armed, leaned there, slowly shaking his head. "Is this some kind of game to you? I want you to stop this! What can I say to make you do that? What can I say to you to persuade you to let this story go?"

Ariel put her hand on his arm. "Jack, you can't—"

"No, listen to me!" He took her hand. Pressing it flat between his palms, he said, "Listen to me because this is important. I'll let it go if you will, okay? As of tonight. I'd already decided . . . This thing's died a natural death. It's decently buried. The mourning period's over, and I'm, finally, back with the living. I'd like to go on from here. No baggage from the past."

"You'd already decided what?" Ariel asked.

"Shh! Let me say this. It's not so easy, so just listen a minute." He touched her cheek, a light, exploratory whisper of the fingertips that got her full attention. He looked as if he wanted to do considerably more. "From what you told me the other night it seems to me you've been in the same boat I am now. Bad things happened to you, and you lived through them. Made the best of things you couldn't change. You don't even seem bitter. If you can do that, so can I, and I . . . well, I've been thinking a lot over the last three days. I almost called you twenty different times. I think we have other things in common, Ariel. If you're at all interested—in me, I mean; not my story—let's find out if I'm right."

The moment was, as they say, pregnant. Appropriately, Ariel's stomach knotted, but it was with the labor of wrestling guilt. "I didn't realize . . ." she began.

"Didn't you? Are you telling me you haven't noticed that we connect? That there's chemistry? Are you saying you haven't felt that?"

"There's a definite . . . affinity."

"Affinity!" Jack broke into an openhearted smile of relief. "You're a regular valentine card, aren't you?"

"But, Jack, I have to tell you—"

He cut in quickly, without taking the time to think about what he was saying. "My God, woman! I've been in hibernation for the last two years. I've been sleep-walking! Like I was paralyzed from the brain down. I know I said I was okay with that. I lied. Or maybe it wasn't a lie. I just didn't get till now what a living death it was. You did that for me. You came along and—"

"No. Please don't say any more. I didn't do anything."

"Okay, maybe it was just time. But being with you . . . it's like the first crack in the shell I've grown around myself. The first little hairline crack. You knew what I'd been accused of, and you didn't despise me. You weren't afraid of me. You trusted me, enough to let me into your confidence. I know you don't go talking about your family tragedies to just anybody. No more now than you did two years ago. That means something to me!"

He grimaced. "Look at you. I've scared you, haven't I?" He cupped her face in his hands, smoothing away the frown lines with the pads of his thumbs. "I should've forgotten the speechmaking and just asked you out, one night at a time." He teased the corners of her mouth into the appearance of a smile. "Look, I'm not crazy. I know we hardly know each other. I'm not asking you to commit to one thing, not the first thing. Not even dinner. Well, maybe dinner. Or a ball game. I know you like basketball. We'll take it slow. I'll send you the occasional Candygram. You can tell me cute stories about how smart your dog is. We'll play Scrabble.

"And if it turns out that this 'affinity' is a fluke, if after a while my laugh's like fingernails on a blackboard to you or the way you chew your food makes me want to lose mine, then so be it. At least we'll have given it a shot. I'll say thanks for jump-starting me back to life and shuffle off into the sunset."

Abruptly, Ariel got into the car. Jack studied her profile for long seconds before he said, "Well, at least you're honest." He closed her door.

When he was strapped into the driver's seat, Ariel put her hand on his, stopping him from turning the key in the ignition. "I'm not so honest," she said.

"About the affinity, you mean? Ariel . . ." Obviously bewildered, Jack said, "I know I'm out of practice interacting with a woman, but am I completely around the bend? Did I *imagine* that there's chemistry here?"

"No, you didn't imagine it, but I was wrong to let it happen. I should have told you before. I'm . . . involved with someone."

"Involved?"

She nodded.

"How involved?"

"Enough."

"I see. You mind my asking why you haven't mentioned this involvement before? No, wait. I don't think I want to hear the answer to that." Jack inhaled sharply, let it out. " 'Enough,' " he repeated. "As in planning marriage?"

"I don't know."

"You don't know? Are you in love with him?"

Ariel struggled for words to explain the depth of her feelings for the man who was her best friend, who a year ago had been her only friend. "Let me put it this way. I can't imagine my life without him in it."

"Well. I guess I don't know what to say to that." In a moment, in a different voice, he said, "This man you can't imagine living without . . . he must be extremely understanding."

"You mean because I'm here with you?" Ariel's sorry little grin was wry. "He's in the news business."

"Ah! That explains a lot. It just about says it all, doesn't it?" He started the engine then and began to back out, slamming on brakes just before colliding with a car he hadn't seen coming. He muttered something and, more cautiously, finished backing.

When he'd paid the parking attendant and they were heading toward Century Boulevard, Ariel said, "I'm sorry. I know you must be angry."

"I'm not angry."

"Really? Tell that to the expression on your face."

"I'm disappointed. And feeling pretty damned foolish. When I think what's been in my mind the last few days, the conversations I've been having with myself." He laughed, and took a curve a bit too fast for comfort. "What a waste of energy!"

• • •

The ride home from the airport was tense, and quiet. Ariel could protest all night long that accepting a date with a man and talking to him a few times was hardly a covenant, but she'd known that she should have spoken up about Henry and she hadn't. She'd lied by omission. She'd seen that Jack was vulnerable. She'd sensed his attraction. She'd been aware of her own. Some people in her business might consider her behavior justified; she didn't. Not that she didn't try. As they passed the Santa Monica turnoff, she said, "I am sorry, and I'm not saying I shouldn't have made my personal situation clear right up front. I absolutely should have. But, in all fairness, Jack, I've never misrepresented myself professionally. You can't say you didn't know I wanted this story."

"No," Jack agreed, "I can't say that, can I?"

Ariel waited, but he had nothing more to say. She held the rest of the conversation in her mind. *No, Jack, I never misrepresented myself professionally, just personally, and not just about Henry. I have this other agenda. I'm after whatever I can manipulate you into telling me about myself.* He stopped the car in her driveway, shifted into park, and stared through the windshield, tapping his fingers against the steering wheel. *That, I can't be straight with you about even now. Much as I like you, chemistry or no chemistry, I'm not fool enough to trust you.* He turned to her. *And this minute, as rotten as I feel, I'd still give a lot to know what "family tragedy" I discussed with you two years ago.*

"Tell you what, Ariel," Jack said. "You want my story? You got it." He reached across her and opened the passenger door. "Call me tomorrow." He waited until she was inside the house, and then he drove away. That he'd decided to cooperate on the story did not feel to Ariel anything like a victory.

Jessie was delighted to see her, and to see dinner in her bowl. Ariel watched her tuck into it, took a deep breath, and called Henry. He didn't sound delighted.

"What's wrong?" she asked.

"Nothing I know of," Henry answered. "How was the trip?"

"Okay. I just wanted you to know: the Spurling story's a go, with his participation."

"The Spurling story? I thought we were talking about Denver. Frozen sperm. New technologies. New moral dilemmas."

Ariel listened to his tone, shifted her feet, and decided maybe she'd better sit down before this conversation went any further. "Are you sure nothing's wrong?"

"I'll tell you the truth, babe; I'm not sure of anything. How'd you get Spurling to play ball?"

"He called and said he wanted to see me. He offered to pick me up at the airport. He did. We talked. He changed his mind. I'm not sure why." Every sentence was true, especially the last one.

Henry sounded, marginally, less like some stranger she'd dialed by mistake when he said, "You're quite a saleswoman, apparently."

"Oh, yeah, that's me: the great saleswoman, 'riding on a smile and a shoeshine.' " Riding for a fall, she said to herself.

21

THE LUCKY SPERM RECIPIENT AND MOTHER OF A CHUBBY six-month-old baby girl made a good interview subject. She came across as a rational woman. The alarm on her biological clock had gone off, there had been no likely mates available, and she'd decided to take matters into her own hands. She'd been efficient. She'd screened the late manufacturer of half her prospective baby's genes as carefully as his parents had screened her. She'd seen the couple as equally efficient; now she saw them as certifiable.

She was better educated than the grandparents Ariel had interviewed the day before. She was more attractive and younger and, certainly, she was happier. She, after all, had the baby; the grandparents had a good shot at a prison term for attempted kidnap.

When the lights clicked off and the cameras rolled away, Ariel shook the mom's hand, chucked the gurgling infant under the chin, and tried to think how to edit both interviews fairly to give the grandparents a fighting chance at any sympathy. Concentration was tough. Her mind was on Jack Spurling, and it was full of questions.

Henry had raised the most cogent one on the phone the night before. "How is it," he'd asked, "that you're so sure this clown's not a killer?" She had no answer Henry would appreciate. *Because I wouldn't respond to a bad guy the way I respond to him?* Ha! She'd responded to Mr. Macho Pete Doyle! Her judgment these days was hardly a litmus test.

She'd tried to reach Jack first thing that morning, before she'd done her interview. A shop assistant told her he was at the home of a client.

As she made her way to her office (the lovely little glass-encased eight-by-eight-foot square of real estate that validated her position with this outfit), Chris Valente, the executive producer, hailed her. The staff members of *The Open File*, especially the correspondents and producers, were like ships in the night, passing between travels. She hadn't seen Valente for over a week.

"I took a look at your interview with the Ellisons," he said, referring to the grandparents she'd been worrying over a few minutes before. "You think they're flakes?"

"Well, not flakes exactly," Ariel hedged. "I don't know that I'd want them baby-sitting my kid, though."

"I thought so. It showed. You want to learn to watch your objectivity on a piece like this one. You've got two grief-stricken people here. Desperate, scared, bitter. They love that baby. She's all they've got left of their son. The mother holds all the cards. They feel betrayed. Keep that in mind when you're cutting."

Ariel nodded, managed a businesslike smile, didn't say she'd already figured all that out.

Valente gave her a politically correct rap on the bicep. "You ever hear of IAD?" he asked. "No? Internet addiction disorder. Yep, no kidding; we've got an acronym already. Interesting symptoms, from what I've been reading. You might want to look for an angle."

Before she could say "Will do" or "Thanks" or "I'm over my head. Help!" Valente was gone. It wasn't lost on her what he'd just done: handing out a gentle (but dead serious) reproach to the greenhorn and then balancing it with a tip.

She went into her office and closed the door. She'd had quite a few calls, she saw; none was from Jack.

While she returned one of the others, she idly fingered an old wooden phrenology head she kept on her desk. A yard sale find, it was one of what Jack would term her "quirky" objets d'art.

"I'll hold," she said into the phone. The head's painted-on eyes stared blankly at her as if to say "Hold what?" There was no such thing as a hold button when the phrenologists' theory was hot. The man who thought it up, Ariel remembered reading, had researched in jails and lunatic asylums. He'd believed the inmates' cranial prominences indicated whether they were thieves or murderers. Too bad it had been humbug. Localizing character traits to little mapped-out patches of skull would sure make life easier; just read the bumps on your noggin, and you've got your personality all worked out. Handy.

"Still holding," she told the phone. The diagram that stretched across the smooth bald pate did look like a map, some unknown continent with weird countries. There was the land of Mirthfulness, there Spirituality, there . . . Ariel squinted. Amativeness? The same thing as amorousness? She felt her own head for that one. Big bump! She felt around for Self-Esteem. Not so big, and shrinking. Her Memory bump was a mere pinhead.

Ariel couldn't remember who it was she'd called. She hung up. She wished she could get her fingers on Jack Spurling's skull.

She was eating a turkey on whole wheat at her desk when he finally called. He was businesslike, even terse. Ariel wasn't surprised by his attitude; she was surprised at the sinking feeling in her stomach.

"I can clear my calendar from midafternoon on if that's convenient for you," he said. She asked if he would come to her office. "No," he said, "and that reminds me. I won't work with one of your assistants or producers or whatever you call them. Just you." She agreed and suggested his office. "No privacy," he said. They finally agreed on his home. Ariel took down the address and said she'd be there at four.

The house was a convenient distance from his shop and about two miles west of her own house. It was a brick two-story, a colonial with a neat lawn. The small semicircular porch was symmetrical: a white column to either side of the door and, standing at attention beside them, conical cedars in weathered stone urns. Ariel rang the bell. She was admiring a fanlight over the door when Jack answered. He had a portable phone to his ear. Gesturing her in, he mouthed, "One minute."

She followed his back down a long entry hall. Tall, white-painted pocket doors on either side were closed. They went through a large formal dining room and a butler's pantry into the kitchen. It, too, was large. Rather forties in feeling. Lots of windows.

While he issued orders into the phone—to one of his assistants, it sounded like—he poured boiling water through a filtered coffee cone into a pot. Ariel set her handbag on the counter and looked around curiously.

Through the back windows and French doors, she could see a small, walled-in backyard. She wandered over to the doors. A flowering quince was in feathery bloom. Mossy stepping-stones led to a fountain. Near it was an old, elaborate metal bench. French, she thought; not cheap, even with a decorator's resale number.

"Tell him he gets paid when the job's done right, Sandy," Jack was saying behind her, "and make sure he doesn't walk off with any leftover fabric. That stuff's seventy-eight dollars a yard." Ariel noticed a potting bench under a jasmine-covered trellis. She hadn't known Jack liked gardening.

He'd stopped talking, she realized. He was off the phone. When she turned around, he was staring at her. The expression on his face in that one unguarded second almost took her breath. "You drink yours black, if I remember," he said.

They took their coffee to a little breakfast nook off the kitchen, where they faced each other in a built-in booth. The window there overlooked a patio Ariel hadn't noticed earlier.

"That's lovely out there," Ariel said. "In here, too. Very nice place. Who's your decorator?"

Twenty-four hours before, he would have come back with something clever. Today, he said, "I'd sell if the market were better. I expect you normally use a tape recorder in these kinds of sessions? I'm going to ask you not to. In fact, I'm going to ask you to agree to what might be an unorthodox way of pursuing this."

"All right."

"Don't say 'all right' until you've heard what you're agreeing to. For now, until I say otherwise, I don't want anything I tell you repeated, not to anybody. Not your boss, not your coworkers, not your newsman friend.

Keep whatever you say to them vague. No personal details. It's the only way I'll go ahead."

"Jack, I can't work a piece in a vacuum. There have to be others involved, technicians at the least. This is TV, not radio. What do you think I'm going to put on the air?"

"What I hope you'll *eventually* put on the air is the truth about who murdered my wife."

The word hit Ariel with the impact of a rock between the eyes. "Murdered," she repeated. "So it was murder."

"When that time comes," Jack went on as if she hadn't spoken, "you can shoot all the interviews you want. I'll make available every photo I've got, and anything else you need. Eve was into shooting home video for a while. You can have the tapes. I'll get them together for you."

Ariel held his gaze briefly before she dropped her eyes. She gave her hands intense, unseeing scrutiny while she thought this through. This certainly wouldn't be the piece she'd intended doing: the "profile of a man in legal limbo" story. *So what? You've already kissed that dog good-bye. This is a real story.*

What was problematical was that she wasn't a freelancer, able to devote days or weeks to a solo investigative effort. How would she fend off questions about details, about her progress, about when the piece might be ready to air? *I'll work longer hours, keep my other stories the focus of attention.*

More problematical, these kooky demands meant a complete waste of *Open File* staff resources. Working solo was ridiculously less effective. Agreeing to do it was the height of arrogance. Being asked to do it could make one wonder whether Jack really wanted the truth to come out. *No way am I going to lose this.*

If the only way I can get him to talk is to agree . . . Guess what.

The bottom-line consideration, though, was this: if, because of whatever information Jack gave her, the mystery (not mystery, she reminded herself: *murder*) was actually solved, it wouldn't even be appropriate for *The Open File.* Eve Spurling's would be a closed file. How would she justify having spent time on a story that couldn't be aired? *So I'll figure out an angle that can be aired. I'll cross that bridge if I ever come to it.*

One thing niggled at the edges of her conscience. She'd promised Max Neely that if she learned anything new, he'd be the first to know. The detective (her good, trusting friend) had been as adamant with that demand as Jack was being with his now. "I'm not kidding," Max had warned. "No judgment calls, no delays." Ariel couldn't come up with arguments for reneging. She'd think of one.

"Okay, fine," she said.

"You're giving me your word?"

"Yes, Jack. What you're asking is dumb. I believe you'll regret it, and I'm sure I will, but I'm giving you my word. I sit on your confidences until you give me the go-ahead."

"I know I can't hold you to a verbal pact. I'll have to trust you. Our short history isn't encouraging in that respect."

Ariel could feel the blood suffuse her face. She wasn't sure if it came from shame or anger. "I don't really think that's quite fair, Jack. I don't lie. I didn't lie to you. If you want to go ahead with this, get on with it. If you want to get back at me for an error in judgment, I think I'll just hit the road."

"You wouldn't on a bet," he said and laughed, the

slightest, most humorless exhalation of breath. "I wonder just what you would do to finally get your story."

His eyes were ice. The contempt in his voice was colder. Ariel set down her coffee cup, carefully. She got up and retrieved her handbag from the counter. She walked through the butler's pantry into the dining room and out into the long, now deeply shadowed hallway. She opened the front door, stepped onto the neat, symmetrical porch, went down the steps, and left.

22

ARIEL DROVE STRAIGHT TO HER GRANDFATHER'S CONDO. She had no idea whether he was in town or back east or in Europe. For the last week she and B.F. had had less communication than at any time since she'd learned he was her grandfather. She missed him so much that it was a physical ache.

The doorman, to whom she was a familiar sight, ushered her in, telling her Mr. Coulter had come in a while earlier, to go on up. "Up," in this case, was not a short journey. B.F. lived in the penthouse, and it was a tall building.

Her grandfather answered the door himself. His blue eyes, bright in a newly tanned face, lit up when he saw her. He looked as if he'd lost a little weight. He looked as good as Ariel had ever seen him look. He was clearly startled when she threw her arms around him and hugged him with the fervor of a shipwreck victim clutching flotsam.

"Well, I love you, too, Ariel Gold," he said. "Get on in here. You don't happen to speak German, do you?"

Before Ariel could decide if she'd heard correctly, he

said, "I'm on the phone with Essen, but communication's about broken down to *'nein,'* which we both understand pretty well. Take off your coat. Go say hey to Sarge. I won't be but a minute."

Following him into the living room, Ariel dropped her coat over a sofa. The floor-to-ceiling French windows faced west, and the sky, she saw, was tuning up for a fairy-tale sunset. She stopped to watch the pinks and mauves blossom as the sun dropped. The view from the balcony would have been even more stunning, but Ariel had never set foot on that little platform perched fourteen stories above Wilshire Boulevard, and she never would. In fact (although she was unaware of doing so), she stood well back from the glass even now.

She sighed, feeling comforted. A Haydn oratorio played softly, the clean, joyous hymn surrounding Ariel as it flowed from speakers hidden strategically throughout the apartment. The place even smelled like heaven. Ariel couldn't put her finger on what was cooking—the fragrance was too complex—but she followed her nose to the kitchen. Sarge was replacing the lid on a large pot.

"I don't know what's in there," she said, "but could I just dive into it?"

The majordomo of B.F. Coulter's four households on two coasts grinned, splitting his new beard. Bushy and darker than his gray crewcut, it gave him the look of a pirate: a short, middle-aged, burly Blackbeard who looked as if he could do damage with a cutlass in his hand. He selected a butcher knife, tested for sharpness, and began mincing something.

Sarge wasn't the demonstrative type, and their relationship wasn't the sort that involved even token hugs, but he did seem glad to see Ariel. Opening the door of the Sub-Zero, he said, "I'll get out another chop. Dinner's in half an hour."

"Best offer I've had all day," Ariel said. "I'd have thought you'd still be dining on fish after your Montana exploits. Did you already run out or didn't you catch any?"

"They practically jumped into the boat calling my name, but you don't keep them. Not allowed to."

"You catch them and throw them back? What's the point in that? Just to cause pain and injury?"

He gave her a disgusted look. "Is B.F. still on the phone?"

When Ariel said yes, he put the Swiss chard he'd been rinsing into a bowl and, in a low voice, said, "Sarah Hardaway—'Sissy' to our love-struck friend out there— was married to a man nine years older than her. For seven years. Martin Hardaway was in insurance. Died of an aneurysm four years ago. On the golf course."

"I *knew* that game wasn't good for you." Ariel scowled. "Too much stress." These were not glad tidings; she'd wanted the late husband to be a codger, rolling in money, and married for a year or two at most. "Did Sarah happen to be putting beside him at the time?" she asked. "A witnessless twosome?"

"She was in the hospital, actually. Hysterectomy."

"Do you know all this for a fact, or did you get it from B.F., who'd have gotten it from her, so it wouldn't necessarily be true?"

"For a fact. Same as what I know about the husband she had before that one."

Ariel's eyes popped. "What?"

"Five years before she married Hardaway, her first husband died in a rock-climbing accident. He wasn't that much older than her, though, and they had ten years of wedded bliss before his piton slipped. And, no, she wasn't on the climb."

"She goes through husbands pretty regularly, though, doesn't she? Was that one wealthy?"

"Comfortable, but not in the same bracket as Hardaway."

"I thought you said Hardaway was an insurance man."

"He was. He owned an agency. It was a big agency."

"Hmm," Ariel said. She grabbed a pencil and pad from beside the phone and did some rapid calculation. "You said she's fifty-six? The merry widow would've been around thirty when she married the rock climber. He wasn't, by any chance, preceded by yet another . . ."

"Nope. She was a spinster schoolteacher, fourth grade. Won a teacher of the year award."

"Big deal."

"I'm relieved by what I've turned up so far. Why aren't you?"

Ariel scowled. "You're not going to stop looking, are you?"

"Hell, no. But what we appear to be looking *at* is a model citizen . . ." He cut his eyes at Ariel. "And a green-eyed monster."

"I am not jealous!"

"Grass green. Your lip's poking out like a two-year-old's."

Ariel clamped her mouth flat. "My attitude's not the issue."

The kitchen door swung open, and B.F. came in grinning. "Finally got a 'Ja' out of the hardheaded booger. Teach him to mess with this cracker!" He plucked a cherry tomato off the counter, popped it into his mouth, and asked, "Either one of you know what *alter Esel* might mean?"

"German, isn't it?" Sarge asked. "The fellow you were on the phone with say that?"

"More than once, mumblin' to himself. I get the feelin' he wasn't complimentin' me."

"Doesn't *alter* mean old?" asked Ariel. "I can look it up when I get home."

"Better not," B.F. told her. "Not while I'm still doin' business with Herr Schiller. Sarge, you need any help out here?"

The offer was unprecedented. Like most Southern men of his generation, B.F. was about as handy in the kitchen as a sheikh. If he'd volunteered to climb out onto the ledge and give the windows a quick going over with a squeegee, Sarge would have been no more surprised. "Uh . . . thanks anyway," he said, "but I can manage."

"Good. Then we'll leave you to it. Ariel, let's you and me go check out the liquid refreshment supply."

He was popping a cork when he said, "You gonna just tell me what's got you so peaked, or you got to work up to it?"

"Peak-ed?"

"Don't act like you don't know what it means, and don't act like it doesn't apply."

"I'm okay. There's nothing you can do anyway, and I'd much rather hear what you've been up to. How're the golf lessons?"

The old man's faint smile said "So we're working up to it" more eloquently than words. "I think golf might be like ballet," he said.

"That's a comparison I don't believe I've heard before."

"I think you might need to take it up when you're about five or forget about it and stick with horseshoes.

Last week I had it tamed." He tapped his forehead. "In the zone. Magic hands."

"And this week?"

He held up his big hands. "Stone."

Ariel laughed. "So Mark Twain was right? 'Golf is a good walk spoiled'? Too bad it's not working out. Looks like golf—or something—is working wonders for you."

"Oh, I'm not lettin' the beast beat me yet. You know me better than that."

"Speaking of golf," Ariel said brightly, "how's Sissy?" The words came out in a squirt, like stomping on a tube of toothpaste.

B.F. ran his tongue around inside his cheek and said, "Sissy's fine."

"Well, that's good. When will we be seeing her again?"

"You know, much as it might stick in your craw, Sissy Hardaway's a good woman."

"And they're hard to find."

"That right? That hasn't been my experience."

Ariel smiled weakly.

"Why is it, exactly, that you don't like her?"

"Now, hold on. I never said I didn't like her. I never said one word against the woman."

B.F. set his glass on the bar counter and rotated it several times, slowly, as though he were admiring the facets of the crystal. "You know," he said, "when you dropped into my life, Sarge was mighty suspicious of you. Jane had just died. You show up and get chummy. I'm clearly taken with you. Taken in *by* you, Sarge was sure. Old agnostic figured you for a slick, lowlife reporter tryin' to weasel your way into the inside story."

"I know that," Ariel said. She and her grandfather's friend had a complicated history of outright suspicion, benefit of the doubt, and, finally, shared trust. "What's your point?"

The old man wouldn't be rushed. At his leisure, reminiscing, he said, "You start to losin' weight, you get rid of those big old ugly glasses and those big old ugly clothes you used to hide in. Fixin' your face like Jane, doin' your hair like Jane, lookin' more and more like her, *actin'* more and more like her. Claimin' to have lost your memory, of all the outlandish things, and, directly, havin' the gall to claim kinship? Why, old Sarge was fit to be tied! He was sure as death you were an out-and-out con artist. A money-grubbin' flimflammer."

Ariel laughed along with her grandfather. "Who'd blame him?" she asked. "An ex-cop? The kind of scams he'd seen? I was about as suspicious a character as he could've dreamed up."

"All he had to do was put his suspicions aside and take the trouble to look at you. Do you know"—he gave Ariel a sly glance from under bushy white eyebrows—"he actually checked up on you? Askin' questions, pokin' around old records? Does that beat all?"

"I know about that." Ariel's eyes flitted away. "But that's all right, B.F. He was just trying to protect you from somebody he thought might be unscrupulous."

"Honey, I didn't need protectin' from you. I don't need protectin', period. Haven't since I was in knee pants, and that was seven decades ago. Now, I was childish then but, so far as I'm aware, I'm not childish now, and I'd be right hurt if I felt like you saw me that way."

"No! Of course, I don't think—"

"Good. Because if and when you ever see any sign of that, you be sure and tell me. That'll be when I take my trusty forty-five and give my addled brains some ventilation."

"Don't say that!" Ariel cried. "God in Heaven, B.F., you're not serious?"

"As a rattler in a bedroll."

"I don't want to hear it! I won't hear it!" Ariel made one agitated circle of the room and then another. "Sarge's concern—my concern—has nothing to do with age or soundness of mind. It's just that nobody's immune to being hood-winked . . . Oh, don't look at me like that. I know Sissy's the next thing to Mother Teresa! But anybody can get mixed up when their emotions get in a stir. You do things you wouldn't ordinarily do. Your judgment might get clouded. After a while you're so addled you hardly recognize yourself. It can happen to anybody. You, me, anybody. 'When love comes in at the door, sense flies out the window.' "

"Is that how that goes? I thought it was love that went out the window when something else came in the door."

"Well, okay, it's poverty that comes in the door—so I adapted the adage, all right?—but poverty sure as heck doesn't come into play here, does it? Which brings me to my point . . ."

"You've made your point, and I'm not a bit addled and I recognize myself just fine."

Ariel sniffed in frustration and made another circle.

"You're gonna wear a trough in that rug," B.F. observed.

She stopped at the windows. The sky was lit not by stars but by the glow of Wilshire Boulevard. The moon was a high, distant, cold nickel, the curves smothered in wispy, fast-moving cloud.

"I'm glad to know," B.F. said from behind her, "that your concern didn't have anything to do with age because Lord knows there's no age limit, down or up, on passions. Maturity doesn't guarantee knowin' which way to go any more than youth precludes it. But once you've had a whiff of . . . let's call it connecting with somebody; once you've had the kind of oneness with another person where you lose track of where you stop and they start, why, you don't want to settle for anything less than that."

The fact that he was talking to Ariel's back didn't stem the flow of his apparently offhand reflections. "You know, your mama followed her heart. Of course, your daddy wasn't worth killin'—forgive me sayin' so—but she wanted him and she went for him. Your sister married for love, too."

"You don't have to tell me your opinion of Jane's choice," Ariel said to the windows.

"No. Now that I recall, from what we know about your past, you went the same route yourself. That didn't work out too well either, did it?"

"What are you saying? That opting for love is a mistake?"

" 'Opting'? The sheer poetry of modern language," B.F. muttered. In a quavering, sarcastic bass, he sang, "You opt for me and I opt for you. True love, true love . . ."

"All right, all right," Ariel said. "Are you saying that *choosing* love is a mistake?"

"Of course not. I was simply sayin' sometimes it doesn't work out. That doesn't keep it from bein' the only way to go if you're lucky enough to get the opportunity."

Bemused, Ariel said, "You surprise me. A tough-minded old brier like you saying love makes the world go round?"

"I didn't say that, but I'll tell you one thing: it sure makes the ride worthwhile." His quick grin came and went. "If you don't have it, no matter what else there is, it's not enough. Sometimes . . ." He eyed Ariel thoughtfully and said, "Sometimes you just have to trust your own judgment—even if the odds are bad."

There came the clink of silverware being laid, heavily, on the table, a polite announcement that other ears were present.

"You about ready to eat?" Sarge called from the dining room.

"On our way," B.F. said. He stopped Ariel as she passed. "If you change your mind about wantin' to talk," he said, "decide maybe I can help with whatever's botherin' you, you let me know, okay? I'm not much for handin' out advice, but I'm a good listener."

23

THE PHONE WAS RINGING WHEN ARIEL WALKED INTO HER house. Hurriedly, fumbly-fingered, she deactivated the alarm and rushed to the nearest extension. Her own voice, delivering the request to leave a message, greeted her. Then she heard a click, dead air, and a whirr of rewind.

She plopped onto the sofa, exhaled tiredly, and replaced the receiver. Jack, calling to apologize? To renew his offer to cooperate? To tell her to go soak her head?

Or Henry? Henry, she realized, hadn't been doing much calling. Unusual in their relationship. But then, their relationship had changed in a fundamental way. She hadn't appreciated just how much of it had been mentor and pupil until the ground rules changed. She missed the security. The confident guidance. The safety net. It occurred to her to wonder how her new position was affecting Henry.

It also occurred to her to wonder where Jessie was. The shepherd was nowhere in evidence. She didn't always greet Ariel at the door, but she usually did.

"Jessie?" she called. She dropped her coat and went back to the foyer to get the mail. "Jess?" She scooped the mail from the box. It was a cubbyhole built into the thick stucco wall beside the front door, slotted outside and fitted with a metal flap inside, and it was one of the many charming little features she loved about her old house.

The gas and electric bill was through the roof. Her credit limit with American Express had been raised to an amount she'd be insane to take advantage of. The neighborhood association newsletter looked to be no more or less ill written than usual.

"Jessie? Where are you, girl? Dinner's coming up."

Ariel laid the junk mail and bills on a table and flicked on the light in the hallway. Stopping to adjust the thermostat on the way, she trudged to her bedroom. The bed drew her like a magnet. She yawned and went into the walk-in closet. Slipped off her dress and examined it for whether it would take another wearing before dry cleaning. Put it into the bag to take along to the cleaners.

Her robe felt like a benediction. Taking off panty hose and heels felt like deliverance. She felt like dried-up leftovers from yesterday's breakfast. She'd been sleeping, on average, four to five hours a night. She almost fell asleep in the closet.

By the time she made her way to the kitchen she couldn't remember why she'd gone there. Jessie's empty bowl reminded her. Even the water dish held only dirty dregs.

"Jessie?" Ariel frowned. Even if she'd been napping, curled up in one of her favorite hidey-holes, she'd have long since been awake. She should be in here, ears up, tongue dangling, checking out the menu.

Ariel hurried through the house calling the dog's name. She looked on Jessie's bed. She flipped on the light in the study, poked her head in, peered at the knee-hole space under her desk where Jessie often took siestas. She checked out the guest shower, a favorite lair on hot days or when the dog just wanted to get away from it all. She looked under her bed. She'd never known Jessie to go under her bed. She didn't believe Jessie would even *fit* under her bed, but by now she wasn't thinking. She was panicking.

The door had been locked when she got home. Was the alarm on? Of course it was! She'd missed the phone call by stopping to turn it off. No one could have come into the house. Jessie had to have gone *out* of the house. She'd gone through her dog door. She was in the backyard. She was . . . Ariel couldn't imagine anything the dog would be doing that would prevent her flapping back through that door the minute her mistress arrived home.

In the time it took her to get back to the kitchen she'd envisioned the side gate accidentally left open by the gardener and Jessie wandering out; the lock on the gate smashed by dognappers who'd lured Jessie out; poisoned meat tossed over the fence by some lunatic, and Jessie lying dead on the grass. She turned on the outside lights. The backyard was empty. She flung open the door and ran out onto the patio.

"Jessie!" she screeched, and listened to answering silence.

Then, distinctly, she heard a scrabbling, scratching sound to her left: claws on redwood decking, over where the umbrella table was. The area was in shadow. Fearfully, Ariel began to cross the patio. She could see that there was nothing and nobody on the chaise longue or on any of the chairs, but she couldn't see underneath them. "Jessie?" she whispered, her voice breaking. She could just make out the darker shape under the chaise now, and she could hear panting. "Are you okay, girl? What's wrong?" It was then that the smell hit her.

"What in the world?" She stopped dead. She knew that smell only from a distance, a faint, unpleasant odor caught through a car window and quickly left behind. It was the first opportunity she'd ever had to appreciate the acrid, eye-watering potency of a concentrated dose.

"Come on, Jess. It's okay. Come here." She waited, breathing through her mouth, and after a few seconds, the shepherd crept from her hiding place. She made a small whimpering sound as she took one obedient step forward. Ariel began to laugh. Her face screwed into a revolted grimace, her eyes stinging, she couldn't help laughing with sheer relief at the poor, shamefaced, demoralized animal. Jessie's tail was down; her head hung low; she stank to high heaven of skunk.

"Come on, baby," Ariel said, nearly gagging, "let's go inside and get you cleaned up."

She realized later that getting Jessie inside had been a mistake. After three baths—one with tomato juice, one with dog shampoo, and one with her own more pleasant-smelling shampoo—the dog only faintly reeked of polecat. Ariel herself and the bathroom and everywhere Jessie had passed on the way to the bathroom smelled rotten. Even the leather band of Ariel's watch was pungent.

Ariel washed herself. She washed her hair. She washed her robe and her underwear and the towels she'd used. She lit fragrance candles—her house looked like a chapel with votive candles winking everywhere—and she built a fire in the fireplace, which someone, sometime, had

advised her to do in such an emergency. When she finally collapsed in front of the fireplace, she remembered
that she'd never fed Jessie. She hauled herself up yet
again. Once Jessie had been restored to her normal,
sated, dignified self, she brought Ariel a favorite ball and
suggested that it was playtime.

"Not a chance!" Ariel told her in no uncertain terms.
"I'm sitting tight until the fire dies and then I'm going
to bed. Or maybe I'll just sleep here; the bedroom's a
long way away."

Jessie dropped the ball in her lap. The bell inside jin-
gled cheerfully. The guilts hit. "I've been neglecting
you, haven't I? I've turned into a self-absorbed jerk."

Jessie grinned broadly.

"Oh, here!" Ariel said, and tossed the ball across the
room. Obligingly, Jessie brought it back.

On the third toss, Jessie didn't come back. Ariel
sighed with relief. Then she heard scratching in the
foyer. After a pause, more insistent scratching. Ariel
stood it for a full minute. Jessie was a tenacious animal.
"All right! Cut it out!"

The ball had rolled behind a potted ficus tree beside
the door. "Well, move so I can get to it." Ariel squeezed
past the shepherd, who was glued to the spot. "Look at
the dust!" she muttered, sliding the pot away from the
wall. She handed Jessie the ball and then noticed a
square of folded paper, fallen, apparently, from the mailbox and trapped on a spiderweb. Muttering "Great
housekeeping, Ariel," she batted a remnant of web from
the paper and unfolded it. The message was short, and
evil. It was written in slashing, angry strokes with a
broad felt-tip pen. It included words Ariel wouldn't
utter aloud.

"Oh!" she gasped, shock sucking the air from her

lungs. She held the note at arm's length, like something nasty that had stuck to her shoe. Reading it was like standing still while someone spit in her face. Reacting, not thinking, she rushed with it to the fireplace. Reason intervened. She propped the singed paper on the mantel, and stepped back to distance herself. Aside from a curse that fell somewhere between gutter denunciation and Pentecostal damnation, it was, in essence, a warning: notice that she should watch her step. The last line, curling into ash, included the words "taste of" (something, something) "medicine."

Ariel studied the handwriting. It was so violently angry, so out of control. Impossible—for her at any rate—to know if a man or a woman had written it. None of the language was specifically derisive of women: no name calling involving female body parts. That *could* mean a woman had written it.

Jessie, Ariel realized, was beside her, the ball in her mouth. Ariel took it, absently fingering the little knobs on the rubber surface. She was profoundly grateful she'd found Jessie before she found the note. It hadn't been mailed; it had obviously been pushed into her mailbox, pushed with such force that it slipped out the other side. The same night as the paint incident? Or had the Canaanites paid another visit? She looked at the note, obliquely, trying not to feel the threat that seemed to emanate from the paper. She recalled something Jack had said, about getting paranoid when you've been "on the receiving end of hate mail."

Jack.

What if the note had nothing to do with Canaan? Not the note or the paint or that godawful creepy phone call. What if they had to do with Jack? Specifically, with her relationship with Jack. He'd thought so. Why? More to the point, who? The vandalism happened the night she'd gone out with him. The phone call two nights later. The note . . . ? She didn't know. Couldn't know. She was carefully slipping it into a Baggie when the telephone rang.

"I called earlier," Marguerite Harris said, "but I got another call just when your machine picked up, so I couldn't take time to leave a message. This week's been bedlam! I'm the proverbial headless chicken. Nervous as a cat. Grumpy as a bear. The whole zoo! I wanted you to know you're welcome to ride with us tomorrow night, although we will be going early, so perhaps you'd prefer to meet us. Would you?"

Tomorrow night? Ariel thought. What day is tomorrow? Friday. Friday night is . . . the opening of Marguerite's new play. "I'll meet you," she said.

"Eight, then, and don't forget supper after. Will you be bringing dear Henry? Should I leave two tickets at the box office?"

"I didn't know I was supposed to invite a date."

"You're to do whatever you feel like doing. One or two?"

"Two. Thanks."

"Rats!"

"Rats what?"

"I just remembered a call I was supposed to make. Wardrobe mistress. I've got to trot. Did you smell a skunk tonight? About an hour and a half ago?"

"Intimately. I'll see you tomorrow night, and, Marguerite . . . ? It's going to be a smash."

"From your mouth," Marguerite said, and she was gone.

Ariel looked up Jack's home number and dialed it.

"Is it true," she said without preamble, "that you still get crank calls, hate mail, all that?"

"Ariel?" Jack said.

"Oh, sorry. Yes it's Ariel. Do you?"

"Sometimes. From one nut case, I think, reminding me that I'll burn in hell or whatever."

"Do you keep them? Do you have any I could look at?"

"No, why?"

"The writer . . . is his or her language pretty foul?"

"I've had those, sure. Why are you asking about this?"

"I want back on the story," Ariel said. "When can I see you?"

24

"THAT'S NOT MY NUT CASE," JACK SAID DECISIVELY.

Once he'd heard about the note she'd found, he'd lost no time in getting to Ariel's house. She'd barely had time to throw on jeans and a sweatshirt before he was there, looking tight with worry and equally hastily dressed.

She took the bagged note back from him now and put it handy to take with her the next morning. She didn't know whether to be relieved or disappointed. If the writer was Jack's ongoing correspondent, it was likely that nothing would come of it but more notes. If not, she was back with the cultists.

"Pathetic," Jack said, "and—" He broke off, scowling, his nose wrinkling, Ariel assumed, with disgust at the note. "Ariel, I don't mean to be rude, and under the circumstances I sure don't mean to be flip, but did something die in here?"

Her lips began to twitch.

"Hey, you're not going to cry?" He touched her shoulder. "Oh, please don't tell me . . . has something else happened? You sure this note didn't come tonight? That you didn't have another visit—"

She burst out laughing.

"Ariel? This isn't funny!"

"Yes, it is," she said and, for one abandoned moment, let her forehead rest against his chest. The laughter died in a hiccup, and with it the worst of the tension. Gently, she disengaged herself. "I should have warned you," she said. "It's eau de skunk."

"What?"

"Jessie the Wonder Dog had a little wildlife adventure."

Jack took in all the twinkling votive candles, sniffed, and, as understanding dawned, shook his head.

"Have a seat," Ariel said. "I'll make coffee, or maybe something stronger? To cauterize your nasal passages."

"Coffee's fine." He gave Jessie wide berth, saying "Dummy!" as he passed her, and followed Ariel into the kitchen.

"So," Ariel said, "this definitely isn't the same person who's been writing to you?"

"No. Different paper, different handwriting, different style of venom. Plus, my notes have always come through the mail, to the shop. I assume the writer doesn't know where I live."

Ariel's head was buried in the refrigerator. She found the coffee beans hidden behind the mayonnaise. She had fit a filter into the cone and was pouring beans into the grinder when she realized that Jack had fallen silent. She glanced up and, on seeing his expression, said, "What is it? What's the matter?"

"It's possible . . ." He was looking slightly ill. "I hope I'm wrong, but I think it's possible that the person who killed Eve wrote your note."

Ariel's hand jerked, the coffee grinder overturned with a splat, and beans spilled all over the counter. "The person who killed Eve?" she repeated.

Jack nodded.

"Do you know who this person is?"

More slowly, he nodded again.

"You're saying . . . are you saying you know for sure or you have a theory?"

"It's no theory. I'm told she admitted it."

"She?"

The kettle began to bubble.

"Jack?"

When the kettle began to hiss and Ariel made no move to turn off the flame, Jack reached for the knob. He twisted it, started scraping coffee beans into his cupped palm, and said, "The same rules still apply. No tapes, no third parties, no repetition of what I tell you until—"

"Jack!"

"Okay," he said, and drew breath as if to begin his story, but he only stood there, staring at the beans in his hand as if he didn't know what they were or what he should do with them.

Ariel said, "Well?"

"It makes me sick, even to think about it. I've never told any of this, to anybody. I don't know where to start."

"Jack, start at the beginning. Or the middle or the end! Here, give me those." She dumped the beans into the grinder, scooped up the rest and did the same, and while the noisy motor whirred, she locked eyes with Jack. "There," she said when she'd finished. "Now talk to me, please! What happened? Who killed your wife?"

He paced for a moment before, finally, he sat himself down on a counter stool. "A woman named Karen Lucas."

"Karen Lucas."

"Yes. She was a member of the cruise party—"

"I know that. Why would she have killed Eve?"

Grimly, Jack said, "Because she wanted me."

"Okay, all right. I see." Ariel frowned, putting one and one together. The sum shouldn't have come as such a surprise. She'd known Jack's marriage was difficult. She knew many a husband less plagued strayed every hour of every day. She certainly knew he was an attractive man, and there must have been many women who'd been happy to offer solace. Still, she was surprised. "You and Karen Lucas were involved with each other."

Jack looked away.

"Well," Ariel said lamely. From nowhere came the thought that one member of the cruise party wouldn't be as surprised as she was. Maura Jameson, she realized now, had suspected, perhaps known, there was something between Jack and Karen Lucas. She'd been disconcerted to hear that the Lucas woman had since vanished.

Ariel wrapped her arms across her chest. It was time—past time—to look at this situation and this man dispassionately. "Were you planning," she asked "to leave your wife?"

"No."

"You were just . . . having a fling."

"It wasn't like that."

"How was it?"

"You would have to have been there to understand."

"It would have been crowded."

"You aren't going to make this easy, are you? I don't deny that I was tired of Eve's neuroses. Tired of her crazed highs. Her apathetic lows. Tired of her drinking and pill popping and tired to death of her little tests of my devotion! How far would I be pushed? How crazy

could she make me before I wanted out? Before I
proved she was right all along. That she was an emotional cripple, unlovable. That she was a physical cripple
who couldn't have a child. That, eventually, I'd turn to
some woman who could."

"And, eventually, you did."

"You want to let me finish? I'm sure I sound like I'm
trying to justify myself—I guess I am—but I'd like to
make you see how it was. How I *thought* it was."

"I'm sorry, please do go on."

"What I thought, Ariel, was that I wouldn't give up.
Give in. She was my wife and I'd loved her once and I
would, by God, do the best I could by her, sick or well.
I'd said I would. I'd meant it. I *thought* that was the
kind of person I was." He shifted restlessly. "Are you
going to make that coffee or not? I could use some."

Ariel turned on the flame under the kettle again and
warmed her hands at it.

"Karen was Eve's friend," he said, "but I could see
she was more interested in being mine. I pretended I
didn't notice. When she made it more obvious, I
laughed it off. After a while it got harder to laugh off.
Eve would pull some stunt or start a fight or accuse me
of giving some other woman the eye. Karen was always
there with soft words, a shoulder to cry on, a look that
let me know there was more than a shoulder available.

"One night Eve's set was together at some club opening. She'd been in a snit because I wouldn't go. We'd had
a rough scene, and she stormed out. A little later, Karen
slipped away from their party and came to the house. She
was . . . so calm. So certain. Eve was wrong about me up
until that night. I'd never slept with another woman or
even seriously considered it in all those hard nine years.
Karen and I made love—coupled—there in the house. In

our bed, Eve's and mine." He picked up the mug Ariel had set before him, studied it absently, and put it down again. "I wonder why the location seems to matter. Surely the act, the breach of faith, is what . . ." He cleared his throat. "The affair lasted a few months. It was during the cruise that I broke it off."

Ariel poured the coffee. Her hand, she noticed, was steady. "You're saying that she seduced you."

"I'm not saying I had no choice in the matter, but yes, she did. She was cool. She was deliberate. Every move, I can see now, was thought out. For whatever reason, she decided she wanted me and she didn't care who got hurt in the process. Compared to her, Eve was the picture of sanity."

"Karen was very strong-willed, apparently."

"Was? Why would you say was? She *is*. I think the psychiatric community would use a different word, but we'll say she's strong-willed. And I was stupid. I thought she was as troubled by what we were doing as I was. That neither one of us had looked for this . . . attraction; it just happened." He stopped abruptly. "You don't believe a word I'm telling you, do you?"

"It's not my place to judge you."

"But that's not stopping you from doing it, is it? You think I'm excusing my behavior? Laying it all at Karen's door? I spent six months beating myself up over what I did. Six months of guilt and doubt and the agony of not knowing what had happened to Eve. I hoped it was an accident. I prayed she'd drowned accidentally. I *feared* that she'd found out about Karen and me and . . . When Mitch told me about the earlier suicide attempts, what I felt then made all the time before—even the trial—seem like a picnic. I spent one solid year in hell, believing I'd been right. Eve had killed herself, and it was my fault.

Not Karen's, not Eve's parents', and not Eve's herself. Mine. I'd failed her. Betrayed her.

"I'd known she wasn't stable. It's not like the word *suicide* had never passed her lips. She'd threatened it more than once. Oh, she'd been in a haze when she did, from one chemical or another, but that didn't mean it was an idle threat."

"You've accounted for a year and a half. It's been two since Eve died. What happened six months ago?"

"It was, to be precise, two months ago. That's when I found out what really happened to Eve."

"That Karen Lucas killed her?"

"Yes, Ariel, that Karen Lucas killed her."

And then, Ariel thought, she just up and disappeared, and now she's writing me dirty notes and, maybe, throwing paint on my house. *And maybe calling me?* She lifted her mug carefully, with both hands, and brought it to her lips. Sipping, she watched Jack over the rim. His eyes were on hers, and what she read there was conviction. That what he was saying was the truth or that he could make her believe it?

"You know," Jack said, "you asked for this. You hounded me for it. You made it clear that 'my story' was the only reason you had anything to do with me. Now I'm telling you what happened, and all I'm getting is attitude. So what do you want? You want me to go on, or would you prefer to continue making up your own version?"

"I'm paid to investigate and report stories, not make them up. How did you find out about Karen?"

"Her husband told me."

"Her . . . ?" Ariel set down her mug. "What husband?"

"Barry Verlyn, the man she was with on the yacht."

"She and Barry Verlyn were married?"

"Not at the time, no. They'd gone out together off and on for a while. It was strictly casual on her part, but he was crazy about her. He'd asked her to marry him more than once. It wasn't more than a month after the cruise that she took him up on his offer."

"Why? You say she was obsessed with you. You were free. She took pretty extreme measures to get you that way."

"If I can be believed, you mean? Two days after Eve's death Karen paid me a visit. She was all commiseration and tears of sympathy, just as shocked and mystified as could be. 'But, Jack,' she got around to saying, 'you did your best for poor Eve, but it's over now. You've got to let her go and get on with living. And you know I'm here for you. I always will be.' " Jack's mouth twisted. "When I declined the offer, she smiled and said, 'You'll feel differently in time.' "

"But then she married Verlyn?"

"We had a few more conversations. They got more pointed. She said she'd have me or no one would. She said something I gave no thought to then . . . a number of things she was saying at the time didn't make a lot of sense. She said she'd 'earned me.' "

"Then I was arrested. I guess she panicked, wondered if she'd be next, decided to cut her losses. Verlyn was a wealthy man. She married him, and they went abroad on an extended honeymoon. I went on trial."

"Where is she now?"

Jack shook his head. "I don't know. I haven't heard from her—not directly, anyway—since Verlyn came to see me nearly two months ago."

"And told you Karen killed Eve."

"And told me Karen admitted killing Eve. That she

flaunted it. Look . . . I'll lay this out as concisely as I can from what I know and what he told me.

"He and Karen lived high and ran with a fast crowd. In the south of France for a while, Rome—I'm not sure where else. Once the trial was over, I began to get postcards and phone calls, every month or so, from wherever they happened to be at the time. And visits. Twice when she was back in the country, she just showed up, once at the house and—"

"Did you keep the postcards?"

"I hardly glanced at them. I threw them in the garbage."

"Would you recognize the handwriting?"

"You're talking about your note? I don't know. It's so . . ." He waved his hand helplessly. "That's the work of a disturbed mind. God knows, Karen qualifies."

"What would she say when she called or showed up?"

" 'Have you come to your senses yet?' That kind of thing. Why wouldn't I listen to her? When would I see that we had to be together? That sooner or later we would be.

"Verlyn didn't know about me, about us, but one night he caught her on the phone. The calls had started to get more frequent, more . . . insistent. Like she could *make* me do what she wanted." Jack thought about that for a minute, and then shrugged it off. "When Verlyn heard her that one time, he took the phone away from her and hung up. But, he said, far from being contrite or even defensive, Karen let him have it with both barrels. Told him she'd never loved him, that he bored her silly. He went for her. She got her hands on this . . . 'dagger,' he said, some ancient decorative thing, and started waving it around, daring him to touch her, saying she'd kill him if he did. He told her she'd never have the nerve. She cut him; drew blood, he said.

"That's when she told him he'd better believe she'd kill, him or anybody who got in her way, that she'd done it before. She told him what she'd done to Eve, taunting him, saying that's how much she wanted me; that she'd killed for me and she would have me."

"What did she say she'd done to Eve?"

"She didn't give Verlyn a play-by-play." Jack ran his hand across his head to the nape of his neck. Kneading the muscles there, frowning, he said, "It had to be that when Eve left the card game, Karen intercepted her. She'd threatened to tell Eve about us more than once. I'm sure that's just what she did. I can't know what she said, but it must have been bad. Her own fantasies, I'd have to believe, mixed in with the truth, which was bad enough."

"Jack, how large a woman is Karen?"

"How large? She's not. Rather short, in fact. Slender."

"Surely you're not telling me that a short, slender woman picked up your wife and threw her over the rail?"

"She didn't have to. There was one place on that boat where a child could've done what Karen said—bragged—she'd done. The swimming platform. You know what that is?"

Ariel shook her head.

"It's down some steps from the aft deck, down below where Eve would've come out of the saloon, and it's blocked from the view of anyone in the saloon. There's no rail, no nothing between you and the water. It's just a foot or so above the water."

"You've really got this worked out, haven't you?"

Jack's face set in hard, bitter lines. "I have given it a lot of thought in the last two months, Ariel. I've imagined every possible scenario. I've visited each one in my nightmares."

Ariel pressed her hands together. She was startled to realize that she'd almost reached out to touch him. She'd almost given in to the urge to press her fingers against that hard, angry mouth, to murmur something consoling. "What do you think happened then?" she said.

"Eve would've tried to leave. I know her. The first thing she'd have done was confront me. She would've been furious and hurt, but she wouldn't have taken it out on Karen. She'd have headed straight for me. I don't know . . . Verlyn didn't know if Karen actually struck her or if Eve slipped and fell. It doesn't matter. What matters is that she went into the water. Eve couldn't swim."

Jack inhaled, a ragged sucking of air. "She must have been panic-stricken, strangling, trying to call for help. Or would the pull of the motor have dragged her under? God, I don't know! I don't want to know. In those last seconds she must have been paralyzed with fear."

He turned away, but Ariel had already seen the tears. The pale, nearly colorless irises shimmered. They seemed to be liquefying. Her own throat involuntarily constricted. This was hard. This was far harder than she could have anticipated. She gave him time, busying herself collecting the coffee beans she'd missed earlier. Getting one that had fallen underneath the kettle and scorched.

"Karen did nothing," Jack said. "She didn't throw a life preserver. She didn't call for help. This insane woman, this *madwoman,* just stood there and watched the water swallow Eve. She let the boat leave her behind, all alone in the dark. She just . . . left her to drown."

Ariel wasn't much of a swimmer herself. The image

horrified her. She felt her skin crawl at the vividness with which Jack described it. As vividly, she thought, as if he'd been there. It was entirely possible. That he, not Karen Lucas, had watched a helpless woman drown was possible. That the two of them had watched together was also possible. That Karen Lucas was no longer alive . . . that, too, was possible.

Had the marriage to Barry Verlyn and all the other details of this conversation ever taken place? Verlyn was in no position to refute anything. This plausible, suffering man in her kitchen might just be accusing another victim—a witness? a troublesome, redundant lover?—of murder.

Hating the hard edge in her voice, Ariel asked, "Where was Barry Verlyn while this was taking place? Do you know?"

It took Jack a moment to focus on her question. "Verlyn?" he asked. "In bed asleep. Why?"

"And where were you?"

"In my cabin, where I said I was."

"I see."

Both answers were lies. Ariel had fervently hoped for the truth. "I need to see to the fire," she said.

Jack found her kneeling on the hearth when he came looking a few minutes later. The fire had long since consumed itself. She was poking at a lost cause.

"You want me to build that up?" he asked.

"No. Thanks."

"Your candles have all burned out, too."

"I should've been watching them. It's a wonder I didn't burn down the house."

"The smell's dissipated some, though."

"Has it? I can't tell anymore. You haven't said . . . why did Verlyn come to you and tell you these things?"

"He said I had a right to know what Karen claimed to have done, whether it was true or not. He'd learned the hard way that she didn't always know what was real from what she imagined. He wanted to warn me, he said, that I'd probably be hearing from her soon, in person. That I should be careful."

"What did he expect her to do?"

Jack shrugged. "There's one fact that makes me believe he knew what he was talking about."

"What fact is that?"

"He was planning to initiate divorce proceedings when he flew back here. The next thing I heard, and it was within weeks of the time we talked, he was dead."

25

IT WAS ONE O'CLOCK IN THE MORNING, THE HOUR WHEN, at whoever's hands, Eve Spurling had met her death. Ariel was dressed for bed. Robotlike, she was brushing her teeth, staring at her pale face in the mirror. The little valleys under her eyes looked like bruises. She was beyond tired. Her skull was hollow with exhaustion.

After Jack had brought up Barry Verlyn's death, she'd tried to think of something sensible to say. Her mind had been blank. Verlyn's death, of course, wasn't news; she'd known about it for days. But hearing the words in connection to all that had gone before had shocked her badly.

There were so many questions begging to be answered that she couldn't count them. She'd managed to ask a few. He'd freely answered. When she realized that she wasn't listening, that she was trying to read his eyes, that she was imagining grabbing him and shaking him until she jarred recognizable truth loose, she'd asked him to go. "I'm sorry," she'd said, "but there's too much ground to cover, and I'm just . . . I'm too tired. I can't focus."

He'd looked as spent as she felt. "I'm not leaving," he said, "until I see no skepticism. Not a trace."

"Jack, whether I'm skeptical isn't the issue. The piece is."

"The *'piece.'* " He bowed his head and, massaging his eyes with thumb and forefinger, said, "Imagine. For a minute I forgot the bloody 'piece.' "

"I didn't. Be glad of that. If I weren't doing my job, if I were being guided strictly by emotions, I can't say that we'd still be talking. Your story's built on air. It's unprovable."

"Brutally honest, aren't you?"

"I don't mean to be brutal. Let me ask you . . . Verlyn's out of the way. You're free. If Karen's so obsessed with you, where is she?"

"I don't know. She may have been here, outside your house, last Saturday night."

"Doesn't that strike you as a pretty oblique form of communication?"

"All I know is that she's made it poisonously clear that she considers me bought and paid for. It's not the first 'oblique' message she's ever sent me."

"What do you . . . Never mind. Tell me, where do you see us going with this? I mean, what do you hope for from *The Open File*?"

"I want that woman," he said. "I made an effort to find her. I couldn't. I don't have the resources to find her by myself."

"What if she doesn't want to be found?"

"She's got to be. She's a cold-blooded killer. I think she's killed twice. Verlyn's death came too soon after he exposed her secret to be coincidence. She's dangerous, to anybody she comes in contact with. She's dangerous to me!"

That last statement, at least, had the ring of utter truth.

Ariel climbed into bed thinking this was going to be one of those nights when she was too tired to sleep. Within seconds her eyes closed. She didn't know another thing until the alarm clock went off at seven.

By eleven, the following Monday night's show was ready to go. Ariel was satisfied that the Ellisons, the grandparents of the sperm bank baby, were getting as fair a shake as the mother. The elderly couple were clearly in pain, and their pain came through as eloquently as their aggressiveness. She was also satisfied that her own post-edit expressions and inflections were, if not constantly sympathetic, nonjudgmental.

She wouldn't be on the show at all the next week—one of the other correspondents would be taking the whole hour with a major investigative piece—and Ariel had two researchers at work on Internet addiction disorder for the week after that. She was on top of things, her bases covered. A few hours here and there on Jack's story wouldn't be challenged. It was officially recognized as her own "investigative piece," worth the time as long as it didn't interfere with any fast-breaking stuff.

Ariel had put a researcher on the two women who'd sworn out warrants against Pete Doyle. She didn't consider staff involvement in that inquiry a breach of her verbal contract with Jack. He knew nothing about Doyle. Furthermore, she didn't intend to drop other avenues of investigation despite what he'd told her about Karen Lucas. At this stage of the game there were too many imponderables.

One, obviously, Jack could be making the whole thing up to cover his own guilt. Two, Barry Verlyn could have made the whole thing up to get back at a hateful, contemptuous wife. Three, Karen Lucas could have made the whole thing up . . . Why? Was she still on coke? Was she delusional? You might as well guess up a tree, Ariel told herself. Meantime, stay grounded.

She had dropped off the bagged note to Max Neely that morning. He'd do his best, he said, to put a rush on getting it checked. She had put in a call to Sacramento; if Karen Lucas and Barry Verlyn had joined in wedded bliss, according to a contact in Vital Statistics, they hadn't done it in California. If they'd divorced, ditto. Verlyn hadn't died in the state either. There was no record of any of those events. She had more calls planned and since it was Friday, she had the weekend to work unquestioned and unobserved.

She'd made up her mind. There would be no more late-night conversations when she was too weak to get it right. No more intimate tête-à-têtes in her home or his. She'd insist on neutral territory, and she'd work with planned questions and she'd write down the answers, the way she should have been doing it all along.

Ariel was making notes from memory of everything Jack had said so far when she looked up to find Henry at her office door. She hadn't seen him since Monday, hadn't even talked to him in two days. He was wearing a shirt she'd never seen before. He looked good. Her heart performed a little trip beat, whether from pleasure or discomposure, she couldn't say. His attitude was as casual as if they were continuing a conversation interrupted minutes before.

"A suggestion on the Ellison piece," he said, and proceeded with typical economy to make it. "Two words: more kid."

"Pardon?"

"Show more of the baby. Open with her. A three-second closeup of her sweet, innocent little face. She's the prize in this heartrending conflict. You've got the footage; I saw it."

Ariel thought it over. It would mean considerably more editing, cutting somewhere else, rewriting the intro. "You're right," she said.

"As usual. You pay more attention to what I say now than you did when you worked for me." He turned to leave.

"Henry, wait a minute. What's your hurry? Listen, Marguerite's play opens tonight. Would you like to go?"

"Sure."

Ariel grinned. "You're easy."

"Too easy. How's the Spurling story coming?"

"It's . . . percolating." When Henry merely frowned, Ariel said, "I'm sorting some things out. It's complicated."

" 'Complicated.' " Henry's frown deepened. "You've got enough problems right now, Ariel, but I'm beginning to get the feeling Leeman Parker and his crew are the least of them."

"I wouldn't say that."

Henry closed the door. "What's going on with you?" he asked.

"With the story you mean?" Ariel tapped her pen against her notepad, a nervous tattoo. Tiny black freckles bloomed. "The thing is, I can't talk about it."

"What the devil does that mean?"

"Just what I said." Ariel sprang to her feet. "I've got to get to an edit bay and see what I can do with the Ellison intro."

Henry's body was blocking the door. An interminable moment passed before he stood aside, saying only, "What time's the play and what's the dress code?"

•   •   •

It was a few minutes past the agreed-upon time of seven when he arrived that night.

Ariel was ready and waiting, was in fact beginning to feel anxious about being late. She reached for her bag, but Henry stopped her. He took it out of her hand and put it back on the table and pulled her to him and kissed her with a hunger that felt almost like anger. It left her a little frightened.

"Let's not go to the play," he said.

"After all the trouble you've gone to?" She tried a smile. "Tying that tie, buttoning all those tricky little buttons. You look mighty elegant."

He let her go, somewhat abruptly. "The tux is why I'm late. It was at the cleaners." He adjusted the fit of the jacket with a little sartorial tweak completely out of character for Henry. "A chili stain from the other night." He was, Ariel realized, ill at ease. His nose wrinkled. "What's that smell?" he asked.

"The powerful and obnoxious smell of mendacity" popped into Ariel's mind. "Skunk," she said. "You think it's bad now, you should have been here last night." Her smile slipped. "Come on. We've got to make tracks."

Marguerite was tense as a tuning fork. Her husband, Carl, appeared to be nonchalant, but Ariel knew better. The other two couples who were their guests had picked up their tension, and Ariel and Henry had brought their own.

The lights dimmed. The audience shuffled and coughed and settled. The curtain rose. The third line in act one, scene one, brought down the house. Carl was holding Marguerite's hand. "Off we go!" Ariel heard him whisper.

By intermission, Marguerite was her cool, veteran self.

Carl was as mellow as well-aged wine, and the rest of the party tittered excitedly. "Look at Carl beam," Ariel said to Henry. "You know they've been married over thirty years? And still in love."

"They're very lucky people," Henry said quietly.

Ariel turned and found him watching, not the couple of the moment, but her. The festive mood hadn't caught on with him, apparently.

"Hey," Ariel teased. "Take your hands out of your pockets. You're ruining the line of your suit."

Henry smiled. "Promise me something, okay?"

"If I can."

"Promise me you'll take care of yourself."

The chime sounded, signaling that it was time for everyone to return to their seats. Crowd noise rose as people hurried to dispose of glasses or find their partners. Ariel didn't move. A woman on crutches bumped into her, knocking her slightly off balance. Henry reached to steady her, grasping her by the shoulders. The woman apologized and thumped on by. Henry didn't let go.

"Promise me," he repeated.

"I don't understand . . ."

"Yes, you do. The last time you pulled this kind of lone wolf stuff with a killer, you almost ended up dead. You're a professional now. I won't insult you by telling you to act it."

"Henry . . . I don't think he is a killer."

"Ariel, I'm not sure you're *thinking* at all. I don't want to see you hurt. In any way."

"We've got to go in. The play's . . ."

"Promise me, dammit."

"Okay," Ariel whispered.

He held her shoulders a moment longer and then turned her toward the doors.

The second half was as well received as the first. The supper afterward was a victory party. Henry and Ariel managed to hold up their ends of the conversation, but Ariel noticed Marguerite sneaking a worried glance their way and redoubled her efforts to be lighthearted.

It was late when they got back to her house.

"Can you come in?" Ariel asked.

"Not tonight. I'm taking Sam hiking in the morning, early."

"*You're* going hiking? This is new!"

"Yeah," Henry said tiredly, and laid his arm along the back of the seat. "Isn't it? An overnight trip complete with rustic cabin in the woods. I'm really looking forward to it."

"Henry . . ." Ariel slid closer, into the shelter of his arm. When she put her hand on the back of his neck, she felt the short, shaved bristles at the hairline. He'd gotten a haircut this afternoon, she could tell, and she hadn't noticed. "Is that really the reason?" she asked. "This trip?"

"It's the easiest one."

"Don't you think . . . wouldn't it be better if we talked?"

He didn't avoid her hand, but he made no move to touch her in return. "I think it would be better if we didn't. You know, I've never felt jealous before. I don't like it worth a damn. I'm finding it brings out the worst in me. Believe me, Ariel, I'd say things you wouldn't like."

"I'm a grownup. I can take that. I need to talk to you."

"No, you need to 'sort things out,' you said, so you do that. Then we'll talk."

Quick tears stung her eyes. "All right, go. But I want you to believe one thing whatever else you may believe. I'm doing the best I can."

"I know that."

There didn't seem to be anything else to say. Ariel opened the car door.

"I'll walk you."

She shook her head.

"Wait a minute."

She turned. "What?" she said over the great painful lump in her throat.

Henry pulled her back into the car. He wrapped her in his arms and buried his face in her neck. He kissed the exact place that hurt. Then he kissed her lips. She wanted never to have to move. She wanted to feel that safe and that loved for all the foreseeable future. She felt the hard, sore knot dissolve.

Finally, hoarsely but firmly, he whispered into her hair, "Do you know how I feel about you?"

"Yes." They would go inside now, Ariel thought. Everything was all right. All the lonely, crazy confusion of the last long week was over.

"Good," Henry said. "Then I don't have to tell you. I won't take part in a dialogue about some other man and I won't make love to you when I don't believe your whole heart's with me. I won't do that to myself. But Ariel . . ." He cupped her face and held her away from him, drinking her in, memorizing every line of her face as though that might have to do him for a long time. "If you need me . . . if you find yourself in any kind of trouble, I'm here."

He kissed her again, the gentlest touch of his mouth on hers, and said, "Now, come on, and I'll walk you to the door."

26

THERE WAS A MESSAGE FROM JACK ON ARIEL'S machine. He hadn't said what he wanted, but he sounded wound up. She didn't return the call. At that moment she wished she'd never heard of him. At that moment she felt too sad to do anything but go to bed.

She was eating breakfast when he called again.

"I got a call last night," he said, "from Karen."

Ariel's grip on the receiver tightened. "Where is she?"

"She ducked the question. Ariel, she was sounding me out. I know it. She doesn't know for sure that Verlyn came to see me."

"What did she say?"

"She asked if I'd heard about him dying. I said I'd read about it. I extended my sympathy. She found that amusing."

"She didn't mention divorce?"

"Maybe she conned him out of it. Or he put it off too long."

"Did she say she'd be calling again?"

"Count on it. I tried to sound receptive. 'Now that

you're free, things are different,' et cetera. But I can't try to lure her. She'll get suspicious. I'll scare her off."

"You ought to get a caller ID, today. If she calls, you've got her."

"Slick. See? This is why I hired a professional. What else?"

"I don't know. With the ground rules you've set, you make it . . . Why are you so adamant about keeping my people out of this?"

"Oh, come on. You can figure it out. I don't know if Karen can be found. If she is, I can't imagine how she's going to be made to admit what she did. I've got no proof. None. I've got no witnesses. I've got hearsay from a dead man.

"Bring in your colleagues, and I'm setting myself up for the same kind of notoriety I barely made it through the first time. Worse! An admitted adulterer, spewing accusations at his lover, like sewage! Do you know how much I hate this? You think I want to talk to strangers about it? To have a lot of newspeople barging around spreading talk. Telling *you* scared the hell out of me!"

"Why did you?"

"I think the explanation could take awhile. I've got a client due in twenty minutes, and I haven't even left home yet."

"Well, when can we talk?"

At Jack's suggestion, they met for lunch at a restaurant across San Vicente from his shop. It was a smart little establishment, with bright winter sunlight flooding through the windows. Ariel was seated beside one. She watched a Jag pull up to the curb. The valet rushed to take the keys, almost colliding with a man walking two emaciated-looking salukis. She saw Jack crossing the street, jaywalking, dodging traffic. He spotted Ariel as

soon as he came in the door and, waving the maître d'
away, started toward her. A chicly dressed diner as rail
thin as the salukis stopped him as he passed her table.
Smiling, shaking hands all around, he was introduced to
the women with her. They all laughed at something he
said, and the skinny lady tapped his arm playfully.

Ariel had her list of questions ready. She felt like a
hangman at a tea party.

"Sorry," he said as he slid into the chair. "Potential
client. Big time."

"Isn't this a bit of a fishbowl for the kind of conversation we'll be having?"

"You said no more private rendezvous."

"Surely there's a compromise in the neighborhood.
Someplace with booths? Poor acoustics?"

"You said public. This is public." Jack's expression
was deadpan, as innocent as spring rain.

Ariel's return smile wasn't innocent. "Let's start then.
You lied about being in your cabin from midnight on.
Where were you?"

"I wasn't killing Eve."

"You and she had an ugly fight within an hour of the
time she *was* killed. What about?"

"We did not."

"You were overheard. Are you saying Leesa Canady
lied under oath?"

"I'm saying she's got moonbeams for brains."

"I'm convinced she heard an argument."

"You're right."

"Well, then? You're saying it wasn't you she heard?"

"I'm saying it wasn't Eve she heard."

"Not . . . It was Karen? And you?"

"Bingo!"

"She said she recognized Eve's voice."

"She's full of crap."

"Ahem." The waiter's smile was discreet. "My name is Wayne," he said, and handed them menus. "May I tell you about our specials?"

Ariel picked something at random. Jack insisted on hearing every special in delicately memorized detail. He asked to hear two repeated. He finally decided on trout, and Wayne departed.

"Happy now?" Ariel said in an exasperated whisper.

"I can't remember the last time I was, to tell you the truth," Jack said quite audibly.

"What's with you? What's going on?"

"See how this strikes *you*. We're here to talk about the night my wife died, the night a crazy woman killed her, and I've spent the morning talking about how 'energizing' red can be. Deep red walls can revolutionize your whole outlook. Did you know that? Great color. How's your newsman friend?"

"That's not up for discussion."

Jack's took a deep breath. "What in the name of sense are we doing?" he said. "You know I ordinarily *have* good sense? And restraint, to a fault. That was one of the things about me that drove Eve crazy." He noticed Wayne the waiter standing a respectful distance away, water pitcher proffered like a question, and nodded. When they were alone again, he said, "I've opened up more to you than I ever have before in my life. Do you realize that? Like some kind of mollusk with its shell ripped off. Quivering protoplasm. Crying, the other night, for God's sake! I can't even remember the last time I cried. And now we're going to solve a crime, you and I. Sleuths, trying to bring a fugitive to justice." He leaned close to Ariel. She noticed that his eyes weren't colorless at all. Tiny silver-blue pinpoints, like chips of mica, flecked the irises. "Don't you find the situation unreal?" he asked. "Don't you feel, just a little, like the Hardy boys?"

"Boys?" Ariel asked. "I don't think so."

"Tell you what. Put your inquisition aside for now, and we'll go for a semiprivate walk after we eat, okay?"

"Tell me why you changed your mind about confiding in me. Why you did a one-eighty."

"You made me mad."

"I don't quite see the cause and effect there."

After a couple of false starts, Jack, quite serious now, said, "I've told you what it's been like these last years. Just staying sane, keeping the guilts at bay took everything I had. Guilt about Eve . . . being half-convinced she'd killed herself. Guilt about the affair, and until I found out about Karen, guilt over the hurt I thought I'd caused her. Even after Verlyn told me the truth, I didn't feel absolved. I felt worse. I agonized over it. Was I responsible? Had I led Karen on? Had I somehow planted the idea that with Eve out of the way—"

"Oh, Jack, spare me! You're not in charge of everybody else. You might want to give some thought to what that says about ego."

Once again, Jack leaned close. "You tell me, honestly, that you never once felt responsible for Jane's death."

Stung, Ariel opened her mouth to protest. She realized he was right. "You know the clinical definition of 'fixation'?" she asked. "I looked it up. It's a person's unreasonable *or even pathological* attachment to another person. If Karen's brains are scrambled, it's not your responsibility. Now, tell me why you opened up to me."

"Before I made my big romantic proposition to you the other night, I sat down and took stock. I came to the conclusion that there was nothing I could do about

Karen, that it was time to stop wallowing in this thing. To let it go. I got the foolish idea that maybe life was worth, not just enduring, but living.

"When you shot me down . . . Don't look at me like that; I'm telling you how it felt. What I was going to say was, it turned out to be a wake-up call. All the anger I'd been too stunned to feel came out. Directed at you at first, I'll admit, but then I saw things for what they were. *Karen killed Eve.* She left me to suffer the dregs of hell— the trial, the not knowing what had happened, the self-recrimination—just like she left Eve to drown.

"Guess what, Ariel. The anger feels good. I feel cleaner and lighter than I have in years. I want her caught. I want her put away. It may be too late for Eve and for poor Verlyn, but she's got to be stopped before she destroys somebody else with her evil."

When they left the restaurant, Ariel and Jack walked two blocks over to the Veterans Hospital, a sprawling relic of the Spanish-American War. The grounds were well kept and mostly unpeopled, but an occasional vet of one conflict or another could be seen. In the north-western corner they came on a small, deserted play-ground. They were, it dawned on Ariel, only a few blocks away from her house. She sat down in a swing with a sagging rubber seat, pushing back and bracing herself with her foot.

"Now this is just what the doctor ordered," Jack said. "Broad daylight, help within screaming distance if I get out of hand, and poor sick veterans nearby to keep everything in perspective. We ought to go get Jessie. She could run around and smell coyotes. They roam pretty freely in this area, you know."

"Do you want to go on with this or not?" Ariel asked.

"We have to. Karen's not going to go away." Jack

leaned against the swing set. "The argument Leesa Canady heard was me telling Karen it was over. Karen called me by name, I'm sure. Thus, Leesa heard 'Jack.' We were talking about Eve; thus, Leesa heard the name 'Eve.' She heard a slap. It happened, all right. Karen was furious. She was beside herself. When I told her I was staying with Eve, she slapped me. I didn't slap her; she slapped me. Leesa heard the word *stupid*? Karen called me that and a few other things."

"Leesa said she recognized Eve's voice."

"Leesa's not an expert on voices. And, Ariel, Karen calls me Jack. Most people since I moved out here to California do. Eve didn't. Ever. She called me by my given name, John. She did from the day we met. So did Mitch. Ask him if you don't believe me."

"I don't have to ask him." Ariel knew Mitch invariably referred to his son-in-law as John; that didn't mean Eve did.

"And I'll tell you something else," Jack said, "although you'll probably have to take my word for this since nobody else aboard that boat seemed to remember it or question it. Leesa said she heard high-heeled shoes on the deck. Eve wasn't wearing high-heeled shoes that night. She was wearing flat sandals."

Could that be substantiated? Ariel wondered. If, say, Maura Jameson were pushed on it, would she remember Eve's footwear? But even if it wasn't Eve on the deck with Jack then, that didn't mean he didn't kill her later. "Did your attorney know—?"

"That the woman I argued with wasn't my wife? That she was my lover? You really think that would've strengthened my defense?"

"But, surely—"

"You're the only person I've told. You're the only

person I've told about Karen, who *was* wearing high heels that night."

"When did this argument take place? What time?"

"Between twelve-twenty and twelve-fifty."

"You've certainly pinpointed it."

"Like I haven't thought about every minute of that night a thousand times? I went back to the cabin at midnight, as I said. I read for a little. I was about to get into the shower when Karen showed up. I was appalled; Eve could've walked in any minute.

"I'd already made up my mind to end it with Karen. I decided to get her out of that cabin and do it then and there. I got dressed again; we went out on deck; I explained, as reasonably and kindly as I knew how, that we were history. As I told you, she didn't take it well. The discussion degenerated into tears and name calling. When she slapped me and stormed off, I went back to my cabin. It was twelve fifty-five when I got there."

That corresponded with what Pete Doyle had said: he'd seen Jack leaving the deck, he said, at a little before or after one. It did not correspond with what Wally Hatcher said: that Jack was not in his cabin sometime between one and one-thirty.

"You've got that 'Is he lying or is he telling the truth?' look on your face again," Jack observed. "Look at you, rubbing your lip, cogitating, trying to decide whether I'm conning you or not. I haven't lied to you once, not once, about anything."

"You lied under oath, Jack."

Jack opened his mouth, scowled, and closed it.

"You said you never left your cabin after midnight."

"I can't explain that without sounding . . . Look, I was scared stupid when they questioned me that first time. I knew I hadn't killed Eve. It hadn't entered my mind that Karen was capable of such a thing. Telling them about us just seemed like buying trouble, and getting her embroiled, too, in a mistake. A nightmare. After I had time to think things through, I thought changing my story would finish me, so I stuck to it. It was the worst mistake I ever made."

"Don't make the same mistake again now."

"What are you talking about?"

"You weren't in your cabin when Hatcher looked in. Where were you?"

"I don't know what time that was, do you? Does he? No. He said he poked his head in for a matter of seconds. I could've been in the bathroom."

"Did you take the shower you meant to take earlier? Could you have been in the shower?"

"No. I paced. I tried to write Karen a note, to tell her how sorry I was to hurt her. I tore it up. I went in and splashed cold water on my face. Then I went to bed. I did not leave that cabin after I came back in from breaking it off with Karen. For all we know, it was as I said at the time: that Hatcher wasn't even looking in the right cabin."

"He must be a pretty confused man, all right. You said Barry Verlyn was asleep at the time; Hatcher said he was with Karen. That they were together. He saw them."

Jack frowned. "Saw them when?"

"When he went to . . . whichever cabin he went to."

"He didn't say that during the trial."

"He said it to me this week. Verlyn's whereabouts are of no consequence, of course, except for one little thing: if he and Karen were together, that pretty much blows your whole story. She wasn't with you. She wasn't then alone to kill Eve."

"He's wrong. That's dead wrong. I was still in

the saloon when Verlyn left, saying he was turning in. It was at least half an hour before *I* left. Karen left with him. He went to bed. It was after he dropped off to sleep that she came to me. She joked about his snoring. No, Ariel. Hatcher's wrong about that.

"Look . . ." Jack went to Ariel and squatted in the patch of dirt under the swing. Resting his palms atop her thighs, he said, "I want you to think about something, and this goes to the heart of the matter. Why would I enlist your help if I were guilty?"

Ariel had asked herself that question before; she didn't have an answer.

"I'm walking free," Jack said. "I've got that to lose. I've got nothing to gain but the knowledge that I tried to do the right thing. Tell me why I'd ask for your help and then lie to you."

"I don't know."

"Then work with me on this, not against me. Stop worrying every word I say, examining it, turning it over and looking under it for something corrupt. Please, either trust me or go away and leave me alone."

Ariel temporarily put away her notepad and her questions. Jack had one thing right: what it all came down to in the end was trust.

27

JACK WENT BACK TO WORK, BUT THEY'D BE GETTING together later. Teasing, he'd suggested they meet at the cosmetics counter at Macy's. "Or"—he'd clicked his fingers—"the Christian Science Reading Room! Public as you could ask for and uplifting literature in case one of us gets moony." Ariel had relented. "Your house," she'd said. "Until the caller ID's hooked up, you should be there in case Karen calls."

Ariel had bought her own machine. They'd both be calling for a hookup. Meantime, she located the brochure she'd gotten from Delafield and studied the layout of the *Princessa Ora*. Jack was right. One of two doors from the saloon led onto the main deck aft. Eve could have exited there. The swimming platform where he claimed she died was directly below. It was at the tail end of the ship. No rails. Right at water level. Only a person peering straight down from one of the aft decks could have seen two women talking there.

She went to work on a time-and-action chart based

on Jack's version of events and what she knew from others. She wrote:

12:15	Karen comes to Jack's cabin
12:20–12:50	Jack & Karen on deck. Jack leaves, is seen alone by Doyle <u>on main deck forward</u>, where Leesa (WHEN?) hears argument Doyle hears heels on deck
12:55	Jack back in cabin
1:00	Eve leaves saloon Karen intercepts Eve They go down to swim platform
1:10–1:15	Game ends. Jamesons to upper forward deck Palmers to cabin
1:15–1:30	Hatcher to cabin: talks to Leesa, goes scouting (Sees Jamesons while en route to the lower deck cabins, Karen <u>& Verlyn?</u> while en route back)
1:40	Lower deck passengers disturbed by Vail & Charvat. Jack discovers Eve missing.

Four things were readily apparent.

One: If Karen was not with Verlyn as Hatcher said, she and Eve could have been aft alone for as long as thirty minutes. Longer than it would take to tell a woman you're having an affair with her husband. To say give him up, he doesn't love you, he stays with you out of pity. It was enough time to strike her, to knock her off balance, to watch her slip into the sea. Enough time, even, to compose yourself afterward.

Two: If Hatcher did see Karen and Verlyn together on

his return from the lower deck cabins, the above didn't happen; Jack was misinformed *or lying*. And if the former was so, three: *Doyle* and Eve could have been alone for that thirty-minute span.

What was, finally, readily apparent was what Ariel had known all along: if Jack was lying, he could have killed his wife any time between one o'clock and one-forty.

She placed a call to Hatcher's Palm Springs residence. The woman who answered *could* have sounded less friendly, say, to the IRS calling to discuss an audit. "My husband isn't in," she said suspiciously. "Who is this?"

"I'm calling from Golf World," said Ariel. "In L.A.? Congratulations! Your husband's the lucky winner of a Big Bertha titanium driver! Isn't that super? I've got it put aside for him, so tell him to ask for me personally, okay?" Ariel spelled her name, made sure the other woman had it right, and left her number.

Her grandfather's new hobby had one benefit, she thought as she hung up. She didn't know what a Big Bertha titanium driver was, but she figured if B.F. had bought one, it must be top of the line.

Ariel took a break, took Jessie to the park, took a shower. Half dressed, still in her slip, she found herself trying to pinpoint the time of the argument Leesa overheard. Could it be done? Leesa had spent time, she said, deciding what to do about what she'd heard. Five minutes' worth? Ten? Putting on her clothes might take five, and putting on her face (amazing but true; Carolyn Palmer verified it, and Ariel had seen for herself the subtle expertise with which Leesa approached that job; that kind of operation took time) . . . fifteen minutes? Twenty? Talking to Hatcher and then awaiting his return, what? Ten minutes? Undressing again (five minutes?) before being seen at 1:40 in her "baby dolls." At the max, fifty minutes, that would put the argument at 12:50, when Jack says Karen stormed away from their fight. At the minimum, forty minutes, that would put it at 1:00, when Eve left the saloon—and could have been involved in an argument herself.

It was useless. Ariel simply couldn't narrow such nebulous activities down that finitely. How long it had taken Leesa to apply makeup, how long she'd dithered in indecision. What time Hatcher had come to their cabin. Had he paused on the way to fix himself another drink? To smoke a cigarette? To go to the john?

Ariel packed her briefcase. She finished dressing (a loose-fitting, midcalf frock prim enough for a librarian—or a newswoman who means to stick to business) and fed Jessie and set the burglar alarm. It was time to go to Jack's house.

He was breathing fast and shallow when he answered the door, his face contorted with fury. "She's been here," he said.

Ariel hurriedly stepped inside and closed the door behind her. "Karen was?" Her eyes darted around the hallway as if Karen Lucas might suddenly materialize clutching a bloody dagger. "Been here when?"

Jack shook his head. "My God, she's sick. She is such a sick, sick woman!"

"Jack, when was she here?"

"I don't know." He slammed the chain lock on the door into place.

"You weren't here?" Ariel pulled her coat tight around her, and not just because she was spooked. It was cold in the house.

"Come on," Jack said. "I've built a fire in the den."

When he'd led her to a small book-lined room, she

said, "No wonder it's cold!" Flames roared in the fireplace, but all the casement windows were wide open.
"It's January, Jack," she exclaimed. Dropping her briefcase on a sofa, she went to the nearest window and
cranked it closed, glancing about uneasily for some evidence of what foul thing would prompt the need to air
out the room. "Tell me what in the world went on here."

Jack had collapsed into a chair. His head rested
against the back, and his eyes were closed. "I got home
. . . I don't know. Fifteen minutes ago. Twenty. I started to go to my room to change clothes." The fire
popped sharply as a log broke. Jack snapped to attention. "I noticed the smell," he said, "the fragrance. I
recognized that perfume and then I saw the bed. My
bed. It was . . . rumpled, the way it would be if someone, if two people had been in it. The pillows indented.
There was. . . ." His mouth twisted. "A rose."

"A rose?"

"On one of the pillows. Wilting. Like it had been
there a while." He began to rub at the palm of his right
hand. Ariel could see a thin crimson line there, a dried
trickle from a puncture on the pad of his thumb, disappearing as he rubbed it.

"Is there some meaning to a rose on a pillow? From
your relationship with—"

"No! Not to me. Not that I remember."

Ariel was still huddled in her coat. "Are there other
windows open somewhere?"

"I'll get them in a minute."

"Why don't I?" She didn't wait for an answer. Pulling
down or cranking windows shut as she made her way
through the house, she climbed the stairs to find Jack's
bedroom. It was cold. The filmy panels between the
open draperies lifted in the night breeze like restless

ghosts. Ariel stood for a moment, sniffing. She thought she might have caught a whiff of something musky, but she couldn't be sure she wasn't imagining it.

The bed was as he'd described it except that it looked less messy than artfully arranged. A perfect shallow valley was centered in each pillow. There was nothing on either of them, but she noticed something small and dark just at the edge of the bed. The single petal was withering to the texture of an old kidskin glove, its color fading to the dull red of dried blood.

Nothing else in the bedroom looked disturbed. Ariel poked her head into a combination closet and dressing room large enough to accommodate a variety of exercise equipment, and then into the bath. There was no obvious damage or disorder in either room.

When she returned to the den, Jack was at the fireplace, at work with a poker. He was ramming the thing into the logs, sending red-hot sparks flying. Karen, Ariel thought, was lucky she'd left before he got home. She cradled her arms. There were chillbumps on them. "It's a horrible thing," she said, "if somebody . . . when somebody breaks into your home. I've been there. I know."

He looked directly at Ariel. "You want to know something?" he said. "I was freaked. This woman who probably weighs all of a hundred and five pounds had me freaked."

"Are you sure it was her?"

He laughed. "I know that perfume. Intimately."

"What did you do with the rose?"

"Trash."

"How do you think she got in?"

"Pretty easy. She has a key."

"*What?*"

"I gave it to her, one time when Eve was gone, visiting Mitch. I didn't think about getting it back—that was the last thing on my mind at the time—but tonight I realized I never did."

"You'll be getting your locks changed?"

"Getting my locks changed, getting caller ID on my phone . . . Should I run quick and pick up a Doberman, too?"

Ariel thought of Jessie, in charge of her own empty premises at that moment, and a small, vague bubble of unease stirred in her stomach. "It's not a bad idea," she said. "An alarm system's an even better one. Given your experiences with the lunatic fringe, I'm surprised you don't already have one."

"I do. She knows the code. I told her at the same time I gave her the key. I know, I know; get it changed."

"I saw you'd hooked the chain on the door in the kitchen. Are there any other exterior doors?"

"Taken care of," Jack said glumly, "and the piranha are in the moat and the barricades are manned. Are you at all hungry?"

"I could eat."

"Then let's do, something to warm our bones. I've got some good soup in the freezer that—"

When the phone rang, they both jumped.

Jack went to the desk, braced himself, and, his eyes on Ariel, picked it up. A few seconds after his hello, his shoulders relaxed, but his expression remained guarded. "For you," he said. "A man."

Henry! Ariel thought, and her heart lurched. Why, oh, why, she asked herself, had she put her phone on call forwarding? Why, when she knew better, had she given in and come to Jack's house tonight?

"Hello?" she asked, putting her back between Jack and the phone.

"Ms. Gold?"

Ariel breathed again. "Yes?"

"You got me all excited for a minute there."

"I beg your pardon?"

"With the tale about the Big Bertha." Wally Hatcher was calling from somewhere noisy. "I was ready to drive to L.A. and claim my prize and then I recognized your name."

"Right!" Ariel flashed Jack a quick smile, mouthing "Forwarded." Into the receiver, she said, "Thanks for calling back."

"Thank *you* for not telling my wife what you were really calling about. Jo would've been stoked if she'd known she was talking to somebody from show biz, but not about that subject! I assume you are still messing around with the Spurling thing?"

With a small movement of his head, Jack indicated the kitchen and left her alone with her call.

"It's Jo's and my anniversary," Hatcher was saying. "We're out celebrating, twenty-two big ones." He laughed. " 'Big Bertha,' for crying out loud! Now I'll have to go buy myself one and pretend I won it. Oh, well, it'll be my anniversary present to myself." He laughed again. The celebration, Ariel deduced, had already involved a number of toasts. "You know, I watched your show after you called before. You were good. Good-looking, too, if you don't mind me saying so. But, look, do me a favor? Don't call again."

"Fair enough. I just need to clarify a couple of minor points with you."

"Okay, but minor's what they've got to be. I left Jo dancing with one of my golf buddies. He's not much of a dancer. If I don't get back pretty quick, she'll come looking."

Lowering her voice, Ariel said, "You told me that when you went down to the Spurlings' cabin, you saw several of the other party members en route, remember? You saw the Jamesons, you said?"

"Yeah?"

"And Karen Lucas?"

"That was the girl with Verlyn, right?"

Ariel closed her eyes. "Right," she whispered.

"He died. Did I tell you that?"

"Yes. Yes, you did."

"So what's your question? Did I see her?" Ariel heard laughter in the background. "Oh, yeah," Hatcher said confidently. "I remember I told her what Leesa said she'd heard, that I'd gone down to make sure everything was okay with the battling Spurlings. She was fascinated, I remember. Hung on my every word. I think she kind of had a thing for me, you want to know the truth."

"You said 'her'? You mean you told Karen?"

"Sure. Isn't that who you just asked me about?"

"What about Verlyn?"

"What about him?"

Her heart bumping, Ariel asked, "Wasn't he with her?"

"No. What made you think that?"

"Karen Lucas was alone when you saw her?"

"I just said that. What's the problem?"

"But you told me—"

"Hey, I've got to go." After repeating his request that she not call him again, Hatcher went back to his party. Ariel plopped into a chair and said a little prayer of thanksgiving before she went through the conversation in her mind, satisfying herself that she hadn't misunderstood this time. She found her briefcase and, among the tapes inside, her first interview with

Hatcher. Within seconds she was listening to his voice saying: "Yeah, coming back I did. Karen somebody. She was with one of the guys."

"Karen Lucas," her own voice said. "She was the companion of a man named Barry Verlyn."

"Yeah, she was with Verlyn. That's right. He died, you know? I saw it in the paper not too long ago."

Ariel rewound the tape and played it again. She'd understood her misinterpretation long since; she just wanted to be sure.

Warm finally, she shrugged off her coat. As she put the tape player away, she became aware of a savory fragrance coming from the kitchen. She found Jack ladling soup into bowls.

"I was wrong about what Wally Hatcher said," Ariel told him.

The ladle stopped in midair. "Hatcher? That's who that was?"

"Karen was alone when he saw her that night. When he said she was 'with one of the guys,' that she was 'with Verlyn,' he meant on the trip, as Verlyn's companion. He didn't mean that she was literally with Verlyn at the time he ran into her."

"I knew it. I told you so."

"My best guess is that it was around one-thirty at the time."

"One-thirty . . ."

"Roughly, so we are talking well after you say she left you, and well after Eve left the saloon."

Jack lowered the ladle back into the soup pot and left it there. "Do you believe me now?" he asked.

"Could we eat?" Ariel asked, smiling.

"No, ma'am. I've been waiting a long time to hear the words. Say them."

"You'd get a fair shake on the show no matter what I personally think."

"Say them."

"You do know that? My personal opinion isn't the issue."

"Don't talk rot. Say the words."

"I believe it was possible for Karen to have killed your wife."

"Well, praise be! At least it's a start. You are the hardest sale I've ever made."

Ariel's smile faded. "Sale?"

"It was a figure of speech, Ariel." Jack went to her, cupping her shoulders as if he were torn between hugging and shaking her, and in fact, he gave her a playful little shake. "Is there any chance we could enjoy one moment of peace, just one, before you start analyzing every careless word all over again?"

"I didn't much like the image that particular word evoked."

He removed his hands, lifting them in mock surrender. "So much for peace," he said.

"Come on, Jack! You're *selling* me? You can see that I might feel a bit manipulated. A bit used."

"You feel used?" he said incredulously. "*You* feel used? Oh, that is good!" He paced away from her, shaking his head as if he couldn't believe his ears. "You go out with me. You give one tremendously convincing imitation of a woman who's enjoying herself. But you forget to tell me that, oh by the way, I'm *'involved'* with somebody else. Sorry, Jack, but the only reason I'm giving you the time of day is because I want an exclusive for my show. And *you* feel used. You are one of a kind, lady. You are something else!"

"I said I was wrong. I will not apologize again."

"I don't give a damn about your apology!" he shouted.

"What do you want from me!" Ariel shouted back. "You think you're the only one who's had it rough? You think you're not causing problems in my life?"

"What problems? Just keep the objective in mind, Ariel. You find that woman, and your problems are solved. You'll get a good show out of it, I promise you that."

"You don't even know what I'm talking about. You have no right to act like this."

"Oh, I know I have no rights to you—I'm clear on that! You know, you're the best I've ever seen at giving with one hand and taking away with the other. You convince me to trust you. To tell you things nobody else could tear out of me. You even return the compliment, confiding in me. Or are you going to pretend that didn't happen? Again?"

"I never said I didn't—"

"If you're going to get the morning-after regrets when you let me in, Ariel, then I've got some advice for you: don't! Save your heart-to-hearts for this man you can't live without."

"You leave him out of this."

"How can I? He is in. He's right where I want to be!" Angrily, he strode to Ariel, placing himself squarely in front of her, and he took hold of her again. This time there was nothing playful about the grip. His fingers dug into the flesh of her arms, and he jerked her so that her face was within inches of his.

"Don't tell me I don't have any rights," he said. "You're not with him, are you? You're with me, and you're here because you want to be. I'm not blind. You think I haven't known the times when you had to hold your own hands to keep from reaching out for me?"

"No. I didn't—"

"Don't lie to me. Don't lie to yourself. I've seen you. I've seen your eyes. And I've wanted your touch so much it was all I could do to keep from begging."

"You're hurting me."

"No, you're hurting yourself. You're cheating yourself. When I asked what you felt for this man of yours, you had to fumble to come up with something. What do you feel? Obligation? Respect? What do you feel?"

"I feel . . ." Ariel couldn't focus on the question. He was too close. She felt her lips part. She thought if he didn't kiss her then, that second, she would scream.

"Ask yourself!" he demanded. "Do you feel safe with him, is that what it is? Let me tell you something, Ariel. Love isn't always safe."

The kiss was not gentle. Then his arms were around her, locking her against him. His kisses covered her face, her eyes, her neck, and she was holding on for everything she was worth because the floor had dropped out from under her. She was free-falling, spinning weightlessly through pure oxygen, and yet she couldn't get enough to breathe. They were wrapped so tightly together that she could feel the heat of every part of him, and her own body seemed to have turned into liquid nerve endings.

He murmured her name between kisses, inhaling the skin of her neck as if he wanted to breathe her into himself. "I knew," he said. "I knew it would be like this."

"I never knew anything could be like this," Ariel found voice enough to say.

She felt his delighted laughter against her ear, a warm tickle that made every inch of her skin quiver. "Oh, love," he said, "trust me. There is so much more to know."

He'd begun, infinitely slowly, one by one, to undo the buttons down the front of her dress, kissing every inch of exposed skin as he worked. "Jack," she gasped, "I can't think." She cradled his head against her, burying her face in his hair. "I can't get my breath." She couldn't remember what she was wearing. What garment did she own that had so many buttons?

Swaying against dizziness, she opened her eyes. She was looking directly at one of the windows she'd closed earlier. Light reflecting off the panes obscured the blackness outside, but she heard a distinct sound, a sharp scrape against the glass, like something scratching to get in. She froze. In the brightness of the kitchen, the two of them were completely exposed.

"Jack . . ."

His lips moved against her breastbone. "It's only the wind. A tree branch."

"I'm scared," she said, and she realized that it was true, on every level.

Jack went still. She could hear his breathing, loud in the silence. Slowly, he straightened and, seeing her face, wrapped his arms around her. "Hey! You're trembling," he said, rocking her, whispering shushing sounds.

"Would you turn off the light?"

In darkness he held her again. The branch still creaked against the windowpane, as if it were irritated by the wind.

"Poor baby," he said. "Scared to death, and not of the wind."

"I'm all right now."

"Uh-huh."

"I am."

"You feel torn, don't you? Your mind's kicked in."

"Stop reading it," Ariel mumbled into his shirt. "You

make me feel worse." It wasn't true. The trembling slowed and stopped. The warmth of his body seeped into hers. She could feel the pumping of his heart against her ear. She wanted never to have to move. For a while neither of them did. Then, quietly, Jack said, "Your lovely, perverse, analytical mind just had to kick in. If I tell you I love you, that's a wrong thing. How can he? you say. He hardly knows me. He's a stranger." He stroked her head, his fingers combing through her hair, as soothing as a lullaby. "A stranger with a murdered wife."

Ariel listened to the words. They were unreal. Mesmerized, she felt more than heard his voice, resonating in his chest.

"And then there's you, my poor wounded Ariel. You've lost so much, haven't you? How can I ask you to give up a man you know you can depend on, a man who's proved himself?"

With obvious reluctance, he detached her from him and held her at arm's length. She could see the line of his jaw, silhouetted by the light from the next room, and the glint of his pale eyes. "He's proved himself time and time again, I'll bet. And I'll tell you what else I'll bet. You've been honest with him, haven't you? About how you're feeling. Feelings you didn't ask for. Unasked for and unwelcome, and confusing."

When Ariel didn't deny it, Jack nodded. "And he's backed off, like a gentleman, letting you work it out. And here I am, pushing."

"You're not. You're fine. Just hold me."

"No, sweetheart, I can't just hold you. I want you."

"And I don't want to feel 'torn' when . . ."

"When we make love? It will happen, you know. But I don't mean I just want to bed you. I want you in my life, after all this is over, when you're sure. When you're not feeling that you're betraying . . . I don't even know his name, this man you have noble feelings for. We keep avoiding calling him by name, don't we?"

Ariel looked down. Absently, she did up a button. "We were supposed to be working tonight."

Jack laughed softly. "Letting you go was the hardest night's work I ever had." He brushed her hand away and continued the buttoning for her. "This dress is downright Victorian. I wouldn't be surprised if you wore it on purpose." He touched her cheek, felt the quick heat, and laughed again. "You did! You are wonderful!" Exaggeratedly, he secured the top button. "There now, ma'am. Your virtue's secure."

"Don't laugh at me."

"I'm not. Well, I am, but I love it. I love that you're strong and brilliant at what you do and brave as a warrior." He nipped at her earlobe, growling. "And all woman."

"Stop it!"

"You are. Soft and fine. My old-fashioned lady."

" 'Pure as the driven slush.' " Ariel forced a grin. " 'A virgin of the psyche' is what Henry once . . ." Her face fell.

Jack didn't have to ask who Henry was. "Well, that's torn it," he said. "Oh, come on, love, it's okay. He exists. Uttering his name isn't a betrayal. Let's eat, what do you say? You can interrogate me; that'll make you feel better."

When they were eating rewarmed soup, Ariel slid her notepad nearer her bowl and said, "I've been curious—"

"As a cat, every minute. It's one of the things I adore about you." Jack reached over to push a lock of hair off her forehead. "Would you like to hear some of the others?"

"I expect . . . another time might be better."

"About what, then, are you curious?"

"What possessed you to go on that yachting trip?"

"You mean with my wife and my crazy lover on the same boat? Because I'm an idiot. Eve was going whether I did or not. I knew Karen would be on board. I couldn't see leaving the two of them together for four days." He smiled crookedly. "I was afraid of what might happen."

"So you were already leery of Karen?"

"She was impatient for me to make a decision, to tell Eve that I wanted a divorce. I had made a decision, and divorce wasn't it. I'd realized by then that Karen was unpredictable. I didn't know she had a screw loose. A machine shop full of screws loose."

"You said you've gotten 'oblique messages' from Karen before. What were you talking about?"

"It was a week or so after the cruise. I'd been questioned a few times by then, but it was before the arrest. I was still working with Mitch. Our corporate offices were on the top floor of our main store in Westwood. I was on the selling floor, working with a designer, and I thought I saw Karen get into the elevator.

"That made me nervous. She'd been very upset the last time we'd talked; she still couldn't believe I meant what I said, that even with Eve dead, she and I weren't going to be together.

"When I got back up to my office, she was nowhere to be seen. I asked my assistant if I'd had any visitors. Sandy—the same Sandy who works for me now was my assistant then—said she hadn't seen anybody, but that she'd been out of the office, too.

"It was the next day before I noticed a picture missing from my credenza, one of Eve. I found the frame in the trash. The picture had been cut into little pieces, and the pieces had been dropped into the water in a vase of flowers."

"Into . . . water."

"I'd almost forgotten about thinking I'd seen Karen. I still wasn't sure it *was* her. This was when I was first getting a taste of how nasty the TV-watching public can be, and I couldn't believe—didn't want to believe—Karen would do such a twisted thing. I believe it now."

"How much into coke was she then?"

Jack's eyebrow shot up. "You knew about that? It was a social thing with her, with most of that crowd. Nothing heavier that I ever saw."

"I still can't reconcile you with that scene."

"You notice I'm not anymore."

Ariel glanced at her notepad. "Where was Karen when Verlyn came to see you? Did he say?"

"No. I know he flew here from New York, but I don't know if he'd stopped off there from somewhere else."

"How did you find out he was dead?"

"Somebody told me. Sandy, the woman who works for me, told me."

"How did she know? Had she seen an obituary?"

"Not in the L.A. *Times.* I looked at a week's worth of back copies. No, I think she just said she'd 'heard.'"

"When exactly would this have been?"

"Sometime . . . the middle of December. He came here toward the end of November."

"What did Sandy say he died of?"

"Heart."

"Wally Hatcher saw it in some paper; he said so. Why do you think Karen waited over a month after his death to . . . make contact, as it were?"

"Maybe the cops wherever she was were suspicious

about his death and she was being careful? Maybe he had other heirs she was afraid would contest his will if she didn't play it cool? With her, who knows?"

Ariel glanced over her pad. She made a complicated doodle, but she couldn't come up with another thing to ask. "Well," she said, "That's it. Time to go, I guess." She didn't make any move to leave. He didn't make any move at all.

"Don't," he said. "If this conversation didn't kill the mood, nothing will. Look, it's still early. Let's go sit in front of the fire. Have an after-soup drink."

"Not a good idea. I will help you clear up in here, though."

That took almost no time. Jack hung up the dishcloth, looked around, and said, "We could clean out the refrigerator."

Ariel laughed. "Definitely time to go."

"No, wait. Do one other thing for me, will you? Keep me company while I change the sheets on the bed."

"You're kidding! That's a worse idea than the drink."

"Please?"

The bed had been an ordinary size when Ariel had been in the bedroom earlier; now it loomed vast as the Sahara. Prudently, she remained in the doorway, leaning against the jamb and watching Jack scrape the old sheets into a bundle and push them onto the floor.

"You want me to tell you a bedtime story, too?" she teased.

"Will you? One with a happy ending?"

"How about Tom Sawyer, the story where he tricks his friends into whitewashing the fence for him?"

"Not what I had in mind."

"You were never in the military, were you?"

"Does this conversation seem at all disjointed to you?"

"You don't know how to make a bed. Are you genuinely that inept or are you trying to trick me into doing
it for you?"

"If I were into tricking you right now, it wouldn't be
into *making* the bed."

"Look at you!" Ariel cried and gave in. "Jack, you tuck
it under like this, and then you fold it . . . thus." She
stepped back from her perfect hospital corner. "See?"

"Maybe you better show me one more time."

"Get out of here!" She grabbed a pillow and swatted
at him. When he danced out of range, something
crunched under his foot.

"Uh-oh," she said, and knelt to feel around in the ball
of sheets he'd stepped on. The envelope buried inside
was heavy and lumpy, and Jack's name was neatly printed on it.

"What in the *hell*?" he said. He tore open the flap
and a locket fell out. It was gold, large and round
and delicately filigreed. "This was Eve's! It was in a
drawer . . ." He glanced at the dresser. "That bitch
pilfered through. . ." Exhaling angrily, he popped the
locket open. Jack's picture was on one side, and Eve
faced him. The glass covering Eve's sweetly smiling
face was cracked where Jack had stepped on it, or perhaps it had been broken earlier, by the person who'd
put the locket into the envelope.

"There's a note," Ariel said.

They read the short, printed message together.

> *A Rose by any other name, my only one, is just
> as fragile.*
> *As you slip between these sheets tonight, remember
> that it's our time now. Not Eve's any longer.*
> *And not hers.*

"What is in her mind?" Jack cried. "What is *wrong* with this woman?"

Ariel looked at the pillows where the rose had been and then at the locket. "The rose was wilted, you said?"

"Dead as a dodo. Do you have any idea what all this means because I sure don't!"

Ariel licked her lips. "I think . . . no, it's too crazy."

"Of course, it's crazy. She *is* crazy."

"No, I mean, how could she know about a name I never use? Never, except on official documents."

"What name? What are you talking about?"

"She's playing with us. See the *R* in rose? It's capitalized, like a proper name."

"So?"

"My middle name is Rose."

Jack put it together. "This isn't a game," he said. "It's a threat."

"I've got to go," Ariel said. "I've got to get to my house now."

28

JACK FOLLOWED HER IN HIS OWN CAR. ARIEL KEPT HER eye out for his headlights, blurred to a nimbus by a fog that had slipped in sometime during the evening. The night seemed colder now with the heavy dampness. The weather had nothing to do with the clamminess that made her hands slip on the steering wheel. When Jack got caught by a light she'd made, she slowed until she could see his car again; she didn't want to face her house alone.

There was a jam-up at the corner of Sunset Boulevard and the little residential street that was the shortest route home. Ariel could see blue and red lights blinking in the next block. Braking, she groaned out loud.

What would she find when she reached her own block? More vandalism? Police cars responding to a concerned neighbor's call? Fire trucks? Horrific images blinked through her mind, each more frightening than the last. "Move it!" she whispered to the cars blocking her way.

She hoped that if Karen Lucas had come to her house

tonight, she was still there. If she'd done anything to Jessie, she would be one sorry woman.

The logjam began to break up, and Ariel inched forward. The van's front tire scraped the curb, mounted it, and bumped back onto the pavement as she made the turn. Jack was right behind her.

Her street was peaceful. Her house still stood. The lights she'd left burning glowed eerily in the fog.

Ariel didn't bother to open the garage. In the driveway, she hit the brakes, jerked the gearshift into park, and cut the engine. She heard Jack's car door slam at the curb, and she'd hardly leaped from the van before he was beside her.

The shutters on the front windows were closed, so it was impossible to see what might await them inside the house, but the outside was intact. "Everything looks okay," Jack said as they hurried to the porch.

"Everything better *be* okay," Ariel replied fiercely.

"Wait," he said when she'd unlocked the door. He blocked her way and went in ahead of her. "It's all right." His voice was a low murmur. "It looks all right. Stay here and let me look around."

"No." Ariel pushed past him, calling Jessie's name. For everlasting seconds she heard nothing but her own blood pumping in her ears, and then the shepherd came trotting from the direction of the bedroom, yawning. She was clearly surprised by the force of the hug her mistress gave her and was quickly infected by the tension she sensed.

"Thank God!" Jack breathed and petted Ariel's shoulder as she petted the dog and murmured foolishness into Jessie's erect ear. "I'll check the rest of the house."

"Believe me," Ariel said with a catch in her voice, "no

one's here." She stood up and deactivated the alarm. "And no one's been here."

"You're right. Of course, you're right." He fell onto the sofa in a relieved heap. "The things that were going through my mind on the way over here . . ."

"You!" Ariel laughed.

"I feel kind of foolish. Did we read something into that note that wasn't there?"

"No." After a moment, Ariel said, "I got an odd call this week."

"What do you mean, 'odd call'?"

"It was a woman. She didn't make much sense and she didn't stay on the line more than a minute. This was two nights after you and I went to dinner."

"After the paint was . . . ? Was this one of those Canaanites or whatever they call themselves?"

"I assumed so. She made a point of the fact that no real damage had been done here. She wanted me to think about that."

"That's all she said?"

Ariel watched Jack's face as she said, " 'He' was sick, she said, but *he* was all she had. She told me to forget . . . him."

Jack did look sick at that moment, and horrified. "Why didn't you tell me about this?"

"I had no reason to believe 'he' was anybody but Parker."

"You didn't trust me. You wouldn't have told me about that filthy note you got if it hadn't panicked you. What else haven't you told me?"

"Trust goes both ways, Jack."

He swallowed whatever he'd been about to say. "I'd never forgive myself if anything happened to you."

"Nobody has a key to my house, and nobody has my

alarm code, and I don't need a Doberman; my pal here will do just fine." Ariel gave Jessie a final scratch, and sat beside Jack. "If Karen knows about me, knows that I've been spending time with you, I wonder how. And how could she know my full given name?"

"I wouldn't put it past her to be watching me. I don't know about the name. Could she have gotten it from somebody at your studio? She's capable of anything."

"How capable is she? Tell me about her. How bright is she? How resourceful?"

Jack thought about it. "It's hard to see beyond the ugliness now."

"You once saw her as appealing. What was it that appealed to you?"

"Her strength."

"Oh, good!"

"Sorry, but living with a woman like Eve made that toughness of Karen's, that strength of will, seem highly desirable. It seemed like steadiness and, well, a passion for life. In a way, she's not unlike you. When she wants something—or someone—she goes after it. The difference is, you're sane; you'd recognize it if who you wanted didn't want you."

"How old is she? What does she look like?"

"She'd be . . . in her early thirties now, I think."

"How early?"

"Or late twenties."

"Oh." Ariel digested that. "Well, go on. What does she look like? Pigtailed and freckled?"

"Auburn hair. Last time I saw her she was wearing it straight, shoulder length. Her eyes are light; gray or blue, I'm not sure which. Fair skin."

"You said slightly built?"

"Maybe five-four, and small-boned. Slender."

Ariel couldn't let the age thing go. "How old was Verlyn?"

"Fifty-something."

"Wow."

"Kind of you not to point out that she's also a lot younger than me. Believe me, she's older than her years."

"What do you know about her background?"

"Never married before Verlyn. Only child. Broken home. Her father deserted her mother, left them in bad straits. Would I be indulging in amateur psychology or stating the obvious to say there's some unresolved anger toward men? Anyhow, Karen borrowed money and made it through a year or two of college before she decided opportunity was where she was. Real estate. She had a part-time desk job. She worked hard. She was aggressive. Ended up a partner. It's no penny ante agency, either. Binns-Harwell."

"So she's tough, determined, aggressive, bright—and young. Isn't that great! Just what I wanted to hear."

"And insane. Don't forget insane. What do we do now?"

" 'Our foe is near, Our choice is clear, Get outa here, Hurray for fear. . . .' I don't know what we do now, do you?"

"Who said that?"

"Maybe the same person who said, 'If you can keep your head when all about you are losing theirs, it's just possible you haven't grasped the situation.' "

Jack sobered. "That's just it," he muttered.

"What?"

"I *can't* grasp the situation." He faced Ariel. "It's foreign to me. Why would anyone want someone who's made it obvious the feeling's not returned? And keep on and on with it? *Kill* for it?" Red mottled his face. "And why me? It's not like I'm some catch. I'm not rich or brilliant. Hell, I'm nothing special."

The point was laughably moot under the circumstances, but Ariel didn't argue it; she'd made her opinion of his attractiveness all too clear. "I know next to nothing about obsession or fixation or whatever," she said, "but I don't think it usually goes hand in glove with rational thinking."

"Well, I'll tell you something. In less dangerous circumstances, I'd find this whole thing embarrassing. It *is* embarrassing! Think about it: how would you like being the love object of a crazy woman? I feel like a freak."

"That's funny. You're funny! The average person would be enraged. You say this woman killed your wife, allowed you to be tried for murder—presumably she was ready to hang you out to dry—and that now she's embarked on a campaign of intimidation, breaking into your home and making threats against someone you claim is near and dear to you, and you're embarrassed? I think maybe you're overcivilized."

"That beats what you *have* thought of me." He gave Ariel a twisted smile. "And what is this 'claim'? You are dear to me." He leaned over and, cupping Ariel's face, kissed her. The touch of his lips was light, but Ariel felt it clean to the pit of her stomach. His tone of voice was mild, even conversational, when he said, "Just because I'm embarrassed doesn't mean I'm not angry, Ariel. If she were to harm you in any way, in even the smallest way, whatever it took, I'd find a way to kill her. I wouldn't think twice about it."

Ariel was as startled by the casual announcement as she'd been by the kiss. "Have you ever killed anybody? It's not as easy to do as you might think."

"You were wrong about my not having been in the military. Lieutenant. Navy. Oh, and I do know how to make a bed, so you can bounce a quarter off it." He stroked her cheek, softly. "And I've killed. You're right: I didn't find it easy, but, then, I didn't hate the Lebanese extremists I was fighting at the time."

"You keep surprising me."

"That's good in a relationship, wouldn't you say?" When he leaned toward her again, Ariel abruptly stood up. "You need to go," she said.

"I'm not leaving you alone. I won't touch you again if you don't want me to, but—"

"See, the problem is I do want you to. I need some distance. And . . ." She moved farther away from where he sat, unnecessarily adjusting the frame of a picture. "You can't stay here forever."

"You don't know how much I wish I could. Be that as it may, I won't leave you alone."

"I don't think there's much chance either one of us will be bothered tonight. The way this is being played so far . . . Nothing that's been done is straightforward. Somebody's having fun—" Ariel caught Jack's sardonic look. "Okay, *Karen's* having fun. I'm betting there'll be more messages. She'll try to get us unnerved and jumpy and make us wonder what she's going to do next."

"Her strategy works."

"Excuse me a second. There's something I need to see to."

When she came back into the room, Ariel took Jack's hands and urged him up from the sofa. "Okay," she said, "listen to me. Nobody's going to get into this house tonight unless they know how to disarm the security system, and if that happens to be one of your lady friend's talents, she'll meet up with a dog that's attack trained and she'll meet up with me. There's a gun on the table beside my bed. I just went to make sure it was loaded. It is."

"And I keep surprising you! This gun . . . you know how to use it?"

"I told you the other night; unfortunately, I *have* used it. Since then, Max, the detective I told you about? He's taken me to a firing range to make sure I know how to use it effectively." Ariel made a face. "I'm a good shot, Jack. Go home."

29

THERE WAS NEVER ANY QUESTION OF WAITING IDLY FOR
Karen Lucas to come after her, not in Ariel's mind;
defense was not her best game. Unfortunately, however, Sunday was not a good day to pursue a missing person. Too many places were closed. All the necessary
government agencies were closed. Even the library was
closed.

It was also a poor day to utilize human resources.
Steve Vanderveer, *The Open File*'s resident computer
expert, would have a dozen ideas, but he was participating in a bicycle race in San Diego. Max Neely was off
duty and not answering his home phone. More times
than once, reflexively, Ariel thought of calling Henry.
He and Sam might be back from their trip, and if they
were, he would take the call. As he'd done so often, he'd
listen to what had transpired. He'd ask incisive questions. He'd point out fallacies in her thinking. He'd suggest approaches. And they'd both be suffering through
every second of it.

Last night's heavy mist hadn't dissipated, and the

morning had a curious, muffled stillness about it. Ariel felt isolated, and as mournful as a foghorn. Sitting with her notepad and coffee and no inspiration, she contemplated fixing a big, cholesterol-packed breakfast. Conversely, she contemplated going for a long fast walk. Continuously, she contemplated calling Jack. Just to make sure he was okay. To make sure nothing more had happened during the night. To hear his voice. She had her hand on the phone when it rang.

"Are you okay?" he asked.

"Are you?"

"No, I'm lonely."

"I told you nothing else would happen right away."

"Something did. Before I'd even left you, I started missing you. It got worse during the night. By morning it was critical."

"Jack, I told you I need some distance."

"You don't sound distant. Say you miss me. I dare you."

"I can't keep giving you mixed signals. It's not fair."

"Break down. Tell me."

"All right, all right."

"Close enough. Can I come over?"

"No. Distance, remember?"

"I'll bring bagels and cream cheese. Or sausage biscuits. How do big hot cinnamon buns sound?"

"Like sugar shock. Go away. I'll call you later."

She realized that she felt measurably better, and hungry. That's when she remembered the doughnuts Max Neely had brought the Sunday before. "Jessie!" she called out before she realized that the shepherd was lying at her feet. "Let's ride," Ariel said.

Ten minutes later she was cruising the streets near Max's stationhouse. She was driving the Darrin. (It was a morning when she needed to keep her cheerfulness bolstered, and the little yellow roadster, even with the top up against the chill, was an upper.) "He said the bakery was near the station," Ariel told Jessie, who was sitting shotgun and looking important. She braked. "And, hey! There it is."

The small establishment was not in a good neighborhood, yuppie-wise—no pedestrian thirty-somethings sipped lattes under sidewalk umbrellas, not on this damp Sunday—but it was perfectly situated for blue-collar workers and police officers and, on weekdays, for businessmen about to battle the 405 or the 10. Max's friend had chosen a smart location. Ariel could smell the pastries from where she sat at the curb across the street. She could also see the woman behind the counter. She looked thin; Ariel had imagined that a woman who ran a bakery would be comfortably padded.

She cut her engine and picked up her handbag. She noticed that a young girl, a teenager, had joined the thin woman who was sacking up an order. That could be the daughter Max mentioned. And then she saw Max. She couldn't believe it. He had on a white bibbed apron. He was laughing. He didn't look like a hardened cop who had probably just come off a night shift. In fact, she'd never seen him look so carefree. The three of them looked like a family.

Ariel put her bag back on the floor of the car. She turned on the ignition and left, heading north.

The shallow beach to which she drove was deserted. She wasn't surprised. It was more rocks than sand, and the waves were too tame for surfers. It wasn't a particularly inviting spot on the sunniest of days, and today was hardly that. The wind moaned in the trees behind her.

Jessie took stock. She liked it fine. When Ariel slipped off her leash, she explored the strange new terrain eagerly. The waves put her off—she didn't trust those—but the fishy smells were evidently riveting. Ariel watched her check out a tidepool. She dug busily at its perimeter, and then stuck her snout into the sand. Hastily, startled, she jerked back, tilting her head as she watched some tiny creature in fascination.

"Bozo," Ariel said, and looked for a dry spot to sit down. Huddled in her coat, trying to absorb what little heat the wan morning sun would spare, she consciously set her mind adrift. For several minutes, she was aware of nothing but sound: the regular, listless movement of the tide, the call of a gull, the complaint of the wind. Distantly, she could hear the hum of traffic from Highway 1, peaking to a whine when a heavy truck zoomed past.

It was good to have time alone. To sort through her conflicting emotions, to give them names, to render them into choices. She let her thoughts range, letting come what would.

She saw again Max's happy face and felt again the surprising pang that little "family" scene had evoked. Envy? It was. Because she was feeling lonely or was it more complicated? Family meant B.F., her grandfather. That's all there was. No sister, whom she missed, acutely, even though she'd never known her. No husband, of whom she had no memory and for whom, regretfully, she had no feelings. And no children of her own.

Heretofore, any children she might bear had been ghosts: vague expectations in some unexamined future. Was that changing? She was thirty-three years old; shouldn't she be feeling some need, some compelling maternal stirring? She could sense no trace of it.

Children, if they came, would be welcome—as the joyous embodiment of a union. It was the union she ached for.

She had assumed that she would have it, *did* have it, with Henry. She faced, finally and full on, that the assumption could no longer be taken for granted. She let that knowledge wash over her, filling her with both sorrow and longing. Longing for what? His presence? The dear familiarity of every gesture, every inflection of his voice? Or for a return to things as they had been?

Abruptly, Ariel got up and went down to the water's edge. The foamy water was thick with silt and, as she'd expected, frigid. When she caught sight of Jessie snuffling around a rotted log some distance down the beach, she began to walk in that direction.

This thing with Jack . . . was this what was meant by falling "in love"? Was what she felt for him another dimension of what she knew with Henry or was it some other thing entirely?

Something glinted in the sand and, idly, she knelt for a closer look when, without warning, one specific moment of the previous night flashed into her mind as vividly as if it were actually happening. The memory of that first kiss, of the urgency of Jack Spurling's body against hers, was like a punch to the stomach. Ariel was stunned by the physical force of the sensation. She hadn't imagined that she was capable of such passion, that such passion existed. It wasn't an especially pleasant feeling. It felt almost like a fever. What fed it? Was it as elemental as fear or rage, some involuntary neural response?

Unnoticed, Jessie had come to investigate. When the rough tongue swiped her face, Ariel flinched and then began to laugh. She sat down where she was, quickly removing something painful from beneath her rump. She threw the bit of driftwood for Jessie. It went into the water, and the dog watched it indecisively before deciding it was dispensable. She trotted back to Ariel, panting, and plopped down beside her. "Jessie," Ariel said, "I am acting like a moonstruck adolescent." Maybe, it occurred to her, since she had no memory of her adolescence, she was doomed to repeat it. She smiled at the foolishness of the thought.

Memories, she reflected. An innate part of the average person's mental equipment, and rarely appreciated. How important they became when you lost them. "You have only to begin to lose your memory," somebody had said, "to realize that memory is what makes our lives." Erase it and you erase more than the minutiae of your history; you erase who you are.

What "private family business," Ariel wondered for the dozenth time, could she possibly have shared with Jack two years before? She'd been "smiling fit to kill," he said, yet he'd also used the word *tragedy*. Crazy. And probably no big revelation at all. Big or small, she'd never know unless she laid her cards on the table. *Anything you can tell me about the woman you met two years ago is more than I know now.* Would that be so bad? Were answers about who she used to be important enough to make herself vulnerable now? To, as Jack said, open up. Again.

"Sometimes," B.F. had said the other night, "you have to trust your own judgment, even if the odds are bad." She remembered something else he'd said. "If you don't have love," he'd told her, "no matter what else there is, it's not enough."

"Well, fine, you old guru," Ariel said. "That's not a philosophy, it's a riddle."

She was back in the Darrin and on her way south when Ariel hung an unplanned, unsignaled left onto Topanga Canyon. The driver behind her sat on his horn, but she was gone, aiming for the San Fernando Valley. Real estate offices were open on Sunday, and she knew the name of the one in which Karen Lucas had been a partner.

Binns-Harwell was a prosperous-looking business. Slick handouts illustrating houses and commercial properties were all over the reception area. "A craftsman's work of heart," gushed one. "Potential limited only by your imagination," Ariel was reading when a well-dressed woman clicked into the room on punishingly high-heeled shoes. She'd reached the door, on her way out, Ariel assumed, when she glanced around, plainly annoyed to see no one at the reception desk. "Was someone helping you?" she inquired.

"No."

"Lindsey Marx," the woman said with a smile less genuine, perhaps, than the fortune in discreet gold jewelry that gleamed from her ears and wrist. Manicured fingers extended, she approached Ariel, bringing the scent of Giorgio with her. "We're short-staffed today. Flu. What can I do for you?"

"If you could point me to one of your colleagues?" Ariel said. "Karen Lucas?"

"Lucas?" Ms. Marx frowned. "She's no longer with us, I'm afraid. I'll be more than happy to help you myself."

"It was a personal matter. Rather important."

"Oh." With a glance at her watch (time having suddenly become a consideration), the realtor said, "Let me get Bill Harwell." She clicked away, to be followed back out, almost immediately, by a thin curly-haired man in a houndstooth sportcoat. After introducing him, the woman realtor grabbed her briefcase and left.

"You were wanting to see Karen, Ms. . . . ?" he asked.

"Ariel Gold." Ariel shook his hand and, as if it had been news to her, said, "I understand Karen's not with you anymore. Did she go with a different firm, do you know?"

"Karen is no longer in the business. I'm sorry, I don't know where she is just now."

Just now? Ariel thought. "Do you ever hear from her?"

"Postcards. The most recent one . . ." Harwell pursed his lips and squinted as though his answer required thought. "Came last year, in the summer, I think, from Milan. But we've had them from all over. St. Tropez, Mont Blanc, London."

The man's attitude puzzled Ariel. He seemed perfectly willing to keep answering questions as long as she kept asking them. "Let's sit," he said, gesturing to wing chairs grouped around a table where more colorful handouts were fanned. Ariel couldn't help herself. "Aren't you curious about why I'm asking these questions?"

"Of course I am. I recognized you."

Ariel was taken aback. This celebrity stuff was still new to her.

"You haven't asked anything," Harwell said, "that could harm Karen or violate her privacy. Postcards are hardly confidential. I post them on the bulletin board, which, I'm sure, is what she intends. She sends them so I and whoever else she wants to show off to know she's living the life of the idle rich. That's fine. I'm glad she's done well for herself. But tell me: why would *The Open File* be interested in Karen?"

"You know, don't you, that she married?"

The realtor blinked rapidly. "Yes," he said. "We were all very happy for her."

I don't think so, Ariel guessed. Figuring he might consider it good news, she asked, "Did you know that her husband died?"

"What? When? What happened?"

"About a month ago of a heart attack. You and Karen must have been close, good friends, for her to be keeping in touch still."

"I haven't heard from her for over five months, not since late August. I didn't know about her husband's death."

Funny, Ariel thought, that you all of a sudden know exactly when that last card came in.

A couple came out of an office just then, shaking hands with a satisfied-looking man Ariel assumed had sold something for them or arranged for them to buy something. Harwell half stood and greeted the pair. Ariel considered the realtor. In his forties, she judged, a serious, colorless man. He must have been dazzled by the bright young Karen. He talked about her, Ariel sensed, because he seldom had the opportunity to talk about her; talking about her was as near as he could get to her. When he'd sat back down, she asked, "Do you remember anything that last card said?"

"About the same as they all did. 'Beautiful here. You'd love it.' " His eyes met Ariel's and quickly skipped away. " 'Won a hundred francs at the tables last night,' that sort of thing. 'Started skiing lessons last week. I'm terrible.' " The phrases had the ring of verbatim recall. Harwell frowned. "Ms. Gold, is Karen in some kind of trouble?"

"Absolutely not. She's an acquaintance of the subject

of the story I'm working on. I'm trying to talk to as many as I can."

"This acquaintance . . . a man?" He nodded at Ariel's reply and, casually, asked, "Has he heard from Karen more recently? Is she . . . getting along well?"

"No one I've talked to has heard directly from Karen for a while. Do you think, sir, that if she were back in town she'd be likely to get in touch with you?"

He couldn't keep the excitement from his voice. "Is she back?"

"I think she may be. Might she call you? Or come by?"

"We'd all love to hear from her."

When Ariel asked if he knew of other friends who might be contacted, she got a surprise. Karen's mother had lived somewhere in North Hollywood during Karen's time at Binns-Harwell. Harwell didn't know if she still did. He didn't know her first name.

Ariel drove the few miles to North Hollywood and, in a phone booth outside a 7-Eleven, found sixteen Lucases listed. Four appeared to be members of one family. Three were businesses, and three were men's first names. One listing was a doctor, unlikely for a woman who'd been left in "bad straits" by a deserting husband. The remainder were either initials or women's names. Ariel copied down those five and went back to her car, where she found Jessie sitting in the driver's seat. "Shoo over!" she ordered and reached for her phone. Acting on the theory that an older single woman would go for the safest listing, Ariel started with the initials. She got lucky on the third call. Unfortunately, "W." was listed with no address.

Wilma Lucas had a thin voice and poor telephone manners. No, Mrs. Barry Verlyn wasn't there, she said.

She did not, however, say that Ariel had the wrong number. She didn't say anything at all for a long moment, and Ariel had the feeling she was more interested in a TV show, loudly audible in the background.

"My name is Ariel Gold," said Ariel. "Do you know, Mrs. Lucas, if Karen's back in Los Angeles? I heard she was, and I'm anxious to talk with her."

"Well, Mrs. . . . who did you say?"

"Ms., but please call me Ariel."

"I don't know where you heard that, miss, but somebody's got their wires crossed. Last call I got, Karen was still in Paris, seeing to her late husband's . . . affairs, I guess you call it. I imagine she'll get home before long; maybe in a week or two."

Ariel frowned. "When did you say she called?" she asked.

"Thursday, it must've been. That's my day at the beauty shop, and I was on my way out, so I couldn't talk but a minute."

Karen could call from next door, Ariel reminded herself, and say she was in Timbuktu. But if she was in town, why wouldn't she tell her mother? Not that her mother seemed especially interested. When Ariel asked for Karen's number in Paris, Mrs. Lucas said, "She didn't give me one. Said she's staying in a hotel while she gets finished up over there."

A shirtless kid in a leather vest had come out of the 7-Eleven toting a small brown bag. Looking at his bare, hairless chest made Ariel cold. When he reached into the bag and popped a top on whatever was inside and then made as if to lean against her front fender while he quenched his thirst, she tapped the horn. "Did she say the name of the hotel?" she asked Mrs. Lucas.

The kid glared and started to express his opinion of

Ariel's inhospitality. When he spotted Jessie, he found another fender.

Ariel heard Wilma Lucas chuckling along with the TV laugh track. "What did you say?" she asked and then without waiting for an answer: "She'll be home soon. You call back in a few weeks."

She hung up, and Ariel called Jack.

"Did Karen ever call you or write you from Paris?"

"Where are you? I've left messages. I need to talk to you."

"What?"

"Not on the phone. Meet me somewhere, will you?"

Twenty minutes later Ariel led Jessie into the sidewalk café area of Brentwood Marketplace, closer to Jack's house than to hers but not far from either. He was waiting at an umbrella table, smoking a cigar. She hadn't known he smoked cigars. He hadn't seen her yet, and she couldn't resist stopping to watch him in that unguarded moment. He did nothing unusual. Scratched his scarred eyebrow. Checked his watch. Took a long puff and exhaled the smoke. And then he did something that brought a grin to Ariel's face. He looked at the cigar speculatively, breathed into his palm, and then smelled the result. His nose wrinkled, and he stubbed out the cigar and moved the ashtray to a neighboring table. Ariel stopped spying and strode to where he sat. There was no way she could not react to the smile that broke on his face when he saw her. She bent and kissed him. "I didn't know you smoked cigars," she said.

"I don't anymore. Please do that again."

"I lost my head." She laughed and sat down opposite him. "Hello, dog," Jack said, and reached to pet Jessie. To Ariel, he said, "I feel as if I haven't seen you for a month."

"Jack . . . You amaze me."

"Good. Why?"

"All of a sudden, you're making yourself so vulnerable. Whether I slam the door in your face or insult you or . . . no matter what I do. It seems too easy. I mean, naive trustfulness after what you've been through? It confuses me."

"It confuses *me*. You think I normally go around acting like a smitten teenager? I didn't act like this when I *was* a teenager. I've never acted like this in my life."

Ariel looked away. "You said you needed to talk to me."

"No, this is bothering you. Let's finish it. I trust you, Ariel. Implicitly. Not only because I care for you. I've found out more than once, as you well know, that because you care for somebody, it doesn't mean you can trust them."

"You said I used you. How could you possibly trust me?"

"I was hurt and angry. Scared, too. I was afraid your honorableness about this 'involvement' of yours would keep you from giving your feelings a chance. I was wrong to accuse you. You haven't done a thing to apologize for, not to me and not to him."

"But still, we've known each other two weeks."

"We've known each other two years. I'm beginning to think I've known you always, from someplace I can't explain. You won't let me down. Hey . . ." Jack tapped the corner of her mouth with a fingertip. "Smile! Don't look as if I just hung a millstone around your neck. Take a lesson from your sister. Trust your instincts."

Instantly alert, Ariel said, "What are you talking about?"

"It was at a Bel Air cocktail party, a potential client's.

A woman who was there recognized me. It happens from time to time, more back then than now. Anyway, this kindly lady—strictly out of concern, no doubt—felt compelled to let her hostess in on the nasty fact that her would-be decorator was an accused murderer. She didn't realize I was within earshot.

"Well, about that time someone came up behind me and, very quietly, said, 'You want me to spill my drink down her cleavage?' "

"It was Jane?"

"She'd just hired me the week before. I thought, well, that's that; so long, both new clients. Turns out Jane had known who I was from the first. 'Then how come we're working together?' I wanted to know. 'Because I don't believe you did what they said,' Jane told me. 'Am I wrong?' When I said no, she said, 'Well, then?' " Jack chuckled at the memory. "And then she started arguing about a color I was trying to get her to consider for her entryway."

Her fist pressed against her mouth, Ariel said, "Why haven't you told me this before?"

"I started to, actually, when I first told you I'd known Jane. You accused me of lying, if you remember. You look like you think I'm making it up now."

"It's not that. It's just . . ." Ariel took a shaky breath.

"I know, love." He covered her hand with his. "Jane could afford to be trusting. She didn't have the kind of job you have, and she hadn't gone through the kind of experiences you have. Also, she wasn't making the same kind of investment; all she was taking on was somebody to decorate her house.

"Now, let me get us some tea or coffee or something, and I'll tell you my news."

When he was back with tea, he said, "I did a keen

piece of detective work this morning." The words were light, but his expression was serious. "I found out how Karen knows about you and how she's known a couple of times when we've been together. Sandy."

"Sandy?" It took Ariel a few seconds to place the name. "The woman who works for you?"

"I got to thinking. Karen's not going to sit around watching me like some cop on a stakeout. Or bug my phones or put one of those tracer gizmos on my car. We're talking about a civilian, a *woman*. How do women get information? Gossip with other women. Don't look at me in that tone of voice. I chauvinistically deduced my way to the right answer. Who knows me, I asked myself, who also knows Karen, who's also in a position to know my comings and goings? I could only come up with one person. At first, I thought: can't be. They met casually, maybe, a long time ago, but—"

"I don't understand. Does this Sandy dislike you? Why would she spy on you? And how does she know Karen?"

"Remember I told you Sandy worked for me when I was still with Mitch? Eve came to the store a lot, to see her dad or me, and Karen was often with her. It seems that when Karen and I . . . when that was going on, she made it a point to cultivate a friendship with Sandy. Later, after she got married, she'd drop Sandy a postcard now and then from someplace exotic, and—"

"Your ex-lady friend is big on postcards."

"What?"

"I'll tell you in a minute. Go ahead."

"So she'd write Sandy occasionally. 'How're you? How's dear Jack? Tell me all the news.' Sandy would write back, et cetera. And then, back around Christmas, Karen called her. She said her husband had died, that she'd be coming back to the States. Since then, their communication's been by phone."

"Sandy told you all this?"

"I called her and got it all out of her. She didn't mean any harm. She's a motherly type. Thinks I need a wife, and it was obvious to her that Karen was interested. Karen, she says, has gotten to be like a 'sweet niece' to her."

Ariel still didn't have all the pieces. "And . . . what? You've been telling Sandy about me?"

"Sure I did, from that first time you called. I was excited. I didn't hide it too well. In fact, I bragged a little. Sandy, as she quaintly expressed it, 'put a bug in Karen's ear.' Told her she better get back here and get busy before somebody 'beat her time.' "

"Can I assume Sandy didn't supply you with Karen's current telephone number and address?"

"The last number Sandy has is a hotel."

"In Paris?"

"Paris? It was down in La Jolla. You asked me about Paris on the phone; what's with Paris?"

"In a minute. She's no longer at the hotel?"

"She checked out Friday the seventeenth."

"A week and two days ago."

"She could be anywhere now." He glanced around edgily, caught himself, and said, "We should be checking into a hotel ourselves, under fake names, and I don't mean that as a proposition."

"What did you tell Sandy?"

"That I had no romantic interest in Karen, that I could scout up my own wife, God and my chosen candidate willing."

That shut Ariel up effectively for quite a few seconds. Jack's smile was joyless. "I also told her I'd like very much to talk to good old Karen, and when she calls again, Sandy should get her number."

Trying to get her mind back on the issue, Ariel asked, "Can she handle that?"

"Sandy thinks of Karen as a 'sweet niece'; she thinks of me as a son. And she loves playing Mata Hari, as we've seen. Now what was all this about Paris?"

When Ariel had told him about both her earlier conversations, she asked, "Did you ever meet Karen's mother?"

"Didn't even know she was still living, let alone in the vicinity."

"I can get her address tomorrow for whatever it's worth. Karen tells her she's still in France when she's within driving distance. They don't seem to have a close relationship."

"So, what do we do?" Jack rubbed his balled-up fist, looking as if he'd like to use it on something. "We can't just sit around and wait. There's got to be some way to find her!"

"What we need to do, and you've got to know this by now, is get people involved. It's enough with this happy-hands-at-home bit, Jack. We've gone as far—"

"What people?"

"The police, or—"

"The police?" Jack's voice rose. "Why don't we just practice what I'd tell the police? The woman I'd been sleeping with when my wife was murdered is after me? To do what? What, Ariel? Come on, think about it. Make me love her? Make me take her back? It's a ludicrous situation! What would I tell them? That this crazy woman killed my wife as a special favor so she could have me, but I didn't have a clue? I was a few dozen feet away, reading a magazine, oblivious? I'd end up back on trial for murder myself!"

"Would you calm down and—"

"Listen to me. She's committed no crime we can prove. Killing Eve is just not in any way, any form, provable, okay? Verlyn's death? Some doctor, somewhere—we don't even know where!—was satisfied that he died of a heart attack. Since then she's splashed paint on my *new* girlfriend's house, *maybe,* and written her a dirty note and left a rose on my pillow." Jack threw up both hands. "What the hell are you thinking of?" He rubbed his face furiously and then, simply, tiredly. "Maybe she's got nothing diabolical in mind at all. She's a rich woman now. She could just show up on my doorstep with a lei and invite me to sail with her to Hawaii."

"Okay, forget the police. My people."

"We've been through that."

"Jack, I don't know what to do. I'm over my head. Look at me; I've wasted this whole day. I didn't learn one single thing that's remotely useful. If you had any sense, you'd listen to me."

"If I had any sense, I would never have involved you. I should have kept my mouth shut and hoped for the best."

"But you did involve me, and you should have known, if you remembered anything about me from before, that I wouldn't let you keep your mouth shut." Ariel smiled. "That much about me hasn't changed. You said so yourself."

Jessie stirred at Ariel's feet, shifting her head from one paw to the other. Ariel gave her a long thoughtful stroking. "I've wondered," she said. "Why did you call me that first time, after my first show? Two years had passed. We were virtual strangers."

"Impulse? Fate taking a hand?" Jack gave the question serious consideration. "You were different from the other newspeople when I was arrested and during the trial. I liked you even then. I was glad to see you were doing so well." Teasing, he said, "I was knocked out to see you *looking* so well."

"Different from other newspeople how? Didn't I shove a mike in your face and ask invasive questions just like all the rest?"

"Invasive, I suppose, but stupid, no. None of the 'How did you feel when your world crashed and burned?' kind of inanity I got way too much of. Not to cast aspersions on your objectivity, but I got the distinct feeling you believed I was innocent. If I'd known how hard I'd have to work to get you back to that point, I'd have thought twice before I dialed your number."

"I did believe you were innocent," Ariel said, remembering Henry had said so. She pressed the flats of her palms together, hard; she could feel the tension all the way to her shoulders. "I wouldn't have had that first heart-to-heart with you otherwise."

"You couldn't have kept your lips zipped that day if I'd been Charles Manson! You were too excited. Ariel, do you wish I hadn't called you?"

She swallowed frustration. "No. Yes. In a way."

Jack smiled. "Can't blame you. If I'd realized I'd be putting you in harm's way, I would never have done it."

"You may be at greater risk than I am, Jack."

"Yeah? Karen wanted Eve out of the way, and Eve's dead."

"Eve was your wife, whom you say you told Karen you wouldn't leave. I'm just a woman you've seen a few times, an annoyance, worth a warning-off. Unless Karen is a woman completely out of control, she wouldn't do anything drastic to me unless she believed I was seriously in her way. She'd confront you first."

"I hope to God you're right. I'll tell her you're nothing to me."

"But what else would you tell her? That you and she will be together?"

"Are you crazy?"

"No, but if everything you've said about her is true, she is. She's owned by her obsession. If she believes you, finally, that there's no chance she'll ever have you, do you honestly think she'll walk away and leave you to some other woman? I don't. I wonder if she'll leave you alive."

30

THE NEXT THREE DAYS BORE OUT ARIEL'S SENSE OF HOW the woman Jack described would play it. Karen didn't phone Sandy. Jack's new caller ID was of no use since she didn't phone him either. Or send a letter or a fax or leave anything on his doorstep. His new locks and alarm code may or may not have prevented her from making any attempt to slip into his house; there was no sign she tried.

She made no move, overt or otherwise, in Ariel's direction. She didn't have to. Ariel's mind did the work. Every time she returned home, she had at least a moment's apprehension about what she might find there. When she retrieved her mail, she flipped through the envelopes quickly, not focusing on any one until she'd made certain there was nothing more offensive than bills. When her home phone rang, she checked her own ID display before she made any move to answer. The invisible and faceless woman could at any given moment be two cars behind her on the freeway or in the same restaurant or store or parking lot, and more than once Ariel had the skin-crawling conviction that she was.

Doubt was the other thing to which, conversely and increasingly, she fell prey. One minute she'd be hearing a noise and watching Jessie to see if the creak or the knock was real or if she'd imagined it, and the next she'd be wondering if imagination (or fabrication—that, too) was all there was to any of it. It is difficult, she came to learn, especially in the midst of daily ordinariness, to maintain a sense of impending threat. Eventually, when nothing happens, you begin to doubt that anything will. You begin to suspect paranoia. You let down your guard.

On Wednesday night she learned how dangerous that was.

Jack had left for Arizona that morning on business. Ariel couldn't deny she missed him—the charged atmosphere of his presence, his frequent touch-base phone calls—but she didn't feel more vulnerable in his absence. On the contrary, she had the feeling that she'd been living in some weird state of suspended animation. In his absence, it seemed to her, reality set in.

She had worked late and come home well after dark. She hadn't felt even a quiver of unease approaching her house. She was tired, and dinner was an effortless cup of yogurt. She was watching TV, a documentary about the *Titanic*, and fighting the onset of the nods. At a few minutes before ten her television picture suddenly sizzled to a single blue dot in the center of a blank screen, and all the lights inside and outside the house went dark. Ariel snapped awake. Even when she saw that her neighbors' houses, too, were dark, she found herself dry-mouthed, fumbling through unnaturally silent rooms, first to the gun, to reassure herself that it was where she'd left it, and then to the phone, to reassure herself that it still worked. The gun was there. The phone was dead.

A power outage wouldn't knock out the phone.

Much faster than she'd made the trip before, Ariel returned for the gun, and this time she didn't leave it on the bedside table. She was setting up candles when she heard the whirr of a helicopter. Jessie had followed her into the kitchen, and the shepherd, like Ariel, looked up as the noise intensified to an ear-shattering racket. A cold colorless light bathed the yard beyond the windows. Jessie was acutely interested, but she wasn't on red alert. The noise abated. The light moved away. Jessie, after a long moment, sat down. Ariel began to relax. There was no one outside, and the police were on top, literally, of whatever was going on. Then she realized: Jessie couldn't understand about the phone. And now the police were gone.

She thought of her cell phone. It was in her car. To get to it, she'd have to go outside. That wasn't an option. And she wasn't going to let anybody in. And Karen Lucas, she reminded herself, was a small woman, short and smaller than she was. And if she came into this house, through door or window, the alarm would go off in the nearest precinct. Ten minutes' response time if it was a slow night. If the alarm hadn't been knocked out, too.

"Okay, now wait," Ariel muttered. "Think." She did. And all that came into her mind was the last time she'd stood in this same kitchen with this same gun and killed a man. Suddenly Jessie was upright, attention riveted to nothing Ariel could hear. "Oh, God," she breathed. "I can't do this." The dog's ears were back, and a slow growl started in her throat. "What?" Ariel cried, and strained to listen herself. The back door slammed open, wood splintering. It wasn't a small woman. It wasn't a woman.

"Stop right there!" Ariel said. "I'll shoot you if you don't."

The door banged against a counter and back, creaking. The man said nothing. He didn't move. Jessie was crouched, silent now, every muscle ready for a command. Eerily, the man's head began to rock on his neck. His eyelids drooped and closed. To one side and then the other, his head swung in some primitive rhythm only he could hear. " 'Behold a pale horse,' " he said, " 'and his name that sat on him was Death, and Hell hath followed with him.' "

"Azrael?" Ariel said.

"They're dead. 'Blessed are the dead which die in the Lord that they may rest from their labours.' "

Ariel held the gun steady. "Who's dead? Parker?"

"The faithful." The cult leader's self-proclaimed right hand man, the "Angel of Death," began, silently and without any change of expression, to weep.

"How many?" Ariel asked, sick with dread. "How many died?"

"They went without me." Tears crept from under his closed eyelids. "Because of you." When he began to raise his hands, Ariel stepped back. His hands, though, were empty. Lifted to whatever deity he served, as if to call down deliverance.

Ariel had no idea what to do next. She held the gun, even if he was behaving as though it didn't exist. She had the dog. He was empty-handed. A failure as an assassin. A deluded, pathetic man who was, after all, just an electrician with a stolen union card. He looked grief-beaten, she thought, dangerous only to himself. On the other hand, she wasn't a complete fool.

"Sit down," she ordered.

He remained as he was, beseeching Heaven.

"Look, Azrael . . ." Ariel wished she knew his real name. "Listen to me. The burglar alarm's bringing the police right now." *Don't I hope!* "The very best thing you can do is sit down calmly. I won't hurt you. I'll tell them you didn't hurt me."

" 'There shall be no more death,' " Azrael mumbled.

"Exactly," Ariel encouraged.

" 'Neither sorrow, nor crying, neither shall there be any more pain' . . ."

"Sit down, Azrael."

" 'For the former things are passed away.' "

Where are the police? With her opposite wrist, Ariel braced the hand that held the gun. He lowered his arms slightly as if he, too, were tiring. His eyes opened, focusing on Ariel for the first time. They were disconcerting eyes. Fixed. The man didn't blink. His mouth curved. He looked beatific. It was a beginning, she thought, and it would all be over soon. He took a faltering step. "Just sit," she said, "right where you are, and we'll all be okay."

When he moved, it was with the swiftness of lightning and the force of divine retribution. His fist slammed into her temple. Her knees buckled. Pain seared through her head as her vision fractured into shimmering fragments that were swallowed by blackness.

She couldn't have been out much longer than seconds. She was astonished to find the gun still in her hand. Azrael or whatever his name was lay frozen to the floor, and Jessie was atop him, his throat between her jaws.

Ariel made it to one knee, raised the gun, and pushed herself upright. When she knew she could remain standing, she called Jessie off. The police, far better late than never, showed up.

● ● ●

Seven cultists had died by their own hand. In an ordinary suburban house in Ontario, California—just west of the San Bernardino National Forest—the police found their bodies. They'd been dead for days; they were all men. Parker was not among them. It was he who had led the police to the scene; "Azrael" and Parker were one and the same.

After two weeks in jail, as stonily uncommunicative as a nameless prisoner of war, he had the day before owned up to his identity. Bail had been arranged, and he'd gone to seek his flock. Without his leadership—during the time of his self-exile in the desert and his time behind bars—the cult had splintered. The greater number, including the women and children, had moved on, evidently under the guidance of a less demanding prophet. The rabid few had stayed behind and drunk lye.

By 3:00 A.M. Parker was back in jail, on suicide watch. He went from gibbering hysteria to near autism. He held Ariel to blame for everything. He'd meant to die; he'd meant to see her dead first. It wasn't clear what was in his mind—there was little clarity in anything he said—but he seemed to believe he was immune to bullets or any weapon until he'd accomplished his mission.

He had been reported tonight, Ariel learned, when he was seen tampering with a utility terminal near her house and lurking suspiciously. He had succeeded in knocking out the power in much of her neighborhood, and he had cut her phone wires. What he had not done was throw paint on her house a week and a half earlier or leave her a deranged note. He couldn't have; he'd been in jail. It was still possible that those incidents and the late-night phone call, too, had been the work of one of the females of the cult. As much as Ariel wanted to

believe it, she didn't. The threatening letters she'd gotten at the studio had been from "brothers." The phone
calls that had come in there from a woman or women,
the calls Tara had intercepted, had stopped within a few
days of Parker's failed attempt on her. And no woman
had been among the "faithful" dead.

Ariel had time to slug coffee, shower, and change
before she went into work Thursday morning. She
hadn't slept. She had a basher of a headache. She was
staring blankly at a transcript of an IAD take-out interview when she looked up and saw Henry passing her
office. He'd been out all week, at a conference in
Toronto. Ariel was fairly certain that attending had been
a last-minute decision. She felt more certain about why
he had chosen to go. He hesitated, noticeably, before he
tapped on the door and came in.

"Hi," she said, and for some reason found herself
standing up. "How was your trip?"

"Could've skipped the meetings, but the hotel was
great. I got to rest up from the great camping adventure." He mentioned the names of a few industry
acquaintances the two of them knew in common and
passed along their hellos. "Heard some good things
about your work so far," he generously added.

"Thanks." Ariel smiled. She saw him take in her less
than fresh-eyed appearance and knew he was misinterpret-
ing it and couldn't for the life of her work up the energy
to relate all that had really happened the night before.

"I'm due in a meeting," Henry said, and turned to
leave. "Oh! Sam said to give you a message. 'Cool
moves,' I think it was. I got the idea he wasn't talking
about basketball."

"No. I expect he put these on a girl he mentioned to
me. Tell him I'm glad if my humble advice worked out."

"Maybe you should write a column," Henry said innocently. With an equally bland "See you around," he went on his way.

Ariel sat down abruptly. "Well, that was fun," she said. She wondered if she could be of any use in the Peace Corps, someplace really, really far away from Los Angeles, California.

Her phone buzzed. It was Sarge McManus. "B.F. said see if you could come for dinner tomorrow night," he told her.

"You're his social secretary now, too?" Ariel joked. "Hope you asked for a raise." She didn't know if Sarge even took a salary. He and B.F. had been friends for most of the younger man's life, sharing ups as well as canyon-deep downs, tragedies in both their families. Almost since Sarge had retired from the LAPD, he'd been B.F.'s voluntary companion, cook, and overprotector, and for all Ariel knew he did it in return for favors owed.

"He's in Tulsa," Sarge said. "Won't be back till tonight. He called and said fix a special dinner and invite you. I'm fixing; I'm inviting."

Ariel had talked to her grandfather on Sunday evening. He'd said nothing about going to Tulsa or about dinner. An impulsive trip? she thought. A special dinner? An invitation to the single family member? "Is she coming back here with him?" she asked.

"Since he also said make sure the guest room's made up, I suspect she is. Oh, and he said bring somebody if you want to."

Ariel was pondering that last, trying to convince herself that B.F. wouldn't extend an invitation to an outsider if he were going to make some disastrous announcement, when the phone buzzed again.

"You okay?" Max Neely asked, concern heavy in his voice.

"I'm still here," Ariel said. "Obviously, you heard."

"Your party last night put a push on the print check, the paint can, and the note. No match on file. They're not Parker's or any of the dead men's either."

Seeing no way to avoid the questions her request would provoke, Ariel said, "Check, would you, against the prints of a woman named Karen Lucas."

"Where do I know that name from?" Max wondered.

"One of the paying passengers on the *Princessa Ora*."

"The what?"

"The yacht Jack Spurling and his wife were on."

A very heavy silence came down the line.

"I've been asking a lot of questions all over the place," Ariel said defensively. "This woman was one of the ones with a record. No biggie. Illegal substances. Three to four years ago? I can't remember exactly, but she broke parole. Ran off. Somebody I talked to said she was back in town, in west L.A., in fact, and that she was on the unstable side. I'm thinking she might not like the idea of my trying to get ahold of her." Ariel realized that she was overexplaining. "This thing . . . the paint and the note . . . might be a strung-out person on a lark, don't you think?"

"I think that's the screwiest reasoning I ever heard," Max commented, "but a direct comparison's easy to check." Ariel knew he'd be checking out more than the prints. "So, am I going to see this story on the air along with the rest of America or are you going to do what you promised?"

"What I promised?"

"Hello? Any new information? Share and share alike?"

"As soon as I have anything more than gossip and theory."

"Sure! When am I going to learn?" Max asked himself in obvious disgust and hung up.

During the week Ariel had followed every lead she could think of, and not only in pursuit of Karen Lucas.

Pete Doyle had been high on her list of unresolved issues. He'd once been charged with harassment. It was true that the charges had been dropped, but if he'd badger or threaten or otherwise harass one woman who wanted him to leave her alone, mightn't he do it with another? With Eve Spurling? It still seemed like an awfully neat fit, and it bothered Ariel.

The researcher she'd put on it first reported that the complainant dropped charges because Doyle had stopped harassing her. Ariel wasn't satisfied. A little more poking around produced what had the ring of truth. Doyle had given the woman money, a loan; she'd considered it a gift. When he broke off with her, he demanded repayment. She retaliated by bringing charges against him. He gave up the money as a lost cause; she dropped the charges.

There had been a second accusation against Doyle, assault and battery, and a conviction. That woman had since married and divorced and remarried the same man. According to officers who'd been called to their address more than once, the couple considered a domestic dispute right up there with movies and bowling as entertainment. The wife was a hot-tempered redhead who gave as good as she got; if neighbors had seen her with a black eye, they hadn't missed the lacerations her spouse had picked up inflicting it.

Pete Doyle's worst failing, Ariel was forced to conclude (choosing to forget he'd shown interest in her), was his taste in women. Any lingering doubts about him

were squelched later on Thursday when she talked with
the crew of the *Princessa Ora*.

Despite having seen pictures, she was unprepared for
how big a hundred-and-thirty-six-foot vessel actually is.
As she watched this one come into port, she began to
understand how people could have been unaware of a
tragedy being played out in their midst.

The captain, Steve Breuer, was a taciturn man, not
ideal, Ariel at first thought, to run a party boat. As she
talked with him, she revised her opinion: if she were
going to abandon herself to high living among a group
of revelers, she'd want just such a person in charge. She
fully expected that she'd have to argue her way aboard.
It didn't happen. Breuer listened carefully to what she
had to say, thought for a minute, and invited her to
board. "That incident still bothers me," he told Ariel,
"a lot."

As he showed her over his domain, taking her from
one elegantly and efficiently appointed area to another,
he went on to say that he'd had one fellow drop dead
from a heart attack while landing a marlin, and, naturally, he'd had close calls with guests who'd done too much
partying or divers who'd suffered cramps, but the cruise
two years before had been a first. "In twenty years," he
said grimly, "that's the only time I ever lost a passenger
to the sea. I still can't believe that poor woman was actually murdered."

Ariel had her time-and-action chart with her, and
Breuer watched with quiet curiosity as she walked
through the movements of the various passengers. The
scenarios she'd put together were possible in every
respect. If Jack parted ways with Karen at twelve-fifty
and Eve left the saloon within ten minutes either way of
one o'clock, Karen would have had ample time to inter-

cept her, invite her for a "private talk" on the swimming platform, and see to her destruction before encountering Wally Hatcher.

Breuer didn't remember which of the cabins had been the Spurlings'. It didn't matter. The lower deck accommodations were clustered together. Some had double beds and some twins, some tubs and some showers, but otherwise, all five cabins were similar. Ariel stood in the doorway of each and craned to see into the bath, to see if anyone at the sink or toilet would be visible from that vantage point. In only two was it possible; in the other three, a person would have to walk all the way into the room and circle the end of a bed in order to see into the bathroom.

When the captain excused himself to see to his crew, Ariel went immediately to the stern and down to the swimming platform. She stood visualizing, as Jack said he'd done so often, the lethal drama that might have happened there. It was, in fact, like a small stage. There was no rail of any kind, just safe, solid surface and then . . . water. It lapped inches from her feet. It wasn't difficult to imagine a shove, a misstep. A desperate woman who couldn't swim, flailing, swallowing water, strangling in the wake, and reaching for a handhold or simply a hand. Ariel wondered how long Eve had remained cognizant. Seconds? Longer? Had she had mind enough to be stunned and disbelieving when no lifeline was thrown, when the yacht simply continued on, the lights gradually disappearing?

Ariel turned. Directly behind her were the stairs she'd come down, one of two symmetrical sets leading up to the main deck, and between them, well above the level of her head, was a sheer, curved wall, a bulkhead, she supposed it was. She couldn't see into the saloon;

no one in the saloon could see her. No one anywhere on the boat could see her here unless they were directly above, aft on the main deck or above that, on the boat deck, looking down over the rails. No one to whom she had thus far talked had been on any aft deck.

Ariel found Breuer with a stocky blond. He was introduced as one of the crew who'd worked the Spurling cruise. He'd been asleep, he told her, until the search for the missing lady was initiated. Another crew member was more useful. Cal Morrisey was his name, and it was he who'd been with Pete Doyle just before the cook had gone up to smoke his cigar.

"Yeah," Morrisey said, "Pete was finishing up in the galley, cleaning up or whatever, having a beer. I'd just waked up, and I was having a cup of coffee before going to relieve Steve, here." Morrisey indicated the captain. "Pete got finished and left."

"And went . . . ?" Ariel asked.

"Probably to smoke a cigar. That's what he usually does last thing before he beds down."

"So you didn't see him again that night?"

"Everybody saw everybody again that night, when the Spurling woman went missing. But, actually, I saw him before then. He came in the cockpit for a little while."

"That would've been about what time, do you know?"

"After one's all I can tell you. That's when my watch starts."

"How did he seem?" Ariel asked.

"I don't get what you mean."

Ariel shrugged. "Was he mad? Sad? Jittery? Sleepy?"

Morrisey sucked his upper lip, poking out his lower one thoughtfully before he shook his head. "He was just Pete, just normal. He's a pretty laid-back guy most of the time. Probably he was talking about the eatery he's going to have some day." He grinned. "That or his latest tootsie."

"He didn't happen to mention any . . . incident that had taken place between him and Mrs. Spurling, did he?"

"Incident?"

"That Mrs. Spurling had shown, um, interest in him?"

Morrisey laughed. "You mean she put the make on him? First I've heard, but I'm not surprised. Wouldn't be unusual." With a quick glance at Captain Breuer and in a more restrained tone, he said, "I don't mean Pete would've hustled her. He wouldn't have to, you know? He's just kind of got a way about him."

Later, Ariel was able to talk to another of the paying guests; she'd finally gotten past Hugh Jameson's protective secretary.

Jameson had seen nothing more than had his ex-wife; in fact, he'd seen less. After the card game had ended, he and Maura had gone out on deck "up front, to get some air." They did that every night before bed, he said. "Those dinky rooms were claustrophobic." If they'd seen Wally Hatcher, Jameson didn't remember it. He didn't remember anything else that had taken place until Jack Spurling had "started carrying on" about Eve being missing.

Bob Vail was out of the country, his office said, and Linda Charvat had moved to Nevada. Ariel didn't follow through; from all she'd heard, those two had been too involved in their own private party to notice what the other guests were up to.

Karen's mother's address had been easy to get; Ariel had had that days before. She didn't know what to do with it, but she had it. She also had a copy of Barry Verlyn's obituary.

It had appeared on December seventeenth in the *New*

York Times, a three-line death notice. He was living in New York at the time he died; he was fifty-six years of age; he was survived by his wife, Karen Lucas Verlyn, and a daughter, Mary Verlyn Green, whose city of residence wasn't given. Cause of death wasn't mentioned, but, Ariel saw, cause of death wasn't mentioned for anyone in the column. There was no way that she could see to locate his doctor.

Ariel wanted to know whether Karen had been in the country when her husband died. For her own peace of mind she wanted to know whether Karen was, in actual fact, in the country now. Passport records were accessible by a third party, theoretically. After several fruitless phone calls, she'd faxed the Department of State. She had yet to receive a reply. She didn't know what to do next. She couldn't think of a thing.

It was Thursday night, and Ariel, exhausted from no sleep the night before, had turned in early. She was struggling out of a nightmare—seven dead faces contorted with an agony inevitable after ingesting something as caustic as lye—when the telephone rang. Reflexively, too groggy to think of checking the ID display, she snatched up the receiver.

"I brought you a souvenir from Sedona," Jack said. "An amulet."

Ariel's heart, already bumping from the dream, did an extra little skip. Jack hadn't called during his business trip, two whole days. "Um," she said, gummy-mouthed, and turned on the bedside lamp. "Perfect to go with my rabbit's foot and asafetida."

"What? No garlic?"

"Haven't had any problem with vampires in this neighborhood for a couple of years now."

Jack asked if she'd turned up anything new in the last

two days. He listened in silence to what she told him, which was not encouraging and which did not include her visit from Parker. The nightmare lingered too vividly. Neither did she mention Pete Doyle, but, then, she never had mentioned him to Jack.

"Have I ever thanked you for what you're doing?" he asked.

"The subjects of my pieces don't usually thank me."

"The subjects of your pieces don't usually insist on your flying solo, and I hope they don't usually put you at risk either. I'm just relieved nothing happened to you while I was gone."

"Right." Ariel smiled grimly. "There was nothing on your machine when you got back, I take it."

"Not here or at the shop. And Sandy hasn't heard from her."

"Had Sandy told her you were going to be away?"

"Sandy didn't know about my trip the last time they talked."

"It doesn't make sense that nothing's happening," Ariel said. "I'd have predicted a clever, nervewracking wait of two days, maybe three. But five? Where is she? What's she doing?"

When Jessie began barking from the direction of the front door, she jumped. "Hang on a second, will you?" she said.

"Be careful," Jack warned as she laid down the receiver. "Don't do anything dumb!"

The doorbell didn't ring, and there was no knock, but there was definitely someone on the porch. Ariel figured letting Henry in qualified as dumb, but she did it anyway.

"Were you planning to ring the bell, or were you just going to stand out there all night?" she asked.

"Yeah," he said ambiguously.

"Come in." He did, to a warm reception from Jessie, and Ariel closed the door. "Let me just hang up the phone."

When she'd assured Jack that everything was okay and told him she'd call him in the morning, she put on a robe and went back to find Henry where she'd left him, squatting to pet the shepherd.

"She'll shed on your clothes," Ariel said. He had on what she knew was his nicest sportcoat, and dark dress pants. He was even wearing a tie, loosened. She could picture him jerking the constricting knot away from his neck; he'd done it, she knew, the second he left wherever he'd been that required such formality.

"I was at a roast," he said, naming the guest of honor, a woman who was an old newspaper buddy. "I was on the way home, and I decided . . ." He stood up. "I heard what happened here last night. Good God, Ariel! Why didn't you tell me?"

"I just . . ." Ariel shrugged. "I don't know."

"What hell it had to be for you. Déjà vu." Neither of them said the obvious: that a few weeks before, he would have been the first person she called.

"I keep thinking about those poor deluded men," Ariel said. "My big debut exposé sure didn't do them any good, did it?"

"If it hadn't been for your story, a lot more of those people might be dead now. Well, I'll go," Henry said. "I just wanted to make sure you were . . ." He scowled. "We've got to talk."

Without realizing she was doing it, Ariel tightened the belt on her robe. She stood a little straighter.

"Look, Ariel, whatever I say is going to sound like wounded feelings and sour grapes, and your . . . your *love life"*—he forced himself not to spit out the words—"is your business, but I can't stand aside and watch you act like a fool and just—"

"In what way am I acting like a fool?"

"The man's wife was murdered, Ariel. Whoever did it is walking the streets. The law thought Spurling was a good enough bet to try him for the killing, and you're in bed with him. That doesn't strike you as just a mite foolhardy? Just the *tiniest* bit dangerous? He was not acquitted, Ariel!"

Ariel swallowed a denial of the bed reference. She didn't know if he'd meant it figuratively, but she'd be damned if she'd rise to the bait and she'd be double-damned if she'd admit how mixed up she was about Jack's guilt or innocence herself. "I'm sorry," she said. "Hurting you—"

"That is not what this conversation is about! And if you have one shred of respect for me, do not say you're sorry again!"

"Don't shout at me."

"Shout at you? I'd like to slap sense into you!"

"That would be the worst mistake you ever made."

"Coming here was the worst mistake I ever made! A complete waste of time. Like caring about you. Like caring that you're letting yourself be used. You've got no history, woman, and very little experience. Because of the amnesia, you are, to put it bluntly, naive. Teenage girls have more savvy than you."

"I'm not backward, Henry."

"No, but you are handicapped. You may be smart, but you're vulnerable. This slick joker is playing games at your expense, and even if he doesn't hurt you physically, you'll end up hurt."

Ariel took a long, calming breath, and made herself

consider just where this was coming from. She forced herself to think of the pain—pain she'd caused—and not the anger. "You're letting your feelings cloud your judgment," she said.

"That's good," Henry quietly said, "coming from you. You've apparently *lost* all judgment, personal and professional. You're being paid to do a job, and you're behaving like the greenest, most ridiculous amateur. I can imagine how much objectivity you're bringing to this story by now. Let somebody else do it. Or forget it altogether; it wasn't that hot a story to start with."

"Is that what you're concerned about? The story?"

"Don't be stupid. Please, stand back and look at him for what he is, will you?"

"It's too bad they wasted tax money on a judge and jury, Henry; they could've just hired you."

He cupped his mouth, dragging his hand down his beard. He gave his head one short impatient jerk before he said, "I give up. Do whatever you please. I don't care anymore."

"Perhaps that's better," Ariel murmured, but she doubted that he heard her, as he was already slamming the door.

31

To her surprise, Ariel invited Jack to the "special" dinner at her grandfather's. Why she was letting herself in for a tense evening of monitoring B.F.'s reaction to Jack while she was facing whatever he had up his own sleeve was more than she could explain to herself. She didn't try. She suspected it was no more complicated than wanting to be with Jack.

She felt awkward when he came to pick her up. A few days apart had made the intimacy between them seem inexplicable if not fantastic. She had half convinced herself that Jack, or rather the qualities with which she'd invested him, were an aberration.

"Hi," she said and, more to distance than welcome him, held out her hand. He shook it. His cheek quivered, holding back laughter. "Even my clients manage an air kiss," he said, and pushed the door shut. He took her other hand, bringing first one knuckle and then the other to his mouth, and then guided her arms around his neck. The laughter in his fine light eyes had died. He pressed her hips against his. He felt quite real.

"If that's what you do with your clients," Ariel said eventually, "it's no wonder if business is good."

"Umm," Jack said. "I'm not letting you out of my sight again. I was beginning to think I'd imagined you."

"Stop that."

"You really want me to?"

"I mean reading my mind. I'd been thinking I'd dreamed this whole thing up."

Suddenly serious, Jack said, "It's real, Ariel."

"I think . . . we'd better go."

He touched the corner of her lip. "I think you'd better fix this first. You're smudged."

When Ariel had made the necessary repairs, she came back to find Jack holding a photograph of B.F. The big old man was sitting on a beach, his pants legs rolled up and his feet bare. His white hair was windblown, and he was laughing.

"This is your grandfather?" Jack asked.

"I took it Labor Day weekend on Kiawah Island. He has a place there."

"That's South Carolina, right? He's from there?"

"Florida originally."

"I'm glad you want us to meet. And a little surprised."

"Me, too," Ariel said, and collected her coat. They were in Jack's car when he said, "What did your grand-dad do for a living?"

"Not 'did.' Does. He's into a lot of different things."

"Well, tell me about him."

"I don't think I can do him justice. You'd better judge for yourself."

"You're a big help. Give me a clue, like, is he a Republican? A Democrat? You say he's Southern. Is he a Dixiecrat?"

"I'm not sure there still is such a thing, but he's not one."

"Well, but he's not ultraconservative, is he? Christian Coalition or whatever. What I mean is, he's not . . . ?"

Ariel laughed out loud when she caught the drift. "He doesn't dress in bedsheets, if that's what you're asking."

Jack was noncommittal in the elevator of B.F.'s building, but his eyes slid to Ariel and his eyebrow lifted as they rose to the penthouse. Sarge, apron-clad, answered the door. Ariel made the introductions. Jack shot her another quizzical look over Sarge's crewcut head, and when the short muscular man turned to precede them through the foyer, mouthed "Who's he?"

His curiosity was nothing compared to that of her grandfather. "B. F. Coulter," he said as he advanced on Jack with his ham of a hand outstretched and interest plain in his face.

"This is Jack Spurling, B.F. A good friend."

"Well, come on in, Jack Spurling. Make yourself at home." B.F. gestured Jack on into the living room and then hugged Ariel, whispering, "Who's he?"

Ariel stifled a giggle. This was beginning to feel like a drawing-room comedy. When she saw Sissy Hardaway, she lost her sense of humor. The petite redhead was again dressed in purple, a royal purple caftan. Hostess garb.

"Ariel," she said warmly, "it's so good to see you again."

"Jack's a 'good friend' of Ariel's," B.F. told her with a sly glance at his granddaughter. "Now, folks, what can I get you?"

The two men and Sissy fell into chitchat, and Ariel, feeling unnaturally alert, as if antennae had sprouted on her head, watched and listened. She should have given Jack a hint of what her grandfather was like: a sleepy-eyed cracker who was sharp as a well-honed blade and who could be just as cutting. She should have told B.F. who Jack was; what if he remembered the name and the trial and blurted something unfortunate? She should have asked Sarge what was going on with Sissy. Was that a secret look that passed between the woman and B.F.? Was that wink significant or B.F. being playful?

"Ariel?"

"What?" She started as if she'd been pinched.

"I'd asked you a question," Jack said. "Where were you?"

By the time they'd taken their places at the table, Ariel knew she needn't waste worry on Jack. He could take care of himself in any kind of social situation, even familial. His former father-in-law had liked him on sight, she reminded herself; Mitch had ended up closer to Jack than to his own daughter. She needn't worry about B.F. either. He was a Southern gentleman; a guest in his home would be treated with impeccable courtesy under any circumstances up to and possibly including drawing a weapon over dessert. There was only one thing left to worry about.

Sissy wasn't acting proprietary; Ariel would give her that. She sat opposite Jack, leaving Ariel the chair at the head of the table. She praised Sarge's efforts like any guest. Perhaps she was smarter than she seemed and knew that playing the part of hostess would be inappropriate. Or, Ariel asked herself, merely premature? She kept waiting for the announcement that warranted a "special" dinner, and over caramel flan with crème anglaise, she got it.

"Where are you, Sarge? Get in here!" B.F. made certain everyone's glass was filled and then raised his.

"We're celebratin' two things tonight," he said, and turned his smile on Sissy. "First, this beautiful woman is havin' a birthday. Many more, sugar," he wished her as Jack and Sarge and Ariel, who could hardly do otherwise, joined in. "She's gon' have the most memorable birthday weekend it's in my power to give her," he went on to say, and Ariel felt sick with dread as she waited for what was coming next.

"Now, please join me in a very special toast." B.F.'s smile at Sissy broadened. "Raise your glasses to the new, as of yesterday afternoon . . ." He paused dramatically and Ariel thought *Oh, dear God! He's married her!* ". . . women's champion of the Colony Creek Country Club of Tulsa, Oklahoma!"

"That is so . . . excellent!" Ariel cried. "Congratulations!" She nearly broke her glass against Sissy's, and the redhead laughed in surprise.

Ariel may have only imagined the expression on B.F.'s face.

As they were driving home, Jack said, "He's one of a kind."

"He is that," Ariel agreed.

"Why didn't you tell me he was B. F. Coulter?"

Ariel regarded him curiously. "Does that make some kind of difference?"

"Probably better you didn't. I would've been intimidated knowing I was going to dine with a legend. He didn't know who I was either, did he?"

"I don't think so, no." It would be an interesting conversation if and when it became necessary to tell him. "He liked you. He cocked his eye at me like a leery old rooster and said you 'seemed like a nice sort of fellow.' "

"That's better than a poke in the eye, I guess." Jack's

faint smile failed him. "His being who he is complicates matters."

"Which 'matters' and why?"

"The matter of trust. You're still tottering on the brink. Once he knows my history, he'll never believe I didn't know you were an heiress, and his opinion is important to you. Ariel, I could read your suspicion of his lady friend like a neon sign. What do you think his reaction will be to me?"

"The money doesn't enter into . . . 'matters.' If he leaves it to me, I'll give it to charity. Start a foundation or whatever."

"Good. Put it in writing. I've got enough going against me without that." Jack couldn't help chuckling a little. "He was as gracious as he could be, but I still felt like he was giving me the once-over. Between his eyeing me and you eyeing the little lady, this was quite an evening. Is he serious about her?"

"I'm afraid so." Ariel crossed her arms and chafed her bicep irritably. She'd had a bad shock tonight when she and Sarge had gotten a chance to talk. "Hate to tell you, Ariel, but I think she's okay," he'd said. "She's a nice lady." Sweet scheming Sissy had another conquest, and Ariel had no allies left.

Jack cut his eyes her way. "Why're you jealous?"

"I am not . . . I don't know." *I've only had him one year, and he's all I've got.* "I can't seem to help myself." She sighed. "She's such a drip."

"Everybody can't be scintillating, my love. Give her a break."

"You didn't like her?" Ariel asked, surprised.

"What's not to like? She's pleasant. Oh, so pleasant." He laughed. "Did you ever see the movie *Harvey?*"

"Jimmy Stewart. I've got the movie and a tape of the play, too. Art Carney."

"Elwood P. Dowd has this line—"

" 'My mother used to say to me, "In this world, Elwood, you must be oh, so smart or oh, so pleasant." For years I was smart. I recommend pleasant.' " Jack joined in as Ariel finished: " 'You may quote me.' " They both laughed.

"Ariel," Jack said, and there was a distinct shift in his tone. "How many people do you run into who're fond of *Harvey*? Who know the movie, let alone that line?" He kept his eyes on the road. "Do you still think you're imagining what we have? That you 'dreamed it up'?"

Ariel was quiet for a moment. "Elwood has another line," she mused. " 'I wrestled with reality for forty years, and I am happy to state that I finally won out over it.' Lucky Elwood."

They approached the turnoff to her house just then, and Jack said, "It's still early. Would you like to go somewhere and hear some music? What do you like? Jazz? Blues?"

"Radio?"

"That's my girl." They caught Sinatra in the middle of "Luck Be a Lady Tonight." "I planned that," Jack said. "And it reminds me, I forgot to bring you your little amulet. We'll stop by my house, and I'll run in and get it, okay?"

When they drove into his garage, and the door rolled down behind them, Ariel asked, "Why'd you park in here if you're just going to 'run in'?"

"It's not an especially bright idea to leave you sitting alone on the street at my house, do you think?"

"I'd forgotten about that."

"I hadn't." He turned off the engine, and the music was cut off mid-note. "I'll be just a minute," he said, but he didn't make any move to get out of the car.

When the automatic light clicked off, it was absolutely dark. Ariel couldn't see even a suggestion of Jack's face. If she'd had any interest in trying, she couldn't have seen her hand in front of her own face. There was no sound but that of the car's motor cooling, and then that began to die down, too. The two of them were reduced to voices, and every nuance was magnified.

"I'll turn the light back on," Jack said, "and the radio. That is, if you want to wait here."

"Or . . . ?"

"Or you could come inside with me."

Ariel had never realized how deep Jack's voice was. She could have picked it out among hundreds, but she'd never really registered the timbre. "For 'just a minute'?" she asked.

"Was that an answer or a question?"

"I think it was . . . the sound of me wrestling with reality."

She heard the creak of the seat as he shifted. "I bought a new bed on Monday."

Ariel laughed softly. "I won't pretend to think that's a non sequitur."

"I wanted you to know. Symbolic. The first purchase but one of a new beginning."

"And I appreciate your thinking of it, but that wasn't really where the problem lay. So to speak." She paused. " 'First purchase but one'?"

"I'll tell you about the other, one of these days."

"Jack? That's not fair."

He didn't answer immediately, and his voice was

much more tentative when he said, "The first was for you. A gift."

"What are you talking about?"

"I expected I'd be carrying it for the next six months or six years before I took the chance of your throwing it back in my face."

"A ring? You're not talking about a ring?"

"I'm talking about how much I want you. It's stupid to bring it up now, I know that. I didn't plan to. Don't say anything, okay? Don't say no. I won't mention it again until it makes sense to." After a long minute, he said, "I just don't feel very sensible."

"Neither do I," Ariel said.

There was one last exhausted ping of the engine. "What?" Jack said.

"I think . . . I seem to be in love with you."

The silence was so absolute that Ariel wondered if she'd heard herself say aloud what she hadn't admitted to herself. "I've never said that. I've never said anything like that, not to anybody, not within my memory, but I've never felt like this either. It's like I'm plugged into some different current than I've ever operated on before." She laughed, a little breathlessly. "I can't explain it, not even to myself. I want to be with you. I want crazy things. I want to watch you sleep. I want to sleep beside you."

She heard a deep exhalation, and when she felt for his face and touched it, she found that his eyes were closed. He kissed her palm and held it against his cheek, and then she felt his smile start. "You're a funny creature, and I love every unique and funny atom of you."

"Funny?"

"Your version of throwing emotional caution to the winds, my darling, is a reckless, headlong, wanton baby step. I know what it cost you, and that's what makes it mean so much. Now, tell me: what's your favorite stone? Gemstone, I mean."

"Oh, Jack, please forget the ring. Hold on to it for me until—"

"Until you're feeling sensible again? No, ma'am! I want you to have it, no strings. Now answer me. Diamond? Sapphire? What?"

"I've never given it any thought. Emerald. No, I don't care. It doesn't matter."

There was a rustle, and then she felt a ring being slipped onto her finger. It fit. "See? Right hand, not left. No strings." His kiss missed her mouth, and they both laughed a little, and on the second try he found it.

A door led from the garage into the kitchen, and Jack guided her to it without mishap. Even the dim light he turned on over the stove seemed intrusive after the perfect blackness of the garage. Ariel looked at the ring that felt cool and strange on her finger. It was a square-cut emerald.

"Jack, how did you . . . ? I'm sorry. I know it's not the romantic thing to say, but this is too freaking weird."

He laughed and hugged her, nearly crowing. "Your sister had an emerald. A lot bigger than that one, incidentally. Something on the order of Plymouth Rock, or that rock your grandfather's lady friend sports, but I remembered Jane's ring. I figured if she liked emeralds, so would you. *Do* you like it? My God, I'm happy! I'd forgotten what it feels like to be happy!"

The phone rang.

As it continued, they both looked at the number on the readout. It was long distance, a 303 area code. "Colorado," Jack said. "Good. It's got to be Mitch."

It was very quickly clear from Jack's expression that it wasn't Mitch Winters who was calling.

"I'm sorry, who did you say this is?" he asked, still on a high. And then his face congealed. He blinked from time to time as he listened, but otherwise, not a muscle moved. He listened for what seemed like a very long time. "I'll be there sometime tomorrow," he said, "as soon as I can. I'll come straight there."

He hung up.

"Mitch is dead," he said, and he had to swallow and swallow again before he could say, "Somebody's killed him."

32

ARIEL WAS TOO HORRIFIED TO DO MORE THAN STARE.
"He's been . . ." Jack tried to say through clamped
teeth. "They think he's been . . ."

"Shhh! Not now." Ariel pulled herself together.
"Let's go sit down in the other room. I'll get you a
drink."

"No, I've got to call—"

"Not now."

She fetched straight whiskey, and he let her drape a
throw over him while he sat with his head in his hands.
He held himself rigidly, but she saw the tremor that rippled through him and made the blanket quiver. "I'll
build a fire," she said.

"In a minute. I'll do it. Just let me sit here a minute."

She sat beside him. "I'm so sorry," she said after a
time.

"It was a priest who called. He's the one who found
him."

Ariel recalled Mitch's mention of a priest who'd
become his friend, who let him get away with no B.S.,

who was helping him learn to forgive himself for not loving his daughter enough.

"They don't know who did it?" she asked.

"I don't remember what he said his name was," Jack said as if he hadn't heard the question. "I don't know how to reach him."

"You mean the priest? You told him on the phone that you'd go 'straight' somewhere . . . ?"

Jack stared at her, focusing. "St. Catherine's. Downtown Boulder. I've got to see about flights." Abruptly, he got up. He drained the glass she'd filled and went to the phone on the desk.

"I want to go with you if you'll let me," Ariel said.

"Why? Afraid you'll miss something newsworthy?"

Ariel couldn't have been more shocked if he'd slapped her. There was truth in what he said, though; she did want to know exactly what had happened.

He didn't wait for a retort. When he had the airline on the phone, he made open-ended reservations for two, efficiently, for eight-thirty the next morning. He hung up, his face expressionless. "No, they don't know who did it. Whoever it was, he let them in. It must have been somebody he knew. No sign of 'forced entry,' this priest said." Jack went to the fireplace where he built up a formidable foundation, lots of kindling and paper and far too much wood. He was, Ariel realized, still in shock.

"He was knifed. Stabbed. So it wasn't necessarily premeditated. It wasn't like somebody necessarily came prepared, like with a gun, and nothing appeared to be taken, the priest said. The place apparently wasn't torn up or anything like that."

"When?"

"They don't know yet. A day or two ago." The fire

caught and began to blaze. "He'd been lying there, all
alone, for . . ." He rubbed at his chin like a man testing
for whether he needed a shave. "A day, two days? Three?
That could make it . . . What's today? Friday. That could
make it sometime yesterday. Maybe even Wednesday."
Without a word of explanation, Jack left the room. He
was back within minutes and, again without any explanation, dropped something—a small rectangular book-
let—into Ariel's lap.

"What's this?" she asked.

"My airline ticket receipt. Round trip to Arizona,
departing Wednesday morning, returning last night.
The destination was Phoenix, not Denver and not
Boulder. Phoenix."

"I didn't even think about—"

"You would have. You will yet. I know that ticket
doesn't prove anything. That I went to Phoenix, yes,
but not that I stayed there for two days. And we weren't
together at all on the night before I left, Ariel—Tuesday
night—or last night either. I was here alone. We talked
on the phone, didn't we? Both nights? But I could've
been calling you from anywhere."

"That's not true. I've had the ID since Tuesday. I
would've known if you'd called from Colorado."

Jack smiled unpleasantly. "See? You're already
thinking."

"That's not fair. I was just pointing out that—"

"Makes no difference. If they're able to pinpoint
when Mitch died and it turns out to be while I was
away, I'm still not in the clear. I could've caught a flight
from Phoenix and then flown back there, couldn't I?
Relatively easily. I can account for just about every hour
of the days and even for Wednesday evening, but not
later that night. I spent it alone, of course. That's real-

ly too bad under the circumstances, but that's the way it is."

"Jack, don't do this."

"It won't be just you. Once the law knows who I am, I'll be a suspect. Again. They'll think I killed Mitch, too. And he won't be around to defend me this time because some murdering bastard stabbed him to death." He closed his eyes and grimaced as a thought hit. "My God. Oh, my God!"

"Jack, what is it?"

His hand over his mouth, he slowly shook his head and then began to laugh. "Mitch," he said, "what have you done to me?"

"Jack?"

"Well, my love, unless he changed his will, I'm his heir. Sole heir. Isn't that just great?" He paced to the desk, picked up the empty glass, and looking as if he were enjoying a huge joke, filled it again. "I told him I didn't want his money. After what happened with Eve, I didn't want to be put in a position to benefit from anybody's death, ever again. He insisted. I insisted. I don't know if he got around to doing anything about it or not. He was stubborn. He loved me like a son, he said; the son he never had. He was hardly even old enough to be my father. He was my friend . . ."

Ariel reached out for him, but he moved away, flinched away. He turned his back on her, and then, again, he simply left the room. She heard a door close, and then she heard nothing for quite a time. She considered leaving him to his privacy and then realized that, short of calling a cab, she had no way to leave. She also didn't want to. She looked at the ring on her finger. No strings, Jack said. The strings existed; they didn't depend on a ring.

When he came back, he said nothing about his abrupt departure. His face averted, he went to refill his glass yet again. His back was to her when he said, "I'm sorry I took it out on you."

When Ariel approached him, he didn't move away. She laid her head against his back and put her arms around him, and he squeezed them tightly and then disengaged himself. "Don't be kind to me right now," he said in a thick voice. "I'll lose it."

"So lose it," Ariel said, and turned him toward her. His eyes were red and swollen, and right now they were swimming.

"I'd just as soon not if you don't mind." He managed a bleak smile. "I hope you saw me at my worst a while ago."

"Bring your drink. Sit down here with me, will you? Tell me about your friend."

"There's not so much to tell," he said, but he did sit. After a sip or two, taken slowly, he said, "During the whole time after Eve died, right up till now, Mitch stood behind me. If he ever doubted my innocence, he never let on. Can you believe that? Where he got that kind of rock-solid faith, I don't know." Jack swiped at his nose with his wrist. He began, awkwardly at the start, to talk about his father-in-law: their first meeting, their deepening friendship through the years they'd worked together, their ultimate partnership. Mitch had been determined, Jack told Ariel, to keep it all together singlehandedly after the arrest and had worked himself nearly sick doing it. Worried about the damage his notoriety was doing the business, Jack had said he wouldn't come back to it, whatever the verdict. Sell it, he'd said. Retire, enjoy life.

Jack smiled faintly. " 'Get yourself some lusty

woman,' I told him. 'Get married again. You've got years ahead of you.' " His mouth flattened into a thin bitter line. "Two. He had two years."

"How old was he?" Ariel asked.

"Fifty-eight last month. I went up there. We celebrated." Jack laid his head against the back of the sofa and, as had happened several times, it seemed to hit him all over again what had happened. Wonderingly, he said, "I just talked to him Sunday."

"He didn't say anything at all that might have . . ."

"Warned me? No! He was in a great mood. I teased him about that, I remember; said he must have finally found himself that lusty woman. He said something like 'I might just beat you to that, sport, if you don't get on the stick.' "

"Was he seeing anyone that you know of?"

Jack shook his head and frowned. "I just remembered, I called him last night, too. Right after I called you. I wanted his advice on an investment."

"That would narrow down when he was—"

"No. He was out. I mean, I thought he was out. I left a message." Jack looked ill. "Joking around about his hot social life. What if he was already dead, and I'm making jokes?"

The night seemed very long at times. Occasionally, Jack slipped into exhausted silence, and Ariel could think of nothing comforting to say or distracting to ask. Then he'd remember some story about his father-in-law, something funny as often as not, and minutes would pass before he'd wind down again. They talked very little about the murder; only occasionally could Jack seem to make himself stop and look at the reality of that.

Ariel was convinced that he'd loved Mitch Winters.

He and his own father hadn't gotten along well, she learned, and his relationship with Mitch had been closer than that of most sons and fathers. "He was hardly perfect," Jack willingly acknowledged. "He wasn't exactly Father of the Year to Eve, as he'd be the first to tell you. He had flaws, but, hell! Glass houses. All I know is he was the best friend I ever had."

"Did he know about Eve's and your troubles?" Ariel asked.

"I didn't talk about it—he and I didn't talk about those kinds of personal things—but he couldn't not know. He wasn't stupid."

"Did he know about Karen?"

Jack shook his head. "I told myself it was irrelevant to what happened to Eve. I told myself there was no point in burdening him with something that would hurt him, that it would be selfish to do it. Mainly, I didn't want to lose his respect. I couldn't have made it without him, I don't think. I'm not sure I would've wanted to."

Eventually, as will happen even in such circumstances, their talk veered on to other subjects, like the climate they'd be encountering the next day—by then, the same day. They even found themselves laughing, when Ariel described the "sharpshooter" attack from the last trip. It was sometime after three o'clock, and Jack was spooning tea into an infuser when he paused in what he was doing and looked up. His face was stubbled, his hair disheveled, and he'd put on well-worn sweat clothes. He was scratching the top of one sock-clad foot with the toes of the other. It was the first time Ariel had ever seen him look anything but almost unnaturally neat. As if he'd had some brilliant flash of insight, he said, "God, I'm glad you're here!"

The time came when Ariel found herself fighting

yawns. The next she knew, she popped awake, disoriented. Her eyes opened to Jack's face. Above her. Watching her. "I won't take the money," she said. She heard herself and blinked. They were on the sofa. The wool throw covered her. She had somehow come to be lying across Jack's lap, in his arms.

"You were dreaming, love," he said, amused. "Go back to sleep."

"I thought . . . I dreamed that what I told you about two years ago was B.F."

"That he was your granddad? And what did I say?"

"You said, 'Oh, good!' " Ariel lay back against him, mumbling sleepily into his shirt. " 'You're an heiress. Lucky me.' "

Jack was quiet for a moment. "God help us," he said then. "You don't even trust me in your sleep!"

"What are you talking about?"

"Your unconscious, I'd say, was connecting dots. I was Eve's beneficiary. Now Mitch's heir . . . and then there's you, who will some sad day be a rich woman."

"That's not—"

"True? It is, but don't worry. I'll insist on a pre-nup."

"It was just a stupid dream. I didn't know about B.F. then, and you didn't know about him till tonight. And what we *did* talk about, of course, had nothing to do with him."

"Of course."

Say it, Ariel! Why not? She could hear the words in her mind: *What did we talk about, Jack? I don't remember. See, I've got this little mental problem . . .* Jack brushed hair from her face, and, absently, gave her a gentle squeeze. His thoughts, Ariel could see, had drifted elsewhere. *Actually, Jack, it's not such a little problem. It's kind of pivotal in my life, but I've never seen fit to men-*

tion it to you. You can figure out why, I'm sure. She'd
waited too long. Or not long enough. There would be
a better time.

"We've still got a few hours," Jack said. "Go back to
sleep."

"I can't. I'm not sleepy."

The next time she woke, the sky was just beginning to
lighten, and he was gone. He was nowhere in the house.
Then she saw him through the kitchen window, a dark
gray shape in the slightly paler gray of a drizzly Saturday
morning. He was sitting beside the fountain in the backyard, huddled in a coat and staring off into the distance.
She left him alone.

She had coffee made and was breaking eggs into a
bowl by the time he came in, bringing a gust of cold
damp air with him. He was clean-shaven and neat again,
dressed for travel, and preoccupied. When she embraced
him, he felt frozen. "This wasn't exactly what I had in
mind," he said against her cheek, "for the first night we
spent together."

"You're a Popsicle," Ariel said and pulled away. She
took a good look at his face. "What?" she said. "What
is it?"

"I remembered who first introduced Eve and me to
Karen. I can't believe I'd forgotten it."

"I'm not following you."

"I can tell you exactly when it was. December sixth,
Eve's and my anniversary, three years and two months
ago. We'd gone out for dinner, unusually, by ourselves.
We ran into Mitch. He was at a table with a couple. A
fourth chair was empty, but somebody had been sitting
there. He was introducing us to the couple when the
fourth person came back. He introduced her as his
realtor."

"Karen?"

Jack nodded.

Jack had dropped Ariel off to change while he went to his shop to leave notes for his staff. He'd be back in forty-five minutes, barely time to shower and dress and take Jessie for a quick, guilt-induced walk after she was fed. Thank goodness for doggie doors, Ariel was thinking, when she noticed her answering machine. She decided to ignore the blinking light. When the phone immediately rang and she saw B.F.'s number on the readout, however, she picked up the receiver.

"Of course, you know who he is," the old man said angrily.

"Yes."

"What are you doing? Have you lost your mind? Where have you been? Don't answer that; I don't want to know. I've left three messages since Sarge remembered where he knew that guy's name from."

"B.F., I want to have a long and reasonable discussion about Jack, but I can't right now. I've got a plane to catch."

"A plane to where?"

"Denver. I'll tell you about that later, too."

"When will you be back?"

"Tonight. Tomorrow at the latest. I'll call and let you know. Will you do me a favor, you or Sarge? Will you feed Jessie this evening? Take her over to your place if I can't get back tonight?"

"Are you going with Spurling?"

"Don't worry; it's not a romantic tryst." Ariel didn't say what it was since that would aggravate her grandfather into an all-out fit. "Will you?"

" 'Don't worry,' " he repeated disgustedly and, nearly choking with frustration, he said, "One or the other of us will get over there in a little while. You call me, and you be careful, you hear me? I want to talk to you as soon as you get back."

Still damp from the shower, Ariel was slipping into her underwear when the phone rang again. She didn't want to take the time to run and check the ID screen or even answer. Then it occurred to her that it might be Jack, calling with some hitch in their plans.

"Didn't you get my message?" Marguerite Harris asked. "See if I ever solve a mystery for you again."

"Hello, Marguerite. What message? What mystery? I'm in a terrible hurry."

"I left a message last night asking you to return my call. Perhaps when you have time, my dear . . ."

"Don't get huffy. Just please talk fast."

"Do you know a man named House?"

"Is this a joke, Marguerite?" Stretching the phone cord as far as it would go, Ariel was just able to reach the wool trousers she'd laid out on the bed.

"Warren House. He lives on Elderwood, two streets up."

"I know where Elderwood is."

"The dead end, uh, end of the block. His wife's named Lila."

"Hold on," Ariel said, and slipped a sweater over her head. "No," she then said, "I don't know anybody named House who lives on Elderwood. What is this all—Wait a minute. The last house on the street? You're talking about a grouchy jerk about sixty? Has a meek-looking wife? Hates dogs?"

Marguerite laughed, a cackle of delight. "That's the one. You didn't happen to have an altercation of some kind with the aforementioned gentleman just before your house got blitzed, did you?"

"I gave him a swift kick in the rear when he tried to hurt Stonewall." Ariel dropped a bracelet into her pocket to put on later, and stuck her feet into ankle boots. "He threatened to sue me, and then I never heard anything else out of the creep."

"Oh, yes, you did."

"He's who made the mess with the paint?" Ariel gave up trying to dress. "How do you know that?"

"You're sure you have time to hear this?"

"Marguerite!"

"I was talking to another neighbor. Marcie Simms on Gladwin. Something of the same sort happened to her after she and Mr. House had a falling out. He said she'd been letting her spaniel poop on his lawn. She'd gotten a couple of crank calls she thinks were him, heavy breathing, do you know, and then she came home and caught him red-handed, so to speak, not with paint but with a bag of manure. I'll bet if you ask around the neighborhood, you'll find hers is not the only house where House—ha-ha—has run amok." Marguerite laughed again. "It might be the last, though. She had some flea spray she'd just bought, and she let him have a faceful of it."

Ariel's mind was racing. No Canaanites at her house—*and no Karen Lucas*. No Karen putting dirty notes in her mailbox. No Karen, she was suddenly sure, calling her up. It had been House's poor desperate wife, begging Ariel to forget her husband's childish destruction; to forgive it, to let it go. Whispering apologies for a "sick" man who was "all she had."

"I've got to run, Marguerite," she said, "but thanks. This takes a load off my mind." It wasn't true. Knowing for sure that Karen had nothing to do with the vandalism directed against her turned things sideways in her mind, but she didn't have time to make sense of it now.

She was trying to dry her hair and buckle her belt simultaneously when Jack arrived. She finished brushing her hair on the way to the airport, and did a few necessary things to her face as well. "Keep your eyes on the road," she said self-consciously. "You're supposed to think all this is my natural beauty."

"What do you call that stuff?" he asked curiously.

"Blush."

"Well, that you don't need." He grinned. "I can't remember the last time I knew a woman who still blushed." An echo of amusement lingered on his face until he made the airport turnoff, and then, as he obviously returned to thinking about the reason for their trip, it vanished.

He hadn't, as far as Ariel knew, slept at all during the night, and he dozed off within ten minutes of takeoff. He was neat in sleep, too, she saw. He kept his arms crossed, containing himself in his allocated space. As his sleep deepened, his eyelids quivered, and once his hand jerked, clenched, and gradually relaxed again. Before long, his head dropped to her shoulder, and he shifted, snuggling in like a cat. Ariel envied his oblivion. She'd had no more than two or three hours' sleep herself, but she was wired. It seemed like weeks, she thought, since she'd voiced a desire to watch Jack sleep; it had been less than twelve hours.

She hadn't told him about Marguerite's neighborhood sleuthing. He'd get a laugh about unrelated and rather ridiculous incidents having caused them such anxiety. All at once, though, it didn't seem funny. The thought—ugly and inevitable—had been nudging at her ever since Marguerite's call. It surfaced. Aside from the Houses' carryings-on, Warren's vandalism and hate note and Lila's phone call, nothing had actually taken place—nothing attributed to Karen—that Jack couldn't have staged himself, or simply made up. A grotesque hoax.

Imagination running wild! Ariel told herself. Too little sleep, too much pitched emotion in too short a time, and too much coffee and tea. She'd lost track of how much she'd consumed. She felt as if pure liquid caffeine ran in her veins. She even felt slightly queasy. *So Karen had nothing to do with your little drama, Ariel. So what? He's not responsible because this woman* didn't *do something!*

But once begun, the doubts metastasized. She was taken by the sudden nauseating notion that Karen Lucas didn't even exist, that she was dead. She'd never seen the woman, never talked to her, never seen one thing that was provably her doing. Who else had seen or talked to her? Jack's faithful Sandy? Ariel had never seen or talked to Sandy; maybe Sandy didn't exist either.

Staring out the plane's window, she fought something not unlike panic. What was she doing here? It occurred to her then and for the first time that not once during the long, unreal night had she questioned Jack's innocence in Mitch's death. She was startled to realize it. Blind faith was not a keynote of her personality. Was she becoming stupidly myopic? Like it or not, it was logistically possible for this man to have stabbed his friend to death. He'd even admitted it was possible. Even volunteering that there were times for which he had no alibi. Even supplying a motive.

Ariel scrunched her eyes shut. "There are two ways to slide easily through life," she told herself, "to believe everything or to doubt everything; both ways save us from thinking." She was going from one extreme of trustingness to rampant paranoia. Karen Lucas was alive. Of course she was. Her own mother had talked to her no more than two weeks before. And Ariel had heard Jack talking with Sandy on the phone. She forced herself to breathe normally. The steel band around her chest began to loosen.

Why would I enlist your help, Jack had asked, *if I were guilty?* She looked at his sleeping face. He looked as vulnerable as she'd ever seen him, totally without defenses. *I'm walking free*, he'd said. *I've got that to lose. Tell me why I'd ask for your help and then lie to you?* She'd had no answer then; she still didn't. He stirred, moving against her shoulder and mumbling something she couldn't understand. It might have been "Mitch."

Ariel had had no time to consider the ramifications of Karen's having known Mitch Winters. That the two were acquainted wasn't surprising. That she had known him independently of her friendship with Eve was.

Had there been anything, Ariel had asked Jack, to indicate that Karen was more to Mitch than realtor? Not really, he'd said, except that Mitch may have seemed a bit uncomfortable when he introduced her that night. If she was his date, after all, he was out with a woman younger than his own daughter. Jack had never seen them together again except as part of a group, and Mitch had never mentioned Karen before that evening or after, but then, Mitch and he didn't chat about their love lives. Jack thought the acquaintance was immaterial; it was long ago, it may have been strictly business, there was nothing to connect Mitch's death to that one dinner they'd had together.

It had been later, when driving Ariel to her house to change, that he said, "This probably has nothing to do with anything, but thinking back, Mitch wasn't himself right around that time." Not himself how? Ariel had wanted to know. "We were talking about opening a new branch," Jack recalled. "I was against it, thought we were overextended. Mitch was pushing for it, though, really enthusiastic, and then—bang!—he lost interest. Said I was right; we were already working too hard and he was . . . 'feeling his age,' he put it. That kind of talk was way out of character. He took a week or two off then; went to the Bahamas."

Coincidence? Ariel wondered. Or depression over a one-sided romance with Lolita? It would have been like Mitch to seek solace in escape; that was the philosophy he'd taught his daughter by example. When life gets unpleasant in one place, he'd said, you go somewhere else. "Forget your troubles, and have a good time." Mitch had matured since he'd espoused a good time as a cure-all. But does anyone's essential character change? Even older and wiser, could he have become infatuated with a woman thirty years his junior? If offered a second chance with her, would he take it? He'd been in a "great mood" on Sunday, Jack said. Because the desirable young woman of his fantasies had contacted him? Ariel acknowledged she didn't have reason one to imagine that, but imagine it she did. Start with the premise that Karen went to see Mitch.

Why? Had she wanted something from him? What? That, Ariel could not imagine, and she couldn't *begin* to imagine what would've impelled her to kill him. Because she hadn't gotten whatever she'd wanted? When Karen made up her mind to go after something—so Jack said—she didn't often fail. It occurred to Ariel that she might be even more manipulative than Jack knew. She'd seduced him, so he said, and he succumbed, not even realizing it was a planned campaign. Jack wasn't unperceptive; he wasn't normally rash. Ergo, she was good.

Barry Verlyn, a successful, wealthy, and, presumably, savvy businessman hadn't just taken her to parties and on a cruise; he'd married her, reproposing after she'd turned him down. And when she'd told him point-blank, so Jack said, that she'd killed for another man, he hadn't gotten around to turning her in or even divorcing her.

Jack hadn't known Bill Harwell, part owner of the agency where Karen had risen, suspiciously quickly, from receptionist to partner. The man still carried an ill-concealed and brightly burning torch for her.

Jack. Verlyn. Harwell. All older men. All relationships cultivated within a relatively short space of time. None casual, not to the men involved. And Mitch? And how many others? The woman wasn't Lolita; she was Lorelei! Ariel suppressed a snort. She was investing Karen Lucas with Machiavellian wiles. Eighteenth-century courtesans expended that kind of single-minded energy, maybe, and nineteenth-century belles, but did any woman in this day and age have the time or the discipline or the need? For what? Power?

Ariel had squeezed in a little heavy reading this week, about obsessive-compulsive disorders. She had thought she was wasting her time; no one had mentioned any such dysfunctions as she saw described in connection to Karen. Moreover, while ritualistic behaviors—eating disorders, compulsive shopping, becoming a workaholic or an exercise freak—might incapacitate the OCD sufferer, they posed no threat to others. What kept Ariel reading was: *"further personality disintegration can and does occur."*

The obsessive personality, she'd read, is driven by a

need for total control. Other people can't be controlled. To need another person, then, becomes a problem— even a threat. If he can't rid himself of the need, the obsessive will rationalize it. He'll convince himself that it is he who fulfills the other person's needs, that the other person is actually dependent on him. "He may tyrannize that person," she'd further and uneasily read, "in order to maintain an illusion of power, and yet, conversely, he may come to see that person as the exploiter."

Ariel couldn't say whether Karen's was an obsessive personality that had broken down into psychosis; she didn't know enough about the woman's behavior or her origins or about the illness to make that judgment. The label wasn't of particular concern, but being able to predict her actions was.

Jack stirred, grumbling. "Ow," he said clearly, and sat up, blinking against the bright daylight and massaging his neck.

"I was just thinking," Ariel said, "about delusions. Do you know the definition?"

"I don't even know where we are. What time is it?"

"A delusion is 'a false belief firmly held despite incontrovertible and obvious evidence to the contrary.'"

"Like believing today isn't going to be a disaster?" Jack unbuckled his seat belt. "God, I'm glad this priest already identified Mitch's body," he said. "If I'd had to face that . . ." He started to get up and then he paused. There was a deep groove along the side of his cheek where the fabric of Ariel's blouse had wrinkled underneath it. "Thank you," he said.

"For what?"

"For a shoulder. For doing this with me." He looked as if that hadn't satisfied him, but he merely said, "I'm going to go throw cold water on my face." Ariel watched him go. She was remembering something else she'd read, something that only now struck her. *Rejection, real or imagined, is anathema to the obsessive. It is viewed as abandonment: feared, to be avoided at all costs.*

However many people Karen had used along the way, Jack might be the only one still living who'd thwarted her. The only man who'd said no.

33

DICK MCRAE DIDN'T LOOK LIKE A PRIEST. HE LOOKED like a boxer who'd had a few bouts too many. His upper front teeth were almost certainly too perfect to be real, and his nose had been broken somewhere along the line. What must have been an impressive physique at thirty was bulk at fifty, or sixty—it was hard to tell his age. He was wearing overalls and a plaid wool shirtjacket that, like him, had seen better days.

Ariel and Jack found him in the basement of St. Catherine's, painting what was obviously a nursery of some sort. A day care center? Cribs and cots had been pulled out from the walls onto which he was rolling butter yellow latex, and toys littered the scarred linoleum floor. They'd been told where to look for him by a woman in his office upstairs; fortunately, she'd also mentioned his name since Jack had forgotten it.

He didn't hear them come into the room. Even after Jack cleared his throat, he was unaware of their presence. "Father McRae?" Jack asked, and the priest jumped, letting out a grunt of surprise and nearly falling off his ladder.

"Sorry," Jack said. "We weren't trying to sneak up on you. You *are* Father McRae?"

The man steadied himself, frowned, and said, "And I guess you must be John Spurling." As he carefully climbed down, he said, "I was in another world there, remembering a fishing trip Mitch and I took last summer." He deposited the roller in a tray and wiped his hands on his overalls. His face was weather-beaten and heavily lined, almost scarred, by deep furrows on his forehead and bracketing his mouth. Finer creases radiated from his eyes, the skin between them pale, as if he spent a good deal of time in the sun without bothering with sunglasses.

Grasping Jack's shoulder with one callused, paint-spotted hand, McRae said, "I know what Mitch thought of you, and I'm sure his feelings were returned. We've both lost a beloved friend."

Jack's face was closed up tight, but he nodded. He introduced Ariel, and the priest shook her hand. He showed no curiosity about who she might be, and, in fact, she thought she saw his eyebrows dip when he heard her name. Mitch, she decided, had told him about her visit.

To Jack, Father McRae said, "Mitch laid out some time ago what he wanted in the way of a service and so on. You're his executor, I know. I think you'll find what you need with his papers at the bank, but I'll tell you about it, if you like."

It didn't take long. The funeral mass would be Monday. A plot had been purchased, but there would be no graveside ceremony. The priest wrote down the name of Mitch's attorney and then said, "There'll be people you want to talk to. Would you like me to go along with you, or would you rather be on your own?"

"I'd like to talk to you," Jack said, "before I do anything else."

They walked to a café, discussing little on the way beyond the weather. It was even colder than when Ariel had been there a week and a half before, and new snow crunched underfoot. Dick McRae looked comfortable enough, but Jack was hunched against the cold and Ariel's thin Southern California blood was gelled to aspic.

Over a varnished wooden table in the café, the priest repeated what he'd told Jack on the phone—that Mitch appeared to have been stabbed to death and that robbery was probably not the motive.

"Where was he, Father?" Jack asked. "Where did you find the . . . find him?"

"Are you Catholic, John?"

"No."

"Mitch called me Mac. You do, too, if it's more comfortable."

The waitress brought their orders—coffee and hot tea; no one seemed disposed to eating—and Dick McRae waited until she'd gone before he said, "I found him in the bedroom."

Jack winced, a minute constriction of the eyes. "In bed?"

"His *body* was lying on the floor, and it was cold. Mitch himself was long gone from there."

Jack glanced Ariel's way, and she wondered if the specter of Karen Lucas was in his mind when he asked, "Was he . . . dressed?"

The priest followed his glance. "He was fully dressed, son," he said, "down to the shoes on his feet."

Ariel sensed again that her presence was a source of uneasiness to the man; she'd been right: he knew who and what she was. His eyes were on her when he added, "I saw nothing that would be an embarrassment to Mitch if it were made known and if he were here to care."

"You said robbery didn't appear to be the motive?" she asked.

"How freely do you want me to speak?" This was addressed to Jack. Ariel wasn't sure whether Father McRae was concerned about Jack's sensibilities or her right to be poking her nose in. Evidently, Jack read it the same way. He answered both questions and, Ariel fancied, a third one as well—a message meant for her—when he said, "We're both all right with the truth."

Father McRae pursed his lips, considering. "Mitchell mentioned your visit to me, Ariel, and your occupation. I was a little surprised, I have to say, at seeing you here with John."

"Did Mitch also tell you," Jack cut in, "that he took her into his confidence? That he 'spoke freely' to her? So have I."

"Fine then. As far as I could see, nothing was disturbed or taken. The police are through out there by now, I expect, and maybe through with the autopsy, too. At any rate, they could tell you much more than I can about what took place."

"You said he 'appeared' to have been stabbed," Ariel said. "Does that mean you didn't see a weapon?"

"No."

No, I didn't see it, Ariel thought, or no, that's not what I mean. "Father," she said, "Mitch told me about you, too. He valued your straight talk. You helped him come to terms with himself, he said. As he put it, you 'wouldn't let him get away with B.S.' "

"Um-hm," the priest said. His mouth may have curved just the smallest bit before he raised his mug and obscured it. When he'd swallowed coffee, he said, "I didn't see a weapon. There was a chest wound. It seemed obvious to me that a knife of some kind had been used, but that's only my opinion. The medical examiner hadn't arrived when I left. I haven't heard anything since."

"How did you come to discover the body?" Ariel asked.

"We had a date for dinner last night. I called to say I'd be late. I got no answer. He wasn't at the restaurant when I got there, so I called again. Same result. After the third time, I got worried. His place is remote. Anything could've happened. An accident. He could've been ill. I went to see about him."

"Was the door open?"

"It was closed and locked. I used the key he kept hidden for emergencies. The house was dark, and it was cold, almost as cold as it was outside. When he didn't answer my hello, I thought, well, he's not here, that's all. He's gone away. He's turned down the heat and closed up the place and gone off on a trip somewhere.

"That bothered me. It isn't . . . it wasn't like Mitch to stand somebody up. To go off without leaving a message. Back outside, I noticed the paper, yesterday morning's paper, still lying there uncollected." The priest sighed, and the lines that scored his face deepened into crevices. "Mitch knew as well as anybody that leaving papers lying around the yard's an invitation to housebreakers. Rural as his place was, it still wouldn't be a good idea, and it . . . well, it just didn't feel right. He would've had delivery cut off. I went back in and looked through the house, and I found him."

Thursday, Ariel thought; he died sometime on Thursday, or before newspaper delivery yesterday morning. She couldn't stop the thought from coming: Jack called me Thursday night, from his home. Before she could start calculating hours—four hours flight time to and from Denver, an hour and a half drive to and from Boulder, and all the rest—she asked, "Were there any signs that he'd had company? That he'd entertained whoever he let in?"

"Not that I saw, but then I didn't look around for fear of disturbing evidence. After I called the police and . . . said my good-byes, I went out and waited in my car."

"Had he mentioned anything to you about expecting company?"

"I'd been gone, doing a little mission work west of here. I hadn't talked to Mitch since Saturday, a week ago."

"And did he say anything then or at any time before to indicate that he had a woman friend?"

"He had several, my dear. Women he'd take to dinner or to a play or concert. I know them all. I can't see any of those ladies harming a hair on the head of one of Boulder's most eligible bachelors." McRae smiled faintly. "I've seen one or two do polite battle *over* him, if you'll forgive the levity, but not with him."

Jack suddenly spoke up. "Father . . . Mac, you said you called him last night and you got no answer. Did you mean that literally?"

"I don't see what you—"

"The answering machine picked up, right?"

"No, the phone just kept ringing. He did have a machine, didn't he? Of course he did. It must be broken."

When the priest said he knew nothing more to tell them, he offered to take them to police headquarters. "I told the detective in charge—Frank Peterson, his name is—that you'd be in town this morning, John. He's expecting you. I think it would be smart," he suggested, "if you go there before you go to the house."

"They probably wouldn't let us into the house," Jack said, "but I get the idea there was a message in what you just said?"

"I told Frank there was no next-of-kin to notify except you, and that I'd call you myself. He asked your name and what your relationship was to Mitch. I told him. He's been around awhile. He's pretty sharp."

Jack drummed the table for a second before his hand clenched into a fist. He'd made that angry fist, Ariel remembered, when he was asleep on the plane, when he was in the throes of a bad dream. "What you're telling me," he said, "is that he recognized my name."

"I'm surprised they didn't have me picked up last night in L.A.," Jack said. Unaccustomed to driving in snow, his attention was on maneuvering. His only discernible emotion was irritation. Ariel didn't buy it. Voluntarily delivering himself back into the hands of the law must be petrifying for him, she thought, like reexposing yourself to an illness that made you sick to death the first time.

"Frank considered it," Dick McRae said mildly from the backseat of the rental. "He held off. Take a right at the next light."

They were no sooner inside the police station than the priest's beeper sounded. He asked the desk sergeant to find Peterson and went off to find a pay phone. He was back within minutes, in time to greet a tall, gaunt, and remarkably homely man who came in through the same street door they'd used. He was probably a decade or two younger than McRae, but he had a similar hard-used look about him, as did the heavy sheepskin jacket and Western boots he wore.

"Frank," said McRae, "John Spurling, and this is a friend of his, Ariel Gold."

The detective shook Jack's hand, said, "Frank Peterson, Mr. Spurling," and nodded to Ariel. If he'd had a hat on, she thought, he would've tipped it.

Surprisingly, McRae, too, reached for Jack's hand. "I'm sorry," he said, "but I've got to leave you. Got a boy in trouble. No, Frank," he said over his shoulder, "not your kind of trouble. I'll be around, John, and don't worry; you'll be fine with Frank." He gave the detective a quick hard look that Ariel read as "Right?" and left in a hurry.

"Appreciate your coming in, Mr. Spurling," Peterson said, "and I want you to know I'm sorry about your father-in-law. I understand from Father McRae that you two were close."

Jack's "Thanks" was terse. Ariel wished she could advise him to go easy, but she could hardly expect him to be anything but wound tight.

"Come on into my office, sir," Peterson said. "Ma'am, we shouldn't be long. The desk sergeant here will get you coffee if you want some."

Ariel hadn't expected to be in on the interview, but that didn't prevent her from feeling left behind and frustrated. Stuffing her hands into her coat pockets, she watched the two men leave through a glass-paned door.

She couldn't see Jack's face, but his back was straight as a plumb line.

"Did you want coffee, ma'am?" the desk sergeant asked.

She didn't—coffee was the last thing she needed—but she accepted the offer, just to have something to do besides wait. Cup in hand, she paced to the door. It was too cold to take a walk. She sat down but couldn't stay still for more than a few minutes. A dog-eared, two-year-old *Reader's Digest* held her interest for about the same length of time.

Jack needed a lawyer. Would he know of one here, she wondered, or would he call the one in L.A., the one who helped keep him out of prison two years ago? Could the police hold him? There was a time limit, she knew. Twenty-four hours? Even if she could remember what it was in California, it might be different here. They'd have to let him go or arrest him. They couldn't arrest him. Not unless they'd found something at the crime scene to implicate him. They couldn't have found anything because he hadn't been there.

Unbidden and unwelcome came the memory of Mitch's lightning-swift reaction to her intrusion the day she'd visited. He'd been more than wary of a stranger trespassing on his isolated property; he'd been ready to defend himself. Whoever had shown up Thursday night—or whenever—had been expected or, at the least, let in. But Jack was hardly the only person Mitch would welcome into his home. Surely, there were many people here in town he would have trustingly admitted. Surely, they were looking into the possibility of some local who didn't like him or—

Ariel dropped the magazine she'd been blindly riffling, and threw the half-full Styrofoam cup into the trash.

There were things this Peterson needed to be told. There were questions she needed to have answered.

"Do you know," she asked the desk sergeant, "if your people are finished out at Mr. Winters's house?"

He didn't.

"I guess you don't know whether the autopsy's been done?"

He didn't think so.

Ariel sat back down. Her thoughts were random, ricocheting like hailstones, and her questions answered themselves almost before she could pose them.

Mitch habitually kept his thermostat turned down. Did they know that? Would that affect their estimation of when he died? No. Father McRae had said it was almost as cold inside the house as out. Mitch didn't keep it that cold, so his habits were irrelevant, but, yes, the cold would affect their calculations.

Had they checked his answering machine? Heard the message Jack left on Thursday night, from L.A.? Was it the type of machine that recorded the time of incoming calls? Would that—and telling about her own call from Jack—help him? Probably not. After a day or two's lapse, they probably wouldn't be able to narrow the time of death down to hours.

Had they found any postcards from Karen Lucas?

Ariel's thoughts found a focus in that question. Karen sent postcards to everybody. She dropped them like leaflets from a propaganda plane. It was how she ingratiated herself, Ariel reasoned, made herself memorable, appeared to communicate while saying nothing of consequence. It was how she maintained her distance from others while staying involved in their lives and, therefore, exerting some measure of control over them, at least in their regard for her.

The police wouldn't attach any significance to mere postcards. Had Mitch received any? Had he kept them? Was she grasping at straws with this whole Mitch-Karen connection?

During the same period of time he'd been seen with her, he'd suffered some sort of depression . . . all right, maybe not a full-fledged depression; Ariel had no way of knowing that. Call it a malaise. He'd made the comment that he was "feeling his age," so Jack said, or so he remembered it three years later.

And then Sunday, when he called and found Mitch in a great mood and teased him about finding himself "a lusty woman," hadn't Mitch said he just might beat Jack to that if Jack didn't "get on the stick"? Or so Jack said.

And—wait a minute! Ariel began gnawing her forefinger as a completely new thought surfaced. Mitch was killed with a knife. When Karen had been confronted by her late husband two months ago, when Verlyn had found out about Jack, she'd threatened him with a knife. A decorative (but presumably functional) dagger of some kind, so Verlyn had told Jack. So Jack said.

Stop it, Ariel! she admonished herself; stop qualifying everything with "so Jack said." You believe him or you don't; make up your mind. He's not even the one pushing this connection and trying to find a way to point a finger at Karen; you are. And one statement Mitch made is *not* hearsay via Jack; you heard it firsthand.

She thought back to the conversation between Mitch and herself. He'd been talking about when he met his future son-in-law, the hope he'd held that Jack would be a stabilizing influence on Eve because he was older. He'd asked Ariel if she believed . . . Ariel closed her eyes and tried to recall exactly, tried to get it right. *Didn't she believe,* he'd asked, *that a man with a little more age on him, a little more experience, could be good for a woman?* Wasn't that it? And hadn't he asked wistfully? As if he wanted to believe it himself? And had he not been talking about Eve and Jack at all?

When Peterson came back through the glass-paned door, Jack was with him. Ariel stood up. She could read nothing from his face. Peterson said something to him, and Jack nodded. He didn't wait for the detective to exit through the outside entrance before he strode to Ariel, took her arm, and said, "Let's get out of this place!"

34

JACK PROPELLED ARIEL DOWN THE STEPS SO FAST SHE almost lost her footing. "Where to now?" she asked.

"Mitch's place. Peterson's meeting us. He wants me to see if I can spot anything they've missed. Something missing, I mean, or added, that they wouldn't know about."

"He's asking for your help?"

"Beats the hell out of tossing me in the slammer," Jack said, unlocking the car door. They both watched the detective back out of his parking space and glance their way before he drove away. "There was a minute or two in there when I was sure that was next."

"What did he say? What did he ask you?"

"Get in, please. I'll tell you on the way."

Peterson, Jack said, had made it plain that he was being thoroughly checked out. He was asked for a detailed report of his activities for the twenty-four-hour period between Thursday and yesterday mornings and the names and phone numbers of everyone with whom he'd been in contact during the time in question.

"The time . . . They're going by the newspaper Father McRae saw in Mitch's yard?" Ariel asked. "Or is the autopsy report in?"

"He's going by the fact that it snowed early yesterday. McRae's were the only footprints, and his tire tracks were the only ones they found."

"Then they were careful with the crime scene," Ariel said. "Sounds like they know what they're doing. That's good."

Jack gave her a quick, impatient look. "The cops in L.A. two years ago weren't slouches either. That wasn't much help to me."

"Shouldn't you have called a lawyer?"

"Of course I should call a lawyer!" he snapped. The car slithered sideways, and it was a few seconds before he got it safely back into the ruts. His hands clenching the wheel, his knuckles white, he said, "I just can't face that whole scene again! I hated it! 'Don't answer this, don't answer that.' Back then . . . every time my lawyer advised me not to answer a question, it made me feel as if I were trying to hide something. It made me look guilty. It made me *feel* guilty!"

A few miles passed before he said, "They've already checked out all the airports—Denver, here, Colorado Springs, even Cheyenne, Peterson said—and all the car rental places. They know I wasn't here, not using my real name, anyway."

"They ought to do the same for Karen."

"Ariel . . ."

"No, Jack, listen to me. It's possible." Ariel told him what she'd been thinking about while she'd waited for him. The postcards, the dagger with which Karen had taunted Barry Verlyn, the question about older men and younger women Mitch asked when she'd visited. "Even you said he wasn't himself during the period when you saw him with her and that he was really up when you called on Sunday, as if he felt good about something and—"

"It's too tenuous. Way too tenuous."

"It's possible," Ariel said stubbornly. "Jack, two people close to you have been killed. You say Karen killed the first. You say she was acquainted with the second. What are the odds that an entirely different killer has entered the equation?"

"Is that supposed to be some kind of logical deduction? As far as I know, Karen hasn't spoken to Mitch in years, since before Eve died. As far as I know, they had no more than a nodding acquaintance then. She had no reason to contact him, let alone kill him."

"Do they have any other suspects?"

"If they do, Peterson didn't share their names with me."

The detective was waiting for them, talking to a uniformed officer in a squad car, who, Ariel assumed, was there on guard duty. The snow was churned up all over the yard and driveway, tire marks giving testimony to the recent presence of many vehicles. Jack didn't immediately get out of the car. His face was stone as he took in the yard and the house and the yellow crime scene tape that barred entrance. "God help me," he whispered, "and God help the person who did this thing if I find him first." He gave Ariel a direct look. "Or her," he added, and opened his door.

Peterson opened Ariel's. "Ms. Gold," he said, "I understand you visited Mr. Winters a week or so ago? You might be some help to us, your having been in the house more recently than Mr. Spurling."

Glad she wasn't expected to wait outside, Ariel asked, "What exactly do you want me to do?"

"Just look around. Anything strikes you as different, say so. Don't worry about touching things." Peterson fitted a key into the padlock on the front door. "We're done in here."

The house, appropriately, was cold as a tomb. Jack entered it with as much dread as if it were. He stopped just inside, and Ariel could see the rapid rise and fall of his chest. She touched his arm, which seemed to startle rather than comfort him. He led them into a living room Ariel hadn't seen before, and she watched as he went straight to an armoire.

Mitch had been an audiophile, apparently. The electronic equipment inside was complex and expensive looking and still there.

A chamois-lined box of sterling flatware was in a drawer in the dining room, and Jack subsequently noted that three TV sets, including a nine-inch black-and-white in a bathroom, were also where they belonged. Peterson followed in his wake, saying little. They were an eccentric-looking trio, all bundled in their coats and wearing faces grim as survivors of a disaster. Each time they went from carpeting or rugs to hardwood, their footsteps seemed unnaturally loud to Ariel.

When Jack got to the master bedroom door, he stopped as if he'd hit a wall and, with a barely audible moan, averted his eyes. The chalked outline on the floor looked like the awkward rendering of a child and, in fact, seemed too small to have circumscribed a grown man. Jack didn't let his eyes stray in that direction again.

The house, throughout, bore evidence that crime scene technicians had been at work, but this room, especially, was a mess. The linens had been removed from the bed, and a grayish-white powder covered every flat surface.

Jack, who was going through a leather box on a tall narrow chest of drawers, asked, "What kind of jewelry was he wearing?"

When Peterson said, "A watch. It looked pricey," Jack gave him a sharp look and inhaled as if to say something. "Oh, and a medal," the detective added, "on a chain around his neck."

Jack's shoulders fell as he let out his breath and dropped cufflinks and studs back into the box. He began to go through drawers, tossing their already churned-up contents, and his expression, Ariel noted, grew more grim as he searched. She tried to catch his eye, to get some idea what it was he wasn't finding, but he either didn't notice or didn't choose to acknowledge her mute question while the detective was breathing down his neck.

When they entered the area of the house with which Ariel was familiar, she stopped watching Peterson watch Jack and let her gaze sweep the room. There was a vase of flowers, now in various stages of expiration, on the dining table. A similar bouquet drooped on an old tea chest beside the sofa on which she had sat the last time. The sofa cushions were askew. "How much have your people disturbed in here?" she asked.

"Vacuumed the hearth, took out the garbage disposal, dusted, checked under cushions." Peterson shrugged. "It's a lot less neat now. In fact, the whole house was about as neat as I ever saw a place. Like a model home."

Not a glass or a dish or a spoon, Ariel saw, was in the kitchen sink or on the counter.

"The dishwasher had been run," Peterson said as if she'd spoken aloud. "No way to know when, of course, or who turned it on, but everything inside had time to dry."

Ariel opened the refrigerator. There were no leftovers, no evidence of a last, shared meal, and no half-drunk bottle of wine to provide telltale fingerprints. The garbage pail, she saw, had a fresh plastic bag inside it.

"Would've been nice," Peterson said with an ironic crimp of his mouth, "if there'd been food scraps with teeth marks or saliva traces. Did he impress you as a meticulous housekeeper?"

"Not especially," Ariel said. "It was 'lived-in' when I was here. But maybe if he expected a guest . . . ?"

"Maybe it was the guest that was meticulous," Peterson said.

Jack was over by a floor-to-ceiling bookcase to the side of the fireplace. "There was a loving cup," he said. "Old. It was silver but probably plated, not worth much to anybody but Mitch."

Peterson looked at Ariel, who shrugged. "I didn't notice it," she said.

"Probably moved sometime or other. You don't see anything else?"

"Yes," said Ariel, who just then did. "A picture, missing. Another photo." She pointed to the tea chest. Beside the dying flowers now were a framed photograph of a woman Ariel recognized as Eve and several of people she didn't know. "It was you, Jack, a close-cropped shot of you with your arm around Mitch."

Jack stared, as if he could will the picture back into place to remind himself what it looked like.

"It wasn't recent," Ariel said. "You didn't have the scar. The one over your eye."

He waved his hand helplessly. "Eve used to take a lot of pictures. Maybe he moved that someplace else, too."

"Or maybe the killer took it," Ariel told him meaningfully. "Detective, did you check the message tape in the machine?"

"I checked the machine. There was no tape."

"Then it was taken, too. Why?"

"Because the killer's voice was on it?"

"She . . . the killer could simply have erased the tape. Jack's voice was more than likely on it. He called here Thursday night. Mitch didn't answer. Jack left a message."

"So he said. And—we may as well get this out of the way now—your name was also on the list he gave us, Ms. Gold, of people he saw or called on Thursday. That right?"

"He called me Thursday night. I don't remember the time, but it was late. He was at home."

"Yes. Caller ID. I heard. Why 'she'?"

"Pardon?"

"You said 'she.' "

Ariel looked at Jack and read the negative in his expression. "Slip of the tongue," she said.

"Really?"

"No, not really. I think Mitch Winters had company he expected, and I don't think a man gets his home all spruced up and gets bouquets of flowers and . . . and puts candles on the table when he's expecting a man."

"There weren't any flowers when you were here before?"

"No."

"Or candles?"

"No. I don't think so," she hedged. "I don't remember those candlesticks, and I would've. I like Portuguese pottery. I think I would've noticed those. Did you check Mitch's desk yet?"

"We did."

"Did you find any sort of correspondence from a woman?"

"No."

"Can we go now?" Jack asked quietly.

"You're going back into town?" Peterson asked.

"I need to take care of some things."

"Yes, Mr. Winters's lawyer's expecting you, I'm sure. Ms. Gold, stop by the station, will you? We need your prints for comparison."

The patrolman who'd been outside was gone. Peterson removed the padlock from the front door, and saying, "Leave word with my office where you'll be," left ahead of them. Ariel looked back at the ranch as she and Jack drove away. It looked forsaken.

Jack waited in the car outside the police station while Ariel was printed. She waited in the lawyer's anteroom while Jack met with him and then waited again while he was in the bank. She waited in the office of the funeral home director while he made certain all would be carried out there as Mitch had dictated, and she stood aside, being given curious once-overs, when the occasional citizen of the small city stopped Jack to express condolences.

"Mitch was well known for having lived here so short a time," she commented after that happened the third time, "and well liked." She glanced at the departing middle-aged woman whose name she hadn't caught. The woman's acquaintance with Mitch was through a book club, she'd told Jack. She seemed genuinely upset.

"He was from here originally," he said. "That's why he retired here." They got back into the car, and he started the engine. "His parents are in the cemetery where he'll be buried. There's a memorial marker there for Eve, too."

"Where to next?" Ariel asked.

"There's nothing else I can do for now; everybody's closing shop. You haven't said; can you stay overnight or did you want to see about getting a flight back?"

"I can stay until tomorrow. If you want me to." What she meant was: I'm feeling like a fifth wheel and not especially needed.

"Of course I want you to. Why would you say that?"

"You've been different today. Distant."

"Distant?" Jack turned off the motor. "I don't think you quite understand, Ariel, and that surprises me. In fact, it blows me away. My best friend has been brutally murdered. It's like I've lost a father and . . . my mainstay, all at once. I don't know who did it, and I can't think of a reason that makes any kind of sense why anyone would do it, and I'm the number one suspect because of my sordid past and the fact that I'm his primary legatee. Ariel, the floor's been jerked out from under me. I'm a little tense. Do forgive me if I seem 'distant.' " Abruptly, Jack sagged, the fight gone out of him. He rubbed his eyes roughly. "I'm sorry," he said.

"Don't be. I was being selfish."

"I'm in . . . call it survival mode. I learned the hard way that, if I wanted to keep going, I had to close up, to shut off. Don't let any feelings in and don't let them out. You understand?"

"Yes."

"This thing happened before I had time to be sure of you, do you see that?"

You said you trusted me, Ariel wanted to say, but the doubts she'd only just managed to squelch too many times during the day were too fresh in her mind. She wasn't that much of a hypocrite.

"If we'd had another month together first," Jack said, "maybe just another week . . . You're dangerous to me, Ariel; you know that?"

"Dangerous?"

"You can hurt me in a way that even these cowboy cops can't." He smiled crookedly. "Stay, please. I do want you here."

"Well, I'm here, and I'm freezing. Would you turn the heater on?"

He smiled then and turned the key in the ignition. The heater, thankfully, was efficient, and the car was beginning to warm up by the time he said, "I had this half-baked hope, you know? That we'd find something at the house. Something that would point to somebody besides me."

"What was it you *didn't* find that you expected to? I'm talking about when you were looking through the drawers in the bedroom."

"At one time Mitch had . . ." Jack grimaced in disgust. "Oh, hell! I can't be sure of anything. How do I know what he might've sold or given away or thrown away?" He put the car into gear. "I guess we'd better see what the hotel situation is."

"Why a hotel? Jack, why not get some kind of take-out and go back to the house."

"Why not get take-out and go sleep at the mortuary? What a cheerful idea, Ariel!"

"No, really, under Peterson's eye, we might've overlooked something." Softly, she said, "I know it's hard on you to be there, but you've done harder things. You made it through this wretched day. It's worth a chance, isn't it? If there's anything, anything at all, you're the only one who knew Mitch well enough to see it."

"I cannot sleep in that house, Ariel, and I need some sleep. I'm beat. I'm dead on my feet. If I saw the murder weapon lying on the dining room table out there, I don't think I'd have sense enough to know it. You've got to be exhausted, too. Come on!"

"Okay, call a hotel, for later. But now, let's at least make the effort, okay?"

"You just don't quit!" Jack said in exasperation. "Of course, for a woman who tracked a murderer for years, that's par—"

"What are you talking about?"

"What do you think I'm talking about? Your husband. His murder. Your one-woman vendetta."

"When did I tell . . . ?" Ariel clamped her lips. She guessed the answer. The conversations they'd had two years before.

"It was no holds barred then, too," Jack was saying. *" 'You're not guilty? Then have the guts to let my show help find out who is!' "* Grudgingly, he said, "Actually, you were kind. Hell-bent on browbeating me out of self-pity. That and getting me on your show."

"We're both consistent, aren't we?" Ariel said carefully.

"Ouch!" Jack chuckled but quickly sobered. "When you told me about your own husband's death . . . what it had been like for you . . . That was a generous thing to do. For you, I know, a hard thing. Which is really why I called you after all that time, you know."

"But you said I was happy."

"Sure. You'd just gotten some new lead. . . ." Jack looked at her quizzically. "You remember. You were on fire! The police could give up, you said, but you knew who'd shot your husband and you wouldn't quit till you got him. And, by God, you did it! All by yourself. That *is* the story you were talking about the other night? The one you'd been researching for a long time?"

"Yes." Ariel waited for more; apparently there was no more. After all her subtle probes, all her guesswork, the big revelation was . . . nothing. She was a hotshot sleuth. The Mounties—and Ariel Gold—always get their man. She swallowed a laugh.

"Hey, Jack," she said, and touched his shoulder.

"What?"

"You didn't listen to me then. Listen now. I don't want you arrested. We can't let that happen. We don't know where Peterson stands or what he might do or when. There may not be time later, Jack. This may be it."

While Ariel shopped the nearest supermarket's deli section, Jack made hotel reservations. The sun was setting as they headed south again, and it was bleak cold twilight when they drove up to the ranch.

"This is probably the worst idea I've ever gone along with," Jack said, and took the groceries from the car.

"What's in that other bag?" Ariel asked, noticing one she hadn't bought.

"Wine. Two bottles of good stuff. I may drink them both."

With the thermostat turned up and a fire blazing, the house was warmer. It wasn't, Ariel privately admitted, much less oppressive. She'd already begun to doubt the soundness of her suggestion to return here, and Jack's grim face wasn't encouraging.

"Shall we eat first?" she asked.

He was in the kitchen, opening and closing drawers. "Second," he said. "Or maybe never. I don't seem to have much appetite for some unexplainable reason."

"What are you looking for?"

"That's the problem. I don't know what we're supposed to be looking for, and neither do you. At the moment, however, what I'm trying to find is a corkscrew."

"Jack, work with me. I can't do any good here without you."

"What the devil is it doing in there?" he muttered, and slammed a drawer shut.

"Would you do me a very big favor? Would you stop banging things around and hold me for a minute? Please?"

Jack set down the corkscrew, bowed his head for a second, and then turned and took her in his arms. He held her for longer than the minute she'd asked for. "I wouldn't blame you," he murmured, "if you took the car and went off and left me."

"Why don't I get us some glasses instead?"

He nodded and let her go, and she began opening cabinets. "The stemware's hanging in the rack behind you," he said, "and you'll find napkins in that drawer. That top one."

She closed the cabinet she was looking in and then stopped, opened it again, and reached inside. "One mystery solved," she said. "Is this the loving cup you were talking about?"

"That's it." He took it from her, smiling at the inscription. "Mitch poked fun at it, but he was proud of this old relic."

Ariel read the gothic script. *First Place Men's Intramural Fencing University of Colorado 1959.* "Fencing?" she asked.

"His one athletic claim to fame. Proved he wasn't a 'spaz,' Mitch said." Jack set the trophy down. "After the trial I spent a couple of weeks here. The first night he

opened a bottle of Moët and Chandon he'd bought for
the occasion. He used this as a chiller."

"He normally kept it on display?"

"Every place he ever lived."

Ariel's eyes went to the obvious empty spot of honor
on the shelf beside the hearth. "Why would he have
stashed it away?"

"I can't believe he would, but what difference does it
make?"

"Was the corkscrew in a different drawer from where
it was usually kept?"

"Yes, or at least if I'm remembering correctly. Well,
no, I know it was. See?" He opened a top drawer.
"Church key, swizzle sticks, toothpicks, et cetera, and
cocktail napkins, right where I told you they were, and
I see where you're going. Somebody else put these
things away." He opened the refrigerator. "But where's
the bottle? It wasn't in the trash."

A flashlight search of recycling bins outside turned up
no wine bottles.

"She took it with her," Ariel said as they came back
inside.

"She?"

"I imagine that your champagne celebration with
Mitch was unusual, don't you? I mean, in the normal
run of things he'd be more likely to entertain a woman
than another man?"

The ringing of the phone startled them both. Jack visibly braced himself before he went to answer.

"Yes, of course I remember you," he said, and, after a
moment, "Yes, he was. Thank you, I appreciate that. I'll
see you there, yes, thank you."

"Sympathy call," Jack told Ariel. "A fellow I met at a
party here once. He and Mitch took an art class together."

"Mitch was an artist?"

"A dabbler, but he enjoyed it. There's an old cabin on this property he's been talking . . . he was talking about converting into a studio come spring."

They were sitting in front of the fire eating sandwiches when Ariel guided the conversation back to the loving cup and wine opener and Karen. "There'll be something else, too," she said. "She was thorough when she cleaned up, but nobody can think of everything. You need to tell them to check for her prints specifically, darling; they're on record because—"

" 'Darling'?" Jack swallowed a mouthful of smoked turkey. "You've never called me darling before. I like the sound of that."

Ariel felt herself coloring. "To the best of my knowledge, I've never called anybody darling before, but to continue—"

"Ariel, listen to me. I appreciate what you're doing, but it's all held together with spit and baling wire. Maybe Mitch had somebody here and served them wine, maybe it was a woman, but we don't know when that was. That bottle could be at the recycling center now, taken there at any time. The woman—or women; it could've been a dinner party—might've helped clean up and put things away in the wrong place. You didn't remember seeing the trophy on the shelf when you were here before. Who knows how long it's been in that cabinet?"

"I didn't memorize every object in the place. What about the flowers? What about the candles?"

"He liked flowers. If he'd had a dinner party, he for sure would've had flowers. And if you didn't see the candlesticks on the table last time—which you weren't really sure about, were you?—it's entirely possible he'd bought them since."

"Why are you so resistant to believing Karen was here?"

"I've just told you, and I told you earlier; all these speculations are too tenuous. They're cobwebs."

"Well, then, we'll just have to find the spider, won't we? In the meantime, here are some more speculations you can poke holes in. Karen took the photo of you and Mitch because she couldn't resist it. It was a truly wonderful picture, but maybe to her it's also a talisman, to keep the object of her fixation lodged, like a poisoned thorn, in her diseased mind.

"She took the tape out of the machine because your voice was on it, joking and loving and happy sounding and maybe the way she remembered you being with her. The way she wants you to be again. She may have been here when you called, you know. She may have heard you leaving the message after she—"

The phone rang again. "Let it ring," Jack said.

"There's no tape in the machine," Ariel reminded him.

Impatiently, he got up and answered. "Can't it wait?" Ariel heard him say, and then, "All right. Give me a half hour to get there."

"What's the matter?" she asked when she saw the rigid set of his shoulders. "Who was that?"

"Some policewoman. They want me back down there. Something's turned up they want me to see."

"Now?"

"If I could have put them off, I would have. It won't take long, the lady said. Are you finished eating?"

"What's turned up?"

"She didn't say. She probably didn't know. She was probably just doing what she'd been told to do. Are you finished or not?"

"I'm not going with you."

"Of course you're going. You don't think I'm going to let you stay here alone?"

"Do I need your permission?"

"We're not really going to have that kind of discussion."

"Jack, I've spent most of the day waiting for you outside offices. It's a waste of time. I can be more useful—"

"I'm not leaving here without you."

"You have no choice short of dragging me. You won't be gone long you said. I'll lock the—"

"Suit yourself," Jack said shortly. He snatched up his coat. "Lock it. Don't open it, not to anybody."

"I'm capable of taking care of myself."

"You're capable of making me crazy," Jack said, and left, slamming the door behind him.

Ariel wasted no time once he'd gone. She headed for Mitch's desk.

35

HENRY PRESSED THE DISCONNECT BUTTON AS SOON AS HE heard the subtle change of ring that signaled a clickover to the answering machine. He'd left one message already, and he couldn't bear to listen to Ariel's pleasant, disembodied voice again.

He slumped in his chair and, violently, kicked the footstool across the room. It rolled true for a few feet, hit an imperceptible dip in the floor, and spun—rather gracefully, not unlike a figure skater's final turn—losing momentum and coming to an anticlimactic stop.

"Hey, Dad?" Sam had come in just in time to witness Henry's childish eruption. "You okay?"

"I'm fine."

"Okay." Sam removed the basketball he carried from under his arm—one-handedly, unconsciously showing off his handspan—and braced it against his stomach. He looked at the stool and then at his father. "You don't look so fine."

"Yeah, well . . ." Henry stood up. "There's nothing

here for dinner, I'm afraid. You rather go out, or have breakfast for dinner, or call for something?"

"Breakfast for dinner?"

"Bacon and eggs. Toast. Like that."

"We had . . ." Sam rubbed his nose and made a conscious, adult decision not to trouble his father with a reminder that they'd had bacon and eggs that morning. "That's okay."

He trailed Henry into the kitchen. "You know what we could have? That chili you made a couple of weeks ago that you froze some of. That night I was gone . . ."

He was dismayed and even a little frightened when his father just stopped, right where he stood, and then, after a second, absently picked up an apple core that Sam had left on a counter that afternoon. The core was brown now and pretty disgusting. Sam braced himself for a familiar dressing-down, as this kind of thing was a sore point. He didn't remember leaving it there, but he supposed he must have. His dad didn't leave apple cores on the counter. He wasn't sure if his dad ever ate apples.

"Good idea," Henry said, and replaced the core as if it belonged there. "I'll thaw it out."

They were finishing up dinner—or Sam was; his father hadn't really eaten much—when Sam decided to get down to issues.

"Are you and Ariel split?" he asked.

His father gave him a level look and, to his surprise, didn't pretend there was nothing to split. "I guess. Looks that way."

"Is it your fault?"

"I don't think so. Maybe in some way . . ." His father shrugged. "No. I don't think so."

"I like her."

"I know you do. I'm sorry."

"I can still be friends with her, can't I?"

"Sure. I hope she and *I* can still be friends."

The phone rang then.

"I'll get it!" Sam said. From the alacrity with which he leaped to answer and the muffled, monosyllabic conversation Henry then overheard, he assumed it was the little girl of Sam's dreams, the girl about whom he'd sought Ariel's advice.

Feeling like a postpeak, baffled old bull put out to pasture, Henry cleared away the chili bowls. What *had* happened with Ariel? he asked himself yet again, hoping this time he'd come up with a different answer. *Was* it his fault? No question, he'd handled his visit two nights ago with all the finesse of a bull snorting a lamebrained swathe through a china shop. He'd been genuinely well intentioned. He'd had no expectations. He'd been thinking of her, not himself. Truly. And it was too late by then, anyway.

He dumped detergent into the dishwasher and closed the door. Maybe Sam had hit on something, seeking Ariel's advice for the lovelorn; maybe he should consult her himself.

He'd called her the night before, several times, to apologize, to express his concerns reasonably. He'd decided at nearly midnight that any further calls, unanswered, would provide more information than he wanted to know.

Dammit! He slammed the greasy, chili-encrusted saucepan into the sink and realized that his son had gone silent in the next room. He turned on the hot water full force.

So she'd fallen in love. So it wasn't with him. She hadn't done it on purpose; it happens to the best of us.

Henry attacked the saucepan with a soap pad, scouring it to a mirror finish. He eyed it critically; his face looked back, distorted by curvature and worry. This wasn't about how he felt, not anymore. He wasn't a superstitious man—the furthest thing from it—but he had the absolute conviction that Ariel was headed for a bad place, and there wasn't one thing he could do about it.

36

LESS THAN A MINUTE OF PLUNDERING TIPPED ARIEL that if there'd been any postcards in Mitch's desk, they'd been removed. She was as disappointed to see that there was no Rolodex, address book, or appointment book; Peterson, she presumed, had taken anything of that sort. In fact, there was very little left in the desk. Either Mitch's files were kept in a computer somewhere or he wasn't much for retaining records or the police had cleaned house. This whole idea was a bust; by coming here, she'd put Jack through yet more grief for damn-all.

She was opening another drawer when she heard something that made the hair on her neck stand erect as needles. A long lonely howl sounded from somewhere in the distance. It was one of the most forlorn things she'd ever heard, and the thought came before she could stop it: *an omen?* Ariel closed the empty drawer and told herself to lighten up: *Jack's hardly out the door, and you're already conceding defeat and spooking yourself out!*

There was nothing in the next drawer but blank stationery and pencils. Another held thin manuals for electric appliances. The last drawer did contain records, old ones; too old, Ariel figured, to have been considered useful. Among them were several plump envelopes labeled "receipts," each with a single year designation. The most recent years were missing or, more probably, confiscated. The earliest was for four years before. Ariel emptied it onto the desk and pawed through restaurant stubs and credit card and gas receipts. One item stopped her. If she could judge by the multipage receipt from the Hotel del Coronado in San Diego, Mitch had spent three days and nights dining well and not alone. It was dated a week before Christmas. Jack had seen Mitch with Karen in early December of that year.

Ariel scanned the phone calls placed from the expensive room. Several were to a number with an area code that included the San Fernando Valley. She dialed it. The recording requested that she call back during office hours and helpfully informed her that Harwell-Binns Realty was open daily from eight until six.

Ariel smiled savagely. This wouldn't convince Jack that Mitch and Karen had been in a relationship—the arguments he'd make weren't hard to imagine—but it was another link to the woman. She began to let out the breath she'd been holding, and then nearly choked on it when the doorbell rang.

She could see no one through the peephole in the back door. The bell rang again, and Ariel hurried to the front door. One of the people who'd offered Jack condolences that afternoon, the woman from Mitch's book club, waited on the porch. She was holding a foil-wrapped dish and looking anxious. Just as she reached to press the doorbell button again, Ariel heard a voice, another female, from a car she hadn't seen until then. "I told you we should have called, Alice," the second woman sang out.

Ariel opened the door.

"Oh!" Alice yelped and jumped as if she'd been goosed. "Oh, hello! We were beginning to think no one was here, but we saw all the lights . . ."

"Sorry to keep you waiting," Ariel said. "I'm Ariel Gold, Jack's . . . Mr. Winters's son-in-law's friend. I'm afraid Jack's not here right now."

"We met this afternoon in town. Alice Carson?" Her breath frosted in the air. "I hope you haven't eaten?"

Ariel smiled her puzzlement.

"I mean," Alice said, "my friend Becky and I just thought you might not have any food in the house." She held out the dish. "Lasagna," she explained. "It's in a disposable tin, so you don't have to worry about returning anything."

"That's awfully kind," Ariel said, and took it.

"Well, we're still kind of small-town in our ways, I suppose. Becky and I live in Nederland. Now that's a *really* small town, just a couple or three miles west."

"Won't you come in?"

Alice declined, saying they wouldn't intrude, they hadn't come to visit. "Just tell Mr. Spurling again, if you will, how sorry we are. Mitch was highly thought of around here. They haven't found out anything, have they? About . . . ?"

Ariel shook her head and promised to pass on the message, and Alice said good night. As she went carefully down the steps, an arm was poked through the waiting car's window, and the hand on the end of it waved. Ariel waved back and closed the door and locked it.

She'd hardly had time to convince herself that there was nothing of further interest among the old receipts before the doorbell rang again. She went back to the peephole.

The woman on the porch was small, or shrunken with age. Age, Ariel decided. She was all bundled up, even to a muffler. Her hair looked like white wool. She held what was obviously a bakery box, and, like Alice before her, she was looking around, checking behind her, as if the place made her uneasy. Mitch's girlfriends, Ariel thought, are brave and well-meaning ladies, or morbidly curious.

She didn't jump with fright when Ariel opened the door. She turned back to face her and, with appropriate gravity, said, "Good evening. Ms. Gold, isn't it? I hope I'm not intruding?"

She wasn't a shrunken old woman; her mother probably wasn't old enough to be a shrunken old woman. She was no more than Ariel's age, and what had looked through the peephole like white wool was, in fact, white wool. A rather smart knitted cap. Holding out the bakery box, she said, "I thought you people might not have had time to shop, so I brought this . . ."

Ariel took the box, sighing inwardly. "How kind of you," she said, and decided it had been a mistake to begin opening the door to the neighborhood. She would have nothing accomplished by the time Jack got back, and she was pretty sure he'd be determined to cut out of here and go to the hotel. He'd also be freaked to know she'd opened the door at all. "I'm afraid Mr. Winters's son-in-law isn't here right now, but I'll tell him you stopped by."

"You're alone out here? Surely . . ." The eerie, faraway howl that came at that moment was so perfectly timed as to be comical, but the woman didn't appreciate the joke. Shivering, she glanced into the darkness behind her. "Surely that can't be wise."

"I don't think the wolves will bother me," Ariel said with a pleasant but, she hoped, dismissive smile, "and Jack will be back any minute. Who shall I tell him—"

"Any minute? Let me keep you company then, until Mr. Spurling gets back. I'd like a chance to tell him how badly I feel about Mitch."

Feeling rude at keeping the woman standing on the porch but even more impatient to be rid of her, Ariel said, "I was exaggerating a little when I said 'any minute.' It'll be a while yet." *Could be days or weeks if he happens to be arrested*, she thought.

"Then that settles it." It was said with the decisiveness of a schoolteacher accustomed to managing young children and, having said it, as if she had every right in the world to do so, she strode past Ariel into the house.

Ariel was caught flatfooted. In the seconds it took her to react, a whole new scenario presented itself. Could *this* be the woman Mitch had in mind when he asked her opinion of older men and young women? Was it this woman and not Karen Lucas at all for whom he'd bought flowers and lit candles? This woman whose company he'd been so happily anticipating? With her heart sinking and her fine theories knocked into a hat, she closed the door.

Unquestionably, the lady knew the layout well; she headed straight for the kitchen area and the hearth. Unquestionably, she felt proprietary; she bent to straighten one of the pictures on the tea chest even as she unbuttoned her coat. And, unquestionably, she looked as if she'd suffered a great loss with Mitch Winters's death. She wore black under the coat, Ariel saw, and her whole demeanor was grave. She wasn't as calm as she'd seemed on the porch.

The phone rang.

"Excuse me," Ariel said, setting the box on the counter. It was Dick McRae: "Just checking in. How's John doing?"

"He's coping," Ariel told the priest. "He's not here right now, though, Father. The police called him back to town."

"They did? That's peculiar. I called Frank to find out where you folks were staying. He didn't say anything about expecting John back there. What's going on, did Frank say?"

Ariel explained, briefly and discreetly, that the cryptic message hadn't come directly from Frank, but that it hadn't seemed to indicate a problem. "I hope," she added.

"Have John call me when he gets back," McRae said, "will you?"

Ariel took down his number and, hanging up, said, "You people hereabouts are unusually . . . neighborly." If there was irony in her voice, her visitor didn't react to it. She was a pretty woman and rather delicate looking, although that might be an impression lent by sorrow. She looked weighed down with it, Ariel thought, and older than she'd first seemed. Her well-formed mouth was tight, and her fair skin was faintly shadowed under the eyes. "That was Father McRae from in town," Ariel went on to say. "Do you know him?"

"I know about him, through Mitch. A good friend, he told me."

"Won't you take off your coat and sit down?" Ariel's curiosity was growing keener by the second. "You knew Mitch well?" she asked.

"I couldn't believe it when I heard this morning. It's . . ." She evidently couldn't find words. "I cared very deeply for him. What a terrible, terrible waste." She still hadn't taken off her outer clothing or even removed her handbag from her shoulder, and she was rubbing her gloved hands together as if she were freezing. "Ms. Gold . . . Ariel, isn't it? Please come sit down here with me."

"Well . . . all right," Ariel said, a little taken aback at being usurped in the role of hostess. "In just a second." She put the lasagna away and, reaching for a fresh glass, asked, "Would you like something to drink . . . I'm sorry; I didn't catch your name."

The woman's composure suddenly and disconcertingly cracked. "Oh, would you stop that and listen to me! It's urgent that I talk to you."

Ariel forgot the glass. "Pardon me?" she asked.

"I know who you are from your TV show. I think if anyone can help, you can. But you need me, too. Please, we don't have much time. Will you come here and sit down?"

"I think I prefer to stand. What do you mean, we don't have much time?"

Abruptly, as if her legs had lost the strength to keep her upright, the woman sat down herself. She clasped her handbag on her knees, and her head fell forward, almost resting on it. She looked, it struck Ariel, as if she were praying. When she raised her face, her eyes were shining with tears, and her mouth was slack. She looked as if she'd gathered every ounce of persuasiveness she possessed to put into her words. "I misled you, pretending to be paying a sympathy call. I didn't see any other way to get in here—to talk to you, I mean. I knew Jack Spurling wasn't here because I'm the one who called him, on my cell phone. I didn't really believe you'd stay behind. I prayed you would, but I couldn't . . . When he finds out it was a wild-goose chase, he'll be back. We lost precious time when those women showed up, and—"

"Who are you and why are you here?"

The woman held up her hand, and Ariel saw that it trembled. "Please! All you need to know now is that I was Mitch's friend, and I'm trying to be yours. I'll tell you who I am; I'll tell you everything, but not here. That man is dangerous, Ms. Gold . . . Ariel. I think . . . no, I'm sure that he killed Mitch. I've put myself in jeopardy coming here to warn you about him, and I cannot be here when he gets back. I will not be. If you won't listen to me . . ." She shook her head helplessly. "I don't know what else to do."

"What are you talking about, lady?" Ariel's foreboding, growing like a mushroom cloud, erupted as anger. It was all she could do to keep from snatching the woman up and pummeling her. "Did Mitch tell you something about Jack? Something that made you think he was afraid of him? Is that what you're saying?"

"What I'm saying is that Mitch found out Jack Spurling killed his daughter."

"What?"

"Now will you take me seriously? Can we get out of here? Look, there's a cabin on this property. He won't think to look there. Just go that far with me. If you won't go back to town with me, just go that far at least, and I'll tell you everything. Then you'll understand why—"

"I'm not going anywhere until you explain who you are and why you're saying these things. Why would you have anything to fear from Jack? Does he even know you?"

"We don't have time for this!" The tears that threatened began to stream. "Yes, he knows me. And I *fear* him because I've known all along that he killed Eve. *I saw him do it!* And now you know it, too—like Mitch. Maybe you'd have been safer if I hadn't interfered, but I couldn't just let . . . I had to warn you, and . . ." She wasn't a pretty crier. She seemed—Ariel couldn't deny it—far too terrified to worry that her nose was running and her pale skin was mottled with red. "And I need help. I'm tired of running. I want to go home, and I'm too scared to, and I need somebody to help me!"

Certainty hit with the force of an iron fist. Two steps took Ariel to the opposite side of the kitchen counter, where—somewhere—there were weapons. Knives. Like the one Mitch Winters had been stabbed with. She said the first thing that came into her mind: "You don't look anything like I expected."

37

"EXPECTED?" KAREN LUCAS VERLYN HALTED IN MID-sob, her mouth open. "You're saying you know who I am?" She opened her handbag and reached inside. "What else do you know?"

Ariel's eye landed on a meat tenderizer stuck in a jar of implements on the counter. It was some kind of pot metal, not much, but it might have to do.

Karen took a packet of tissues from her bag. She seemed oblivious to Ariel's reaction. It threw Ariel. She didn't know whether she was overreacting or underreacting, but either response seemed dramatically wrong. Her hand hovered near the inadequate weapon. Faster than thought came gut reaction: *if the woman meant any harm, if she had a weapon, she would have used it already. Except . . .* she wants to know what I know, what Jack knows and what he's told me. And she can't afford another body found in this house. One could've been some crazy with an unknown motive, a tragic mystery; two's a crime wave.

But why this elaborate charade?

Karen clutched the tissue in her closed fist, pressing it against her sternum, against her full breasts. She glanced nervously toward the door.

Why? Because she thought I'd jump at the chance to get her version of Eve Spurling's death, that's why. She thought her accusations would frighten me into bolting. And . . . Ariel had a flash of insight. *Because she enjoys the power that manipulating people gives her. She thrives on it.*

"What did Jack tell you about me?" Karen asked. She bit down on her lower lip. It was full, to the point of lushness. Her teeth were straight and white and small, and her nose, pink now with crying, was so perfect that a plastic surgeon could have used it as the deluxe model. She didn't look remotely psychotic; she looked about as threatening as a storybook princess.

She could have made me leave by force, Ariel thought. *She didn't. She's got no weapon.* "What did he tell me?" she repeated. "Nothing bad, Karen. Nothing bad at all. You wanted to talk to me? Fine. I'm listening."

Karen blew her nose and made a visible effort to calm herself. "You sound like a tough person, Ariel. I'm not. Since he did this to Mitch, I'm scared out of my wits. What if he turns around and comes back for some reason?" She glanced at her watch. "I've spent two years staying out of his reach. I'm not going to sit here and wait for him."

Ariel looked at her own watch. "Jack's barely reached town by now. We've got at least twenty-five minutes before he can possibly get back. Tell me what you saw the night Eve Spurling died."

"Not here."

"Here or nowhere. We've got plenty of time."

"All right! But just . . ." Rattling out the words, almost tripping over them, she said, "Do you know about . . ." She began to twist the tissue in her fingers. "About Jack and me? I don't know how it happened! Eve was my friend. I was engaged to be married.

"I don't know how well you know Jack, but he's . . . persuasive. Like some kind of sorcerer. He can make you believe anything. He made me believe he loved me. I've never, ever wanted a man the way he made me want him.

"That night, the night Eve died, he and I were out on the deck. Things got . . . heavy. I was nervous. I wanted to go in. Barry, my fiancé Barry, was asleep, but Eve wasn't. She was in the main room. Too near. This is too risky, I told Jack." Her eyes slid away. "I was half undressed. All of a sudden, Eve was standing there. Looking at . . ." The tissue was by now in shreds. "I was so ashamed, I just ran.

I don't know what happened then, but somebody heard them fighting, and . . ." She moaned. "Oh, God," she said, "this is taking too long!" and she began to talk even faster.

"And then I was even more ashamed of being such a coward. I went looking for them, to try to explain to Eve, to ask her to forgive me. They were down on this platform thing at the back of the boat. I looked down, and I saw them, and then I saw him hit her and then hit her again. She stopped fighting back. The next time he hit her, she went into the water, and she just went under."

Karen licked her lips, over and over. "I ran down there. I couldn't even see her anymore. I said, 'We've got to stop the boat!' He stood there looking down at the water, at the wake, the boat's wake, like he was in a trance. 'Do something!' I begged him! I started to run back up the stairs, to—I don't know—to find the captain. Somebody. Jack grabbed me and held me. Pinned my arms. He said, 'Isn't this what you wanted? Tell me it isn't.' "

Shaking her head, staring wildly, Karen said, "I didn't want her dead. God forgive me, I wanted him, but I didn't want her dead. His eyes were . . . You know what his eyes are like? They were ice. He must have seen how . . . appalled I was. She would never have given him a divorce, he said. 'She'd have seen me dead first!'

"I just wanted to get away from him. To get away from those eyes. And then . . . I don't know . . . He knew it was a lost cause, I guess. He said—I remember *this* verbatim—'What you saw didn't happen. Do you understand? You tell anybody, ever, about this, and I'll kill you, too.' "

For the first time since she'd arrived, Karen was still. Ariel was stone. At that moment she felt nothing. The barrage of words had hit her like blows. She'd been knocked senseless by them.

"Why are you here?" she asked quietly.

"I told you why!"

"No. I mean why are you in Boulder? What are you doing here?"

Karen seemed then to remember the circumstances. She made another check of her watch and started to her feet. "I'll tell you once we've—"

"Now, please. We've got time."

"I came to tell Mitch what Jack had done."

"Why would you do that?"

"Mitch was good to me. I once did some work for him—I used to be in real estate—and he and I became friends. He was almost like a father to me then. He deserved to know. It wasn't right that Jack pretended to care about him, to use him after what he'd done."

"Why didn't Mitch deserve to know two years ago?"

"I was too scared to tell him or anybody two years ago! I believed Jack when he said he'd kill me!"

"What changed?"

"My husband died."

Ariel raised her eyebrows. "So?"

Karen did stand up then. She popped up from the hearth, looking as if she wanted to stamp her foot with frustration. Ariel tensed, but the other woman made no move toward her. "Why are you acting like this?" she said. "What's wrong with you? I should never have come here."

"No, you were right to come. I'm glad you did. I'm sorry about your husband. What, exactly, was it he died of?"

"His heart. He had a heart attack."

"What did his death have to do with your visit to Mitch?"

"Barry knew about . . . the affair. I told him about that, but that's all I told him. He didn't push—he could see how shaky I was, that I was ready to break—but I think he guessed what Jack had done. Barry took care of me. He took me away, and when . . . I was in a clinic for a while, more than once. I . . . unraveled. He helped me get back on track. Then in December he had a heart attack. I was . . . I was rudderless, don't you see? Devastated. I wanted to come home!"

Hugging herself into her coat, Karen began to pace: two jerky steps one way and two the other like a toy soldier, a windup sentry. "Somehow, Jack heard about Barry. He'd let me be as long as I stayed away, but he must have been afraid I'd come back then. I wouldn't have said anything, but I guess he couldn't believe that, couldn't be sure of it. He called my mother, trying to get information out of her, wanting to know where I was.

"I didn't know who to turn to, but then I thought of Mitch. I would help him and he would help me. So I flew here, and I told him. It was a mistake. He must have confronted Jack. He should never have done that! He should have just gone with me to the police the way I begged him to."

There was a noise outside, and Karen jumped. "We've got to go!" she cried.

"It was just a limb cracking," Ariel said. "Probably with the cold." She felt icy cold herself. Nerveless as steel. She would find out whether this woman was lying, she thought, if it was the last thing she ever did.

One thing she didn't doubt: Karen was scared. Of Jack, just as she claimed? Because of what she knew about two murders? Or because she committed those murders—one right in this house—and she couldn't afford to be caught returning to the scene?

And can't afford to be caught with me since she means to get rid of me, too?

It would take too many questions and too many answers to recognize the truth, and Karen wasn't going to hang around to be interrogated. And she couldn't be allowed to leave.

And I'd be a fool to go with her.

"I can give you everything, Ariel," Karen was saying, "all the details, for your show. I'll tell you tonight. All I ask is that you help me hide."

The words hardly registered. Could she be telling the truth? *And everything Jack's ever said a lie?*

"Will you? Help me hide until he's convicted? I've seen how you distort faces on TV to protect your sources, how you disguise voices. Can't you set up some kind of protective custody, too?"

Every word? And every touch? Every caress?

Hurrying across the room, Karen said, "Please! Why are you just standing there? We're running out of time!" She grasped Ariel's elbow. "We've got to get out of here!"

Ariel's eyes dropped to the hand on her arm and then back to the desperate, tear-stained face. *She's not unlike you*, Jack had said. *When she wants something—or some-one—she goes after it. The difference is, you're sane.*

"Karen," she said, "I'm afraid I just don't believe you."

38

KAREN'S LARGE, EXPRESSIVE, AND REALLY QUITE LOVELY eyes underwent a series of changes so swift Ariel would have been hard pressed to describe it even seconds after she watched it happen. She saw shock. She may have only imagined anger. She recognized understanding.

"You're in love with him," Karen stated flatly. She dropped Ariel's arm as if it had become contaminated, slowly and distastefully brushing her gloved palms one against the other. "I thought there was a chance . . . I hoped it was the story you were after, but it's him."

Ariel braced herself. She'd been monumentally stupid to voice her disbelief, and she'd realized it before the words were out of her mouth. But Karen merely began to button her coat. "I won't call you a fool," she said bitterly. "I've been there."

"You're jumping to conclusions. I only meant that I can't believe Jack could do these things. You're guessing about Mitch. You must have misinterpreted what happened with Eve. Let your imagination run away . . ."

With an eloquent roll of the eyes, the other woman finished buttoning her coat.

"No, really, Karen! Think about what you've told me. The only reason you've given for believing Jack's interested in your whereabouts is that he called your mother. Come on! Maybe he simply wanted to express his sympathy about your husband. Maybe he wants to see you again."

"He wants to see me, all right!"

"Look, let's say, just for argument's sake, that what you've told me is true; Jack's not going to do anything to you with me right here, is he?"

Karen laughed. It struck Ariel as patronizing, but she may have wanted to interpret it that way; it may have been pitying. "Not tonight, maybe. But are you going to be my bodyguard forever? Protecting me against a man you're in love with? A man who probably has you convinced he cares for you, too?" There was no mistaking the pity now. "Jack Spurling's incapable of genuine feeling. Trust me, he's using you somehow, you and your TV show, I'd bet."

"You're not making sense. If all Jack needed was *Open File* resources, why would he take the trouble to make me believe we were an item?"

"How about because he can?" Karen said, her voice breaking on the "can." "Because he is exceptionally good at it. Because he enjoys the power it gives him to be able to convince just about anybody of just about anything."

The argument was uncannily similar to the one Ariel had used on herself only moments before—against Karen. Either this woman was very, very good, she thought, *or I'm very, very wrong.*

"I think," Karen said, "I'm starting to understand

what's going on. He's told you some outrageous lie about me, hasn't he? God knows what."

Ariel watched the other woman's brow furrow. Her own mind raced. *Can it be? The whole time Jack was refusing to be involved with finding "Eve's killer," he meant to use me to do it?*

"What was it?" Karen asked. Her hand went to the collar of her coat, and she pressed it against her throat protectively. "What would he tell a newswoman that would reel her in like a fish?"

He sought me out deliberately? Everything, from the first call to the first "accidental" meeting, all planned? To find Karen, not to make her talk but to make sure she didn't!

"He told you *I* killed Eve, didn't he? Oh, my God! That's it. The only thing it could be. He's been using you to find me, you and your people."

No, no "people." Just me. He was adamant about that. The jailhouse chat Ariel had finally heard about popped into her head. Was it, after all, a revelation? *He knew I'd stop at nothing to find a "killer." If it matters enough to me. If I have a personal investment. I've done it before. Without police. Without help. Without witnesses?*

"And I waltz in here," Karen muttered to herself, "under my own steam! Hand myself over like a prize fool!"

Ariel took a deep breath, let it out, and lied. "You're wrong, Karen. He hasn't told me anything like that."

"I think he did, and he's got you believing it, too. He's that good! Ariel, the man convinced a sufficient number of jurors that he didn't kill his wife! He's so good, I wouldn't be surprised if he's convinced himself of the same thing."

That one was a jolt. "Why would you say that?"

"It's nearly impossible to believe, isn't it, that he could come across so plausibly otherwise?"

At that moment the only thing Ariel was sure of was that Karen couldn't be allowed to leave. "I'm telling you," she said, "that Jack's said nothing about you remotely like what you're imagining."

"All right, good. Fine! I'm glad to be wrong about that, but that doesn't really change anything else, does it?"

"Yes, well, I think you're wrong about what you think you witnessed, and about Mitch, too, okay? You said you've had emotional problems. I think you're—"

"Crazy? I'm thinking more clearly than you. You tell Jack I was here, and he'll guess I told you the truth. Look at the position that puts you in! You think he's going to let you walk around with that knowledge? A smart newswoman like you? You've been blinded by your feelings, I expect, but you've started to wonder now. He'll know that. Doubt's there; it'll fester. He's not going to sit around and watch that happen. You can't stay here, Ariel!"

"I'm not afraid of Jack."

"Then you're the one who's crazy." Karen's face set. "I'm through talking." She reached into her purse, and Ariel heard keys jangle, metal against metal. "You're coming with me."

Ariel gripped Karen's arm. "No, listen, we—"

The smaller woman reacted furiously. She slung off the restraining hand, her own gloved hand slamming into Ariel's nose in the process. It hurt. Quick sharp tears stung Ariel's eyes, and her fingers flew to the wetness already beginning to trickle. The red she saw then wasn't only blood. "Well, that tears it!" she said. "You . . ." She stopped, listening.

By Ariel's reckoning, it should have taken Jack another five, maybe ten minutes to get back there, and for a second she thought she'd imagined the sound of hurrying footsteps on the back porch, conjured it with the intensity of willing his return. The footsteps were real, and so was the sound of the lock turning.

Her back was to the door, her face toward Karen. Even as she turned, her mouth opening to form the words *Thank God!*, she caught the other woman's expression. It was naked panic. The words died on Ariel's lips.

Jack's breath was coming fast from what had to have been a headlong race and, despite the arctic cold that clung to him, he was sweating. He didn't look surprised. Even as he struggled to catch his breath, there was something like a smile on his face. Ariel saw the fury behind the grimace, and fear, too, she realized. Both were barely in check.

"Well, Karen," he said. "So it was you!"

Out of the corner of her eye Ariel saw Karen's hand rise as if to reach out to him, or fend him off. It faltered in midair before dropping to join the hand that clutched her purse. "Jack . . ." she said, and a world of desperate uncertainty was contained in the one syllable.

"All the way back here," he said, "I was trying to put together who it was who'd played such a trick on me. I couldn't think of a soul who'd do something like that but you."

"I heard about Mitch, Jack. So horrible! I got here as fast as—"

"What are you doing here, Karen? What have you been up to?"

Karen glanced at Ariel—to reassure herself of a protective witness? to beg not to be given away?—and stood straighter. She managed a shaky, quizzical smile. "I told you. I heard about . . . I just got here a few minutes ago. I was waiting for you. I know you must be surprised I came, but—"

"You don't know how many times I've imagined this moment," Jack interrupted, and on a long deep breath, his smile disappeared. "How I've waited for it."

Karen took a half step backward.

Ariel frowned. What exactly was happening here? Jack hadn't spoken to her, hadn't acknowledged her presence at all. Except for the briefest glance when he'd come through the door, an unreadable flick of the eye that might have been to check whether she'd been harmed or to see where he now stood in the equation, he'd ignored her completely.

"You must have wanted to get Ariel alone badly to go to so much trouble," he said. "Why is that?"

"Jack?" Ariel said. "She hasn't done—"

"Ariel, shut up! This is between Karen and me. It's time for you to go."

Ariel swallowed shock. She caught the flash of grim triumph that crossed Karen's face. *I told you so!* that look said. *And you thought he cared about you!*

"You're in the way," Jack said and reached into his coat pocket. "Sorry, but that's life." Ariel made no effort to catch whatever it was he then tossed at her. There was hardly a *click!* as the keys to his rental car hit the floor.

If he had assumed some alien form or begun speaking in tongues, Ariel couldn't have been more stupefied. She recognized the sudden urge to laugh for the hysteria it was. Everybody sure wanted her out of here!

Jack had turned his back on her, as if she were already gone. "What have you been filling her head with,

Karen?" he was saying. "She's not your problem, you know."

"I don't know what you're—"

"She's nobody. You're the problem. And your problem, Karen, is me."

"Jack," Ariel tried again and actually did laugh a little. Raw nerves. "Why don't you—"

"Get out!" He said it savagely. Ariel felt a sickening thud in her stomach as if she'd been kicked from the inside. Both Jack and Karen seemed, suddenly, far away, sucked into the wrong end of a telescope. She reached out for the back of a chair, the nearest solid, unmoving support.

"Jack, Jack . . ." the Lilliputian Karen said from her distance, "listen to me. There's no problem with me. There never was. There never will be. You don't know what you're saying. Don't think that. Don't say it."

"No," Ariel said. When neither of the others reacted, she realized she must only have thought it. She wasn't even sure what she'd meant by it. Karen looked as if she were shouting, but her voice came to Ariel as a hollow, remote echo. "I am not a problem! After all this time, you have to know that! Don't you understand that by now?"

Jack didn't answer. The silence rang in Ariel's ears, a bright, high-pitched vibration. The silence was smothering her, and when she saw Karen's lips move again, wordlessly, she thought she'd been struck deaf. It seemed as possible as anything else that was happening. Then Jack cracked his knuckles; the sound was perfectly audible. She blinked fiercely, shaking her head to clear her brain. He swam into clear focus. He was rigid, a stranger, as oblivious to her as if she'd ceased to exist. All his attention was focused on Karen, who, though she kept her distance, seemed almost to sway toward him as she said, "Jack? Why all this anger? This mistrust? Have you forgotten all the good things?"

His eyes darted from Karen's face to her hands, still clutching her purse, and back to her face, so quickly Ariel might have imagined it. To Ariel's utter confusion, his shoulders relaxed, and his expression softened. "I haven't forgotten," he said.

Karen went still.

"Have I been wrong all this time?" Jack asked quietly. "Wasted all this time we could have been together?" He slowly shook his head, and took a step toward her. "I've been a fool, haven't I, to believe . . . ?" He seemed to catch himself then, and he pressed his lips together into a rueful smile. "I've been a fool, haven't I?"

Karen swallowed. She looked as if she couldn't credit her ears, as if every word he spoke was a jewel beyond price.

"Come here, Karrie." Jack held out his arms. "Let's talk, just you and me."

The intimacy in his voice was excruciating to Ariel. Why was he doing this? *How about because he can?* Karen's explanation floated to the surface of her mind. *Because he is exceptionally good at it.*

"It's been too long, hasn't it? Since we've been together?"

Because he enjoys the power it gives him to be able to convince just about anybody of just about anything.

"Just the two of us, the way it used to be."

Ariel felt so disoriented, so sickened, she honestly didn't know if she imagined that menace lay beneath the words.

And Karen began to move toward him.

Ariel couldn't believe it. What she was seeing had to be a need that ran deeper than reason; deeper, even, than fear. The woman was actually letting herself be persuaded that she'd somehow been all wrong all along, that now everything was miraculously all right. Or . . . the question flitted through Ariel's mind: was it Karen who had been persuaded?

With a glance Ariel's way, Karen hesitated. "But . . . what about her?"

"She's leaving." Jack closed the space between himself and Karen, and wrapped her in his arms. The crown of her head came just to his chin. He looked straight at Ariel, and his eyes were ice, just as Karen had described from the night Eve died. "Why are you all bundled up?" he murmured into Karen's hair. "Hanging on to your bag like a little old lady?"

The disparity between those eyes and that voice was as unnerving a thing as Ariel had ever experienced. It came to her suddenly and certainly that if she left this house, Karen was a dead woman. She heard Jack's promise made that very afternoon. *God help the person who did this thing if I find him first. Or her.* As vividly, she remembered Karen's words, repeating the threat she claimed he'd made. *You tell anybody, ever, about this, and I'll kill you, too.* He intended to kill her, either because of what she'd done, or what she'd seen and, perhaps, told. Ariel didn't know which was true, and just then she didn't care.

"Jack!" she said. "You can't do this."

"Get out, Ariel."

"Can't do what?" Karen whispered. "Jack . . . ?"

"You can't do this," Ariel repeated. "I won't let you. This is not the way to handle it. Whatever she's done"

"What I've done?" Karen asked, and pulled away from Jack's shoulder. "What's she talking about?" She turned to Ariel. "What are you talking about?"

"For once, Ariel," Jack ordered, "do what you're told!"

"No, wait." Karen backed away, looking from Ariel to Jack. "Just wait a minute." She was still holding her purse, clutching it to her chest like a shield. Ariel could see the struggle behind her eyes: what she wanted to believe; what she'd said and couldn't take back. "You mean what I told you," she said to Ariel. "Is that what it is? You think he's going to hurt me?"

"What you told her?" Jack asked. "What was that, Karen?"

"It's nothing. I was . . . hysterical." Karen laughed, a girlish hiccup, dismissing all the accusations as if they were quibbles. "I was a little jealous, I admit it. I got it all wrong, just as you said, Ariel. Just forget all that! Jack's not going to do anything to me. Tell her, darling. Tell her you love me."

"I'm calling Frank Peterson," Ariel said. "Right now." She turned and strode to the phone.

"Who is that?" she heard Karen ask from behind her. "Who's she calling?" And then in a higher voice, "What are you doing? Jack!"

Receiver in hand, Ariel turned. Over Jack's shoulder, she saw Karen's face. Her mouth was an O of disbelief. Before Ariel could make sense of what was happening, Karen lunged toward Jack, and he slammed her against the wall, pinning her to it with his body. Grunting, the two of them writhed briefly in a struggle that from behind looked like some kind of manic coupling. Karen's face was a tortured grimace. She could have been a woman in the throes of passion.

The phone dropped with a clatter as Ariel flew toward the couple. "Stop it!" she cried just as the explosion came. It was shockingly loud. It was so totally unexpected, Ariel couldn't absorb the fact that there was even a gun between them, let alone that it had gone off. She had no time to wonder who, if anyone, had been hit before Jack jerked backward as if he'd been shoved.

A sharp hot stink filled the room. Ariel couldn't hear herself moaning above the ringing in her ears. She plastered her palms over them, almost tripping over an ottoman as she stumbled backward. She was righting herself when Jack took another step back, panting heavily, staring at Karen, whose eyes were wide with shock, who, as if she were overcome with curiosity, looked down at her chest. Ariel only glimpsed the ugly dark wound before Karen's hand pressed against it. She looked as though she were taking an oath. Blood began to seep through her fingers. And then, slowly and oddly gracefully, Karen slid down the wall. Her eyes fluttered. When her body made contact with the floor, she crumpled and lay still.

Jack glanced Ariel's way, hesitating before he knelt to touch Karen's neck, and then it was the briefest of touches. He wiped his hand against his pants leg as he straightened and turned away. His face was twisted with emotion that could have been anguish or disgust. It was purely her imagination that the small gun in his hand was still smoking.

"You stubborn fool!" he said. "You should've left when I told you to! Why the hell didn't you leave when I told you to?"

39

ARIEL'S KNEES HAD TURNED TO SPONGE. IT TOOK ALL her strength to remain upright. She couldn't take her eyes off the gun. "What?" she asked stupidly.

Jack took a step toward her. "There's blood on your face."

Ariel moved backward, crossing her fists on her chest.

He halted. "What did she do to you?"

Ariel merely shook her head.

"Come here to me!"

When she didn't move, his eyes narrowed and then followed hers to the gun in his hand. "The question, I guess, is what did she *say* to you?"

"Do something for her!" Ariel cried.

"Do something for her?" he repeated. He glanced at Karen's body. It was slumped over, and her face was turned away. The bullet hole, too, was hidden. Except for her stillness, she could have been a vagrant, peacefully asleep in a doorway. Jack's mouth turned down as he faced Ariel again. "What is it you want me to do? She's not Lazarus, and I wouldn't raise her if I could."

"But are you sure? We need to call—"

"There's no urgency, Ariel."

Ariel had no concept of what was in her face at that moment, but it must have been horror.

"What?" Jack said. "You think I should be sorry? I should be wallowing in remorse? She killed my wife. She killed Mitch. For the longest twenty minutes of my life tonight, I was terrified that I'd be too late, that you were dead, too. I told you once that if she were ever to try to harm you, I'd kill her and I wouldn't think twice about it. I meant it."

Ariel was standing beside a wing chair; she stepped behind it, grasping the leather with fingers that were almost too cold to bend. "But she didn't—"

"She didn't manage to kill you—yet? Why do you think she was carrying Mitch's gun around? Who do you suppose she meant to use it on?"

"Mitch's gun?" Ariel frowned. She hadn't seen where the gun came from. Its ownership at that moment was more distraction than she could deal with. "*She* had the gun?"

"*What?*" Jack gave his head an incredulous shake. "Yes, Ariel, she had the gun."

"How could you know that?"

"I didn't *know*—I hoped to hell I was wrong—but I saw the way she kept hanging on to that purse. And when I hugged her . . . I could feel the thing."

"She might've had it," Ariel said, "for protection."

"Protection against whom? She killed Mitch, Ariel, and then she calmly straightened and cleaned as if there'd been a party. While he lay dead on the floor, she pawed through his belongings and she found his gun—the gun I looked for and couldn't find and hoped to God he'd sold or gotten rid of somewhere along the way. He didn't. This is it. She took the gun, Ariel, along with her other little souvenirs, and she brought it back here tonight to use on you! Why do you think she arranged for me to be gone? Why do you think she was wearing gloves? Why did she fight me for the bloody gun? All I wanted to do was get it out of her sick hands!"

"But she didn't use it. She was here plenty long enough to use it if she meant to."

"Evidently, she was here plenty long enough to twist your mind into . . ." Jack made a sound of disgust. "She told you I killed Eve, is that it? And what about Mitch? Am I supposed to have done that, too? Well, my darling Ariel, she lied."

"Why?"

"Why did she kill him? I do not know, but the fact that she's here in Boulder . . ." He waved the gun. "The fact that she had this thing ought to be enough for you." His closed his eyes then, and rubbed them tiredly. "Evidently, it's not. Believe whatever you want," he said. "I'm not going back to square one with you. I'm not going through that again."

Ariel looked at Karen's inert body. It looked pitifully small, and the jaunty knit cap was askew. She'd seemed so frightened of Jack, yet she'd been as helpless in his hands as an addict. "She said you'd kill her," Ariel murmured.

"Did she? That's one thing she told the truth about, then. Look, I don't want to hear about it. It all comes down to trust, Ariel. Either you do or you don't."

Ariel couldn't deny that. She felt frozen to the spot.

Jack's face hardened. "Well," he said, "you'll make this next meeting with Peterson and his pals interesting, won't you?"

"Jack . . ."

He raised the gun, caught the tensing of Ariel's body, and laughed, soundlessly and mirthlessly. Then, with exaggerated care, he laid the gun on the nearest surface, the ottoman that had tripped Ariel up. Holding out his empty hands, he said, "All gone. Excuse me while I use the phone."

He was lifting the receiver when Ariel moved out from behind her chair. She crossed to where he was and put her finger on the disconnect button. "I'm sorry," she said. "It's just that she seemed so frightened of you. She seemed . . . sane."

"And I seemed otherwise?" He moved her finger.

"You were like a different person. You were so ugly."

"I wanted you out of harm's way." He punched in 911. "I wanted her attention off you and on me. I thought you'd have wits enough to catch on to what . . . Hello," he said into the phone. The call was short. When he'd hung up, he let out a long, ragged sigh. He stood there staring at nothing, looking defeated. "So, what are you going to tell them?"

"I told *her* I didn't believe her."

He looked at Ariel then, curiously. "Did you? Why?"

"Because I wanted to believe you."

"Was it that hard?"

"She was credible, Jack. You of all people have to admit that. I may have been tempted to fall for her line, but you fell for her. And you'd have been a lot more credible yourself if you hadn't kept hanging on to that gun."

He was quite serious when he said, "I could still be lying, you know, the biggest ruse yet, to make sure you're on my side when the cops get here."

"You could have shot me dead and said Karen did it; then you wouldn't have to worry about what I might say."

"I didn't think of that."

"It's not too late."

"Ariel," Jack said, "what am I going to do with you?" He held out his arms and, feeling as if she were laying down a very heavy burden, Ariel started into them.

Later, she went over those next seconds so many times that, in the end, she couldn't be sure of what had actually happened or what she thought had happened— or what she desperately wished had happened.

The noise of the gunshot was less real a memory, strangely, than was the jolt of Jack's body and the astonishment on his face. She learned afterward that the bullet had barely grazed his shoulder. A half inch to the right, and it would have missed him altogether. The second blast, a wild shot that shattered a kitchen window, came before Ariel could register the first. Jack had already moved in front of her when the third shot hit home.

He didn't look one last time into her eyes. There were no final words. His head, bloodied, fell forward, and he went down, and Ariel went down with him. She was sprawled on her knees, her body sheltering his. She looked across the room to where a white-faced, drunken-looking Karen knelt.

Both her hands gripped the gun. It was braced on the ottoman. She moved it ever so slightly, and it was aimed, more or less, at Ariel's head. It listed to the side. Karen steadied it, held it for what was probably no longer than a second, and then, fumbling, turned it around. There was no way Ariel could have reached her in time to stop her even if she'd tried. Karen's aim was more accurate close up.

40

THE *OPEN FILE* STUDIO was dark, DESERTED FOR THE weekend. Henry stood some distance from the windows of the edit bay, but he could see Ariel clearly. Bathed in the greenish light of the equipment at which she was working, she looked like some ghostly aviator, soloing through the night. She was staring at one of the monitors, her arms crossed over her chest, unaware, he was sure, that there was anyone left in the building but her. She hadn't moved for several minutes. He hoped she'd finally finished editing the wretched damned episode.

He laid the correspondence he'd stayed to complete on his assistant's desk. It hadn't been urgent, and he had no reason to put off leaving any longer. He sighed. He wanted to go in and sit with Ariel; if not work with her, then keep her company. He knew she wouldn't welcome company, his in particular. He was alive, and Jack Spurling was dead, and the videotaped monument to his stamped-out life was Ariel's baby, hers and hers alone. He was afraid it was becoming her obsession.

She'd let no one in on this story from the beginning.

A month now? Longer? She'd let no one near any of the edited footage during the five days she'd been closeted in the bay, which was where she'd stayed when she wasn't plugged into the phone in her office or dashing out for some related interview. Such free rein was unusual for a comparative neophyte, but this was Ariel's story. You couldn't argue with that. If she hadn't sold it here, she could have sold it anywhere. How often is a news correspondent confidante to a notorious shooting victim— and the only living eyewitness? Obviously, she'd said nothing but "Sorry, no comment" to every reporter who'd stuck a mike in her face.

Henry had called her on Sunday, the minute he'd heard the news about the double killing. She was still in Boulder or en route home. By the time he finally reached her that night, he'd learned that she was present when Spurling and this Verlyn woman were shot, and he was worried sick. Ariel had thanked him, assuring him that she was okay but too tired to talk. She'd see him at the studio, she said, the next morning. Henry was surprised. He'd figured she'd take a few days off. He was even more surprised when she had announced that the Spurling piece would air in one week.

Every day Ariel had come in early and left late. The only day she'd missed was when she'd flown back to Colorado, taking a film crew with her. She'd guarded every aspect of the piece like a miser, reminding him more and more as the days went by of the person she'd been back before she'd lost her memory: closed off, grim, and brittle as glass.

She was down to the wire now; Monday night and airtime loomed. But Henry sensed that, probably unconsciously, she didn't want to finish the piece, that as long as she held on to it, she somehow held on to

Spurling. He ached for her. He didn't know which was worse, missing someone you'd never see again or someone you were forced to see every day.

Hardly aware he was doing it, he'd drifted toward the door of the edit bay. He would just stop to say good night, he told himself. Her back was to him, and she looked totally absorbed; he hesitated, afraid of startling her.

"Come in, Henry," Ariel said without turning. She reached out to touch a button, and the image at which she'd been staring fractured into demented reverse action. She looked up and smiled faintly. "Got a minute? I'd appreciate your opinion on this."

Henry sat down, stealing a careful glance at her face as he did. She looked impassive. He'd like to have believed her feelings for Spurling hadn't gone as deep as he'd thought; his gut knotted with certainty that the opposite was true. "You about done with the rough?" he asked.

"I've been thinking for the last two hours that it's too cut and dried; now I'm convinced its heart is bleeding. Pure melodrama."

"You don't have to supply the drama, God knows." Henry braced his elbows on the chair arms and leaned over his clasped hands. "I heard you did have to get pretty inventive, though."

"Inventive?"

"Why no tape on Spurling after all this time? Not even audio?"

"He wouldn't let me; it was a stipulation he made. No tape, no staff involvement."

Henry raised an eyebrow.

"And the truth, Henry, as I imagine you know, is that it had ceased being a story to me."

"Yes, well . . . Yeah." The videotape had rewound back to staticky leader. When she reached to hit another button, the emerald on her finger flashed in the light. Henry had noticed the ring first thing on Monday. He supposed the fact that it was on her right hand should have made him feel less sick every time he saw it. "I didn't expect that you'd end up *doing* the story," he said. "Why did you? Catharsis?"

"Necessity. I owe it to him. He'd still be alive if it weren't for me."

Henry frowned and grew uneasier but let it go by. "Let's see what you've got," he said.

The intro had been shot outside a rambling ranch house that looked as if it was in the middle of nowhere. It was the father-in-law's place, Henry assumed, where Spurling had been killed. The weather suited the tone of the story; the sky was smothered in ominous low-lying clouds and the ground was blanketed by snow.

Ariel wore black: coat, boots, and gloves. Her nose was red with the cold, and she was forced to press her hair to her skull to keep it from blowing into her face. She looked composed. Henry wondered what that had cost her; he wondered what returning to that house had cost her.

"Two years ago," she said into the camera, "John Spurling—Jack to those who knew him—was a successful Los Angeles businessman; his wife, Eve, a beautiful young socialite. They'd been married for nine years when, with a group of friends, they chartered a motor yacht, the *Princessa Ora*, and set sail for a holiday. Eve Spurling never returned. There were no witnesses to her drowning, and her body was never recovered. Her husband was tried for manslaughter. It ended in a hung jury, and the decision was made not to retry.

"When *The Open File* decided to follow up on Jack Spurling's story a few weeks ago, we expected to profile a man in a highly unusual social and legal limbo. He hadn't been proven guilty, but neither had he been acquitted. He could have been retried at any time. What we did not expect was that, by the time our show aired, Jack Spurling would be dead."

Ariel turned to look at the house beside which she stood. Henry had the absolute conviction that she took that second to force down doubt about what she was doing. He'd bet anything they'd gotten this in one take, flat.

"This Boulder, Colorado, house belonged to Jack Spurling's father-in-law, retired businessman Mitchell Winters. Mr. Winters was murdered here a week and a half ago, and it was here, too"—she faced the camera again—"that Jack Spurling was shot to death two days later. I was beside him at the time."

Ariel had cut then to what was obviously home video. She'd killed the sound, and she'd left in glitches, like the camera's jiggle as it had been locked into position. Both were clever moves, investing the silent little twelve-second scene with an innocent poignancy. There wouldn't be one amateur cameraperson in the country who couldn't relate to it.

Framed was what looked like a patio. Spurling, dressed in white shorts and shirt, relaxed at an umbrella table on which a tennis racquet lay. His wife, presumably having set up the camera, hurried into view. Her mouth moved as she spoke to someone out of camera range, and the lenses of her dark glasses glinted in the sunlight. She looked young, a California girl, tanned and blond, without a care in the world. She was laughing as she rested her chin on the crown of her husband's head, hugging him from behind. Just as he reached up to cradle her cheek, she made a "come here" gesture, and a distinguished-looking older man appeared, pulling a dark-haired woman by the hand. He was smiling; she was rolling her eyes in mock exasperation.

"Jack Spurling," Ariel, voice over, named them, "and Eve Spurling. Her father, Mitchell Winters, and her friend and fellow passenger on the *Princessa Ora*, Karen Lucas Verlyn. All four are dead; two, we know—Jack and Karen herself—by her hand."

Ariel hit freeze frame. "I couldn't find any footage with Karen's husband, but by the same criterion, he should be there, too. That's just my opinion at this point, but we'll know for sure once they exhume his body."

"They're exhuming based on . . . ?"

"The information I gave them and the cooperation of his daughter. She didn't like Karen. She didn't like some scenes she'd witnessed between her father and Karen or a couple of things he'd alluded to shortly before his death. There was no autopsy. Exhumation's planned for next week; I'm fighting to get it pushed up."

"Where'd you come up with the home movie?"

"A box in Jack's office. He'd put my name on it, and a woman who worked for him found it and called me. Eve Spurling was into 'capturing the moment' earlier in the marriage. She took a lot of pictures, video and still."

Ariel pressed a button, and they got a last glimpse of the happy quartet before a cut to Jack Spurling's face. He was no longer laughing; he was being escorted into a courtroom by his lawyer.

For the next eleven and a quarter minutes Henry watched a combination of still shots, old news film and new footage, tightly scripted stand-ups and narration and interviews shot aboard the *Princessa Ora,* at Jack's shop, at Karen's mother's home, at Boulder police headquarters. It was a painstaking balance between pathos and restraint. It was also a scrupulously objective presentation of Spurling's and his former lover's versions of what had taken place prior to the night they'd both died. One version was true, the other, consequently, an aberration, and one was no less chillingly possible than the other.

Henry covered his smile, one of pure relief. Although he itched to refine a few rough edges (he would, by God, before it was over!), it was damned fine reporting, dramatically pieced together; he wondered who she'd learned it from.

The closing had been shot in the studio: Ariel seated, facing the camera, her expression serious as she began with a re-ask.

"Did Jack Spurling coldbloodedly allow his wife to drown and then threaten his lover if she told what she'd seen? Did he stab Mitchell Winters because Winters had learned the truth, and did he return to Winters's house last Saturday night fully intending to kill the woman from whom he'd learned it?

"As for Karen Verlyn, it could be argued—in fact, it has been argued—that she fired in self-defense or retaliation or fear, and that, wounded and confused, she shot herself unintentionally. I don't think so."

The camera came in for a close-up as Ariel said, "During my investigation, I came to regard Mr. Spurling as a friend. We, therefore, considered whether it would be appropriate for one of my colleagues to handle his story. We opted otherwise, and what you've seen tonight, I believe, is unbiased." She smiled slightly. "So far.

"I am convinced by the facts I reported as well as the tragedy I witnessed that Jack Spurling was the victim of a fixation as deadly as the gun Karen Verlyn ultimately used to kill him. She deliberately punished the man who wouldn't have her, and she deliberately chose not to live without him. Let me be clear: this is commentary. It does not reflect any position except my own."

After a moment's pause as if for thought, Ariel said, "One

last comment. As you have seen and heard, Ms. Verlyn's husband died just two months ago. His death was sudden and unexpected, and it occurred after his wife allegedly confessed to him that she had killed Eve Spurling.

"Barry Verlyn's body will be exhumed and autopsied this week. If he did not die of natural causes, his murder will almost surely be laid at his wife's door, and we will be one step closer to closing the file on an innocent man."

The monitor faded to black, and Henry let a heavily weighted minute go by before he said, "Hmm."

" 'Hmm' okay or 'hmm' rot?"

"It isn't rot."

"You thought the whole thing was going to be a testimonial, didn't you? It would be if I could get away with it."

"Yeah, well, you left yourself hanging out without a net there at the end. No way will it air unless you tone it down."

Matter-of-factly, Ariel said, "That close is a starting point for negotiation."

"Have you given any thought to what's going to happen if you're wrong?"

"No."

Henry's lips folded into a thin unhappy line. "This woman . . . you have any theories why she killed Winters?"

"Theories?" She pinched her lower lip between thumb and forefinger, absently toying with it. Henry noticed that her fingers shook. "I've got theories out the wazoo. What I want are answers."

"You'll get one when Verlyn's body's exhumed. Some answers you're not going to get, ever. Tell me why you think she killed Winters."

"A fact-finding mission that went awry."

Henry waited, and after a moment prodded. "Yes?"

"Karen was afraid Jack knew about her, that Verlyn

might've told him. She called Jack to feel him out. He said he didn't give anything away, but the fact that he was suddenly more receptive to seeing her—as much as she wanted to believe that—must've sent up her antennae. She had to be sure, to see how to play it.

"She knew how tight Jack and Mitch were. If Jack knew, she reasoned—erroneously—then Mitch knew, too. She went to Boulder to find out, and, somehow, she gave herself away. Maybe she let slip how she felt about Jack. Mitch put two and two together. He guessed what happened to his daughter. She killed him."

"Ariel, if she didn't feel safe showing herself to Spurling, why would she with Winters?"

"I'm convinced Mitch once had an affair with her, and unlike Jack, didn't get over it. She figured she could handle him. Karen's will was . . . indomitable. I think she truly couldn't conceive of anybody else's not just bending before it."

"That's . . ." Henry hesitated. "Wild," he finished kindly.

"Wild?" Ariel said with a lift of eyebrows. "You didn't see her face when I said I didn't believe her. You didn't see a note she left in Jack's house. She snuck into his house. She left a note in his bed. 'It's our time now. . . .' " Ariel was quoting, Henry assumed. Her voice trailed off.

Forcing his mind away from the circumstances under which the note must have been found, wondering how much longer he could stand this, Henry recalled that there'd been nothing in the story about a note. He figured he knew why. "You know, I suppose, that the note actually came from her?"

"I didn't take it to be analyzed. At the time we found it I wasn't thinking in terms of proof, and I don't know what became of it."

"Was that all it said?"

"No. The note made it clear that I was expendable if I was in her way. When she saw me there in Boulder with Jack, she decided I was."

"What do you think she had in mind for you Saturday night?"

"I know what she had in mind. She mentioned a cabin on Mitch's property that she wanted me to go to with her, to be 'safe from Jack' while she gave me all the lurid details. I found the cabin Sunday morning. There was an old, dry well there. It had been covered, but the cover was lying on the ground, and it hadn't been there long. There was snow under it and no snow on top of it and fresh *small* footprints around it." Ariel's mouth twisted. "It was all ready for me. One bullet—or two; her aim wasn't great—and into the well. No body to worry about, no explanations to make. It would've been months or years before I was found—if ever."

"She thought Spurling wouldn't notice you'd disappeared?"

"Not her problem. If she'd gotten me out of that house before Jack got back—and, Lord knows, she tried—nobody would've known she was anywhere in the vicinity. She was the woman who wasn't there. If she was staying in a hotel or motel in town, she wasn't registered in her own name."

"What about the rental she was driving?"

"I suppose that was in her name—she couldn't avoid that—but the point is, nobody would've been looking for her. Nobody knew she was there. Even Jack didn't believe she had anything to do with Mitch's death."

Ariel reached to snap on the overhead light, wincing at the brightness, and there was a moment of awkward silence. Henry shifted in his seat. "You did a good job here," he said, "and a tough one."

She hit a button, and, abruptly, her image on the monitor shrank to a dot. "But you still think I'm wrong about Jack."

Henry fervently wished he could say that he thought the man was guilty as sin and got just what he deserved. "No," he said.

"No?"

Henry shifted again. Gruffly, he said, "It was Winters's gun, right? And the woman had it in her possession." He shrugged, palms up.

"Yes, it was Mitch's gun—it was registered to him— but I couldn't actually swear that it was Karen who had it. I couldn't see where it came from."

"It had to be her. Spurling couldn't have brought any gun on the plane with him. If it had been there in the house, the police would probably have confiscated it when they searched. But say they didn't. Say they missed it and Spurling found it; I seriously doubt that he—a murder suspect—would've had it in his pocket when he went to the police station."

"He couldn't have found it," Ariel said thoughtfully. "I was with him every second we were in that house." She was picking at the skin by her thumbnail, Henry noticed; it looked raw. He itched to stop her. "Is that the only reason?" she asked.

Henry sighed. "One other little thing. You'd probably be dead."

Ariel stopped mutilating her thumb and stared.

"If Spurling was the stone-cold murderer the Verlyn woman claimed," Henry said, "and he'd been after her to shut her up, he'd have made sure she was dead, even if it took a second bullet. And as for you . . . you were vacillating, halfway convinced he was guilty, and ready to call the cops if he didn't. What was to stop him from shooting you both and saying he found you that way?" His voice softened. "You were right about him, Ariel. Thank God."

"If I'd trusted him when it mattered, he'd never have put that gun down where Karen could get at it."

Henry cleared his throat, considered what was on the tip of his tongue to say, and thought better of it. "Ariel, that's enough for tonight," he said instead. "Go home. Rest. Forget this for a while. Rent a Peter Sellers film or . . . anything. The Three Stooges, for crying out loud."

Ariel continued what she was doing, straightening the work surface. She tossed him an offhanded ghost of a smile. She'd stopped listening.

"When have you slept?" Henry persisted. "When have you eaten?"

"What did you think of that cut from Peterson's . . . from the Boulder detective's interview? Would it work better to have—"

"Ariel!" Henry placed his hands on Ariel's, capturing them. "Stop it. You're going to make yourself sick."

Ariel looked at their hands and then at Henry. "Stop mothering me, Henry. I'm fine."

"Oh, you're dandy! Your hands shake. Your eyes look like black holes in a white sheet. I'm not trying to mother you; I'm trying to be your friend."

"The friendliest thing you can do is leave me alone. You can't fix this!"

"Nobody can fix it! It's unfixable. The only thing you can do is face it and suffer and let it go. The last time we talked, I told you I felt like slapping sense into you. I may do it yet. You didn't kill the man. You're not responsible for his death. You can't change the fact that he's dead. Grieve . . . fine! Cry. Scream. Get mad. Break things. But don't break yourself."

Ariel's forehead lowered, and she set her mouth, and

for a split second, Henry thought what he was seeing was rage. Then, suddenly, her head began to tremble uncontrollably. The muscles of her neck tautened, fighting to control the spasm, and he felt her hands clench to fists. She moaned. It was an ugly guttural sound, like something being torn loose inside her.

"Let it go," he said, "before you break."

In a voice he would never have recognized as hers, she said, "Leave . . . Me . . . Alone!"

"No." It was all he could do to restrain her fists. The skin in the deep crevices between her eyes turned red with her efforts to free her hands. She looked as if she wanted to pound him. She had already lost the battle. Her eyes filled. Her face twisted, and the tears began to fall. For a few seconds she made no sound at all, and then, against the last vestiges of her will, the awful low keening began.

Henry pulled her fast against him and, because he couldn't think of anything at all to say—and because his own throat was too tight to speak if he could—he simply held her.

He'd rarely seen Ariel cry. He could count the times on one hand, maybe one finger. It was a very long time before she grew still against him, and even then, neither spoke. With one hand, he fumbled in his pocket and found his handkerchief. Without lifting her head, she took it. When she'd blown her nose and dried her face, she lay slack against him, depleted.

"Crying makes me feel sick," she eventually murmured, her voice thick. "I hate it."

"Are you going to be sick?" he asked seriously.

"No."

He patted the back of her head, and she sighed, mumbling something unintelligible. She sounded like a child about to drop off to sleep.

"Listen, Ariel, last time we talked I said some things"

"We both did. Just don't stop being my friend."

"I was your friend a long time before . . . anything else. I've had more practice at it."

Finally, sighing with exhaustion, she lifted her face from his chest. "Don't worry," he said, "I'll keep practicing till I get it right."

The buzzer that sounded then startled them both. Henry recovered first. "Front door," he said. "You expecting anybody?"

Ariel shook her head, and Henry left, returning shortly with her grandfather in tow. He was mauling the knot of his tie, dragging it away from his neck, and chuckling. He sobered at the sight of her. "Lord, baby," he said. "You look like somebody jerked a knot in you."

"Somebody jerked one out," Ariel said.

He studied her face worriedly. "You need nourishment," he decided. "Get your things. You're comin' for supper."

"Says who?" She smiled a little, and hugged him. Fingering the lapel of yet another new sportcoat, she said, "Hey! Nice threads. The accessory's a little iffy, though."

"What's wrong with it?" B.F. set the Braves cap he wore at a jauntier angle. "Got it from Bobby Cox himself. Come on, now, time to hit the road."

"Not tonight, B.F. I'm tired. And I need to get home and feed Jessie."

"We'll pick her up on the way to my place. Sarge's making his special beef roast; she can have some. Come on, Henry. You, too."

"Thanks anyway," Henry said, "but—"

B.F. scowled at both of them. "You two mad at each other?"

"Not for a minute." Henry jammed his hands in his pockets. "I just need to get on—"

"Henry," Ariel interrupted. "I'd like it if you would. Really. You said you'd keep practicing. . . ."

"So I did." Their eyes held for a long moment. "And 'practice makes perfect,' right?"

" 'Nothing is perfect. There are lumps in it.' "

"Bless God," B.F. said, "she's quotin' again. Let's get out of here."

Ariel was shouldering her purse and briefcase when she had an awful thought. "This will be just us and Sarge, right? You don't have any company coming?"

"Like who?"

"Like Sissy Hardaway."

"Sissy's not in the picture anymore."

Ariel frowned. Had the blasted woman dumped B.F.? Blown him off for a richer man? A younger man? She'd find her and tear her hair out by the hennaed roots. "What happened?"

"Woman was too mature for me. Nice—sweet as she could be, and good-lookin', too—but too confounded set in her ways. I could see boredom down the road, you know what I mean?" He sighed and trundled toward the door. "Sometimes, you just got to trust your instincts."

Ariel reached for the light switch. "Yeah," she said. The room went dark, and no one saw her first genuine smile in a long time. "Poor old Sissy."

JUDY MERCER

Praise for
Fast Forward

"One of the best suspense novels of the
year....inspired, provocative....makes John Grisham's
thrillers seem like the work of a rank amateur...."
—Les Robert,
Cleveland *Plain Dealer*

And look for

Double Take
and
Split Image

Available now in paperback

**POCKET BOOKS
PROUDLY PRESENTS**

Blind Spot

Judy Mercer

**Coming in hardcover from
Pocket Books**

**The following is a preview of
Blind Spot. . . .**

One

GOOD NEWS DOESN'T COME AT 4:00 A.M.

For those unlucky enough to lie wakeful, that silent predawn black is a lonesome place. Worries nibble at the mind. Old regrets come home to roost. As sleep eludes, just beyond grasp, every minute stretches. The clock ticks. Fears that would seem foolish by day take hold of the imagination and grow.

It isn't the dead of night, 4:00 A.M., but it can, nonetheless, be deadly. Ask a nurse on the graveyard shift. Ask any priest. It is the hour, you'll learn, when the body's purchase on life is at its weakest, when those sapped by age or illness will often, finally, surrender.

It is an hour when the earth itself is unreliable. Predawn—historically, quirkily, and inexplicably— is favored by earthquakes.

And when the phone rings in the last dark hours of the night, chances are it's bringing trouble.

It wasn't the phone that woke Ariel Gold at 4:06 A.M., and it wasn't the rumble of a quake. It was, in the first disoriented second, just as shocking. She'd been deeply asleep. She'd gone to bed alone. She no longer was. Something cold bumped against her cheek. She jerked awake, still half-mired in a nonsensical dream. The noise she heard then was a low, anxious murmur, so close it was like a moist breath on her face, so close it almost stopped her heart. That was when the phone rang.

Later, she questioned whether she could have the sequence of events right: that her dog nudged her awake *before* the phone actually rang. How was that possible? Did telephones emit some sound undetected by human ears in the split second before the ring? Was it coincidence? Or did animals have an early warning system for tragedy on the way? The time came when Ariel stopped questioning. Weirder things were entirely, proveably possible. Whatever the big German shepherd may or may not have sensed, tragedy had already happened.

"Hello?" Ariel said, her voice hardly audible over Jessie's panting. She stroked the dog's neck, invisible in the dark, but warm, softly furred and familiar. "Hello?" she asked louder. "Who is it?"

She heard the *thwack!* of a receiver being

dropped, banging against something, and she snapped on the bedside lamp, squinting against the brightness of the hundred-watt bulb. This wasn't a wrong number; she was somehow sure of that. It wasn't a creep of the heavy breathing variety either, although Ariel could, faintly, hear the sound of someone breathing. The receiver was evidently retrieved, for the breathing grew loud. It was ragged, the desperate, greedy mouth-breathing of a woman in labor.

"Ariel? Oh, God! Ariel?"

The voice was a woman's. Thin. At the very edge of a scream. It took Ariel a second to place it. She'd never heard this particular woman sound anything but serene, even detached. "Laya?" she asked. "Is that you?"

Ariel heard a whimper, and then, faintly, "Help me!"

"Laya? What's happened?"

Horribly, Ariel's friend had begun to moan. *She's been attacked!* Ariel thought. *Raped.* "What's happened?" she cried, but the moaning, a litany of pain, overrode her. "Hurts!" Ariel made out, and the words "come" and "please."

"Stop it," she ordered, "and tell me what's happened."

Laya made a strangling sound and then swallowed noisily, more than once. It sounded as though she were forcing down stones. "I can't," she said. "I can't—"

"You can't what?"

"See. I can't see!"

"What do you mean?"

"Don't you understand English?" The hysteria broke loose then. A flood. "I can't see! I can't see anything! Ariel, I'm blind!"

Two

THE KINDEST THING THAT COULD BE SAID ABOUT the hospital's waiting room was that it was neutral. The muted Muzak piped in through some unseen speaker was vanilla: white noise, par for Otis ups and downs. The only other occupant of the room was a spent-looking middle-aged man. He was snoring quietly, mouth ajar, emitting delicate little puffs as if he were blowing dandelions, and his head had dropped back at an angle that was sure to mean a crick when he woke up. Ariel had seen him earlier down in the emergency room comforting a woman on a stretcher. A crick, she thought, might be the least of his troubles. He had her sympathy. She didn't know much about her first thirty-two years, but the last one had packed more trouble than most people faced in a lifetime.

It was 6:05 A.M. The sun was presumably up,

but since there were no windows in the room, it was impossible to know what the new day looked like. Ariel was reluctant to take even a short walk outside for fear a doctor might come looking for her. Paramedics had turned Laya over to the emergency room staff over an hour ago. An hour and twenty minutes ago. Ariel had no inkling of her condition, and she still had no inkling of what had taken place before that horrifying call.

Her race to Laya's apartment had been little short of suicidal. She'd beaten the paramedics, whom she'd phoned en route. The front door had been closed and locked. Ariel used the key she knew was kept beneath a particular potted plant outside the door, a fishtail palm that reigned over a small, carefully tended oasis of palms and succulents. The plants were among Laya's few personal indulgences. Two others Ariel knew of were her cat and, idiosyncratically, a love of fine fountain pens. Otherwise, the tall, handsome black woman traveled lightly.

She was a yogi: Ariel's teacher as well as her friend, a woman always in possession of herself and, Ariel was sometimes convinced, the secrets of the universe as well. Laya seemed unaware of her quiet charisma and unconcerned about her looks, which were arresting. (Ariel once remarked on her resemblance to Poitier. "Poiret?" Laya had teased. "Wrong accent," Ariel had said, straightfaced.) There was a trace of the West Indies in Laya's cadences, as elusive as its origins. Her graying hair was left to its natural tendencies and cropped within an inch of her skull. Her wardrobe was utilitarian—the comfortable leggings, T-shirts, and sweats of a yoga teacher—or, on occasion, exotic—some flowing garment likely to be plucked from a secondhand rack.

Her home was as spartan as a transient's. This morning, in the dense gray predawn, it had appeared abandoned.

Ariel had had trouble with the key. When at last she'd gotten the door open, she'd called out. There'd been no answer. Reassuring herself that if anyone had been here—a burglar? a rapist? (a lover who'd turned violent? Who knew? There were whole chunks of Laya's life about which Ariel knew nothing)—they were long gone. She had hurried into the living room. It was dark. She was feeling for a light switch when she heard music, jazz, turned very low. It was coming, she thought, from the bedroom. So was a faint shaft of light.

At first she saw no one but Arthur, Laya's fat marmalade cat. He was in the middle of an unmade bed, a tightly tucked, unhappy-looking orange mound. Normally the most lethargic of animals, his ears were back and his eyes watchful. His tail switched once, an emphatic arc.

Then Ariel spotted Laya.

She was on the other side of the bed, on the floor with the phone beside her. She was in a sitting position, slumped against the wall, dressed in an oversized T-shirt. Her eyes were closed. She was inert. Ariel was sure for a blank bright moment that she was dead. Then a sprawled leg twitched, the tiniest contraction.

Calling her name, Ariel rushed to kneel beside her. Laya didn't stir. The eyes weren't just closed, Ariel saw; they appeared to be swollen shut. Both dark cheeks bore long scratches. In the stingy glow of the bedside lamp, Ariel could see the vertical welts below each eye: not deep, she thought—the blood beading and beginning already to dry—but angry. There were red smears on the front of the T-shirt.

Ariel reached out, unsure what to do. "Laya!" she said sharply. There was no response at all. She touched her fingers to Laya's neck. The flesh was cool, but the pulse beat—it seemed to her—strongly. Gritting her teeth, she lifted an eyelid. The eye was hideously inflamed, as if it were bleeding internally. Very gently she let the lid close. There were no other obvious signs of injury. She stood and looked around. Other than an overturned desk chair, there was no sign that anything of a violent nature had taken place.

Ariel pulled the comforter from the bed, dislodging Arthur, who thumped gracefully to the floor and vanished. She was tucking the cover around Laya when she became aware of the sound of running water. Careful to touch nothing, she went into the bathroom. Using a tissue to handle it, she turned off the cold water tap.

Laya was as oblivious to the noisy arrival of the

paramedics as she'd been to Ariel. "Shock," guessed one of the EMTs after a swift glance.

It wasn't until they were lifting her insensible friend onto the gurney that Ariel noticed the small plastic bottle in Laya's hand. It contained eye-drops, a generic over-the-counter brand. She pocketed the bottle.

All the way to the hospital, pushing her minivan and risking a ticket to keep the ambulance in sight, Ariel speculated. Because she couldn't even begin to imagine what had happened, every theory she came up with was less likely than the one before. None made sense.

Laya, she told herself, must have simply scratched her cornea. Corneas. Badly. Very badly. *Idiotic!* Ariel pushed her glasses more securely onto her nose. She didn't wear them often, but she hadn't taken the time to put in her contacts. *Contacts.* Did Laya wear them? Maybe the old, nonair-permeable kind that stuck to your eyeballs like glue if you fell asleep with them in? And when you tried to peel them off . . . more *idiotic.* Well, then . . . she'd gotten soap or some cosmetic into her eyes. *Soap? Cosmetic? Her eyes looked flayed!* An allergic reaction? No. An accident . . . some house-hold cleaning solution. *Laya was cleaning house at four in the morning?* Maybe. It wasn't impossible. And didn't every bleach and detergent and polish caution against contact with the eyes? But surely, if that was what happened, Laya would still have been frantic—hysterical as she was on the phone—

not . . . comatose. Out of it. Or whatever she was. Just . . . gone. *Where?* It was then that Ariel remembered something she'd read in a book about yoga.

Ariel was a neophyte, strictly into the physical benefits of yoga; still, the more esoteric aspects of the discipline held a certain fascination. The passage she recalled had to do with something called kundalini. As nearly as she'd understood, it was a force or power activated while one was in a profound trance state. Adepts, she'd read, could stop their own hearts. They could enter into a state of suspended animation. They could curl up on a bed of nails or stroll around on burning coals without pain. *They could escape pain!* Was Laya capable of willing herself, meditating herself, into such a trance?

If she herself were in severe pain, Ariel reasoned, in severe distress, and could remove herself to oblivion or bliss or at least absence of pain, she'd be *Om*ing fit to kill.

She was clutching at straws, avoiding thinking about those facial scratches.

What were those all about? *Was* Laya attacked?

What kind of attacker would scratch rather than strike? Or had Laya been struck? A head blow, knocking her unconscious and impacting whatever portion of the brain affected vision?

Ariel hit the brakes, narrowly missing a car determined to beat the light. She frowned, not at the car but at what was suggested by the water that had been left running. Someone cleaning off blood, the evidence of attack? Or Laya flushing out her eyes, trying to rinse out some foreign matter. The eyedrops. They must have been a desperate, last-ditch attempt at finding relief.

In the bedlam of the emergency room, Ariel almost forgot to give the bottle to the ER doctor. He'd barely glanced at it, saying only that if the lady's problems stemmed from any kind of chemical burn, he hoped she'd used more than a few drops. "Should've irrigated with water," he'd said tersely, "and lots of it!"

Remembering the questions he's fired at her, Ariel surmised that he'd been more concerned at that moment about Laya's unresponsive state.

The old man who shared the waiting room exhaled forcefully, one noisy snort. He woke himself up. Smiled sheepishly. Glanced at Ariel and then at the nurses' station, and then, starting slightly, at Ariel again. She smiled back, sympathetic acknowledgment of a fellow passenger in the wait-and-worry boat. He turned pink and suddenly found his fingers of interest. Lacing them carefully, he watched himself rub the pad of one thumb against the other. After a good thirty seconds of this fascinating exercise, he blurted, "Excuse me, but you're somebody, aren't you?"

"Pardon me?"

"I'll get it in a minute. Somebody . . ."

Ariel almost turned to look behind her. Preoccupied as she'd been, dressed in last night's wrinkled clothes, her hair at odds with her head and her face bare of makeup, she honestly didn't get it for a second.

"Open File!" he cried. "You're the lady from that TV show! A celebrity!"

Wincing, Ariel admitted that the first part, at least, was true. She still wasn't used to being recognized. She found it incredible, at the moment, that she had been. She looked more like a gummy-eyed bag lady, she imagined, than a "celebrity."

In Los Angeles one spots them—celebrities, even legends—regularly, on the street, in the dry cleaners, at the car wash. A major box-office draw blocks the grocery aisle with his cart, studying the ingredients on a cereal box. A sitcom lead sees your look of recognition and gives you a wink as he passes on the sidewalk. The woman rummaging through old linens at the next flea market stall is an Academy Award-winning singer-turned-actress. Ariel wasn't in that league. It was a fact, though, that since she'd gone from producer to correspondent on a network newsmagazine three months before, she did get surreptitious glances and even, like now, the occasional autograph request.

"My wife watches your show faithfully," the man said, patting his pockets, pulling a pen from one of them and what turned out to be a phone bill from another. "She even tapes it when we go out. We square dance." He faltered, and seemed to sink into himself. "Diabetes, she's got. Bad. They may have to amputate . . ."

Ariel took the envelope and scribbled inadequate best wishes. "Tell you what," she said. "When your wife's feeling better, you call the studio, Mr.—"

"Morris. Charles Morris. Merle, that's my wife."

"Ask for me. I'll arrange for you two to tour the studio, if you'd like to do that." Jotting the studio number and wishing him luck, Ariel got to her feet. "I need to check on my friend," she said, and started for the nearest nurses' station.

The ER doctor intercepted her. After asking questions Ariel couldn't answer about Laya, like her last name (the hospital's red tape snarled hopelessly on a patient who went by a single name), her next of kin (Ariel knew of only one, a sister in New York whose last name she also didn't know), and Ariel's credentials for being given information, he volunteered only, "An ophthalmologist is with her now. We've got saline drips going to irrigate the eyes. We'll know more later."

"Tell me what you know now, please," Ariel begged.

The doctor (whose name, Ariel later thought, she must surely have heard or read on his ID badge but didn't remember) considered his reply. Blinking rapidly and addressing his answer through half-closed lids to some point behind her (a nervous and probably unconscious habit she put down to shyness—or having delivered bad news a few times too many), he said, "Chemical burn, of course. Damage to the left eye looks like it might be limited to the outer layer of the cornea." He went through the blinking routine again. "Other eye's not so good. Cornea's cloudy."

Ariel felt herself grow cold. "Which means?"

He tried falling back on his earlier bromide. "We'll know more a little later."

"But what happened?"

He sighed. "What actually took place, you mean? Since the patient's out of it—something I have *never* seen in these situations—I can't answer that. We can't get any information from her. I can only tell you that some form of acid was introduced into the eyes." He blinked. "I'm having the contents of that bottle you gave me checked out."

Look for

Blind Spot

**Wherever Books
Are Sold**

**Coming Soon
in Hardcover
from Pocket Books**